BATTLECRUISER

DOUGLAS REEMAN joined the Navy in 1941. He did convoy duty in the Atlantic, the Arctic, and the North Sea, and later served in motor torpedo boats. As he says, 'I am always asked to account for the perennial appeal of the sea story, and its enduring interest for people of so many nationalities and cultures. It would seem that the eternal and sometimes elusive triangle of man, ship and ocean, particularly under the stress of war, produces the best qualities of courage and compassion, irrespective of the rights and wrongs of the conflict . . . The sea has no understanding of the righteous or unjust causes. It is the common enemy, respected by all who serve on it, ignored at their peril.'

Battlecruiser is Douglas Reeman's thirty-second novel under his own name; he has also written twenty-three bestselling historical novels featuring Richard Bolitho, under the pseudonym Alexander Kent.

D0615744

Also by Douglas Reeman

Battlecruiser

Douglas Reeman

ARROW

Published by Arrow Books in 1998

5 7 9 10 8 6 4

Copyright © Bolitho Maritime Productions Ltd 1997

First published in the United Kingdom in 1997 by William Heinemann

Arrow Books Limited
20 Vauxhall Bridge Road, London, SW1V 2SA

Random House Australia (Pty) Limited
20 Alfred Street, Milsons Point, Sydney,
New South Wales 2061, Australia

Random House New Zealand Limited
18 Poland Road, Glenfield,
Auckland 10, New Zealand

Random House South Africa (Pty) Limited
Endulini, 5a Jubilee Road, Parktown 2193, South Africa

Random House UK Limited Reg. No. 54009

A CIP catalogue record for this book is available from the British Library

Papers used by Random House UK Limited
are natural, recyclable products made from wood grown in sustainable
forests. The manufacturing processes conform to the environmental
regulations of the country of origin

ISBN 0 74 932350 7

Typeset by Avon Dataset Ltd, Bidford-on-Avon, Warks

Printed and bound in Great Britain by
Mackays of Chatham, Chatham, Kent

For you, Kim, with love.
'Save thou my rose; in it thou art my all.'

Escort the brave
Whose hearts, unsatisfied
With the kind stairs and tender hearths of love,
Are loyal to the cunning of the waves,
The sparse rule of the tide.

Fly over these,
Humble and brave, who sail
And trim the ships with very life. Their lives
Delineate the seas.
Patrol their deathless trail.

John Pudney
Flight Lieutenant, R.A.F.
1942

Contents

Prologue

In peace or war, the launch of a great ship is like no other experience, and to have been a part of it, to have shared the creation from idea to blueprint, and then to follow it over the months to this moment, must be unique.

For the many men who helped to build this particular ship, it is a time for pride and satisfaction. Day by day, they have seen her grow and take shape until she dominates all around her, just as she has ruled their working lives. Unlike the days of unemployment and depression, when the completion of such a ship would represent loss of work until another order could be won and another keel laid down, this slipway will not be empty for very long.

And here on Clydebank, you can feel the excitement on every side. Even in neighbouring yards, men have stopped work to watch this great ship, bedecked with flags, built for war but as yet without weapons, her bridges and superstructure strangely bare and unfinished. But some will say that she already has a character of her own.

Sailors have always been prone to claim that different ships have different characters. Happy ships, where the line between wardroom and messdeck is flexible, ready to adapt, and others where the opposite is equally obvious. Men under punishment, with lists of defaulters as further proof of the discontent which can harm any ship. And those other, rogue ships, with their unexplained accidents and breakdowns, and the inevitable aftermath of recriminations from on high, usually leading to a court-martial.

But now there is a hush, as if some one has raised a signal. The figures on the platform, dwarfed by the towering grey stem that rises high above them, come to life. A small girl curtsies and presents a bouquet to the woman in white, an admiral's wife, who is to perform the final honour. She is well supported by senior naval officers and dockyard officials, one of whom takes her hand and places it gently on the lever; another takes the bouquet from her. For a few moments she stares up at those great, graceful bows, the empty hawse pipes like eyes.

Below her, the band of the Royal Marines raise their instruments, waiting for the first stroke of the baton.

Her voice is strong, loud even, on the improvised speakers.

'I name this ship . . .'

Her voice is completely drowned by the thunder of cheering, the crash of drums as the band breaks into *Rule, Britannia*.

'God bless her . . .'

There is one stark moment when some of the yard engineers glance at one another with alarm, until, with something like a sigh, the great ship begins to move, so slowly at first; and then, with the chain cables holding her under control in a rising cloud of rust, she touches the Clyde for the first time.

'And all who sail in her!'

In war, a ship can fall victim to mine or torpedo, shellfire or dive-bomber, impartial killers without conscience or memory. Or they can live on, to end their days in some breaker's yard, suffering the indignity and the contempt after years of loyal service. But this ship is a machine, a weapon, only as good or as bad as those who will command her. A ship has no soul, and can have no say in her own destiny. Or can she?

1

Back from the Dead

The journey from the railway station to the church in the one and only taxi seemed to pass within a minute. Huddled in a heavy coat and scarf, the driver occasionally glanced at the passenger reflected in the mirror, a stranger now in his naval uniform, but one who had grown up in this small Surrey town. Like all those other boys, like the driver's own son, who was now driving a tank in the Western Desert.

For something to say, he called over his shoulder, 'Might still make it, sir. They could have been delayed.'

Captain Guy Sherbrooke turned up the collar of his raincoat and said something vague in agreement. The weather was cold despite the bright, clear sky, but it was not that. He was used to it, or should be, he thought. He glanced at the passing houses, and a pub with some soldiers standing outside, waiting for the doors to open. It was unreal, coming back like this; he should have known that it would be. The raincoat felt stiff and unfamiliar, like the rest of his clothing, all new. Like the cap that lay on the seat beside him, its peak bearing gold oak leaves. A captain. The dream . . . that was all it had been, in those days.

He should not have come. He had been offered an excuse at Waterloo station. The train was delayed; there had been a derailment; local slow trains were held up to make way for others more important. A familiar story. He had gone into the station buffet and had a cup of stale coffee. A drink, a proper drink, had been what he had really wanted.

He smiled unconsciously, a young man again. It would hardly do to arrive at a funeral smelling of gin. He turned to gaze at the great, green sprawl of Sandown Park racecourse, where his grandfather had taken him as a child to watch the jockeys urging their mounts around the last bend before the post. Only a memory now. This was the second day of January, 1943, another year of war. Sandown Park was no longer witness to the raucous bookmakers and jostling punters, the tipsters and the pickpockets. It was part of the army for the duration: stones painted white, sentries on the gates, lines of khaki stamping up and down in a cloud of dust, the home of a training battalion of the Welsh Guards.

He looked ahead and saw the familiar church spire; you could even see it from Kingston Hill on a fine day, they said. There had been some bombing around here, but not much, unlike the cities he had seen where hardly a building remained undamaged.

The taxi turned into the narrow road by the church, and stopped. The driver, who sported a moustache like the Old Bill character of the Great War, turned in his open seat and said, 'We were all sorry to hear about your ship, sir . . . losing her like that. Tim Evans, the postman's son, was on board.'

'I know.' Would it always be like this? 'He was a nice lad.'

Was. So many had died that day, in that bitter sea that robbed a man of his breath, his very will.

The driver watched him thoughtfully. A youthful, clean-cut face, with little to show of what he must have suffered.

5

But the steadiness of his eyes and the tightness of the jaw made a lie of it. The driver had been a sapper in that other war, in Flanders, no less a graveyard than this one on the other side of the old stone wall.

Sherbrooke knew what he was thinking, and was moved by it. Air raids, rationing . . . it was bad enough for the civilian populace without those hated telegrams. *We regret to inform you that your husband, father, son . . .* And yet this old taxi driver was always at the station, whenever he had managed to get away for a spot of leave.

Now there was nowhere to call home. Perhaps it was just as well: a new start. No doubts or misgivings. *Just do it.*

He got out of the taxi and glanced across at the church. The doors were opening; he imagined he could hear the organ. He was too late. He should have stayed away.

He reached into his pocket: even that felt different, alien, like a stranger's garment. The old driver shook his head.

'No, sir, not this time.' He looked grimly at the church. ''Sides, I brought *him* from the station this last time.'

Then he smiled. 'I'll be seeing you, sir. Just like the song says!' He swung away from the kerb. Back to the station.

Sherbrooke straightened his cap and pushed open the gate.

The coffin was being carried around the church, the mourners following in small, separate groups. Several naval officers were among them, one walking with a stick, a tall, unsmiling Wren close beside him. He was obviously feeling the cold, despite the heavy greatcoat with its gold vice-admiral's rank markings. It was hard to imagine him as a captain in that great ship, in that vanished world of the peacetime Mediterranean fleet. Sherbrooke could not accept it. *Dead men's shoes . . .* not yet.

The man being buried today was Captain Charles Cavendish; he had been a lieutenant with Sherbrooke in those far-off days. A quiet, private funeral, with only a White Ensign draped over the coffin as a token of respect. The coroner's verdict had been 'death by misadventure'. Cavendish had been a brave and respected officer, who had commanded one of Britain's most famous ships. His death had been a sad one, even pointless, following a few days of leave, while the ship was in the Firth of Forth for work to be carried out on board. He had been found sitting in his beloved Armstrong-Siddeley car, his pride and joy, bought when he had married Jane. Another flash of memory pierced Sherbrooke. They had all been there, smiling, happy to be part of it, their swords drawn to form an arch over the bridal couple: Cavendish, tall and rather serious, even as a lieutenant, and the lovely Jane, who could win a man's heart as she could freeze another, with a mere glance.

The older people were looking at one another warily, seeking comfort, clearly ill at ease. The naval officers were here to show their respect to Captain Charles Cavendish, D.S.O. and Bar, who had died alone in his car, with the engine running and the garage door closed.

The local police sergeant had explained that it had been a very windy day, that the door had probably been blown shut; there could be no other explanation. Jane had been in London and had known nothing about her husband's unexpected leave. Otherwise . . .

That same sergeant was here now, erect and unsmiling. He was well acquainted with the family, and had been known to drop in for a glass when the captain was at home.

Sherbrooke turned his head, and saw her looking directly at him. As the vicar opened his book and began to read, his breath hanging in the clear air like steam, she gave the

7

merest nod. Even in this setting she stood out, as she always had, tall, slender, striking. She appeared calm, very contained, her fingers holding her black coat tightly shut, the diamond naval crown brooch glittering in the hard sunlight.

Then the gaunt-looking undertaker and his team moved away, as though following the steps of a well-rehearsed dance. The coffin was gone. People were gathering round to offer condolences, some doubtless wondering what had really happened. The vice-admiral joined Sherbrooke, and poked at the loose gravel with his stick.

'People think this is an affectation, dammit. I can assure you it isn't!' Then he dropped his voice. 'I'm glad you accepted command, Sherbrooke. Keeps it in the family, so to speak.'

Sherbrooke smiled, something he had not done much of late. He knew what the vice-admiral meant; he had been retired soon after his promotion to flag rank, *put out to graze*, as he himself described it. But he had never forgotten those days, when he had been the captain. There had been four lieutenants in the wardroom during a carefree commission, when life had seemed always to be sunny and easy in retrospect. John Broadwood, killed eighteen months ago in command of a destroyer on the Atlantic run. Charles Cavendish. Sherbrooke dragged his mind back to the present as the men with spades moved toward the grave. And there was Vincent Stagg, now a rear-admiral, the youngest since Nelson, one newspaper had trumpeted. *And me*.

He had reached her without realizing he had moved. Her hand was soft, but strong, and like ice.

'It was nice of you to come. I thought about you a lot when you lost your ship. We all did.' She smiled at somebody who was trying to get near, but her eyes were without warmth. 'Is it true you're taking Charles's ship?' She studied him thoughtfully. 'I'm glad for you. No sense in brooding.' She looked away. 'When do you take command?'

'Right away,' he said.

She released his hand, and smiled. 'Good luck, Guy. You could use it.'

She moved through the crowd of mourners, and the vice-admiral said, 'Coming up to the house, Sherbrooke?' He recognized the doubt, the sense of loss. 'Just for a few minutes, eh? Spam sandwiches and sherry. God, I've been to a few recently!' He touched his arm. 'I can run you up to town afterwards, get things started for you. Might be a drop of Scotch in it, too. Do you good!' His stick slipped from his hand and the Wren stooped down to retrieve it for him. The vice-admiral sighed. 'Everybody's so bloody young! If only . . .' He glanced at the tall, unsmiling Wren. 'Eh, Joyce? If only.'

She said patiently, 'That's right, sir.' But she was looking past him at the captain in the new, uncreased raincoat. Afterwards, Sherbrooke thought she had been thinking of someone else, and perhaps, what might have been.

They walked slowly across the village green toward the larger houses on the hill. Jane had money of her own, plenty of it. He found himself glancing at the garage beside the house as he approached the double doors.

They had just watched a secret being buried.

He recalled her voice, so cool and assured. *No sense in brooding*.

Suddenly, he was glad to be leaving.

The naval operations and signals distribution sections at Leith were situated in a dispirited-looking building that faced out over the great Firth of Forth. The stiff wind,

9

across the water and the many moored warships, cut like a knife, and made any sort of outdoor work a misery.

Inside the operations room, it was almost humid by comparison, the broad windows misty with condensation.

The duty operations officer got up from his desk and moved to the nearest one. Old for his rank, and put on the beach between the wars, he had come to accept this day-to-day work on the fringe of what he considered the real war. He wiped the glass with his sleeve and saw the moisture running down the criss-cross of sticky paper which, allegedly, offered protection against bomb-blast, should any enemy aircraft be reckless enough to attempt a raid. These days, there were so many warships here at any given time that their combined anti-aircraft fire would deter anybody in his right mind.

He half-listened to the endless clatter of typewriters and teleprinters in the adjoining offices: signals, codes, instructions, orders, the demands of a fleet at war.

It would be Twelfth Night tomorrow. He glanced at the tattered Christmas decorations hung above the framed portrait of Winston Churchill, and the fake holly beside the operations board. He peered harder at the blurred outline of the Forth Bridge, that vital link, which must have offered such a tempting target in the first months of war.

He told himself often enough that he was lucky to be doing something useful, important even, that his age and experience carried a lot of weight with his team of Wrens, most of whom were young enough to be his daughters. But occasionally that sense of satisfaction at being *back*, being a part of it again, was not enough.

He remembered the small escort destroyer, which had nearly failed to make it back to base. He had watched her creep in, her bows so low in the water that her forecastle was almost awash. By luck or by mischance, the destroyer, a veteran from the Great War like so many, had confronted a U-Boat, surfaced, and about to attack a slow-moving convoy.

The operations officer had pictured the confrontation, as if he himself had been there: the sudden realization, the U-Boat, taken by surprise and unable to dive, opening fire with her heavy machine-guns in a last attempt to stave off the inevitable. There had been small bundles laid out on the destroyer's listing deck that day, each covered with a flag: there was always a price to be paid. But the destroyer had kept going, and had rammed the submarine at full speed, driving it down, until only an oil slick and the remains of her deck party were left to mark the spot. The Admiralty was far from keen on escorts ramming U-Boats. Even if successful, it meant that the ship involved would be in dock for months, at a time when every escort was worth her tonnage in gold.

But the cheers that day from every ship in the anchorage must have made each man in her company feel like a giant, and he had been surprised that he could still be so moved. So envious.

'Tea, sir?' He turned and looked at his personal Wren, a petty officer writer who had been with him for four months. It was a long time in the service these days. He wondered what she would say if he asked her out for a quiet meal in Edinburgh, for a Twelfth Night celebration. Probably make some excuse, and then ask for a transfer.

She smiled to herself. She knew exactly what he was thinking, or could make a good guess.

She said, 'The battlecruiser's new captain is due today, sir. I wonder what he'll be like.'

He looked at her. How different from the time he had found her crying in that very chair, the telegram gripped in one hand. Her fiancé had been killed in some

11

godforsaken place in North Africa. Was she over it? So many such telegrams . . . thousands, probably millions.

He considered her remark, and replied, 'I know something of him. It was just before you joined us here at Leith. He's Captain Guy Sherbrooke – young for his rank. He was in command of the cruiser *Pyrrhus*, Leander class, like the *Achilles* and *Ajax* of River Plate fame. Smart ships, small by today's standards, of course. Six six-inch guns as main armament.' Without looking, he knew she was sitting down in the chair, listening, as she had that day when he had found her with the telegram. 'She was part of the escort for a convoy to North Russia – that damnable place. The Admiralty had been expecting trouble, even with *Bismarck* sunk and only *Scharnhorst* as an immediate threat, and they had ordered heavier units to stand by off Iceland, just in case.'

'I remember, sir. I read about it in the papers. Three German cruisers came out of Norway and went for the convoy. But the *Scharnhorst* never appeared.'

He touched the cup on his desk. The tea was cold. 'The convoy was ordered to disperse, not "scatter", as some might have had it. *Pyrrhus* placed herself between the convoy and the enemy.' He added with sudden bitterness, 'But the heavy units never arrived, and Captain Sherbrooke's challenge was in vain. *Pyrrhus* managed to maul one of them, but she was hopelessly outgunned. Swamped.'

'But the convoy was left alone, sir?'

He did not hear her. 'I remember seeing *Pyrrhus* at a fleet review before the war. I couldn't keep away, even then. She had a ship's company of four hundred and fifty. They picked up eight of them. One was Sherbrooke. You don't last long in the Arctic in September.'

'And now he's here, sir.'

'And now he's here.' A small Wren hovered at the door with a signal-pad in her hands.

The operations officer was glad of the interruption. He was only speculating, in any case. Nobody knew for certain what had happened that day. He wiped the window again. He could not see the ship from here, but he had already watched her at her anchorage, surrounded by barges and lighters, boats coming and going like servants. She was there: he could feel her. A ship so well known in peace and war, part of the legend, a symbol of all the navy stood for.

Her previous captain, Cavendish, had died suddenly, not on his bridge but at home. An accident, the report had stated. Cavendish would have known the truth. He had been in command of that great ship out there when *Pyrrhus* had gone down, guns blazing, in seas as high as this building. Now Sherbrooke was taking his place. In command of a legend . . . the ship which had left his *Pyrrhus* to perish.

The Wren petty officer came back and said, 'Nothing important, sir.' She saw his face, and exclaimed, 'What is it, sir?'

He turned his back on the streaming window and the choppy waters of the Firth.

He said bluntly, 'I wonder if you could spare an evening for dinner in the city? Nothing fancy.'

She said, 'I'm sorry, sir. I'm tied up for the next few runs ashore.' Then she smiled. 'I'd love to. Really.'

The operations officer beamed. 'I'll cadge some transport. Rank hath its privileges!'

Then he turned again, and stared across the busy anchorage. He still could not see her through the haze and drizzle. But the ship was there. Waiting.

Captain Guy Sherbrooke stepped down from the staff car

and turned toward the Firth. He heard the operations officer giving instructions to the driver about something, and wished he could have been alone for these last free moments. Taking command, even joining a ship for the first time, was always a testing business. All the way from London, changing trains, holding onto solitude even in crowded compartments, he had thought about it. This was very different from all the other times. At the Admiralty they had tried to make light of it, for his sake; it had only made it worse, in some ways.

His new company would be much more worried about what their new captain would be like. *Think of it that way.* The old vice-admiral at the funeral had also said as much. 'She's a fine ship, a great ship. I'd give my whole life to command her all over again.'

During the journey he had found himself recalling the funeral and the aftermath, the sandwiches and the sherry, and the first nervous laughter as the tension had begun to wear thin. What had he really expected?

And why could he not accept that nothing would ever be the same? *Pyrrhus* was gone. All the faces, the weaknesses, and the rough camaraderie which made any ship were no more. *Eight survivors.*

He had passed the journey north going through his notes, putting names to people who would soon become an everyday part of his life. Whenever he had glanced up from his papers, a ruddy-faced brigadier had tried to force him into conversation about the war. What the navy, 'the blue jobs' as he called them, really thought about it, while he took occasional sips from a silver flask which certainly did not contain tea. He had not offered it to Sherbrooke. He felt his mouth relax into a thin smile. *Just as well. I'd probably have told him!*

The operations officer was speaking again. He had seen

the glances passing between him and the Wren petty officer: like the old vice-admiral and his Wren driver, wanting to be the man he once was.

Sherbrooke turned towards him. He was doing his best: they all were. *It's me.* 'What is it?'

The operations officer replied, 'Nothing, sir. Just a young chap joining the ships. Asking about boats. I told him to report to . . .'

'I'll take him.'

He caught sight of a young lieutenant with a pile of ill-assorted luggage and an instrument case, a banjo, by the look of it. His stripes were wavy: another R.N.V.R. officer, hostilities only, who overnight had become the largest part of the navy.

But there was something different about this one, a gold-laced letter 'A' in the curl of his upper stripe, and when he responded to the operations officer's reluctant offer, Sherbrooke saw the pilot's wings on his left sleeve.

'Great! Thanks!' He stared, obviously dismayed as he saw the oak leaves around the peak of Sherbrooke's cap. 'Gee, I'm sorry, sir! I didn't realize!' He added helplessly, 'I'm joining the *Reliant*, you see.'

Sherbrooke nodded, momentarily off-balance. The easy use of her name. Had he really been avoiding it?

Then he smiled. 'So am I, as it happens.'

The lieutenant slipped the raincoat off his shoulder and saluted.

'Rayner, sir. R.C.N.V.R.'

Sherbrooke returned his salute, and glanced at the word *Canada* on the lieutenant's shoulder. It was a different navy now: errand boys and bank clerks, brick-layers and bus conductors. A miracle which had been performed without any one noticing, or so it sometimes seemed to him.

15

The operations officer looked up from his watch. 'The launch is coming, sir.'

Sherbrooke shivered again, but not because of the cold. 'Right on time.'

The operations officer sounded relieved. His part was almost over. 'She would be on time, sir. In *that* ship.'

Sherbrooke barely heard him. He was feeling in his pockets, half expecting to find his pipe there, but that had gone too, probably when they had cut his frozen clothing from his body. All the time, he had been trying to hold onto the other man, hearing his voice. *Help me. Somebody help me.* And another voice, a stranger's. 'No use, Captain. He's gone.'

'Excuse me, sir.'

'What?' He swung on the Canadian almost blindly. 'What is it?'

'I just realized what a stupid goddamn fool I am. Who you are. What you did.' He shook his head. 'And all I do is . . .'

Sherbrooke held out his hand. 'Don't say it. This is an important day for both of us.' He slipped out of his new raincoat, feeling the bitter air through his uniform, and stinging his face. This young Canadian temporary lieutenant would be the replacement pilot for the ship's Walrus amphibian, affectionately known throughout the navy as 'the Shagbat', which was used for both reconnaissance and rescue. He had made a good start; he had just rescued his captain, without even knowing it.

He heard the throaty growl of the launch as it swung around a ponderous tug and headed straight for the jetty.

Very smart: it could have been Spithead in peacetime. The bowman with his raised boathook, a petty officer as coxswain, and some other face beside his in the cockpit. There was a rear-admiral's flag painted on either bow.

16

Stagg was doing him proud. He would . . . He almost smiled. In *that* ship.

Sherbrooke watched as the boat's engines coughed astern, and the hull came to rest against the jetty's fenders with barely a shudder.

A midshipman scrambled ashore and saluted. 'Ready when you are, sir.'

Sherbrooke turned to shake hands with the operations officer. A few passers-by were hanging about to watch. He could almost hear them.

All right for some, eh?

He found that it did not worry him. 'Thanks for your help.'

'Good luck, sir.' The other man saluted.

The midshipman was staring at the Canadian lieutenant, confused, angry perhaps, that something unrehearsed was happening. The pilot was gathering up his bags, and lastly the banjo, if that was what it was.

'After you, sir.'

Sherbrooke did not raise his voice. 'It's not vital, Mr Rayner, but senior officers go *last*, right?'

More confusion, until a seaman ran to help carry the bags into the launch.

He could feel the scrutiny, the curiosity, perhaps the understanding, too. The navy was a family, after all.

He touched the peak of his cap and stepped down into the boat.

'Bear off forrard! Let go aft!' The midshipman's voice was just a little too loud. He would be watching everything, preparing what he would say to his fellows in the gunroom when he was dismissed from this duty. *The new captain, what's he like?*

The boat tore away from the jetty and caught the Canadian off-balance; Sherbrooke heard a twang as the banjo fell onto the deck. A face he would get to know, and the man behind it, like all the rest of them. He gripped the safety rail until his hand throbbed. But not too intimately. Not again.

He thought suddenly of his last visit to the Admiralty, the barrage balloons like basking whales in the washed-out sky, uniforms everywhere, representing every country imaginable, all fighting the same war with their homes under German occupation.

When he had been told about *Reliant*, he had heard himself ask, 'Why me, sir?'

The admiral's face had crinkled. Relieved, perhaps, that it was a question he could answer without personal involvement.

'Her flag officer, Rear-Admiral Stagg, asked for you himself. Insisted, I should say.'

Spray lanced over the glass screen, and he wiped his face with the back of his hand. It was exhilarating, without threat. What had he expected? The question always repeated itself.

Fear, perhaps? Some manifestation of the horror that might have scarred him more deeply than even the experts realized?

He looked up again, and saw her for the first time. It had happened so suddenly that it was hard to take in, to accept. H.M.S. *Reliant*, a battlecruiser, one of the giants, and to the public a surviving symbol of a world which would never be the same again.

She was huge but graceful, with the speed and agility of a destroyer, and the fighting power of a battleship. At the outbreak of war Britain, with the largest fleet in the world, had retained four battlecruisers. The *Hood*, and *Reliant*'s two sisters, *Repulse* and *Renown*. The *Hood*, probably the most beautiful warship ever built, and in her day the largest afloat, not only represented the strength and majesty of the peacetime Royal Navy, to the general public she *was* the navy. But she was a battlecruiser, built for speed, for a style of warfare already outdated at Jutland, if not even before that. In 1941, she was destined to meet with *Bismarck*, Hitler's most powerful battleship, and unsinkable, as her German builders had claimed. On that bitter day in the North Atlantic, *Hood*, in company with a battleship, *Prince of Wales*, so new that she still carried dockyard workers on board, had opened fire on the enemy. It had taken only one direct hit from *Bismarck*'s great shells, which had exploded inside a magazine after piercing *Hood*'s thinly armoured deck, to sink her like her fore-runners at Jutland. Out of a complement of some fourteen hundred men, only a midshipman and two ratings had been found alive. Just months later, off the coast of Malaya, *Repulse*, in company with the same ill-fated *Prince of Wales*, was attacked by Japanese aircraft. Within an hour, both great ships were sunk, with terrible loss of life. A different theatre of war, but the same sacrifice, the same fatal weakness.

The launch was slowing down but Sherbrooke did not move, although his reefer jacket was shining black with spray.

The young Canadian, Rayner, stared at him, wanting to understand, needing to remember this moment for all time.

A full captain, he thought, a sort of god to most junior ranks, and yet so youthful himself. A face you would trust. Believe.

Sherbrooke saw the figures on the battlecruiser's quarterdeck. Marines, officers, people whom he must meet, and who should see him before the darkness closed in across the Firth of Forth.

Then he stared up at the grey superstructure, still

graceful and unaltered, without the massive tower-bridges given to several of the older capital ships.

It was like being held, taken over; like nothing he had ever experienced.

'Hooked on, sir!' They were waiting, and up there on deck the boatswain's mates would be moistening their silver calls. Ready for the captain.

The king is dead. Long live the king.

Captain Guy Sherbrooke was thirty-nine years old, twenty-seven of which he had been in naval uniform. Whatever had gone before, and no matter what it had cost him, this was his future. Perhaps his only future.

Pride, then? Satisfaction? If anything, he felt only disbelief. He saluted the coxswain and reached for the safety lines.

He might have spoken aloud. 'I survived.' He looked up at the after funnel, and the mast with the rear-admiral's flag standing out in the breeze like painted metal. 'I'm back.'

2

Welcome Aboard

Captain Guy Sherbrooke leaned his elbows on the desk and massaged his eyes with his fingers. Like the nearby chairs, the desk was almost covered with books, folders, and separate pads of signals, arranged in order of importance or urgency. He stared around the day cabin, where he had been working without a break since he had been piped aboard only this afternoon. The cabin was huge, but *Reliant* had been built at a time when allotted space was often measured by rank. And so quiet. Even with half the ship's company on a week's leave, there were still enough people aboard to be heard. *Reliant* carried a total of twelve hundred officers, ratings and marines, and yet beyond the cabin bulkhead he could barely hear the occasional tannoy announcement, or the twitter of a boatswain's call.

He tried to remember the ship as she had appeared when he had first stepped aboard in peacetime. The Mediterranean, regattas, parties, and receptions. Showing the flag. Like the time when the squadron had been at Naples: he could see it as if it were yesterday, perhaps because he wanted to erase what had happened so recently. Suntanned shoulders and daring gowns, officers in their 'ice-cream suits' falling over one another to entertain and impress all the ladies. One had been Jane, in Italy with her father, who had been on some important trade mission. Another world . . .

He was on his feet, although he did not recall having left the desk. He looked at the ship's crest, an upraised double-edged sword surrounded by a victor's laurels. And her motto, *Cedemus Nunquam*. We will never give in.

It must have been in this same cabin where he had said goodbye to the captain of the day, the vice-admiral he had met at the funeral. Surely he was not that old . . . But then, all senior officers had seemed ancient to him in those days.

There was a picture of the King in uniform, and several spaces left by others which had been removed recently. He glanced at a pile of boxes and packages, discreetly covered with a tartan rug near the door, the personal effects of his predecessor, Charles Cavendish. In a separate cardboard box was a photograph of Jane in a silver frame; the glass was broken. The captain's steward had told him that Cavendish had always taken the picture to the upper bridge with him when the ship was at sea, in an oilskin bag. He had added as an afterthought, *just in case*.

Sherbrooke held the photo to the desk light. The same poise, the candid eyes. The woman he had once hoped . . .

He swung round. 'Yes?'

It was the steward, Petty Officer Arthur Long, doubtless nicknamed 'Dodger' by the members of the petty officers' mess. The navy's way. Long had been in the ship since she had recommissioned at the outbreak of war, and had already served two captains. Prematurely bald, with bent ears, he had the appearance of a mournful pixie. When Sherbrooke had asked if he would like to continue with the same duties, he had not even hesitated.

'Of course, sir.'

At first, Sherbrooke had wondered why he had accepted

the job so readily. It would not be a soft number, with some captains.

He was glad, nonetheless. All his new clothing, uniforms and shirts had been pressed and stowed away as soon as they had arrived: it seemed as though a part of him had already been here. Waiting, like the ship.

Long paused in the doorway and regarded the tray, on a small table, still covered with a napkin. He shook his head sadly.

'Won't do, sir. They've just piped Rounds, an' you've not eaten a scrap!'

Sherbrooke sat down and glanced at his gleaming new pipe, and the tobacco pouch. He had used neither. He touched his face. Not since . . .

'Sorry. I got a bit bogged down.' He stared at the mass of books and ledgers, brought and sometimes removed by another face he would soon come to know. A chief petty officer writer, a dry, austere man, who had not once looked him in the eye.

Another visitor had been Commander John Frazier, *Reliant*'s second-in-command, The Bloke, as he was known to wardroom and lower deck alike. Another one who seemed young for his rank, he had a serious, intelligent face, and Sherbrooke supposed that women would consider him very good-looking. He knew from his confidential file that Frazier had been due for a command of his own, but had remained instead with Cavendish for some reason. He might well be regretting it now, he thought.

Long was saying, 'Scrambled eggs, and a slice or two of bacon, sir. I'll tell the chef.' He almost winked. 'He's a mate of mine.'

Suddenly Sherbrooke found that it sounded very appealing.

Long was studying the tartan rug. 'I'll have this lot sent

ashore tomorrow, sir. I'll fix it with the baggage-master.' He shook his head. 'Very sad.'

Sherbrooke looked penetratingly at him. He was obviously a man who knew more than he was telling, at this point, anyway. The broken photo glass. Not dropped, but smashed to fragments. Here, or in the adjoining sleeping cabin. Another secret.

Long said, 'Captain Cavendish used to fancy a Horse's Neck when he got a spare moment, sir.'

Sherbrooke looked away, troubled that it affected him so much, and afraid Long would notice it. 'Yes. I remember now. I'll have the same, please.'

Long brightened as much as was possible. 'Something similar. That's the ticket, sir.'

The glass suddenly appeared on the desk, and Long was gone, doubtless to see the chef, his mate.

Sherbrooke sat down, and stared at the new jacket with its four bright gold stripes, the blue and white ribbon of the Distinguished Service Cross on the breast. He raised the glass, forcing himself to do it slowly. Had he died with the others, he would probably have been awarded a posthumous V. C.

He switched off the desk lamp and opened the nearest deadlight, and, after a slight hesitation, unclipped the big polished scuttle. The cold air in his face was refreshing after the canned air of the elegant quarters he had inherited. But everything was so still . . . like being on dry land. Only occasionally he felt a slight tremor, like a nerve, some remote piece of machinery, perhaps a pump or generator inside this great hull. Thirty-two thousand tons, and almost eight hundred feet from flared bows to graceful stern. Even *Reliant*'s beam was over one hundred feet. A ship of war, a weapon, but she was more than these. She was a way of life to the men who served her from bridge to boiler room, from flag-deck to the ungainly Shagbat balanced on its catapult abaft the funnels, soon to be piloted by a young Canadian who said 'gee'.

Now, in the darkness, with the chill of salt air across his mouth, he had the sense of her, the powerful armament of six fifteen-inch guns, which could drop high explosive on a target twenty miles away at the rate of seven tons a minute. He touched the glass. If the target was obliging. And she had the power to do it. Turbines which could give her quadruple screws twenty-nine knots or more, and which could leave some modern destroyers astern. A battlecruiser, an idea, a dream which had ended at Jutland.

He heard singing, and inclined his head closer to the scuttle to listen. One of the many motor fishing vessels, M.F.V.s, used as tenders by the fleet, this one carrying returning libertymen. A run ashore, too much to drink, with the hope of sneaking past the eagle eye of an officer-of-the-day or some hard-fisted petty officer. It was the sailor's way. Tomorrow could wait.

'Roll on the *Nelson*, the *Rodney*, *Renown*,
This long-funnelled bastard is getting me down!'

He slammed the scuttle and screwed down the deadlight. He had heard the libertymen singing much the same thing many times in *Pyrrhus*.

He looked at the empty glass in his hand, as if he expected it to be trembling.

At least Vincent Stagg had not been aboard when he had arrived. In London, The Bloke had informed him. Something important. It would be.

But tomorrow Stagg would be flying back, no messing about with trains or other wartime delays. What would he be like now, he wondered. He was a man who had always

25

been full of surprises, even as a lieutenant. Stagg had taken the appointment of flag lieutenant to an admiral with royal connections and little else to recommend him, while they had all pulled his leg for missing a chance at proper sea-duty.

As he had been in London, it was strange that he had not turned up at the funeral of his own flag captain.

He heard Long humming to himself, and the cheerful rattle of yet another tray.

Tomorrow was Sunday. He examined his feelings. There would be Divisions; *Reliant* even carried her own chaplain, the Reverend Beveridge. Sherbrooke had already heard that he was nicknamed 'Horlicks' by the lower deck.

It would be the first real test. All those faces, watching, assessing him, considering how they might be affected by the man who stood alone before them, under the scrutiny of thousands of eyes. And in the afternoon, the rear-admiral would come aboard.

'Ready, sir?'

Sherbrooke touched the ship's crest. *We will never give in.* It was somehow apt.

He looked at the tray. There was a bottle of wine on it, opened and ready.

Long shrugged glumly. 'From the wardroom, sir. Welcome aboard.'

Sherbrooke sat down, and tried not to watch as the balding steward poured.

It was a small thing: it might even have been only Frazier's personal gesture. But to the new captain, as he raised his glass to the ship's crest, it meant everything.

Any visitor or guest in *Reliant*'s wardroom would usually receive a first impression of size, and an austere dignity. But, like all ships of war, the wardroom had several personalities, rarely seen by strangers or the casual observer. Rowdy mess nights when the young bloods went wild, turning the place into a mock battlefield or practising field-gun drill, with chairs and anything else movable used to charge across tables laid down as barricades. The aftermath of huge mess bills and punishing hangovers acted as some deterrent, until the next time. Birthdays and engagements, toasts to scarcely remembered victories, and to lost friends too soon forgotten. And those other grim times at sea, when this same wardroom became a hospital for sick and wounded, men picked up from yet another butchered convoy. Men burned and poisoned with fuel oil, men without hope, and beyond fear. A different face.

But Sunday in harbour showed the other side. It was, after all, rare enough.

Officers who might be seen only occasionally, because of their varied watchkeeping schedules or their stations deep in the hull or behind armour plate, were free on this one day to meet and share an hour or so of normality: men who were scarcely recognizable in their best uniforms and dazzlingly clean white shirts, instead of the usual scuffed Wellington boots, grey flannel trousers, and old seagoing reefer jackets, with rank markings so tarnished and worn by salt and wind that they often looked like survivors themselves.

The stewards, too, were different on Sundays, bustling around amongst the various groups with a quiet efficiency reminiscent of some pre-war hotel.

One corner of the wardroom retained a semblance of privacy because of what appeared to be a curved pillar, like a partition. It was, in fact, the casing of a shell-hoist, which led directly from one of the lower magazines to a triple four-inch gun mounting on the after superstructure, far above the din of voices and the enclosing fog of pipe and cigarette smoke.

Any member of the wardroom mess, no matter how senior or lowly, was entitled to sit anywhere he liked, except on special occasions. Officially, the mess was democratic. But this particular space, known to *Reliant*'s officers as *The Club*, was, unofficially, for the ship's senior officers, the heads of departments, where they could sit, talk, drink and complain, without any chance of a word being overheard or misinterpreted.

In a corner, close to a sealed scuttle, one armchair was occupied by Commander (E) Hugh Onslow, 'the Chief' as he was known here, as in most ships. He was a large, heavy man with a round, jowled face, and bushy eyebrows which were almost white. The face could be cheerful or angry as the occasion dictated but it was not one to cross at any time. The engine room department in any warship was separate from all the rest; exclusive, some might say; bloody-minded, others would describe it. In *Reliant*'s massive engine and boiler rooms, with their teams of stokers, artificers and mechanics, the Chief was like a god, and his word was law. Not only was he the most senior member of the mess, but he was the oldest man in *Reliant*'s company. He was quietly proud that he had, he said, come up the hard way.

He glanced around at the crowded wardroom, and wondered briefly what their new orders would be. A vital convoy to protect, a bombardment somewhere, or perhaps another spell in Arctic waters in case *Scharnhorst* came out of her lair. He saw the commander, The Bloke, standing characteristically with feet apart, one hand in his reefer pocket, a drink in the other, while he listened to the ship's chaplain, Beveridge, going on about something or other.

The Chief signalled to a steward for a refill, and

frowned. This was their third consecutive Sunday in harbour. It was too much, especially for the chaplain. It had gone completely to his head.

This morning at Divisions, for instance. The lines and lines of seamen and Royal Marines, the stokers and the supply branch, gathered together to hear the Word. He wondered cynically if Beveridge really thought it did any good. Did he still not know that when the air rang to the well-known hymn, *What a friend we have in Jesus*, the old sweats, who were careful not to sing too loudly and alert their divisional officers, used their own version?

> 'When this bloody war is over,
> Oh, how happy I shall be . . .
> No more queuing in the N.A.A.F.I.,
> No more waiting for my tea . . .'

And then there had been that bit about Cavendish. *The sad tragedy of it*. Had Beveridge forgotten that many of *Reliant*'s people had lost relatives and friends, wives and girlfriends? Some had lost everything.

He had studied the new captain, Sherbrooke, his features calm, and betraying nothing while he had stood before his ship's company for the first time. They said he had been a friend of Cavendish's, and in this ship, too. Onslow's eyes moved to a framed photo of the battlecruiser as she had looked before the clutter of new weaponry, signals equipment, and the secret, invisible eye of radar with all its additional fittings. She was a beautiful ship, and still unspoiled by the modern box-like bridges they had built on other old veterans: she had even retained the original tripod mast, and the slightly raked line of her unmatched funnels.

Everybody aboard above a certain rank had heard of

Captain Guy Sherbrooke, but who really knew him? He had an introspective, attentive face, and when they had met, only briefly, Onslow had noticed the eyes. Blue, but not hard like some, and not cold. Eyes that did not forget. Or did not want to forget . . .

The steward said, 'Gin, sir.'

He grunted. A good lunch shortly, but no nap afterwards. His department was on top line, and his staff knew what was expected of them. All the same, like other heads of department, he would probably go round and check a few items before *the great man* returned on board sometime this afternoon.

He thought of Sherbrooke's impassive features while Beveridge had been droning on, and wondered how he felt about Stagg. *Reliant* had always been a very pusser ship, even in peacetime, and without an admiral's flag.

He looked across at the commander. His glass was empty, but his position and expression were unchanged.

He knew that Frazier had been offered a command of his own. He was good; for one so young, better than most. He would make a competent skipper anywhere. But he had stayed. His jowls moved into a grin. *Like me*.

Frazier would be weighing up the new captain as well. As second-in-command, his main purpose was to present his captain with an efficient, reliable, fighting ship. But his duties encompassed far more. The promotion or selection of key ratings for advancement or courses ashore, which would improve their own skills but weaken the ship's self-dependent team, matters of discipline and punishment, or recreation and training, all fell on his shoulders. It was like being the mayor, quartermaster and magistrate of a small town. But know him? That was something else.

He turned, his train of thought disturbed as somebody came to an empty chair and asked, 'This taken, sir?'

Onslow contained an angry retort. This was the new boy. Wavy Navy, wings on his sleeve, and the innocent good looks which would soon get him into trouble.

He relented. 'Take the weight off your feet. Settling in?'

Lieutenant Rayner looked at him, perhaps warily.

'Getting the hang of it, sir.' He shook his head. 'All that spit and polish, though. I thought that was over for the duration.'

Onslow grinned. 'In the navy, it's never over. The war is just a bloody inconvenience!' He chuckled. 'Have a gin. On me.'

Rayner smiled. 'Juice, please.'

Onslow waved to a hurrying steward. 'You would! Costs twice as much as gin!'

The commander walked over to the Club, and raised an eyebrow.

'I'll join you, Chief.' His eyes said, *you must be slipping*. 'What did the God-bosun want this time?'

Frazier smiled. 'One of your stokers, actually. Lucas. His wife's having a baby.'

Onslow snorted. 'Doesn't know his arse from his elbow! I'm surprised he managed it!'

Frazier took a glass. 'Wants the kid to be baptised in the ship's bell.'

Onslow tapped the young Canadian's knee. 'Told you.'

Rayner stood up and excused himself. 'My observer has just arrived.' He smiled gently. 'Another foreigner, I'm afraid. From New Zealand.'

Onslow sighed. 'Take it off your back, son. They mean no harm. You'll see.'

As he left, Frazier said, 'Are you giving him a hard time?'

Onslow ignored it. 'How's the Old Man?' Then he

grinned hugely. It seemed ridiculous to call Sherbrooke that.

Frazier hesitated. 'He's . . . different.'

'How so, John? From Cavendish? Don't keep it a secret!'

Frazier leaned back, his face relaxed, but his mind buzzing with details, lists, people to see, work to be completed before they left the Firth of Forth.

'Something's driving him. I can't explain. But I could feel it.'

'So long as it's not revenge. When I first went to sea, I was with a skipper who'd lost his ship. *I'm out for revenge*, he told us.'

The long curtain was drawn aside; officers were making their way to the tables, pausing to collect a napkin from the rack by the entrance, watched closely by the chief steward, as if he expected one of them to steal something.

They downed their drinks, and Frazier asked, 'And was he?'

Onslow grinned. 'Christ, we were blown up ourselves within a week!'

Frazier sat down. It was hard to accept that the Chief had served in that other war. He must have been just a kid, like some of the midshipmen and junior ratings in this ship. He glanced over the bobbing heads and thrusting soup spoons. *Reliant* had been there, too. All those years, all those miles. It was surprising what he had learned about this ship in the eighteen months since his advanced promotion. He had even heard about the most important day for any captain: when his ship, new from the builders, had been commissioned. He had discovered that *Reliant*'s first captain's wife had waited for that particular day to announce that she was leaving him. Just like that.

And what about Cavendish? A tragedy, Beveridge had

called it. Well, possibly. But an accident? It didn't ring true.

And now a new captain, as screwed up as everybody who had preceded him. What was it about this ship? *I'm a fine one to talk.*

He turned and saw a midshipman, his face red with cold, standing self-consciously behind his chair.

'The Officer-of-the-Day sends his respects, sir. Signal from Operations.' His eyes were moving along the busy plates: midshipmen did not change much in any century, where food was concerned.

Frazier prompted, *'And?'*

'The admiral will be coming off at 1445, sir. An hour earlier than expected.'

'Thank you, Mr Potter.' A steward dragged back his chair, and Frazier stood. 'I'll tell the captain.'

Onslow mopped up the last of his soup with some fresh bread. You could say what you liked, he thought, but you couldn't fault the big ships when it came to bread. They baked their own.

'Trouble, John?'

Frazier touched his fat shoulder. In his heart, he somehow knew that by next Sunday the Chief would be back in his immaculate white overalls again.

'I have a feeling, Chief, that the balloon is about to go up.' He saw some of the others looking over at them, guessing. 'Again.'

Onslow reached for another piece of bread. War *was* a bloody inconvenience.

The piercing shrill of boatswain's calls had barely died away when Rear-Admiral Vincent Stagg appeared at the top of the long accommodation ladder, his hand to his cap in salute. Sherbrooke saw his eyes flit briefly but

33

searchingly across *Reliant*'s broad expanse of quarterdeck, to his flag at the masthead, and back again, taking in the rigid side-party. It was a steep climb from the launch alongside, but Stagg was not even breathless.

Their eyes met for the first time, and Sherbrooke said, 'Welcome aboard, sir.'

Stagg nodded. 'And the same to you, Guy. Good to have you. Capital!'

Sherbrooke remembered the eyes well. Hazel, very clear; like the man, full of energy and questions. Despite the flag officer's thick band of gold on his sleeve, and the double row of oak leaves around his peak, Stagg seemed much the same as when they had last met, at Scapa, between convoys, about eighteen months ago. At first glance he appeared tall, taller than he actually was, but he was careful to hold his trim figure erect at all times, and his personality did the rest. He had always distinguished himself in matters of fitness, and sport of a decidedly personal nature. As a young subbie, he had proved himself to be a fierce and skilled fighter in the boxing ring, and the legacy of a broken nose still gave him a raffish, almost jaunty appearance, which had made him popular with certain newspapers and war correspondents. He had also made his name in competitions throughout the fleet, at squash, where he was rarely beaten, and fencing with both foil and sabre, where he never lost a contest. A man's man. And, in time of war, the sort of no-nonsense leader the country had too long been denied, or so the press insisted.

Stagg was moving again, his hands emphasising various points as he strode toward the lobby, which led the way to his quarters aft. A small procession seemed to flow in his wake: Howe, his flag lieutenant, a tall, harassed-looking officer with a bulging briefcase, who had been ashore to meet his master at the local R.A.F. station, and another lieutenant with a paymaster's white cloth between his stripes, also trying to keep up. He was Villar, the rear-admiral's secretary. There were others too, including a chief writer and an anxious midshipman, whose sole duty appeared to be to take the admiral's cap and gloves.

Sherbrooke sighed inwardly. He would soon know all of them. Stagg had never been one to tolerate ignorance where the men under his charge were concerned.

Stagg strode into the huge day cabin and glared around. 'Open some scuttles! This place is like a tomb!'

He walked to a table and glanced at some letters arranged on a silver tray.

A voice said, 'The commander is here, sir.'

Frazier entered, his cap under one arm, his eyes questioning.

'Sir?'

'I'll want a full report on the replacements for men drafted to other ships, or ashore for training. I'm not happy with the way their lordships are ignoring our need for top-quality personnel.' He looked up, his eyes bright, impatient. 'Officers, too.'

'Yes, sir. We've been lucky so far.'

Stagg turned toward a long mirror on one bulkhead. 'This is a flagship. Luck doesn't come into it.'

Sherbrooke was very aware of the tension, and that the others in their various postures around the big cabin were trying not to notice it.

'Another thing.' Stagg touched a lock of hair which had been flattened by his cap. 'When I was coming out to the ship just now, I saw some ratings on the four-inch director platform. They were smoking.'

There was a loud click as the flag lieutenant opened his briefcase, and took out a pair of binoculars.

Frazier said, 'It is Sunday, sir. Some of the hands have

been doing extra work because of the leave period.'

Stagg did not turn from the glass. 'I don't care if it's bloody Christmas, John. I'll not abide lower standards in this ship.'

The use of Frazier's first name made it worse, in some way.

Stagg faced them. Even that movement revealed a restless energy. Senior officers often went to great lengths to appear absolutely aloof and remote, even in the presence of danger. Rear-Admiral Vincent Stagg was the very opposite. As if he could barely contain his vigour, like something too powerful to be controlled.

'You will know Captain Sherbrooke, by reputation if nothing else. Together we will make this ship, *this command*, an example to others. We are entering a phase of the war which may well determine the strategy of final victory.'

The secretary was handing out sealed envelopes to his minions. Stagg waited until Frazier had returned his attention to him, and said, 'About leave, John. Not too many compassionate cases, right? If any man is a malingerer, replace him. I'd rather have a bunch of new, eager recruits than a collection of moaning barrack stanchions.'

Frazier swallowed. 'There were two bad air raids last night. London and Portsmouth. There are bound to be more requests for leave.'

Stagg grinned. 'Ignore them. Carry on, if you please.'

They moved from the cabin, lastly the midshipman, who handed the admiral's gleaming cap to a steward.

Stagg spread his arms. 'That's more like it.' He looked keenly at Sherbrooke. 'You think I was a bit hard on Frazier? That, as captain, any censure should come from you? I can see it written all over your face!' He paused while Price, his own chief steward, placed a tray of glasses

36

and a decanter on the table, and then said, 'You're absolutely right, of course, or will be, when you've found your feet. You've been hard at it since you came aboard – yesterday, right? You'll soon get the weight.'

He looked at the framed picture of the ship. 'That's why I asked for you to replace poor old Cavendish. I know you've been through it – I read all the reports about *Pyrrhus*, what you did to save the convoy. Against odds. *What I need*, I thought, the right man. Determination and guts. What they respect in the end, you know. Norway, Greece, Crete, and all too often in the Atlantic, we've both seen enough bloody waste and incompetence. Old women dressed as officers, men who learned absolutely nothing from the experiences of the Great War, or ever since, in some cases.'

Sherbrooke watched him. Who did he mean? Frazier, because he had overlooked some small flaw in the pattern when Stagg had come on board? Or Cavendish?

Stagg said sharply, 'Scotch, right?' He nodded to the steward. 'The sun's long past the yardarm!'

Then he said, 'You went to the funeral, I hear.'

Sherbrooke tried to relax. This was more like the man he had known as a lieutenant, full of surprises, perhaps secretly hoping you might be disconcerted by his private knowledge, or its source.

He tasted the Scotch, like fire on his tongue, and noticed that Stagg had not touched his. Another test, perhaps? To see if his new captain was bomb-happy, still back there with his old ship and her silent company?

He said, 'I was in London, too, sir.'

Stagg grinned. 'Well, I had better things to do that day.' He glanced at his watch. 'I'll be ashore again tonight. I expect they'll ask you to the wardroom. To size you up. See what they're in for.'

It was no assumption. Stagg already knew, had probably ordered it.

'The ship seems in good hands, sir.'

Stagg swallowed some whisky, frowning slightly as if he detected some inferiority.

'Can't always tell by the ship's books – but then you know that, of course.'

The door closed, as if to some secret signal. They were alone.

Stagg said, 'The fact is, Guy, I shall be getting more scope for this command. That's why I was up at the Admiralty. Doesn't do any harm to show them what we're doing to fight this war.'

He turned to the mirror again, his eyes almost cold as he examined his reflection, as if it were some subordinate who did not quite measure up. Like Frazier.

He said over his shoulder, 'And don't worry about Cavendish – what happened, I mean. Dead men's shoes. As far as this ship is concerned, it's just so much history.'

Sherbrooke realized that the reflected eyes were fixed upon him.

'It crossed my mind, sir.'

Stagg did not smile. 'Just make certain the shoes don't pinch, right?'

Sherbrooke put down the glass, to give himself time. They had been lieutenants together; they had both been captains.

Today we are as different as two languages.

There was a painting of Beatty beside one of the doors, a battlecruiser, like some great phantom ship, in the background: Sir David Beatty, who had commanded the battlecruisers at Jutland, a generation and another war ago. The battlecruiser had been a new concept, a dream, and a legend: at Jutland, it had become a nightmare, when these great ships, with too little armour, had been blasted apart by superior German shells and gunnery.

He looked at Stagg as he turned away from the mirror. Was that how he saw himself? Another Beatty?

Stagg asked suddenly, 'You never married, did you, Guy?'

'No, sir.' He found he could answer without anger, without the terrible grief he had once suffered. But Stagg knew that also, that she had been killed in an air raid, while *Pyrrhus* had been on one of her runs to North Russia.

Stagg nodded, as though privately satisfied. 'A new beginning, then.' He glanced at the picture of his flagship. 'She'll not let you down.'

Sherbrooke was reminded suddenly of the churchyard in Esher, close to Sandown Park racecourse. And the tall girl in black. *No sense in brooding . . .*

No better epitaph.

3

Coming to Terms

It seemed to take an age to drag his mind back to reality, to the present. *Now*. And yet Sherbrooke had come to know from bitter experience that it was only a matter of seconds. Almost without thinking he had rolled over on the narrow bunk, his feet planted on the deck, his ear and mind adjusting, taking stock. He glanced at the small clock. It was just after six in the morning, halfway through the morning watch. Surprisingly, he had been able to sleep, for a while anyway, the small bunkside reading light left on as a precaution. A link with routine, a barrier against the nightmare which could strike without mercy if he dropped his guard.

Perhaps he was mistaken, and it would never return.

He pulled on his sea-boots, and glanced around at the small sea-cabin which had been his home for most of the time since *Reliant* had weighed anchor on a cold, misty morning, slipping silently from the Firth of Forth to join her destroyer escort without fuss or ceremony. That had been five days ago, steering north into these familiar, hostile waters. Sherbrooke stood up and waited for the deck to tell him the motion, as it would have done immediately in *Pyrrhus*. It was there all right, but slow and steady, in time with the sea, like deep breathing. He leaned on the small wash basin and studied his face in the mirror. He had shaved before turning in, a habit he had developed somewhere along the way, when the real edge of war had shown itself. It did not do the watchkeepers any good to see their captain unshaven and bleary-eyed when he first appeared on the bridge. Like that morning when they had weighed anchor: the forecastle party, shining black like beetles in their oilskins, and seemingly miles away from his lofty position on the upper bridge. Two tugs hovering nearby in case the new captain made a cock-up of it. At least Rear-Admiral Stagg had stayed away during the manoeuvre, although his presence was very real, nevertheless.

The great bows swinging, as if the land and not the ship was gliding past, while the Jack was hauled down and the anchor appeared above the water like a giant pendulum. And so quiet. The coxswain and telegraphsmen far below the bridge, hidden behind armour plate, the officers on the lookout for unexpected harbour craft, the navigator, Lieutenant-Commander Rhodes, a great, bearded figure bending over his chart table, his big fingers supple and almost delicate as they worked busily with dividers and parallel rulers. In *Pyrrhus*, the pilot had been an R.N.R. officer, an ex-merchant navy man with a master's ticket. During some of the long night watches Sherbrooke had found a form of escape in listening to him and his tales of another world, of cruise ships and long voyages, of money, and of the passengers, many of whom reappeared every year for one cruise or another.

In time he would get to know Rhodes, too. But even that memory opened the wound again.

There was a tap at the door. 'Captain, sir?'

It was a bridge messenger, a mug of tea carefully balanced on a tray. Sherbrooke had been surprised, moved, when for the first two mornings at sea his own steward,

41

Petty Officer Long, had brought the tea himself, as if he did not trust anybody else, or perhaps for other reasons at which one could only guess. Either way, he had got out of a warm bunk to do it.

He sipped the tea, the typical navy mixture of sugar and tinned milk: stuck to your ribs, they said. It would be going round the upper deck positions now, the secondary armament, and the anti-aircraft gun crews. Even up here, they were manned. Not even a battlecruiser could afford to be careless.

He could picture the chart exactly in his mind, as if he had just examined it. They were three hundred miles south of the Icelandic coast, Seydisfjord to be exact, and some two hundred miles west of the Faroes. A wilderness, but a jungle, too, where hunter could so easily change roles with the hunted.

Their destroyer escort numbered six, some of the new M-class, probably the largest of their type yet built. Even so, they would be finding it hard going in these waters, keeping station on their giant consort, men trying to stay on their feet with the hulls bucking and plunging, attempting to cripple the unwary.

'What's it like out there?'

The seaman hesitated, surprised that the captain had spoken to him.

'Bit rough, sir. She can take it, though.'

He looked away as Sherbrooke glanced at him, afraid, perhaps, that he had gone too far.

But Sherbrooke had caught the man's sense of belonging, of pride. How old was he? Certainly not yet twenty, or old enough to draw his tot.

The seaman left quietly. And there were twelve hundred more like him crammed into this great hull. There had been a few absentees when *Reliant* had left the Firth of

Forth, a couple of men who had been sent on compassionate leave, their homes and families wiped out in air raids, and another who had gone south to see his wife. The welfare people had reported that she had been having an affair with somebody else. It was common enough in wartime, but no less heartbreaking for the one involved. Neighbours had heard screams, and the local police had discovered the woman more dead than alive, with a real chance that she might not recover. The naval patrols would be out looking, and the police would know all the likely hiding-places by now. That was one face he would rather not see across the defaulters' table. A good seaman, to all accounts. Now he was a deserter, and far worse.

And there had been the usual ones who had overstayed their brief liberty. Too much to drink, a woman maybe: it would all drop in Commander Frazier's lap. He smiled and reached for his cap. *The Bloke*.

He slid open the door and glanced back at the small, businesslike bunk. Stagg would have slept down aft in his own lavish quarters. He closed the door. He probably had the right idea.

He turned and listened to the muted stammer of morse, the occasional rasp of static. *My ship*. It was still hard to accept, let alone take for granted.

They would know he was on his way. They always did. *The Old Man's coming up. What's he like today? Roll on my bleedin' twelve!*

Sherbrooke stepped into the gloom of the upper bridge and waited to get his bearings, as the ship's bows sank slowly into a bank of solid water. Icy spray dashed across the bridge windows like hail, and the clearview screens squeaked in protest.

He was slowly becoming accustomed to the breadth and size of this bridge, the place of command, the nerve-centre, the eyes and brain of the ship. Dark figures stood around in their familiar positions, although to a layman they might appear casual, or unemployed. Messengers at the rank of polished voicepipes, a boatswain's mate by the tannoy microphone, somebody gathering up empty mugs from the deck. The navigating officer had the morning watch: he always did. As the senior lieutenant-commander, he was always ready for the dawning of a new day, a time when fatigue and thoughts of breakfast, no matter how ordinary, could make a man careless, vulnerable. And it only took one man.

Rhodes's assistant was a young lieutenant named Frost, very keen and eager, who had his leg pulled mercilessly because of the beard he was trying to grow, without much success. At the moment it looked more like something a child might stick to his face for a school pantomime.

Sherbrooke said, 'Morning, Pilot. All quiet?'

Rhodes stood massively beside a clearview screen and gestured toward the rising bank of water. In the faint light, it was the colour of charcoal, but the troughs were like black glass. Higher and higher, so it appeared that the battlecruiser was sliding abeam down an unending slope, unable to resist.

Then the bows dipped once more and Sherbrooke watched the sea bursting over the forecastle deck and spurting through the hawse pipes, until, barely shaking, the ship raised herself again, the water boiling away over the side, or exploding against gun positions and other fixtures like froth. It looked almost yellow in the poor light.

'We had a signal from *Montagu*, sir, but nothing really bad. One of her boats came adrift and she requested permission to go and search for it.'

'You refused?'

Rhodes nodded. 'They know the orders as well as we do, sir. No stopping.'

Sherbrooke gripped the tall chair which was bolted down on the port side of the bridge. Rhodes made light of it, but many officers in his position, orders or not, would have awakened the captain, if only to keep a clear yardarm. He would make a fine commanding officer when the chance came.

He glanced through the side windows, which opened onto the flag deck. More anonymous figures in oilskins ducked and pounced, as if taking part in some ritual dance. Occasionally a flag would be unfolded, the bunting very bright against the sombre backdrop before it was stowed away. The lights were ready for the first signal of the day. *All ships will exercise action stations.*

It was hard for men who had just been on watch, as well as for those who had barely slept during the brief respite in their stuffy messdecks, to obey the urgent clamour of alarm bells, even though everyone knew it was an exercise.

Sherbrooke touched the arms of his chair and felt them press into his ribs as the great hull swayed upright again. *Reliant* had been described as a lucky ship. Compared with some, this must be true. It was said that when Günther Prien, one of Germany's first U-Boat aces, had forced his audacious and seemingly impossible entry into Scapa Flow and torpedoed the battleship *Royal Oak*, with appalling loss of life, his sights had first been on *Reliant*. And at Jutland, when the battlecruiser squadron had come under direct and heavy fire, her steering had inexplicably jammed, the rudder helpless to prevent her from steering in a wide circle, away from the embattled squadron, and almost certain destruction.

Unfortunately, luck was not always enough.

There were more voices, low, contained, formal.

Because of me.

It was Frazier, his face reddened by the wind and icy spray.

'Good morning, sir.'

'Morning, John.' He waited. Frazier would have been right around the ship already: he never took anything for granted. But Sherbrooke felt no closer to him than at their first meeting.

'Any special orders, sir?' He did not even bother to hold onto anything, he was so used to the ship.

'Damage control, John, but this time replace the officers and petty officers with more junior ones. Good training.'

He glanced at the radar repeater in the forepart of the bridge. The invisible eye. In the early days, it had been just a dream.

'And let the Royal Marines exercise Y Turret with local control. We may not always be able to rely on miracles.' He saw the young Lieutenant Frost peering at the bridge clock, the boatswain's mate examining the tannoy. It was almost time. *To be cursed by every man aboard.* He smiled. It might even bring Stagg to the bridge.

A messenger lowered his face to a voicepipe. 'Fore-bridge?' He turned toward Sherbrooke. 'From W/T, sir. Signal.'

'Send it up.' It was probably a ship in distress some-where, a convoy under U-Boat attack, an R.A.F. plane down in the drink. Important, but outside their concern.

A figure appeared on the bridge: it was the chief telegraphist, Elphick, another man up and about early, making sure his department was on top line.

Sherbrooke opened the signal, feeling their eyes upon him, sensing a certain relief at the break in routine.

Afterwards, he tried to recall exactly how long he had

sat with the signal pad in his hands, the neat, firm printing meaning nothing, as if it were mocking him.

Eventually he said, 'Immediate from Admiralty. Air Reconnaissance report that the German cruiser *Minden* is at sea.' He was conscious of the coldness of his voice, the flatness. 'Believed to have left Tromsø two days ago.'

Rhodes, the professional, was the first to speak. 'It was reported to be foul weather at that time, sir.'

Frazier said, 'She could be anywhere by now.' He looked at the others. 'Not here. Anywhere.'

Sherbrooke scarcely heard. He picked up the solitary handset opposite his chair, the one with the small red light on it, like a baleful eye.

Stagg answered immediately, as if he had been expecting it.

'Bloody people! Don't they know how important it is to watch every single move?' Then there was a short pause. '*Minden*, eh? The one you met up with?'

Sherbrooke said, 'Yes, sir. The one that sank my ship.'

He replaced the handset, and said, 'Exercise Action Stations, if you please.'

Frazier hesitated. 'I'm very sorry, sir.'

Just for those seconds, they were alone. Not captain and subordinate, but two men.

Sherbrooke laid one hand on his sleeve. 'I hope to God it never happens to you. It's something . . .'

The rest was lost in the screaming clamour of alarm bells and the slam of watertight doors.

Sherbrooke slid from the chair and walked to the chart table. It had been a damned close thing.

Rear-Admiral Vincent Stagg sat comfortably on a chart cabinet and crossed his legs. 'Weather's easing. Should be at Seydisfjord on time.' He glanced sharply at the navigating officer, the only other man present besides Sherbrooke. *'Right?'*

Rhodes picked up his notebook from the table. '1100 tomorrow.'

Stagg looked around the chart room, a quiet refuge after the bridge and the comings and goings of watchkeepers and working parties.

'Good.' He added, 'You can carry on, Pilot. I expect you have a few things to do.'

The navigator smiled. 'A few, sir.'

As the door closed behind him, Stagg remarked to Sherbrooke, 'Useful chap. Don't want to lose him, if I can help it.' He unbuttoned his jacket and took out a leather cigar case. 'You can stop worrying, Guy. There's been no more news of *Minden*. It's somebody else's headache anyway, until she's buggered off back to Tromsø or some other godforsaken place. Things are moving at last – and as I told them at the Admiralty, it's not a moment too soon. We need smaller but more powerful units, like Force H, for instance. Our sister ship *Renown*, a carrier, and a strong set of escorts have worked wonders. We can do better. I just told them to get their fingers out!' It amused him, and he lit a cigar, smiling reminiscently at some thought of London. 'I can be tough when I like, you know, Guy. Nice as pie if I get treated with respect, but call me pig and I'm pig all the way through!'

He glanced up at the deckhead speaker as it squeaked into life.

'Watchkeepers of the afternoon watch to dinner!'

He corrected gently, *'Lunch.'*

Sherbrooke, gazing at the chart table, barely heard him. Nearly six hours had passed since the signal had been brought to the bridge. *Minden* was out again. There had been three of them that day, when *Pyrrhus* had gone down.

And I still cannot remember. One second on the bridge, the steel plating buckled inboard like wet cardboard, voicepipes calling and calling, unanswered by the men who lay dead or dying at their stations. *And then?* He stared at the chart lying uppermost on the table, *The approaches to Iceland*, but he did not see it. There must have been another massive explosion, and yet he could recall nothing more, only breaking the surface, gasping and shouting, crushed by the cold, the numbing pressure of icy water. And the ship had gone. *Nothing*. Only a handful of choking, floundering shapes. Men he had known. *Men who trusted me*.

Stagg leaned forward, a lock of chestnut hair falling above one eye.

'You've done well, Guy. Damn well. To take command at such short notice.' His tone hardened. 'But I wanted you as captain. I knew your record, your style of leadership – it still matters, you know.' He was suddenly on his feet, the uncontrollable energy manifesting itself again. 'In every war it takes *time* to get rid of the deadwood. Look at the last one, for God's sake! Ideas that had scarcely changed since Trafalgar, rules that went out the window when the first U-Boats put to sea! *Winning* is what matters, what counts. Rules are for losers!'

He paused beside the table, and Sherwood could smell his after-shave lotion, strong and powerful, like the man.

'In Iceland we shall be joined by *Seeker*, a new escort carrier.' He smiled, and watched his cigar smoke being drawn into the overhead fan. 'She's no giant, but it's a start. We'll be a small, self-dependent force. There'll be a lot more before long.' His smile broadened into a grin. 'But there's only one *Reliant*!'

The grin vanished, as though its effect had been calculated. 'I shall want you with me when we visit the admiral-commanding in Iceland. Our destroyers can refuel, and I'll want a full report on why *Montagu* lost a boat. Her commanding officer has a very inflated opinion of himself . . . that'll stop him farting in church.'

There was a sound, and he turned and exclaimed, 'Oh, for Christ's sake! I told them I wasn't to be disturbed!'

The door opened slightly. It was Rhodes again. 'Signal from Admiralty, sir. *Minden* is reported back in harbour. She was sighted heading for the Lofoten Islands.'

Stagg asked sharply, 'Where do *you* think she is, Pilot?'

Rhodes answered without hesitation. 'Bodø, sir. A big fjord on the Norwegian mainland. The Jerries built a military airfield there.' He saw the rear-admiral raise his eyebrows. 'It was in A.I.s, sir.'

Sherbrooke said, 'What else?'

Rhodes looked at him directly. '*Minden* made contact with a Russian destroyer and some minesweepers.' He turned to the rear-admiral, but Sherbrooke knew he was still speaking to him. 'She sank all of them. No survivors.'

Sherbrooke repressed the memories. There was nothing they could have done. It was far more important to discover why *Minden* had come out and had headed for the one anchorage where there was strong air cover, and where she would be better placed for another sortie further south, or even an attempt to enter the Baltic and return to Germany.

But the cold reason of strategy eluded him. All he could see was the dark, crouching shape of the cruiser, her guns firing and reloading with the precision of a machine, a single weapon.

Stagg said, 'Keep us informed, Pilot.' He looked at his watch. 'I shall stroll aft . . . for some *lunch*.'

Then he replaced his cigar case in one pocket, his face deep in thought.

'We shall be working-up with *Seeker* for a few days until the two big convoys are through. Who knows, we might get a crack at your bloody *Minden*, eh? But I doubt it. Now, if it was *Scharnhorst*, that would really be a feather in the proverbial cap.'

Sherbrooke felt the tension draining away. Perhaps Stagg was right after all. Hold personal feelings at a distance. Eyes always on the main chance . . . He almost smiled. Stagg would be a vice-admiral at this rate before anybody realized what had happened!

Stagg remarked in an almost matter-of-fact tone, 'We've been so damn busy I didn't have a chance to speak to you about the funeral. Many there?'

Sherbrooke shook his head, seeing again the drab clothing, the vice-admiral and his unsmiling Wren driver.

'Just a few relations – some of our lot, too.'

Stagg regarded him thoughtfully. 'What about Jane . . . ah, Mrs Cavendish? Was she taking it well?' He laughed, without humour. 'Of course – I forgot. You were quite keen on her once yourself, weren't you?' He picked up his cap, regarding the two rows of bright gold leaves. 'Well, now's your chance, Guy.'

When he had gone, still smiling, Sherbrooke waited for a few moments, signing Rhodes's log book, giving himself time.

He thought of her face when they had spoken together, the poise and the strength of the woman. He thought, too, of the smart Armstrong-Siddeley car in which Captain Charles Cavendish had died alone. Like the shattered photograph, it had been no accident, and Stagg knew as much.

He heard feet outside the door, probably Rhodes, waiting to announce the next alteration of course. The ship needed him, but not as much as he needed her.

He strode out of the chart room, and saw the relief on Rhodes's bearded face. After all, ships were bombed, torpedoed and sunk by shellfire every day of the week. It was their world: survival was the only prize.

He climbed into his chair, realizing that he had not eaten since the previous evening. 'Dodger' Long would not be happy about that.

He leaned forward to peer at the wide, flared bows, the sea lifting and falling away on either side as the stem sliced through it, the deck glistening with spray.

'Time to alter course, Pilot?'

Rhodes gave a broad grin. 'Course to steer is zero-one-zero, sir.' He watched the captain's hand touch the arm of his chair: something personal, private. Like his eyes, when the Chief Tel had brought up the signal about the German cruiser. It was something Rhodes knew he might never share, or truly understand.

'Bring her round. Make a signal to the escorts to alter course in succession.' He thought of Stagg's obvious pleasure at the missing boat. 'And signal *Montagu*'s C.O. to report on board when we reach harbour.'

Rhodes was already busy, and on either side of the bridge the signal lamps clattered in unison, each destroyer acknowledging instantly, the lights like bright chips of diamond.

Sherbrooke recalled the words of the elderly operations officer. *They would. In that ship.*

He touched the chair again. So be it.

The smart launch with the rear-admiral's flag painted on either bow dashed across the water, the roar of her engines echoing from the sides of the fjord. Fragments of ice tinkled and broke from the stem like glass, and when Sherbrooke stood up in the cockpit he felt the breeze cutting his face, and wondered how people managed to live normal lives in Iceland.

He heard Stagg's angry voice from the small cabin. His flag lieutenant, Howe, was getting the rough edge of the admiral's tongue again. Stagg could not be an easy man to serve.

Everything had gone wrong, from the moment *Reliant* had dropped anchor. Their consort-to-be, the escort carrier *Seeker*, was not ready for sea. While making her final approach, she had been in collision with a local fishing trawler; it was not much, but enough to cause some damage to *Seeker*'s lower hull. Repairs had already begun at Reykjavik, but how long they would take was anybody's guess. Stagg had been furious, especially when the admiral in charge had told him that the Icelandic authorities were considering taking action against the Royal Navy for severely damaging one of their fishing fleet.

Stagg had been unable to hide his fury, even from the officers of the local headquarters.

'Bloody Icelanders, they hate our guts anyway! Would have preferred the Germans to get here before us! By God, I'll lay odds that Admiral Donitz would have taught them a sharp lesson!'

They had gone aboard *Seeker* and met her captain. It had been a tense visit.

Seeker, a *Smiter* Class escort carrier, was neither beautiful nor as grand as the big fleet carriers. A product of the Anglo-American lease-lend agreement, and converted from merchant-ship hulls, with wooden flight decks, they were unstable in any kind of bad weather, and would not last five minutes in the embattled seas of the Mediterranean, or with the Americans in the Pacific. But *Seeker* and her growing number of consorts, graceless and uncomfortable though they might be, were achieving

53

something which, eighteen months ago, people would have believed impossible. In the vital Battle of the Atlantic, with the mounting toll of losses of ships and their desperately needed cargoes, there had always been a vast spread of ocean where air cover could not reach. Whether the convoys originated in the U.S.A. and Canada, or from Britain and the base here in Iceland, there had always been that gap, *the killing ground*, as the old Atlantic hands called it. U-Boats had been able to surface with impunity, and use their superior speed to pursue convoys and charge their batteries at the same time. Then, at night, they would close with the slow-moving lines of merchantmen and attack. Losses rose higher and higher, outpacing the shipyards' ability to build vessels to replace those sunk.

The little escort carrier had changed that. U-Boat crews were suddenly confronted with fast fighters and bombers hundreds of miles from any kind of base, and the lesson had been learned. Now the enemy was forced to spend more and more time submerged, and at reduced speed, their ability to track and torpedo the plodding merchantmen seriously impaired. The monthly list of kills had, at last, diminished, in the Allies' favour.

Sherbrooke wiped his face with his gloved hand and saw *Reliant* lying directly ahead. Against the bleak side of the fjord, she looked completely white, and seemed to shimmer in the hard glare, her powerful hull, high bridges and funnels covered with a sheen of ice, and so still that she could have been an extension of the land itself, with only the flags and a thin tendril of smoke from one funnel to reveal her latent strength.

Stagg climbed up beside him. 'A beauty, eh?'

Sherbrooke glanced at him. Calm, or resigned, he wondered.

Stagg muttered, 'Might be weeks before we get *Seeker*

in company, Guy. Bloody poor show!'

The bowman was in position, boathook at the ready. Sherbrooke saw the side-party at the top of the accommodation ladder, frozen stiff, probably, after A.C.H.Q. had sent a signal to announce their return aboard.

'Waste of a day!' Stagg's eyes gleamed. 'I'll see *Montagu*'s captain when we get aboard. Just in the bloody mood for him!'

The calls trilled, and Sherbrooke noticed that Stagg made a point of climbing aboard without his greatcoat. The flag lieutenant would carry it himself.

Commander Frazier was ready to meet them.

Stagg said, 'I'll let you tell him the great news, Guy. I'm going aft.' His glance shifted to a small group of seamen who were attempting to splice some eyes in a tangle of wire from the boatswain's store. They were all very young ordinary seamen, some of the most recent replacements, and still completely lost in the new surroundings of this, their first ship.

Stagg strode over to them and nodded abruptly to a leading hand who was in charge.

To one of the new recruits he said curtly, 'Name, boy?'

The youth stared at the broad lower stripe on Stagg's sleeve, and seemed almost tongue-tied. 'Baker, s-sir!'

'*From?*'

'Leeds, sir.'

Stagg smiled. 'Ah, well.' Then he took the wire from the young seaman's nerveless hand and a marlin spike from another. 'Like this, see? Take charge of it! Show who's boss, right?'

It was a perfect piece of wire splicing. He thrust his hand into his pocket.

'Like riding a bicycle, boy – you never forget!'

Sherbrooke had seen the blood on his fingers, and

wondered why he had bothered. He was respected, admired, even feared; he did not have to impress, or prove anything to any man.

Stagg strode aft, his cap at a jaunty angle.

Like Beatty, he thought. Perhaps that was it.

Frazier followed him into his cabin, where Petty Officer Long was already waiting expectantly.

'Drink, John?' His eyes fell on the file Frazier was carrying under his arm. 'What's that?'

'Operational reports. They came out from A.C.H.Q. while you were in *Seeker*.' He paused. 'Pity about her spot of bother, sir.'

Sherbrooke, looking through the file, did not answer. Then he said, 'The admiral will want to see this.'

'I thought it could wait, sir. There's nothing that concerns us.' Frazier sounded defensive.

Sherbrooke looked over at Long. 'Later – but thanks.' To Frazier he said, 'I'll take it to him.'

He found Stagg having a drink, his feet propped on a chair.

'Oh, for God's sake. Can't it wait, Guy?' He was smiling, but there was no warmth in his eyes.

'Operational folio, sir.' He looked at him evenly. 'And no, I don't think it can.'

'Oh, very well. Get on with it.'

Sherbrooke turned over a page. 'Admiralty reported that one of our submarines torpedoed a German cruiser in the Skaggerak, believed to be the *Flensburg*.'

'Well, bully for our gallant submariners! I told you the Jerries were more than likely going to try to move ships to the Baltic. Their troops will need all the support they can get once the weather improves.'

Sherbrooke regarded him gravely. 'The *Flensburg*, if it was her, was heading west, sir.'

'Let me see that.' Stagg merely sounded annoyed that his drink had been spoiled.

Sherbrooke watched his eyes moving quickly across the folio, then more slowly, until he could almost feel the force of Stagg's concentration.

'The same time as *Minden* made her move.' He shook his head. 'No, they'd never risk an attack on another Murmansk convoy with the ice edge so low. Later on, April maybe . . . when our ships get scattered up to Jan Mayen or Bear Island.' The hazel eyes lifted from the papers. 'You've made up your mind, I take it.'

'I think the cruiser intended to join *Minden*, sir, maybe with others, for all we know. Air reconnaissance is never reliable at this time of year.' He saw the lingering doubt, resentment even. 'I think they're coming this way, sir. After the big convoy, the one nobody talks about.'

Stagg lurched to his feet. 'They wouldn't dare! With us here, and a cruiser squadron under Admiral Simms? Never.'

Sherbrooke waited. Seeing it. Wondering why Frazier had not thought it important enough to make immediate contact.

'The cruisers are probably five or six hundred miles to the northeast of here. As for us . . .' He almost shrugged. 'We wouldn't have been here if *Seeker* had kept out of trouble.'

Stagg nodded slowly. 'You're bloody right, you know. They'd not hesitate to throw a couple of cruisers to the wolves if they could get amongst that convoy.' He stared at him, his eyes hard. 'How many troops will it be carrying?'

'An army, sir.'

Stagg put his hand to his mouth. It was still bleeding from his display of wire-splicing.

'Do you think we could do it?'

'If we weigh anchor this afternoon – yes, I do. If you ask the Admiralty to send heavy units from Scapa, it could be too late.'

Stagg said coolly, 'You never forget your old tricks, do you?'

Sherbrooke stared at the icy slab of land visible through the nearest scuttle. He was surprised that he sounded so calm. So confident.

'Like riding a bicycle,' he said.

4

Lifeline

The middle watch, from midnight to four a.m., was hated more than any other. It began too early for watchkeepers to snatch more than an hour's sleep before going to their stations throughout the ship, and came to an end at a time when another dawn was already on the horizon. It was a demanding four hours, when men had to concentrate even on the most routine and boring duties and remain alert, when sleep was a constant threat.

On *Reliant*'s broad bridge, protected as it was from the spray and wind, the problem was the same. Lieutenant-Commander Christopher Evershed stood with arms folded in the centre position, his ears and eyes reaching out to the muffled figures around him, to the occasional sounds from voicepipe or telephone, and the blurred panorama of the sea beyond the bows. By rocking forward slightly on his toes, he could expect to see the overlapping muzzles of the twin fifteen-inch guns in A and B turrets, a sight which had once afforded him pride and satisfaction.

Evershed was *Reliant*'s gunnery officer, and as such was a key member of the ship's 'team', as Rear-Admiral Stagg liked to describe them. He had been in the battle-cruiser almost since she had commissioned at the outbreak of war, three years, broken only when he had left her to attend advanced courses, which had eventually made him the senior gunnery officer. He thought the others in his department probably envied him, as he had once envied his superior.

He turned his head sharply and saw a seaman in a duffle coat straightening up, away from the voicepipes, very aware of his scrutiny.

Evershed tried to find comfort in the fact that, during those watches when he was the O.O.W., there was neither slackness nor any irresponsibility for which he might later be blamed. His guns and the training and efficiency of their crews were his reason for being, and the ship's own strength and purpose. It was a demanding duty at any time, even in a private ship, but with a flag officer aboard, he could never afford to relax.

He watched the clearview screens being wiped again, but not of spray or ice this time. It was fog, an element which, in those early days, would have caused something like panic as this great ship and her six invisible escorts pounded along blindly with no slackening of speed. His eyes moved to the small radar repeater on the port side of the bridge, close to the captain's empty chair so that he could have seen it without moving.

He could feel the huge hull lifting almost contemptuously to thrust through the fog-shrouded water, and imagined the attendant destroyers spread out on either beam, Asdic machines sweeping in slow, cautious arcs. There were no U-Boats reported in this area, but you could never be sure.

Evershed unfolded his arms and moved them briskly in the still, damp air. He always tried to keep fit, something he considered essential for any officer who intended to set an example to others. He saw the bright blink of light from the screen and wondered if the chance would come, not one day, but soon, for a command of his own. All those destroyers were commanded by officers of his own rank, except for the leader, *Mulgrave*, which carried a full captain.

He heard somebody whispering, and saw his watch-keeping assistant, Lieutenant Gerald Drake, pausing to speak with one of the signalmen. Evershed contained the spark of irritation with an effort. He was tired, feeling the strain of working watch-and-watch, even though he would never admit it to anyone.

He knew there was nothing really to dislike in Drake, or for that matter even bother to consider. Drake was an R.N.V.R. lieutenant, a temporary wartime officer, something so rare as to be almost unknown in *Reliant* and in other big ships at the outbreak of war. Now they were everywhere; many of them even held commands of their own, the ones that made headlines, the destroyers and battered corvettes of the Atlantic, the Glory Boys of Light Coastal Forces, M.T.B.s and motor gunboats. Even Rear-Admiral Stagg, who had at first been quick to criticize the Wavy Navy, had changed his tune.

It was deeper than a mere dislike of amateurs. Drake was young, in his twenties, but he radiated a confidence and calm assurance totally at odds with his rank and inexperience. He was a barrister in civilian life, and there had been several judges in his family, according to Commander Frazier.

Evershed could almost hear his own father's voice. *Privileged.*

Like that time at Scapa, where there had been a reception for the press and some war correspondents, held in *Reliant*'s wardroom. He had seen Drake being greeted by one of the correspondents, a man well known on newsreel and wireless alike, the pair of them behaving like old friends. They had, apparently, been at school together.

And he had not been the only one: the rear-admiral had noticed it, too. Evershed strode to the chart room. It was all so bloody unfair. *Privileged* . . .

He heard Drake chuckle; he would have to have a word with him about gossiping with the ratings. Perhaps he wanted to be popular. He would soon learn the truth about that. They would laugh at him behind his back.

Evershed caught sight of his own reflection in the door of a first-aid locker: a narrow, alert face, hair cut short, brushed straight back. The gunnery officer of a famous ship; a legend, he told himself.

He frowned and stared at the chart. Three days since they had weighed and had quit Seydisfjord. Southeast and then further south, the blustery weather making station-keeping a nightmare, even for the crack destroyers. The Admiralty would not stand for much more of it, he thought. His eyes moved to the jagged coastline of Norway, only one hundred and fifty miles to port, with the carefully defined *Declared Mined Area* as a warning to any captain, friend or enemy, who might lose his way. And there was Stavanger, a known German air base. Surely Stagg must be aware of the additional hazard?

He listened to the ship around and below him, the beat of fans, the steady vibration of her engines and her four great screws, considering the new captain, Sherbrooke, and wondering what he was really like. He always seemed so calm, and yet so aware, as if he were part of the ship. What must it have been like when his ship had been blown from under him?

It had been different with the last captain, Cavendish. Very approachable, ready to listen, and he had hinted more than once at a chance of promotion for Evershed. But even Cavendish had not truly understood that he had not wanted to end up in command of some gunnery school, or in charge of advanced instruction. Classrooms and diagrams. *Not with my own ship . . .*

And Cavendish had changed, towards the end. Evershed was not an imaginative man, but he was intelligent enough to appreciate it and to know when the change had occurred. Either just before, or immediately after the German cruisers had attacked the Russian convoy, and Sherbrooke's *Pyrrhus* had broken formation to engage them unaided. *Reliant* had had steam up and had been ready, awaiting the signal that would have told them that *Scharnhorst*, or even the mighty *Tirpitz*, imprisoned so long behind her booms and nets deep inside a Norwegian fjord, was coming out to challenge them. But *Reliant* had not moved. He had seen Cavendish leaving Stagg's quarters, and the captain's expression had held something he would never forget. Anger, astonishment; if anything, it had seemed like grief.

He looked at the chart room clock and stifled a yawn. Three days would be long enough. Tomorrow . . . he grimaced, *today*, Stagg would be ordered to break off the hunt. The German cruiser was probably back in her fjord, her company peacefully asleep. *Lucky devils . . .*

Another hour and a half, and the watch would change, and Rhodes would take over. Nothing ever seemed to get to Rhodes.

He turned and snapped, 'What is it?'

The boatswain's mate stared in at him, his face carefully blank.

'I think Mr Drake would like to speak to you, sir.'

Evershed glared. 'I'm out of sight for two minutes and . . .' He saw the sudden uncertainty. 'What is it, man?'

The seaman followed him across the bridge. Everything was exactly as before, except that a rating was collecting mugs for another round of tea.

'Well?'

Lieutenant Drake turned away from the radar repeater. 'I just lost *Mulgrave*, sir.' He sounded quite calm, possibly wary, like the opening words of a cross-examination of some unknown witness.

Evershed leaned over the repeater and watched the steadily revolving beam. The escorting destroyers appeared and faded again, in perfect formation.

He said, 'Well, *Mulgrave*'s there now, right?'

'I thought you should be told, sir.'

So poised. Evershed had noticed more than once the perfect cut of Drake's uniforms; he had a greatcoat which would have looked well on an admiral. *Privileged* . . .

He said sharply, 'You have to learn about these things.' He did not care if the other watchkeepers were listening. Drake had to realize that he was not God's gift to the Royal Navy, and nor would he . . .

'*Christ!*' A leading signalman could not contain it. 'She's gone again!'

Evershed pushed him aside and stared with disbelief as the pale green images on the screen faded, and then merged like spectres in some wild dance. He said, 'Get the senior radar mechanic up here, *chop-chop*!' He was about to turn on Drake again when the radar repeater gave a quick flicker and went dead. Nothing.

But all Evershed could see was the great battlecruiser hurtling at almost full speed into the fog. Completely blind; and at any minute the slightest alteration of course could bring her into collision with one of the escorts.

'*Half ahead!*' He caught Drake's arm. 'No, let me do it!' He leaned over the voicepipe's bell mouth and said, 'Half ahead both!'

It seemed an age before the wheelhouse acknowledged, although it was only seconds. The quartermaster, staring for so long at the gently ticking gyro repeater, his fingers moving the polished wheel without conscious thought, sounded remarkably normal.

'Half ahead both, sir!' The clatter of telegraphs echoed faintly up the tube. 'Revolutions one-one-zero!'

Evershed pressed his face to the sloping bridge windows. The fog was thicker, as though they were charging into a solid barrier.

He heard himself snap, 'Slow ahead! Reduce to seven-zero revolutions!' He saw Drake watching him. *'Bloody do it!'*

He steadied himself against the captain's chair and felt the pressure against his thigh as the great ship began to lose way. The destroyers, provided they were awake and their radar was working, would see what was happening. If only . . .

He winced as the red eye began to flicker, and the admiral's handset gave its usual unpleasant squawk.

He snatched it up. 'Bridge, sir! Officer of the watch here.' He got no further.

Stagg sounded querulous. 'I know who you are! Why the hell have you reduced speed?'

Evershed tried to swallow but his mouth felt like sand.

'The radar, sir.' He looked up as a hand reached past him and took the handset. It was Sherbrooke.

'All right, Guns. I've got the weight.' He raised the instrument to his ear. 'Captain, sir. Radar's on the blink. I shall signal the escorts. I'd like to sound action stations, then clear lower deck, just in case.'

He paused, expecting an argument or worse. He could feel the others watching him, and had sensed the sudden tension even as he had entered the bridge.

Stagg muttered, 'If you think so.' Another hesitation. 'Good thinking. I'll come up.'

Sherbrooke looked round. Rhodes, the navigating

officer, was already here, perhaps summoned by the same instinct which had spoken to Sherbrooke himself in his small sea-cabin, as clearly as any human voice.

'Sound off. Call up Commander Frazier and put him in the picture. Boats and rafts, just like the real thing.'

He saw the lieutenant, Drake, watching him. 'Nothing to do?' Then he smiled. 'See if you can rustle up something to drink, will you?'

He could feel them relaxing. So easily done. Like his men on that day when so many had died. *Trust*.

The bells were screaming between decks and men were stampeding to ladders and watertight doors.

Sherbrooke glanced at the gyro repeater. 'Steady on one-six-zero.' Then he touched the arm of the chair. 'Easy, girl, you've made your point!'

Only Evershed heard him, but still it did not register; all he could think about was the moment when something had failed, snapped, and he had been left helpless, unable to move or think. Like somebody who had discovered a terrible affliction in himself, a weakness he had always believed could not exist.

Figures were moving about, the newcomers hurrying to their action stations, the voicepipes and telephones stammering and buzzing like beetles in a tank.

The navigating officer was beside him, his eyes in shadow.

Rhodes said quietly, 'Better get going, Guns. Your control team will be waiting for their lord and master.'

Evershed strode past him without a word. They could have been strangers.

Sherbrooke climbed into his chair and listened to the final reports coming in.

'Ship at action stations, sir!'

Sherbrooke had been aware of Evershed's confusion

even as he had entered the bridge: it was as if he had already sensed it, and the sensation that something in the pattern was wrong had brought him from the stuffy privacy of his sea-cabin.

It had been a long night; maybe Evershed was feeling the strain.

We all are.

Several things had become clear. *Minden* was out of her anchorage, and the Admiralty signals had hinted that she might be heading west. Their information had probably been received from agents in Norway, people who daily risked their lives and those of their families and friends to send off vital information as quickly as possible before the German military police could fix an exact radio bearing on their transmission. The rest was too terrible to contemplate: doors being smashed in, men and women being dragged away to face the interrogation and torture of the Gestapo. No wonder these members of the Resistance were hated and feared by many of their countrymen. The margin between terrorist and freedom-fighter was a narrow one, and anything that might rouse the fury of the occupying forces should, some would suggest, be avoided.

Other signals had been even more guarded. The main part of the troop convoy had been rerouted around Scotland, and would eventually be escorted into the Firth of Forth, where Sherbrooke had taken command less than a month ago. He was beginning to feel that he had been aboard for years.

Stagg had received each report without comment, leaving Howe, his hard-worked flag lieutenant, to carry the messages back and forth like a trainee midshipman. Howe had even been provided with a rickety camp bed, which was placed in the small lobby adjoining Stagg's quarters so he could be on call.

With the radar out of action, they must return to port. By maintaining radio silence, *Reliant* was a law unto herself, but their lordships, roused from their beds by *Minden*'s reappearance and the rerouting of the big troopships, would soon call Stagg to account and order him to break off his search. Without radar, and in this dense fog, there was no sensible alternative.

Sherbrooke considered the elusive *Minden* again. Next to *Prinz Eugen*, she was reported to be the best gunnery ship in the German navy: she had proved that when she had destroyed his command. He was almost surprised that he could contemplate it so calmly; but what had he really expected? This was what he was, what he had been trained for, year after year, from schoolboy to *Reliant*'s captain. Should he feel hatred, a desire for revenge, a blessing on whatever action he should decide to take from those men who had died with *Pyrrhus*?

Circumstances, not strategy, turned *maybes* to brutal reality. The troopships were former liners, fast, and well able to outpace the U-Boat packs, provided their destroyer escorts could keep the enemy submerged. The cargo they carried was men, from Australia and New Zealand, and from Canada, like the new Walrus pilot who had brought his banjo with him.

Like most serving officers, Sherbrooke was suspicious of too much optimism and confidence. But things were changing, and for the first time the German Afrika Corps was falling back, and on the defensive. The R.A.F. and the American squadrons based in England were hitting the enemy hard, and at his own back door. Factories, U-Boat pens and shipyards were bombed day and night, something which would have been impossible a short while ago.

So the next step had to be invasion, the long haul back. They would need more men than ever before, and the deployment of such numbers of troops was not something that could be kept a complete secret.

It was unlikely to be sheer coincidence. The German High Command would consider *Minden*'s risk totally justified, like *Scharnhorst* slipping through the English Channel under the noses of the Royal Navy, and the mighty *Bismarck* breaking out of her lair to head for a more strategic base in occupied France. The Home Fleet had caught her, and had eventually put her down, but not before the German gunners had sent *Hood* to the bottom with one devastating shot.

A voice said, 'The admiral's here, sir.'

The door slammed back and Stagg strode into the dim glow of shaded lights and winking repeaters.

Sherbrooke slid from the chair. 'I'm waiting for the mechanic's report, sir.' He thought it strange to see Stagg so untidy, wearing a crumpled duffle coat which must have been the first thing he snatched up for the long walk along the upper deck necessary to avoid the sealed watertight doors.

Stagg made a contemptuous sound.

'Fat lot of use that'll be! Just a potmess of technical jargon that nobody else understands!' He stared round at the others. 'I'll skin those bloody radar people alive when we get back to base!' He strode to the chart room and waited for Sherbrooke to close the door; in the chart lights he looked unusually strained, and his cheeks were unshaven.

Sherbrooke paused while he examined the chart and the neat calculations beside the log, then he said, 'Captain Cavendish was unhappy with the last refit, sir. Too much of a hurry . . .'

Stagg stared at him. 'Who told you that?'

'It was in his own log, sir. I read it, when I was going

through the ship's books and signals.'

'I see.' He swung away angrily. 'Well, he's not bloody well here now, is he? It's the first I've heard about it – I can't do everything.'

Sherbrooke said, 'I still think this is too much of a coincidence, sir.'

Stagg seemed to drag his mind back with an effort. '*Minden*, you mean.'

'If she gets amongst those troopers, they won't stand a chance.'

Stagg muttered, 'If it hadn't been for that bloody fishing boat we'd have our own carrier with us!'

Sherbrooke let it pass. The admiral was tired and short-tempered, but he was not a fool. Even he could not believe that any carrier could fly off aircraft in this weather; the planes would eventually run out of fuel, and then ditch. There was no air-sea rescue in these bleak waters between Norway and the Shetland Islands. Their crews would not last more than a few minutes.

The telephone buzzed and Sherbrooke picked it up. Obviously, no one wanted to risk disturbing Stagg by opening the door.

'Captain.'

It was Rhodes. 'In contact with Captain (D) *Mulgrave*, sir. They have full radar contact.'

Sherbrooke repeated the message aloud. Stagg was leaning over the chart again.

'Blind leading the blind. I'm going to lose that bastard, Guy.' He sighed. 'We'd better code up a signal for Admiralty.' He saw Sherbrooke's face as he moved closer to the lights. *'What?'*

'I think we should go for the convoy, sir. Fog or no fog.'

Stagg opened his mouth as if to object, but said only, 'Go on.'

'*Mulgrave* can lead, showing a stern light. It might be enough, but we can rig a telephone line to the eyes of the ship and put an experienced officer there to make sure we don't run down the leader.'

Stagg rubbed his chin, his hand rasping on bristles. Sherbrooke sensed his doubt.

'Iceland will have put the Admiralty in the picture about us, sir.' He heard the fittings and navigating instruments rattling, an unusual sound in this ship. At reduced speed, she was rolling very slightly, and every turn of those screws was taking them further south.

He said, 'I think *Minden* has passed us already, sir. She has the advantage, and her intelligence is probably more accurate and more current than ours.'

Stagg watched him, his eyes without expression, cold.

'It's my responsibility, Guy. I don't have to do anything . . .'

The telephone in Sherbrooke's hand murmured, 'Are you still there, sir?'

Stagg reached out impulsively. 'Let me.'

He said, 'Dust off your Operations folio, Pilot, and estimate a course to rendezvous with the special convoy. Captain Sherbrooke will tell you what's needed.' He put down the telephone, and stared at it for several seconds.

He said, 'I hope to God you're right, that's all.'

Sherbrooke walked out to join the others. A glance told him that the radar was still out of action.

'This is what I want done right away. Send for Commander Frazier.'

One of the shadows moved. 'Here, sir.'

'We shall follow *Mulgrave* on the new course. I want to make a signal to Captain (D). Now.'

The yeoman of signals held his pad close to one of the shaded lights, and wrote carefully as Sherbrooke explained what was required of him and of the other escorts once they had turned on to their new course. As the yeoman made to leave, Sherbrooke called, 'Wait, Donovan. Add, *good luck.*'

The chief petty officer looked at him impassively. 'All done, sir.' He hesitated. 'My name is Yorke, sir.'

Sherbrooke reached out and touched his sleeve. 'Of course. I'm sorry.'

He did not have to explain. If the navy was a family, then the signals branch was its mainstay. They would all know that Donovan had been *Pyrrhus*'s yeoman when she had gone down.

Stagg strode out among them. 'You can fall out action stations, I think. Get some hot food and drink sent round defence stations. Jack always works better on a full belly!' He glanced across at Sherbrooke, excluding all the others. 'So do I, as a matter of fact!' He sought out the exhausted figure of his flag lieutenant. 'Come on, laddie, jump about! Lot to do!'

Some of the men were grinning surreptitiously at one another. Pleased, or perhaps proud to be a part of it.

Sherbrooke walked to the chair, setting his thoughts in order before he shared them.

He had recently read a highly-coloured article about Stagg in one of the popular newspapers. The reporter had described the rear-admiral's charisma, his ability to inspire the men he commanded. He had just seen it in action.

It was like watching a film being reversed, images of those years when they had been lieutenants together in this same ship, learning and training for the inevitable, from escorting royal tours of the Empire to the misery of the Spanish Civil War, and at naval reviews when they had met and enjoyed the company of many German officers. *Minden*'s captain had probably been one of them.

He heard the voice in his mind, with startling clarity: the old vice-admiral at the funeral, who had been their captain in those bright, unreal days.

It had been here, in this bridge, the causes lost in time, but the words suddenly clear, vivid.

'You might try to bluff others, Mr Stagg, but you don't deceive me!'

Surprisingly, it seemed to calm him. He looked at their expectant faces. Rhodes handed him his small pad, waiting, his eyes filled with questions.

Sherbrooke said, 'Allowing for the weather and our speed, which will depend on it, by noon tomorrow and according to *the writings of Pilot* . . .' Their glances held again. Like a firm handshake. '. . .we shall know if we have lost the enemy, or sunk him!'

He turned away, unable to watch their faces. There were too many others which should not be here, like the yeoman Donovan, and Cavendish, and so many more. Ghosts.

He said abruptly, 'Let's get started.'

It is what I am. He was ready.

Lieutenant Dick Rayner, Royal Canadian Naval Volunteer Reserve, pulled up the zip of his fleece-lined flying jacket. It was early morning, and when he had last looked out, the sea had been pitch-black. It was bloody cold, he thought, even by Canadian standards. Apart from the sluice of water along the hull and the occasional movement from one of the gun positions, the ship was very quiet. Just another boring day, or was this really a time for action? Nobody seemed certain: if the admiral and the skipper knew something, they were keeping damn quiet about it.

There had been very little fuss. The hands off watch had been called, then the duty watch had been relieved, and tea had arrived, with corned beef sandwiches you could barely get your teeth around. An early breakfast; probably their last, some wag had said.

Rayner glanced around 'the readiness room', as it was called. It reminded him of a large, cheerless biscuit tin, full of files, photos and details of enemy ships and aircraft, one box for last-minute letters home, another for first-aid gear. At the solitary table his companion and observer, Sub-Lieutenant Buck, a New Zealander from Wellington, was sitting exactly as before, his pen poised over an empty sheet of paper. Rayner was twenty-six years old, and in the company of some of *Reliant*'s junior officers, he felt ancient. Buck, Eddy to his friends, was nineteen and looked about twelve, likeable, thoughtless, untroubled by anything more than the various girls to whom he wrote. There seemed to be quite a few of them.

Rayner thought of his own family in Toronto. It would be freezing there, too, right now, the wind off the lake like a knife. There were three boys and a girl. His father was doing well, and they lived in an old and spacious house. He had often wondered how his father had managed when the depression had knocked Canada sideways in the thirties, after the stock market collapse: he had owned a small trucking company then, and had somehow scraped through, investing in two small, bankrupt factories. War had brought him prosperity. The factories made weapons now, and his trucking company was known from coast to coast. It had been hard for him to understand when two of his sons had volunteered for the navy, and harder still for Rayner's mother.

Rayner's older brother, Larry, had also been selected for the Fleet Air Arm, although he had claimed it was the only way he could escape from endless training ashore. He had been shot down while defending a convoy on its way to embattled Malta. His younger brother, Bob, had gone up to Kingston and volunteered for the R.C.A.F. Just a kid, like Eddy there. He knew his father would have asked the same question. *Why did they volunteer?* And his mother would have looked at him, loving the man who had given everything for her and his family, and answered, *Why did you, in the last war?*

He heard the mechanics chatting together beyond the closed steel door. They were bored, too, but not for the same reasons. *They did not fly.* They all worked closely together, with only the slightest formality evident. But they did not fly. That was the real divide.

He thought of the large, ungainly Walrus amphibian perched out there on its catapult. Few people understood how a brilliant designer like Reginald Mitchell, who had created the Spitfire, probably the most beautiful aircraft in the war, could have conceived the awkward, lumbering Shagbat.

Fired by his brother's example and the reports about the Battle of Britain, Rayner had seen himself as a fighter pilot from the very beginning. He had put up with the endless drills and inspections, learning naval terms and even struggling with the mysteries of bends and hitches, with his eventual goal acting like a beacon. Even when he had finally transferred to the Fleet Air Arm for training as a pilot, with the solitary wavy stripe on his sleeve, he had still believed it was what he wanted.

Until he had let it slip that he was already a qualified pilot, and had flown two kinds of float plane on Canada's west coast. The senior instructor would have been astonished if he had told him he had been flying one of those little float planes while he was still under age.

'So you *are* used to landing on water?'

That had settled it. They had sent him to Halifax and then across to England, and the Fleet Air Arm station at

Yeovilton. To Scotland and to Scapa Flow, flying the real thing, where the training was hard and relentless. *Join the navy and see the world. Join the Fleet Air Arm and see the next.* Then he had been ordered to a big, old-fashioned County class cruiser, with three spindly funnels. It had been like going in at the deep end. If the navy had taught him to be a pilot, then the old cruiser had taught him how to fly.

Everywhere she had gone, the fighting had been bad; at best, they were always on the defensive. She had acted as heavy escort for convoys to and from Canada and the United States, to Gibraltar, and the deceptively kind blue waters of the Indian Ocean, but mostly it had been the bitter Atlantic. Ships sunk, left to die alone because no one was allowed to stop for them. He could not now believe how many times he had been flown off in his battered Walrus, scouting for surfaced U-Boats, one of which, on one occasion, they might have even sunk with their depth charges. But the cruiser's wild-eyed captain had snapped, 'No evidence! No claim!'

The British sense of fair play, he supposed. He would get used to it. Maybe. It had almost lost them the war. It still could.

And yet, in his heart, he did not believe that. On leave in London, and in Plymouth near the naval air station, where the bombing had been heavy and merciless, he had sensed the shabby determination about which his brother had written before he had bought it.

That was something else he had learned. The callous dismissal, the cover-up, when one of their number went missing. You didn't brood over it, or you were likely to be the next.

Sometimes they had landed on the water to rescue dazed and barely conscious survivors. When the dead and the living wore naval uniform, it was like seeing a reflection of yourself, gasping and sobbing, past gratitude, and beyond hope.

He recalled his uncertainty when the cruiser had been ordered into dock after several near misses in Western Approaches, and he had been sent on a brief and unwanted leave, before joining the battlecruiser *Reliant*. It had been an unexpected wrench to leave the old, long-funnelled cruiser. He had just managed to get to know everybody in her company; even the captain had wished him well, and had told him that his promotion to lieutenant had been confirmed.

He had said, '*Reliant*'s a fine ship. But she's big, so take it a step at a time.' It was the closest Rayner had ever been emotionally to his captain.

And now he was learning all over again. Names and faces; where they all fitted in the ship's geography.

And he still had the awkward Shagbat, for which he felt a grudging affection. He had been deeply touched when he had seen that one of his fitters had painted a bright red maple leaf on the outside of the cockpit. Nobody had mentioned it; it had not been done openly to impress, or to gain favour. He had learned that at least, in the old cruiser.

He felt a grin on his face at the old dream of himself as a fighter pilot. Now, he couldn't imagine flying anything else!

He saw Eddy Buck jump as the solitary telephone buzzed noisily.

He said, 'You take it, Eddy. I'm going out to the plane.'

The slightly-built subbie from Wellington spoke briefly, and then covered the handset.

'It's for you.' He grinned. 'I could hardly say you were out!'

He took it. 'Rayner.'

'Captain. Come to the bridge, please.' The line went dead.

Rayner said quietly, 'It was the Skipper. Not one of his minions. Can you beat that?'

Buck sealed an envelope and popped it into the little box.

'He must like you. Probably thinks we colonials are a bit quaint.'

Rayner picked up his cap, recalling Sherbrooke's old-young face when they had first met. Waiting for the same ship. Externally, his experiences had left no mark. Except, perhaps, in the eyes. But how much could any man suffer and seal away, and remain unchanged?

Eddy said, 'When we finish charging about the bloody ocean for a while, we'll do a run ashore together. I'll get you fixed up. A nice girl, you know?'

'Yeah, I can just about remember.'

The subbie grinned. 'Okay, Dad!'

It was a long climb to the bridge, and on his way Rayner saw all the preparations for action, the gun crews in duffle coats, with their helmets and anti-flash gear close at hand. Six fifteen-inch guns in three great turrets, and twenty four-inch guns, some in triple mountings, to form a massive cone of fire against aircraft and fast enemies on the surface.

He had reached the flag deck, where oil-skinned signalmen were staring across at the nearest destroyer. The fog had almost gone, but there was still low mist clinging to the deep swell now visible alongside, where the bow wave creamed away like half an arrowhead.

Into the bridge itself, with its murmuring voicepipes, and a sense of intense watchfulness as figures trained their glasses on the leading destroyer's stern light, a misty blue eye reflecting in the leader's own frothing wake.

Lieutenant Frost, with his absurd beard, glanced toward

him. 'Never fear, Biggles is here!' Nobody laughed.

Sherbrooke turned in his chair. 'Long climb, isn't it?'

He looked and sounded quite relaxed, although from what Rayner had heard, he had been on the bridge for hours with hardly a break.

Rayner stood beside the chair, and stared at the great forecastle rising slowly and then dipping again, tossing up spray like pellets.

The captain said, 'No more news of *Minden*. Might have lost her in the fog. But no news of the convoy, either.'

He could have been discussing the weather, Rayner thought. He studied his profile, youthful and clean-cut, the cheekbones high, and well formed. A face you would see in a crowd, and remember.

'The fact is, there was a signal.' He twisted round in the chair, his eyes questioning. 'A U.S. Airforce plane has ditched. Iceland Base reported it when they got the Mayday. Probably the mail run from there to Scotland.'

Rayner nodded, seeing it. 'Probably a Dakota, sir. Most of them are. Pretty good kites, reliable . . . but then . . .'

'Crew?'

'Four, sir. Might be passengers, too.'

'There was no mention of any.'

The screens began to squeak again and Rayner watched as Sherbrooke thrust one hand into his pocket. A reaction? A habit? Perhaps a memory.

He said, 'They wouldn't last long in this, sir.'

'I know.'

Rayner almost flinched as the blue eyes searched his face.

'I'm sorry, sir. I only meant—'

Sherbrooke grasped his arm, the four new, bright gold stripes seeming strangely out of place.

'I understand what you meant. I was wondering.' He

looked at the screens again. 'In this visibility.'

Rayner heard himself reply, no hesitation, no doubts. 'Yeah, I could do it, sir.' He thought of his father again. *Why did they volunteer?* 'The sea's not too bad, is it?'

Sherbrooke released his arm. 'Good lad. Go and get ready.' He looked at him in that direct way again. 'No heroics. But if they *are* here . . .'

He watched Rayner leave, some of the watchkeepers turning to share it.

He heard Rhodes rasp at his lieutenant, 'If your face was where your arse is, I'd kick it right through that bulkhead!' He saw Sherbrooke looking at him, and said, 'I'll send down all the info I've got, sir. Possible bearing and search area. It's not much, but it might help.'

Sherbrooke nodded his thanks. Stagg wouldn't care. He had already written off their chances of catching *Minden*, if indeed she was anywhere in the vicinity, or ever had been.

'Take it down yourself, Pilot. He'd appreciate that. So would I.'

Ten minutes later, after a preliminary misfire, the Walrus was hurled from her catapult.

Sherbrooke stood on the bridge wing, oblivious to the cold as he watched the top-heavy flying boat with the solitary engine, the pusher, as it was nicknamed, lurching above her own murky reflection as if about to drop hard alongside. Then she was climbing, her engine like an express train in a cutting as she slowly gained height and ploughed sedately above the nearest destroyer.

Someone gave a cheer. The risks to Walrus and crew were not hard to imagine.

But at least they were doing *something*. All of them.

He slung his binoculars around his neck and returned to the bridge.

And somebody, maybe only one survivor, would hear the Shagbat coming, and know he had not been forgotten.

He tightened his grip on the unused pipe in his pocket. A lifeline.

5

Rendezvous

There was no other feeling in the world quite like it. Flying on and on, seemingly into nowhere, with occasional glimpses of the sea, at first like black, molten glass, and then, as the Walrus lost height for a few moments, another change, to a hard, shark-blue which reached out on either beam. Forever.

Rayner sat comfortably, and quite relaxed, at home in his own private world. They were still heading due north, but for one quick alteration of course to investigate what he had thought was drifting wreckage. It had risen, no doubt screaming a noisy protest: a flock of gulls resting until full daylight, outraged by the flying-boat's unexpected appearance.

Rayner glanced at his watch and saw Buck turn his head to look at him. He smiled. It was a very expensive watch, a birthday gift from his parents before he had left for England. The youthful New Zealander probably imagined, like some of the other young members of *Reliant*'s wardroom, that he was just another spoiled son of some rich tycoon. If only they knew what it had been like. Even he did not really understand how his father had come through, when so many of his friends and their businesses had gone under during the depression.

His father had once tossed out a hint that not all of his

ventures had been completely within the law, and Rayner knew that at one time he had used his small fleet of trucks to run booze down to the parched Yanks during Prohibition. Risky, but it had paid off.

He said, 'Time to alter course in a few minutes, Eddy. We've been out here an hour.' He tried to make light of it. 'Don't want to lose the ship now, do we?'

Buck leaned forward in his harness to peer at the water. 'Ah, daylight, at long last!'

Rayner listened to the dull roar of the big Pegasus Radial engine, above and behind his seat. The pusher was a real deterrent against baling out without taking full precautions. You could be chopped into mincemeat by those formidable blades.

He sensed the other two crew members moving restlessly behind him. Rob Morgan, a pug-faced ex-milkman from Cardiff, was a telegraphist air gunner, and the other, a trainee gunner, was James Hardie from London. The Smoke, as he called it. Rayner had never asked about the previous pilot, and nobody had ever spoken of him. It was the navy's way.

He imagined the great battlecruiser steaming along as they had left her. With the radar out of action, the Walrus was an extension to the captain's range of vision. Another eye, even if only in the forlorn hope of finding some ditched airmen.

He spoke into his mouthpiece again. 'O.K., Eddy, open the thermos. Then we'll alter course.'

He thought again of the ship, the very size of her, the chain of command. He had met the rear-admiral on only one occasion, after they had left the Firth of Forth. Stagg had appeared to be conducting an unannounced, personal inspection, accompanied by his flag lieutenant and Frazier, the Bloke. He smiled again. They really did have some weird slang.

Stagg had walked around the catapult and asked Rayner a few questions about himself, his previous experience and personal background. He had had the feeling that Stagg had known most of it already, just as he had sensed that the visit to the flying area had been no spur of the moment decision.

Stagg had displayed an immense knowledge about the aircraft and the Fleet Air Arm in general, the strategy of attack and defence, and the growing deployment of small task-forces, in the American style.

During a brief pause, Commander Frazier had commented mildly, 'I'm surprised you never became a flier yourself, sir.'

Rayner had seen the rear-admiral's eyes fasten on him in an unwavering stare.

'Too busy. Never had the time!'

Buck said, 'What d'you think, Dick?'

He moved the stick slightly, his eyes on the compass. 'Doesn't look too good. We've been up here an hour. We'll try another leg and then go back to the ship. The Skipper won't want to hang around while he's hoisting us inboard.'

He leaned over to watch the cloud streaming beneath the wings, the first glint of sunlight on the water, some four thousand feet below. A cold, hard light, and across the gently heaving surface there were still traces of departing fog. He was glad about the increased visibility. The Shagbat had a range of six hundred miles; it sounded a lot, but it was little enough when you were searching for your parent ship. His crew seemed relaxed and at ease, the mugs being carefully prepared for the thermos and some hot, sweet tea.

It would be strange when they eventually got together with the escort carriers and he finally met the others. All the bright, boastful types, the fighter pilots, shooting lines about how good they were, probably looking with pity or sarcastic delight at his ungainly Walrus.

Buck snatched up his binoculars and strained against his harness.

'What is it?' Rayner swore to himself as more cloud enveloped the wet perspex.

Buck looked at him, his eyes bright, confused.

'A light. A flash. I'm not sure.'

Rayner shrugged. 'Ready, you guys – I'm going around!' He added, 'Hold onto the tea, Rob!'

It was probably nothing. No survivor would have a light strong enough to be seen at this distance, even if he had the strength to aim it.

He was reminded of the captain's face when he had mentioned the chances of finding anybody alive. He would know better than any of them. One of eight survivors, they had said. Everything lost, wiped out in a second.

'Coming on course again, Dick.' Buck was speaking through his teeth, unusually on edge. Uncertain.

It was still worth a try. He tilted the aircraft, and saw the first real sunlight on a hostile sea.

Buck shouted, *'Aircraft! In the drink!'*

Rayner eased the controls again and watched the scene fade away into another bank of bumpy cloud.

'*On* it, Eddy. Not in it.' He was surprised that he sounded so calm. But for Buck's alertness, they could so easily have missed it. Just seconds, but Buck's warning had given him time to pull out his powerful glasses even as they completed their turn. Just seconds . . . that was all it took. The flash Buck had seen must have been sunlight reflected from the wing as it tipped and rolled on the uneasy swell. A float plane, single-winged, edging slowly past a small yellow dinghy. Seconds. He had seen the twin black crosses on the shining wing. He had met one before. An Arado 196, the kind carried by large German warships. Ships like the *Minden*.

Buck asked hoarsely, 'What should we do?'

Rayner said, 'He hasn't seen us, and with his engine going he won't have heard us, either. When he does, he'll come after us.' He saw the sudden comprehension in Buck's face. 'He's a hell of a lot faster than we are, and he has twenty-millimetre cannons, and machine-guns. We'd never make it.' He twisted round to involve all of them, so that they should understand. 'He'd have us for breakfast.' He thought of his brother Larry, going down in the Med. Quickly? Slowly? Had he known? Had he suffered?

He heard Morgan, the ex-milkman, clear his throat on the intercom.

'Then the old *Reliant* would never know about it.'

Rayner tried to ease his fingers on the controls. Morgan had spoken for them all. The German float plane had put down to investigate the drifting rubber dinghy. For reasons of intelligence, because of the fellowship of one pilot for another? It must not matter now. This plane and these men were his responsibility. The rest was a myth, as his brother must have found out for himself.

He said shortly, 'Stand by depth charges. I'm going in. We'll only get one chance.'

Buck said in a small voice, 'All set!'

Hardie, the trainee gunner, murmured, 'Steady the Buffs!'

It was unreal, hurtling through the cloud, the engine's roar rising to a scream, protesting like those disturbed gulls. Then the bright, hard sunlight, and more cloud, ripping through the wings and struts like pressurized steam.

And then there was only the sea. It seemed to be hurtling to meet them, even though the Shagbat's top speed was a hundred and thirty knots at best.

It was all there. The float plane, no longer swaying uncomfortably in the swell but already moving, the twin floats cutting razor-sharp furrows as it continued to gather speed. The abandoned dinghy was already drifting away, its solitary occupant lying over one side, as if he had fallen asleep.

Rayner felt his jaw crack with concentration. *He'll have us for breakfast.* His own words echoed back to mock him.

Fifteen, ten seconds . . . they roared over the moving plane, the Walrus's crooked shadow blotting out everything.

'Now!'

He felt the aircraft jump as the two charges were released. Thank God for a good crew to check every small detail. If only one charge had jammed, it would all have been too late.

'Come on, old girl!' He felt his seat lean over, and was in time to see the other plane altering course violently as pilot and crewman realized their danger.

They had missed. With one eye on the compass, he swung the Walrus into another turn.

He stared down, startled, as Buck's gloved fingers fastened on his arm like a vice. He was shouting into his mouthpiece, but no sound was coming through.

Rayner watched, the moment frozen in his mind as the two depth charges exploded almost simultaneously. Not that near: any U-Boat commander would have merely crossed himself and grinned. But close enough for the finely balanced float plane. The explosions had blasted off one wing completely, so that the plane was turning over onto its side, the sea thrashing around the propeller until it, too, came to a sudden stop. Like a dead bird. No menace. Nothing.

Buck was switched on again. 'You did it, Dick! *You clever old bugger!'*

Rayner allowed his nerves to settle. 'You're not so bad yourself, kid.' He added more sharply, 'Now give me a course to steer. We'll head back.'

What the hell is the matter with me? They could have shot us down without a thought. Would have, if they hadn't been so curious about the dead airman in the dinghy. Or were they just doing what he himself would have done, out of humanity?

The thoughts disturbed him, and he dismissed them.

They climbed steadily into the cloud again, each man reliving privately what they had seen and shared.

Hardie was crouching beside the controls, a mug of tea in one grimy fist.

'Char, sir?' He watched as Rayner dragged off one glove with his teeth.

Then, almost shyly, he said, 'Nice to have you as skipper, an' no mistake.'

Rayner leaned back in his hard seat and sipped the tea. It was the finest he had ever tasted. Later on, maybe much later, they would set up the drinks and celebrate, and somebody would paint a little symbol on the side below the cockpit to represent their kill. After this, he would be accepted. One of them. And later, he knew how much it would mean to him.

But now, all he wanted to do was find *Reliant* and report what they had found, and where. At the same time, he knew he would never forget how he had felt.

'Aircraft's hooked on, sir!'

Sherbrooke walked to the extreme side of the bridge and peered down at the surging water, so far below, after his last ship. He could see little of the Walrus but for the tips of the wings, but the great arm of the aircraft hoisting crane was turning slowly inboard, where the handling party would be waiting to secure the plane to the catapult again.

The Walrus pilot had done well, and he sensed the relief all around him when the garbled signal had been received and the plane was sighted, flying within feet of the water. It had all taken time. Slowing the ship and turning to provide some sort of lee while the Walrus had manoeuvred carefully alongside. One false move, or a sudden change in the weather, and the aircraft could have been smashed against the hull like a toy.

Once, Stagg had called up from his own private bridge beneath this one, a small nerve-centre which was connected to the main communications systems and transmitting station, and complete with its own radar repeater.

When Sherbrooke had told him that the Walrus was ready for recovery, Stagg had said tersely, 'Taking long enough!'

'All secure, sir.'

Sherbrooke walked past his chair and looked through the forward screen. It was misty: perhaps more fog was on the way. If so, Rayner was luckier than he knew.

'Resume course and speed, Pilot. Inform Captain (D) that we have recovered our aircraft.'

He could picture the senior destroyer captain very well, a stocky, almost square figure, who had been in destroyers for most of his service, from picking up terrified White Russians at Odessa after the revolution, to the battles of Narvik and the bloody evacuation of Crete. Sherbrooke liked what he had seen of him, although he had sensed that Stagg was less than enthusiastic. The Captain (D) had been tipped for promotion to flag rank, and possibly that was the rub, although Stagg surely had no reason for jealousy.

'Course two-nine-zero, sir. Engines half speed ahead.'

Sherbrooke joined the navigating officer by the gyro compass repeater.

Rhodes said, 'Visibility's falling again, sir.'

Sherbrooke wanted to return to his chair, but every muscle was telling him how much he needed to rest. It would be fatal.

'I'll see what Rayner has to say, then I'll speak with the admiral.'

There had been another signal from the Admiralty, brief and unhelpful. *There are three U-Boats in your vicinity.* That could mean anything. When Stagg had been informed he had snapped, 'Probably heading up to Iceland. I'm not breaking radio silence to ask!'

A door slid back and Lieutenant Rayner walked into the bridge.

Sherbrooke said, 'You did well. Tell me about it.'

'An Arado float plane, sir. I couldn't just leave it. If it had climbed after us, we wouldn't have stood a chance.'

For one so young, who had already proved his skill as a pilot, he looked drained, and unusually downcast.

Sherbrooke said, 'Go on.' He saw Rhodes step back, as if to offer some privacy in this crowded bridge.

'They were looking at a dinghy, sir. There was a dead airman in it. They were doing what we would have done.'

Sherbrooke watched him gravely. What *you* would have done, he thought. So that was it. Like shooting someone under a flag of truce. But it was not like that.

He said, 'They would have done for you, given the same opportunity. You must know that. Accept it.'

Rayner forced a smile. It made him look young and vulnerable.

'I guess so, sir.'

Sherbrooke heard the sounds resuming around him, felt the bridge returning to normal. He said, 'One enemy aircraft destroyed. I shall see that it goes on your report. Well done.'

Another door crashed open and Stagg strode into the bridge. Was it simply that he found his own small, private bridge too restricting, or did he hate to feel like a mere bystander?

He stared keenly at Rayner, still in his flying jacket, and said, 'So you destroyed a German aircraft, eh? It's not a lot for me to act on, is it?'

Sherbrooke prepared to interrupt, but there was no need. Rayner answered, very calmly, 'It was an Arado 196, sir. It could only have come from a sizeable German warship. It's too far to be from anywhere else.'

Stagg regarded him coldly. 'You think?'

Rayner said, 'I *know*, sir.'

Stagg bent his head, apparently frowning. When he looked up, his teeth were set in a grin. 'Good lad! I like your style!' He turned to Sherbrooke. 'But it's not enough, is it?'

Sherbrooke said, 'I have a feeling about this one, sir.'

Stagg shrugged. 'That's not enough either, Guy. There's too much at stake. Now, if we had that ruddy carrier . . .' He thrust his hands into his reefer pockets, his thumbs jutting over the front like horns. 'It's no go. Not this time. Come to the chart room. We'll be ordered to Scapa – I can almost see the bloody signal!'

He glared at the mist beyond the damp glass. 'And this damned stuff isn't helping!'

They both stared at a bridge speaker as Evershed's voice intoned, 'Director Control to Bridge. Radar transmissions are returning. Some repeaters still out of use.'

Sherbrooke looked questioningly across at the repeater whose failure had so unbalanced Evershed. It was still dead.

Stagg rasped, 'Wait till I get my hands on those mental cripples!'

'T/S – Forebridge.' There was no mistaking Frazier's calm, unruffled voice. 'Repeaters are now in use.'

Sherbrooke took a handset and said, 'This is the Captain. What are the prospects, John?' He could feel Stagg's impatience and frustration. If they were not recalled by the Admiralty, he would make the decision himself. Sherbrooke could almost pity him. Almost.

Frazier replied, 'Got every mechanic on to it, sir. This isn't the first time it's happened.' That was as far as he would commit himself.

Sherbrooke replaced the handset, feeling Stagg's eyes upon him. Eventually Stagg said, 'I shall break radio silence. It will be up to the Admiralty and the C-in-C Home Fleet to decide what to do next.'

It was the first time Sherbrooke had ever seen him look so deflated. He had not even attempted to bluff his way out of it with the usual style.

The speaker again, a different voice, sharper, and intense.

'Contact, sir! Ship bearing three-two-zero, range two-two-oh!'

It was as if an electric shock had ripped through the bridge, momentarily rendering every man incapable of movement.

Then the voicepipes began to chatter, and even the radar repeater showed a faint sign of life.

'Start plotting!'

Sherbrooke returned to his chair and gripped it, his mind reaching out as if it were unrolling an immense chart. A ship. Somewhere out there, eleven miles away.

'Target is moving left. Range steady at two-two-oh. Rate two hundred – closing!'

He could picture Evershed, all his doubts forgotten for the moment, while his brain, eye and mind reacted to each range and bearing. Eleven miles, and closing at the rate of two hundred yards a minute. Fast, then. Committed.

The enemy had altered course, probably heading due west on a slightly converging track. *Reliant* must bring all three turrets to bear, and at once.

Stagg was suddenly beside him, his face very grim. 'I'm going to my perch, Guy.' He looked at him with fierce intensity. 'Fight the ship, Guy! Destroy that bastard!' Then he was gone.

Sherbrooke said, 'Alter course, Pilot. Steer three-zero-zero.' He reached for the red handset and imagined the Chief snatching up his own telephone, his boiler suit spotlessly white as usual.

'Captain. We are going for the enemy. Starboard bow. Full revs when I call for them.' He did not wait for a reply. Nobody knew his job like Onslow.

'Make a signal to Leader. *Enemy in sight. Prepare to engage with torpedoes.*' He saw the yeoman in his wet oilskin coat watching him from the bridge wing: the one he had called Donovan.

'Bright enough, Yeo?' He saw the sudden understanding, and a faint hint of something like sadness. 'Hoist Battle Ensigns!'

He took the tannoy handset from a midshipman, and felt the youth's hand accidentally brush against his. It was ice-cold, trembling. But when he looked at him and asked quietly, 'Ready, Mr Crawford?' he saw the quick determination, the dissipation of fear.

The midshipman murmured, 'I'm all right, sir. My first time.'

Sherbrooke pressed the button. The captain had to be above all traps like sentiment and sympathy. There was no room for it: war did not permit such luxuries. He saw that Rayner was still beside him, strangely out of place in his leather jacket, his goggles hanging around his neck. He had killed some of the enemy. But in his heart, he had seen them only as airmen, like himself.

He said gently, 'Stay, if you like.'

Their eyes met in a peculiar sympathy, as they had that day aboard Stagg's launch.

'Thanks, sir.'

'This is the Captain speaking. We are about to engage the enemy.'

Rhodes unclipped a small vent in the screen and looked over at him. Even above the roar of fans and the surge of water along the hull, Sherbrooke heard it. They were cheering: men leaning out of their gun positions, rigged in anti-flash gear and unfamiliar steel helmets, cheering as they had at Jutland, when *Reliant* had swung defiantly away from the savage bombardment. Men he barely knew, some he had never seen. And they could cheer. It was like a madness, or some wild drug, where everything was larger than life and somehow unreal, even the huge White Ensigns streaming from each mast to match Stagg's flag, bright red and white against the dull mist and cloud.

'Target bearing two-seven-zero, range two-one-five, rate two hundred, *closing*.'

Sherbrooke gripped the rail below the screen and watched as the two forward turrets swivelled slowly to starboard, each pair of guns lifting, as if to sniff out the target. Down aft, the third turret, manned entirely by Royal Marines, was already training hard round onto the same bearing, the long barrels angled differently for the first testing shots. Each great turret weighed hundreds of tons, and yet they moved soundlessly, without effort.

From turret to magazine, quarters officers, gunlayers

and trainers, Evershed's hard-drilled crews moved in time with the machinery which, from the moment the first order to *Load – Load – Load* had been yelled, had taken over their lives. The six guns were each loaded with a fifteen-inch shell, massive semi-armour-piercing projectiles which were timed to explode even as they tore into the enemy's armour.

Sherbrooke saw one seaman duck and shield his face as a great gusher of grey water exploded high over the port bow, the sea fired with a brief orange glow like some volcanic eruption on the seabed. Sherbrooke glanced at the clock. The *Minden* had opened fire. In firepower, the German cruiser was no match for *Reliant*, but it took more than a broadside to win a battle.

Now. Like another voice, or was it some memory? He called, *'Open fire!'*

The bridge seemed to reel as if struck by gunfire. All three turrets had fired together, and even now, as the shells ripped toward the clouds before the final descent, the smoking breeches would be open like hungry jaws, while the next shells, the next long charges, were thrust into position.

Lights would be flashing; more ranges and deflections would be pouring in from the Director Control, the gun crews sweating despite the bitter, clammy air.

Sherbrooke said, 'Full revolutions, Pilot. Signal the escort . . .'

He felt the immediate response, the raked stem smashing through the water as the Chief opened his throttles, until the destroyers would barely be able to keep station on the flagship.

'Layer on! Trainer on!' The merest pause. *'Shoot!'*

Again and again, with another fall of shot from the invisible *Minden*, exploding perhaps where *Reliant* might have been, but for her impressive increase of speed.

'Up two hundred! *Ready! Shoot!*'

Somebody cried out as metal cracked across the bridge shutters, and something broke through part of the screen.

Sherbrooke said, 'Report damage!' He saw the midshipman staring at him, his eyes wild, terrified. *Reliant* had been hit. But the guns were still training round, the stained barrels like long grey fingers opening to seize their target.

'Shoot!'

'Damage Control reports one hit in the forrard messdeck, sir.' It was Lieutenant Frost, Rhodes's assistant. He sounded calm, detached even, as he added, 'Three casualties, sir.'

Evershed again, his self-control momentarily gone. 'Captain, sir! A *straddle!* Target is slowing down!' A gong rang tinnily in the background as the six guns thundered out again. They had the target in a straddle. Her fate was already decided.

'Shoot!'

'Target is stopped, sir!'

Sherbrooke raised his glasses and stared at the nearest destroyer. She was clearer now, and her flags looked very bright against the dull water. The mist was lifting. Even as he watched, he saw the white-painted anchor cables on the forecastle deck, some huddled seamen in helmets dragging a hose around the port side, the damage control team going to support their companions where the shell had exploded, perhaps prematurely, before it could penetrate more deeply into the hull, to fuel bunker or magazine.

Shells ripped overhead, and exploded harmlessly far beyond the destroyer screen.

A signalman was holding out a telephone. 'The admiral, sir.'

Sherbrooke lowered his glasses. He had not even heard

Stagg's call. He had just seen the enemy for the first time since that terrible day. He knew it was *Minden*, even though *Reliant*'s gunnery had transformed her into a smoking wreck. Guns pointed impotently to the sky or towards the open sea, several fires blazed unchecked, and were visible through great gashes in the lower hull. But one gun was still firing, although the shots were few and far between.

Stagg said, 'Finish it. Signal *Mulgrave*. Attack with torpedoes.' He could not hide his excitement, his pleasure. 'I shall make a signal to Admiralty.'

Sherbrooke raised his glasses with one hand; they felt as heavy as lead. He heard the clatter of the signal lamp, and saw the destroyer's diamond-bright acknowledgment.

The big M-class destroyer was already breaking away, torpedo tubes swinging across her streaming deck, her captain, who had been tipped for flag rank, going in for the kill.

'The enemy has ceased firing, sir.'

Sherbrooke saw smoke pouring from the nearest muzzles. Evershed would fire no more, unless so ordered.

Rhodes asked, 'Will we recall *Mulgrave*, sir?'

Sherbrooke shook his head.

'When it's over, Pilot.'

He saw Rayner watching him, feeling it, perhaps sharing it.

Sherbrooke walked to the bridge wing and out into the bitter air.

A seaman gunner, strapped into one of the bridge Oerlikons, swung round in his harness and called, 'We done it, sir! *We done it!*'

They were staring at the enemy, hugging one another; they had made a small part of this war's bloody history.

And the convoy was unharmed, those thousands of soldiers saved, for some more impressive fate.

But all Sherbrooke saw was a ship dying. Like watching himself, watching *Pyrrhus*. There was a muffled explosion, and then another. Two torpedoes would be enough: *Minden* was starting to go fast, the smoke changing into steam as the sea burst into her engine and boiler rooms. The destroyer was thrashing away from the sinking cruiser, and seconds later the dullness was torn apart by a great flash, so vivid that even the sea regained its colour.

Sherbrooke watched the stern section of the cruiser rising very slowly, some tiny figures, like ants even through his powerful binoculars, as they tried to clamber higher and higher, some madness making them believe there was still safety for them if they remained with their ship. Perhaps sailors never changed . . . He felt *Reliant* give a long shudder. As if she knew: as if she had always known.

He said, 'Signal *Mulgrave* to pick up survivors.'

There was another massive explosion. When he looked again, the destroyer had the sea to herself.

He remembered the words he had used to Rayner on the subject of *Minden*'s seaplane. *They would have done it to you, given the same opportunity*. Or the moment when he had given the order to open fire, as if the words had been spoken for him.

A victory, then? *Minden* was no more, and some of her people, who were out there gasping and crying now for aid, might know what his own men had suffered when their ship had been blasted from under them.

There was so much to do, signals to be prepared, damage to be assessed, casualties to be comforted.

He touched the dripping steel as he turned away from the sea. It was a moment he could share with no one, except with that other captain.

But victory? Not yet.

6

Spreading the Word

Captain Guy Sherbrooke blotted the letter carefully and placed it in the tray on his desk with all the others. This one was so different from the rest, official letters which required his signature, forms about stores, and a pad of signals for operational approval.

But the letter in his own handwriting, with an Edinburgh address, was personal. Part of the ship, therefore a part of him too. Of *Reliant*'s three casualties, one had been killed outright by blast as the shell had exploded prior to penetrating the empty messdeck. All three men had been stokers, members of the damage control section. It had been bad luck, when the enemy cruiser had already been too badly mauled to survive much longer. Of the other two, one had lost an arm; the other had sustained only a cut above the eye.

He stood up restlessly and walked to the nearest scuttle. It was strange to feel the ship so still, trapped in this great spread of noise, rust and vivid welding torches. Like any other busy naval dockyard, Rosyth was filled with ships being repaired, rebuilt, or patched up in some cases, when they had already been worked to death. Rosyth Dockyard was also headquarters of the vice-admiral commanding the coast of Scotland.

Hard to believe he was seeing the same old Forth Bridge

again, last viewed from Stagg's launch when he had taken command of *Reliant*. Leith lay on the other side of the Firth of Forth, lost in mist and the steady drizzle which had accompanied their noisy return, sirens and whistles, and welcoming cheers from ships' companies and dockyard maties alike. *Reliant* must have made a proud sight, her hands smartly fallen in forward and aft, her flared bows peppered with splinters, and the jagged shell-hole in her side, which Stagg had insisted, with his characteristic flair for the dramatic, should be uncovered for the occasion.

He glanced at the letter again. Should he tear it up? Leave it to officialdom and the welfare people, who were far more used to such delicate matters? Edinburgh. The dead man's wife might even have seen *Reliant* coming in, have known it was her man's ship, and believed that all was well. He could not recall the man in question, but he had heard the Chief and Commander Frazier discussing the possibility of his first child being baptized in the ship's bell. No, the letter would not help. But later on, perhaps . . . A sound from the door interrupted his troubled thoughts.

'Come in!'

It was Frazier, cap beneath his arm, eyes moving quickly around the cabin as if he expected to find some personal revelation in it, some clue to distinguish this captain from Cavendish.

'Libertymen are all ashore, sir. I've granted local leave for the others.'

Reliant was to remain at Rosyth until the repairs were completed. Ten days, they said. He listened to the ceaseless rattle of rivet guns, like metallic woodpeckers, and the occasional crash as something heavy was dropped onto a jetty or dockside.

'You're off then, John.'

Frazier watched him uncertainly. 'Unless you need me, sir?'

Sherbrooke shook his head. 'No, make the most of it. You've earned it.'

Frazier did not seem to hear. 'I wish you could meet my wife, sir. She's staying in Edinburgh – until things get more settled. But I expect there'll be a lot to catch up on. You know how it is.' He glanced at the clock. 'You're not married, are you, sir?'

'No.' It always came out like that, like a door slamming. There was nothing to say. It had been finished before it had even begun.

'Pilot's taking over, sir. If you need anything . . .'

Sherbrooke heard thuds overhead and knew that the chief boatswain's mate, the Buffer, would be hounding the dockyard workers every hour they were aboard to make certain they did not scratch, scrape or stain one single plank of *Reliant*'s immaculate quarterdeck. It was always an uphill battle.

Frazier said, 'It was on the news this morning, sir . . . about us.'

'I know. They made it sound like a real battle.' He glanced at the ship's crest. 'She did well, though.'

He had left the bridge after *Reliant* and her escorts were clear of the arena where that brief but fierce engagement had been fought. Most of the German survivors picked up by *Mulgrave* had been transferred to the flagship. *Reliant* not only had better facilities for dealing with casualties, but also carried a senior medical officer, Surgeon Commander Farleigh, a formidable man who brooked no interference with his department, and was unintimidated even by Stagg.

He had greeted Sherbrooke without warmth. 'Fifty-two, sir. A few more still in *Mulgrave*, but they're not expected to make it, and can't be moved to us.' He had followed Sherbrooke among the tiers of bunks.

Some of *Minden*'s company had seemed remarkably cheerful, smoking duty-free cigarettes, only their voices marking them out from all the other survivors *Reliant* had picked up during three years of war.

The officers were separated from the others, one with his eyes and hands bandaged, although his head was moving as though he were trying to hear what was being said. Another, a lieutenant, attempted to rise when he recognized the rank on Sherbrooke's sleeve.

Sherbrooke had reached out and touched his shoulder, then shook his head.

'No. Rest. You are safe now.'

If he did not speak English, then at least he had understood the tone. He had nodded weakly.

'Danke, Herr Kapitän. Danke sehr!' Some of his companions had leaned closer to listen, as though uneasy, or perhaps surprised.

Sherbrooke asked abruptly, 'Was their own captain not saved?'

He had realized that the surgeon commander was studying him. Perhaps disappointed that the captain did not fit his diagnosis.

He thinks I came down here to gloat. It made him unreasonably angry. He was deathly tired, and it was catching up with him, but he could not help himself.

Farleigh said, 'He was killed, sir.'

'I think I knew.'

He had walked back through the large sick bay, feeling their eyes on him. Did they know who he was? Did they care? They were out of the war. They were the lucky ones.

So this is the enemy. Perhaps it was better, safer, never to meet them face to face.

He realized that Frazier was speaking to him. *Must be worse than I think*. Round the bend, bomb-happy, the sailors called it. He could not imagine what psychiatric handle Surgeon Commander Farleigh would put on it.

'I'll be off, sir. Got a taxi coming.' But still he hesitated. 'Must make the most of it, as you say.'

Sherbrooke sat down again when he had gone, wondering, rather dully, what Frazier's wife was like. What would they talk about? The fight with *Minden*, the ship? He smiled disparagingly. *Me?*

The door opened slightly and Petty Officer Long stepped into the day cabin, a tray balanced on one hand.

Sherbrooke said, 'Perfect timing. Thanks.'

Long was arranging the glass and some ginger ale. 'Bit early, sir, but as we're on our own, I thought, well, where's the harm?'

On our own. Stagg was speeding south to London again. It would be interesting, not to say illuminating, to be a fly on the wall at the Admiralty, and observe the rear-admiral reliving the hunt for, and the destruction of the cruiser *Minden*.

Dodger Long watched the first Horse's Neck being sipped, appreciated.

'Nearly forgot, sir.' He took out an envelope: there was a vice-admiral's flag displayed on the flap. 'This just come aboard, sir.' He saw the reluctance with which Sherbrooke was opening it. Long knew what it was, right enough: captains' stewards knew everything. They had to. And he knew the captain wasn't going to like it one little bit. They said he had hardly slept while the ship had been at sea. This was certainly not the time.

An invitation to the vice-admiral's house. It was not a request, but a command.

Sherbrooke said, 'How can I get out of this?'

Long sucked his teeth. 'You can't, sir, an' that's a fact. Rear-Admiral Stagg's not 'ere, so there's no way out, so to speak.'

Sherbrooke stood up and walked to the scuttle again. It was still raining. He should have expected this. Stagg had probably arranged it himself. Meet the captain who had been sunk by *Minden*, and had evened the score . . . He would not put any manipulative stunt past Stagg.

Long was right, of course. A captain's duties did not begin and end with the ship. He stared at the handwritten summons.

There *was* no way out.

Long saw him glance at the empty tumbler, and then visibly change his mind. The new captain, no matter what he had gone through, had the makings, he thought. From Petty Officer Long, there was no higher accolade.

The vice-admiral was waiting to meet Sherbrooke the moment he stepped from the staff car which had collected him from the dockyard. He was a stocky, bright-eyed little man with a weathered complexion and a youthful face, another veteran brought back from retirement, but with more vigour than many younger men Sherbrooke had known, and an impressive rectangle of medal ribbons.

He took Sherbrooke by the arm and led him through a pair of tall doors. He wasted no time.

'Sorry to drag you over here, Sherbrooke. I haven't forgotten what it's like to bring a ship into a dockyard after a fight – unlike some, eh?'

He was shown to a chair. He had the pleasing impression that the apology was genuine.

'Fact is, I've got an important visitor on my hands. Sir Graham Edwardes.' He put his head on one side like some quizzical bird. 'I can see it on your face. You thought he was long out of it!'

Sherbrooke smiled, suddenly liking the small vice-admiral. The man in question, 'long out of it', might even have been dead, but his name would never be forgotten: Edwardes of the Dover Strait, a hero in every schoolboy's eyes for his exploits in the Channel and the North Sea, at the Dogger Bank and Jutland.

'Something like that, sir.'

'Well, he has an important job now, with the Admiralty's blessing. He goes round the country, spreading the word on behalf of the Royal Navy, persuading people to put their savings into funds for building warships, adopting the ships, too. It's all good for morale, or whatever they like to call it.' He grimaced. 'And now he's here. He was expecting to see Rear-Admiral Stagg, but apparently nobody informed him that the First Sea Lord has called Stagg down to London. Right hand not knowing what the left is doing – you know the score!'

'How can I help?'

'*Reliant* is a famous ship, and she's just destroyed a German cruiser. It's the stuff people want to hear, to share. They don't have the opportunity all that often.'

'Propaganda?'

'If you like, yes. We're the Silent Service too bloody often if you ask me!'

A steward in a perfectly pressed white jacket entered and waited, eyes discreetly averted, a tray in his hands.

The vice-admiral said, 'My usual, Wilson. Horse's Neck for you, eh, Sherbrooke?'

He remarked, 'Not much is secret here, sir.'

The vice-admiral called after the steward, 'Large ones!' Then he said, 'Dinner later. I just wanted to put you in the picture beforehand. Tomorrow you'll be interviewed by

105

two tame journalists, and there will be some photos. You know how it's done.'

Sherbrooke did not know. No wonder they had wanted Stagg. He seemed to thrive on this sort of thing.

The drinks arrived and the vice-admiral said, 'Sir Graham likes a dry ship, so I thought we'd get in first!'

He seemed to notice Sherbrooke's uncertainty. 'It's all been cleared, and your Rear-Admiral Stagg will have been told by now. Cheers!'

Sherbrooke thought of Long's obvious concern, the relief when he had declined that second drink. Afraid he might let the side down, or perhaps the ship.

The steward's head appeared round the door. 'In the drawing room, sir.'

The vice-admiral glanced ruefully at his empty glass. 'Ah, well, let's get on with it. Don't be fooled, he's still pretty sharp!'

The drawing room, like the rest of the house Sherbrooke had seen, was large, gloomy and indefinably damp. There were several paintings of famous sea-battles, much of the detail lost in the grime of years. There were three people waiting, one of them Sir Graham Edwardes, straight-backed and severe in a very dark suit. Sherbrooke had seen so many photographs of him over the years, all in uniform, that his appearance in civilian clothing was something of a shock. He looked so *old*. There was a younger man, vaguely scruffy, no doubt one of the tame journalists, and the third was a woman. Sherbrooke had a quick impression of very dark eyes, and hair pulled back severely to reveal her ears. Younger, much younger than himself. She returned his handshake, and Sir Graham introduced her as, 'Mrs Meheux, my assistant. A real treasure.'

She sat down and crossed her legs, and Sherbrooke saw

the other man turn to stare openly at them. As expected, he *was* a journalist, from the Ministry of Information.

'I'm glad you agreed to step into the breach, Captain Sherman . . .'

He turned, frowning, as the girl corrected quietly, 'Sherbrooke, Sir Graham. Captain Sherbrooke.'

Surprisingly, Edwardes laughed. 'Of course. Been working too hard, that's my trouble, what?'

The vice-admiral said gently, 'Please excuse me, Sir Graham. My other guests are arriving.'

Sherbrooke could still taste the brandy on his tongue. Whatever it was, it was better than his own stock in *Reliant*.

It seemed warmer in the room; the giant, old-fashioned radiators must have suddenly come to life. He saw the girl loosen her heavy coat, which she had not removed, as though she had intended to leave soon, and light glinted from a brooch fashioned like a regimental badge on the blouse underneath. The Royal Engineers.

So Mrs Meheux was married to a sapper. She looked no more than twenty-five, and he wondered if her husband was like Frazier, fretting over separation, fearful of growing apart.

Sir Graham Edwardes said, 'Good show about the *Minden*, Sherbrooke. A top gunnery ship, I believe. Those Jerries certainly know how to design gunsights and rangefinders – that I do understand!'

Sherbrooke tried to relax. It was a wonder that Edwardes had not referred to the enemy as The Hun.

He said, 'Her captain stood no chance, in my opinion, Sir Graham. He was outgunned, and too far from support.'

Edwardes pressed his fingertips together and commented, 'Rather like you when you last met up with him, eh?'

The little admiral was right. This one was pretty sharp.

Sherbrooke said, 'I had destroyers too, sir. It's often a matter of coincidence, luck, if you like. I had flown off our Walrus to look for some downed airmen. The pilot found *Minden*'s seaplane instead. After that, I knew. It was that convoy or nothing.'

Edwardes smiled. Strangely, it made him look older. 'Being a bit modest, I'd say.'

Sherbrooke saw that the journalist was making notes, his foot tapping as if to some soundless music.

He glanced at the girl again. She was trying not to yawn, and he had seen her peering at her watch. All in a day's work.

He said abruptly, 'German intelligence is good, Sir Graham. They knew about the convoy and its importance, and they had homed a whole U-Boat pack to intercept it, hence the emergency route around Scotland.'

'Well, that's it, surely?' He was smiling again, like a patient schoolmaster with an inept pupil. 'We got 'em through, and that's what counts!'

Sherbrooke said, 'Seven escorts were sunk, Sir Graham.'

Edwardes said, 'We're getting away from the bones of the matter. You destroyed one of Hitler's last big cruisers. If you hadn't, *Minden* would have been amongst those troopers like a fox in a chicken-run. It would have been bloody murder!' He glanced at the journalist. 'Got that?' He came sharply to his feet. 'Excuse me for a moment. Got to pump the bilges!'

Sherbrooke watched the girl, but she showed no sign of having heard. An older version of Stagg, then. Had he said it to shock, or to embarrass her?

The journalist murmured, 'For the record, Captain Sherbrooke, I'll just ask a couple of questions.'

Sherbrooke said evenly, 'Fire away.'

'I've genned up on most of it, of course. Your last ship

was sunk while you were defending a Russian convoy, and there were only eight of you saved. It must have been a terrible experience.'

Sherbrooke sat very still, but saw the girl twisting the wedding ring around her finger. Eager to leave.

'Yes. It was.' He seemed to hear the voices again. Calling out, pleading, then dying finally, in silence, while the cold tightened its grip. He shut his mind against them and said, 'Our sailors face that risk every day of their lives.'

The journalist hurried on, as though closing the chapter on it. 'Then you were given the *Reliant*, a much bigger ship. Were you . . . um . . . in awe of it?'

Sherbrooke said, 'I suppose so. She's a fine ship, almost the last of her class. I feel I've known her all my life. And I've served in her before, like a lot of others. To me, she *is* the navy.'

How easily it had come out, and he knew that he had meant it.

The girl said, quite suddenly, 'I have to go now. Tell Sir Graham, John. I'll see him as arranged.'

Sherbrooke stood up. 'I'll walk with you, and make sure about the car.'

She looked up at him, her eyes very steady. 'I can manage, Captain, but thank you. It was good of you to alter your arrangements for us.' A cool, firm handshake. 'I can appreciate what it cost you. You're full of surprises.' She saw him begin to smile and added, 'No . . . I mean it. I didn't really want to come. Like you, I'm rather tired. But I'm glad I did. I don't really know very much about ships, you see.'

Sherbrooke glanced at the brooch. 'He's a sapper.'

She gazed at him, as though searching for something. 'Yes.'

There were voices outside, and she said, 'You're not married.'

'I see you've done your homework, too.'

She shook her head. 'No, I just listen. I hear things. It goes with the job. It was rude of me. I'm sorry.'

The vice-admiral entered the room, his bright eyes everywhere. To Sir Graham he said, 'We can finish this over dinner. You've got the picture now. Should work out well.'

They all walked into the entrance hall. It retained some of its former beauty, despite the blackout shutters, and a clutter of stirrup pumps and the attendant buckets of water and sand in case of incendiary bombs.

The girl was speaking with a Royal Marine driver, giving him directions, and Sherbrooke imagined her going to meet her husband. In some hotel, he thought, or maybe he was stationed nearby. Greeting each other, forgetting everything while the moment lasted . . .

As if she sensed that he was watching her, she looked round at him.

'Enjoy your dinner, Captain.'

She turned to follow the driver, and he said abruptly, 'Will you be coming aboard tomorrow, Mrs Meheux?'

Edwardes, observing her hesitation, chuckled. 'If it's allowed, you might find it interesting.'

The little vice-admiral beamed, rubbing his hands briskly, glad it was almost over.

'I'll deal with that, Sir Graham.'

She said, 'Yes. I should like that, Captain.'

Edwardes called after her, 'Better wear some trousers, Emma. There are a lot of ladders to climb in a battlecruiser, and you know what sailors are like!'

She looked over her shoulder, her eyes curiously remote. 'I can manage, Sir Graham.'

Then she was gone, and Sherbrooke heard the car growling away into the darkness and the rain.

The vice-admiral was saying, 'I've arranged a few drinks with the other guests, Sir Graham. Can I tempt you this time?'

Edwardes said something, and strode away to confer with the shabby journalist. The vice-admiral murmured to Sherbrooke, 'Not too bad, was it?'

He thought of the girl in the staff car, returning to a life he barely understood.

'I gather Mrs Meheux is married to someone in the Royal Engineers. Lucky chap.'

The vice-admiral cleared his throat. 'Not too sure about that. He was at Singapore when the Japs marched in.'

'Prisoner of war?'

'Missing. Not a bloody word from anybody. There are a lot like that, of course. It must be hard – on her, I mean.'

Sherbrooke heard a gust of laughter, and the clink of glasses.

The vice-admiral grunted. 'Just think of it as another bloody convoy. Something to get through in one piece!'

He smiled, scarcely listening, glad that he had come despite the questions, the obvious insincerity of it all. It was absurd, and he knew it, but he would think of her when he eventually got back to the ship. *Emma* . . .

The noise and greetings washed over him, and he summoned yet another smile when he heard someone loudly welcoming 'a real hero'. But it was Edwardes of the Dover Strait who was gravely acknowledging the salutation.

The same steward asked, 'What can I get for you, sir?' He dropped his voice and said confidentially, 'My brother, sir, 'e's a leadin' 'and. 'E's in *Reliant*!'

Sherbrooke saw Edwardes staring at them.

He thought of all the others . . . the young woman not far away in Edinburgh, with her baby and a photo of her husband, who had wanted the baptism in the ship's bell . . . of Rayner's unknown airman, floating alone in his dinghy in those freezing waters . . . of the wounded German who had thanked him. Of so many. Too many.

He clapped the steward on the shoulder. 'Horse's Neck, please. Large one!' He saw the man grin. The story would soon go round, and would probably reach Dodger Long before the day was out.

And of Emma, whose husband was missing.

He recalled the sadness in her eyes when Edwardes had made his coarse remark about trousers. It was because she understood, too well, that all Edwardes had left was the memory. The rest was so much sham.

The forenoon passed better than Sherbrooke had dared to hope. A camera crew and several photographers roamed the ship, taking pictures of the upper deck, particularly the long grey barrels of A and B turrets, while working parties moved about their duties and became stiff and self-conscious whenever they found themselves being filmed.

Even the interview went reasonably well, conducted by a highly professional war correspondent who turned out to be an old school friend of Lieutenant Drake, *Reliant*'s young ex-barrister.

The day had begun badly with Sherbrooke fighting a nightmare, thrashing and crying out, and waking to find his pyjamas soaked in sweat, and Petty Officer Long's hand on his shoulder, with a cup of black coffee on his tray.

He had had too much to drink at the vice-admiral's party, and he was paying for it now. He also realized that his uniform, which he had thrown aside before falling into unconsciousness, had vanished, to reappear on a hanger, pressed and brushed, for today's event.

Long had said impassively, 'There was a shore tele-phone call for you, sir. Near six o'clock, it was. I told the caller to leave a number.' He had given his pixie-like smile. 'Mayfair number in London, sir. Very posh.'

It had obviously been Stagg, and he was equally sure that Long had known. The man would have made the perfect valet.

It was not easy to get a priority call through to London during the day, but he had told the O.O.D. to do what he could.

He saw Sir Graham Edwardes standing below a four-inch gun mounting, his eyes studiously grave and compelling as he completed an interview of his own. What had happened to the hero of Dover? His own father had aged, but had remained the same man until he had died . . . He rephrased the thought, brutally. Had been killed.

Commander Frazier was beside him. 'I hope you'll join us in the wardroom, sir.'

In theory, a captain was always a guest in his officers' wardroom, although he had often wondered if any captain had ever been refused entry.

It seemed more spacious than usual, with some of the officers absent on this unexpected leave, and others ashore to beg, borrow or steal items for their own departments.

He had seen Emma Meheux come aboard with the others, but had not had a chance to speak with her. She had been wearing the same heavy coat as yesterday, but now, holding her own in conversation with several officers, she wore a plain green dress, and the Royal Engineers brooch.

The Canadian pilot was explaining something to her, his hands in the air, the others grinning at him. The only other women present were two Wren officers from the base, very smart and self-assured in a world they understood and shared.

Frazier coughed politely, and the others melted away, except Rayner, who said, 'I was just telling Mrs Meheux how to cook lobsters, sir.'

She said, 'Thank you, Lieutenant. I shall try and remember, if the opportunity ever arises.'

Sherbrooke said, 'I hope they've all been looking after you.'

She looked at him directly, avoiding the polite preliminaries.

'I think it went quite well, don't you?'

So calm, so confident; no wonder the easy-going Rayner had been getting along with her so well.

'I'm not really used to it,' he said. 'I suppose it does some good. Does it?'

She said, without smiling, 'We hope so. It's all some people have to hold on to.'

Was she really so assured, so in control?

He asked, 'Are you staying in Scotland for long?'

She shook her head, and for the first time he realized how long her hair was. The colour of chestnuts, newly broken, the colour of autumn. She kept it tied back, almost severely.

'No. I'm going back to London tonight.'

'I had hoped to show you around the ship.'

'I'm afraid I can't. Perhaps some other time.'

She was ending the contact before it had begun. Any woman with her looks would always turn a lot of heads. A wedding ring was no protection in wartime, when loneliness was often the greatest hardship.

He said, 'Do you like your work?'

She shrugged, and raised one hand to wave away another tray of drinks. 'I'm a civil servant, that's all. My father

114

and brother are both doctors. I never had the inclination.' She smiled. 'Or the opportunity, either!' She paused, perhaps considering whether to continue. 'We lived in Bath, and so when I was appointed to my first proper post it was to the Admiralty office – where else? At Bath, of course.'

Just for those few seconds, Sherbrooke had glimpsed the young, untroubled girl. It was like sharing something secret.

She said quickly, almost curtly, 'If I'd been doing the interview, I would have asked you some rather different questions.'

'Tell me.'

She looked away. 'About how you felt when you lost your ship . . . if you think we'll win this war. I was watching you today when you were speaking with some of your men. Not when the camera was intruding, but the other times. And I thought, a great ship like this, and yet they seem to know you, as if the previous captain is forgotten.' She faced him again. 'There, I've said too much. Gin before lunch is never a smart idea.'

'Excuse me, sir.' It was the Officer-of-the-Day. 'We have that call on the line.' His eyes moved to the girl and back again. It would make a good story.

Sherbrooke acknowledged it, and said, 'Don't go until I get back, Mrs Meheux. Please. I'll be as quick as I can.'

The O.O.D. said helpfully, 'I've had it transferred to the lobby, sir.'

She watched them leave, and then glanced at her watch. Edwardes would understand, and anyway . . .

'Can I get you anything?' It was Frazier.

He felt drained, and vaguely sickened. Something had happened on this leave which had never occurred before. He had had a row with his wife, a hushed, angry argument, subdued out of pride and a regard for the thinness of the hotel room's walls.

She answered, 'I shall have to make my excuses, Commander Frazier.'

He smiled, trying to play the part. 'I'm sorry, Mrs Meheux. I haven't seen the Captain so relaxed for a long time.'

She half-turned. 'I like him. I'm surprised he's not married.'

Frazier shrugged. 'I don't know the whole story, but the Andrew's like a family, so I've heard some of it. His father was a serving officer for years, then he became ill and was forced onto the beach . . . and when the war came, he insisted on moving to Portsmouth. I suppose he wanted to be near the world he'd loved, or something like that. Then, two years ago – I expect you heard all about it – there was a series of air raids on the city, and a great part of it was destroyed. The Captain's father was killed in one of those attacks.' He hesitated. 'The girl the Captain was going to marry was visiting at the time. She was killed, too. It must have been tough on him.'

She said, very quietly, 'Thank you for telling me. It will go no further.'

Frazier said, equally gravely, 'I know.'

The stewards were looking at the wardroom clock; some of the officers were already heading for lunch. A break in the routine was always welcome.

Sherbrooke strode back into the wardroom, and said, 'Sorry about that,' and to Frazier, 'It was Rear-Admiral Stagg. Checking up on today's event, needless to say.'

To the girl, he said, 'Are you sure you can't stay longer?'

'I'm afraid not. I have a reserved seat at Edinburgh Waverley for the night train.' She turned to speak to Frazier, but he had gone.

'He's a nice man,' she said.

'John? Yes, he is. I don't know what I would have done without him.'

She was looking round again, preparing her escape, he thought. She said, 'He's very fond of you, isn't he?'

Then, in that direct manner, as she had spoken to him at their first meeting, she said, 'He told me about your father. I'm very sorry.'

There was a silence, which he found difficult to break. At length, he said, 'My last command was a Portsmouth ship.' He glanced around the wardroom, a stranger again. 'Like *Reliant*. There were many broken hearts after those raids.'

'I think you've just answered the questions I would have asked in my interview.'

He said, 'I'll see you over the side, Mrs Meheux.'

'Over the side. You even make that sound so polite.' She laughed, but there was something in her eyes that revealed the lie.

He said, 'I'll make sure your transport is here.' He watched her cross the wardroom to say goodbye to the vice-admiral, and to the Hero of Dover.

He was making an idiot of himself. Missing or not, she had a husband, and in any case she would barely remember this visit once she was back in London.

He walked out onto the damp planking and saw the quartermaster and side-party come to life. The O.O.D. was present, and there was a car waiting on the jetty, the driver chatting to a Royal Marine sentry.

He thought of Stagg's interest in this interview, which had been so badly timed as to have happened in his absence. He was sure Stagg thought he would have done a much better job.

But the other aspect of it remained fixed in his mind,

117

irremovable, like a fish-bone in the throat.

A woman had answered the telephone, her voice brusque, impatient.

'Vincent! It's the *Reliant*!'

On such a bad line, he could have been mistaken. Then he recalled the churchyard, the flag draped on the coffin. He was not mistaken. He would have recognized Jane's voice anywhere.

He walked to the guardrail and stared down at the abandoned, rusty cables and piles of old armour plate, so much scrap now.

Reliant would be repaired and at sea very soon. Rosyth, like every other dockyard, needed the space.

He heard her shoes on the planking, and prepared himself to face her.

'I hope we meet again, Mrs Meheux. I mean that. I might still get a chance to show you *Reliant*. Perhaps in London—'

She looked at him steadily, curious, defiant, guarded.

'I think it would be unwise, Captain Sherbrooke. For both of us.' She held out her hand. 'Take care of yourself. I shall not forget this visit.'

He gripped her hand, and could feel, almost physically, the eyes of the side-party on every move.

He had offended her, or worse, she was embarrassed by his clumsy attentiveness, or his arrogance.

She released her hand, and fumbled with the collar of her coat.

He said, 'Hold on to the rail. The brow is very steep.'

She looked sharply at him again, as if surprised by his solicitude.

She said, 'It's starting to rain again!' She seemed to make up her mind. 'If you really want to . . .' She paused. 'My office number is in orders.'

Sherbrooke saluted as she went down the side, very small against the grey steel and the welders' blinding torches. She did not look up at the ship, but he himself watched the car until it was swallowed by the dockyard. And, somehow, he knew that she would know it.

7

Friends

Much to everyone's surprise, *Reliant*'s repairs were completed at the promised time, although it took another day to work the ship out of dock and to a new mooring. Re-ammunitioning and the replenishment of stores began at once. That was the day on which Rear-Admiral Stagg chose to return, and from the moment he strode aboard, it was evident that he was in a foul mood. The talks at the Admiralty and with the chiefs of staff had solved nothing, as far as Stagg was concerned.

'And all because of that bloody carrier, *Seeker*! She's still stuck up there in Iceland – one damned delay after another. It might be weeks before she's ready to join us! And their lordships are so shit-scared after the *Minden* affair that they want *my* flagship to escort another major troop convoy they've approved for next month. Australian and New Zealand divisions this time. Coming from Ceylon via the Cape. They've got raiders on the brain!'

Sherbrooke watched him, seeing the anger, the resentment.

'I can understand their point, sir. If anything happened in those waters . . .'

Stagg snapped, 'God damnit, Guy, you're as bad as they are! I want a separate force, an active group – something that would have some significance at this stage of the war! The First Sea Lord made it plain that it's this year or not at all for an invasion. I don't intend to be used as a convoy escort. Any clapped-out battleship could manage that!'

He glared at his flag lieutenant as he rearranged the files of signals on his desk. '*And* I read your report about the bloody radar. Nothing wrong with it, they said, eh? They should have been there, eh?'

Sherbrooke did not understand it, either. A fluke, an unexplained temporary fault: after all, radar was still in its infancy.

The stark fact remained, that had they been using their radar at full strength, *Minden* might have detected *Reliant*'s position with their own form of r.d.f. *Minden* had not been in her expected position, nor had she been on the estimated course. But for Rayner's sighting of the Arado seaplane and their sudden loss of radar transmission, the enemy might easily have fired the first destructive broadside. He recalled the answers he had given the untidy journalist. Luck, coincidence: that was often true. But this had been different. Like fate.

It was ridiculous, of course. He was tired, and Stagg's mood of intolerance had done nothing to help.

Stagg was saying sharply, 'But once we get *Seeker* in the group, things will be different, believe me!'

Sherbrooke considered the long haul south. Gibraltar, the South Atlantic, probably to relieve other heavy escorts at Cape Town. Away from the ice, the dark, angry seas.

Stagg said, 'Oh, and this just came in. That chap you met, Sir Graham Edwardes.' He took time to pick up a signal. 'Two days after his visit to *Reliant* the poor old chap popped off, slipped his cable. Heart attack, apparently.' He smiled sarcastically. 'Must be the effect you have on people.'

Sherbrooke saw the flag lieutenant's eyes moving between them. He had been aboard during the event: Stagg never seemed to take him anywhere of importance.

He recalled the vice-admiral's warning that evening. *He's still pretty sharp.* And now he was dead.

Stagg said, 'You've been working your pants off since you took command. You haven't had a break – I'll lay odds on it.' His humour was returning. 'You know, Guy, I'm going to be pretty tied up, and as you made such an impression with your interviews and everything else in my absence, I think *you* should go south in my place. A sort of tribute.'

Sherbrooke stared at him. 'A memorial service?'

Stagg almost winked. 'Their lordships expect it. Always like a good piss-up. And I'd certainly appreciate your doing it for me.'

Sherbrooke heard feet marching across the quarterdeck, the ship asserting herself after the invasion of dockyard intruders.

The flag lieutenant said gently, 'It's at Portsmouth, sir.'

Stagg snapped, 'Don't fuss, Flags.' To Sherbrooke, he added, 'I shall see that the R.A.F. fly you most of the way. Least I can do, eh?'

Sherbrooke hesitated. 'When will this be, sir?'

Stagg was tiring of it. 'Thursday next. No problem. Fix it up, Flags. Then tell my secretary to come in.'

Sherbrooke walked to the door. It was true that, apart from Iceland and the dockyard, he had barely stepped ashore since taking command. Frazier could take care of things; he had done it before. He seemed to hear her voice again, at the wardroom reception. *He's very fond of you, isn't he?* He had never seen Frazier in that light before. A perfectionist at his work, but always slightly withdrawn, on occasions quite remote, except for that brief moment on the bridge. *Perhaps we're all learning something.*

Stagg said, 'Meant to tell you, Guy. I saw Jane Cavendish in London. Took her out to lunch. She's looking well, considering.'

Out to lunch. Petty Officer Long had told him that the first shore telephone call had been at six in the morning.

Sherbrooke heard himself say, 'I'm glad she's all right.' It might have been a coincidence.

Stagg said indifferently, 'Oh, she'll get over it.'

Sherbrooke left the day cabin without risking another word. So it was true, and all he could think of was Cavendish sitting in his beloved car, with its engine running in a sealed garage.

She'll get over it. But he had not.

Further forward in *Reliant*'s great hull were many of the ship's offices, where everything was arranged from issues of rum and tinned coffee powder to protective clothing and station cards to give identities to new arrivals.

In one of these offices, Paymaster Lieutenant James Villar, the admiral's secretary, sat at his desk, his legs crossed, while he endeavoured to complete a crossword puzzle. He was a late entry into the Royal Navy, with a background so unremarkable that he sometimes found it necessary to embroider it. He was thirty years old, senior when compared to most of *Reliant*'s wardroom, and had a dark, almost swarthy face with restless, penetrating eyes which missed very little. As officers and ratings came and went, to take courses for advancement, for promotion, or to fill gaps left by men who had died or deserted, he had watched them all. It was not merely a hobby; it was a dedicated pursuit. Officers of his branch, of the supply and secretariat section, distinguished by the white cloth between their gold stripes, were considered by the others to be necessary evils, and that was as far as it went. The executive officers, the gunnery types, and the fliers saw themselves on another planet.

But Villar was the admiral's secretary, and he considered that that placed him in a different sphere entirely.

Everyone had a story somewhere inside him, and Villar would often make it his business to uncover it.

He turned his head slightly as something squeaked, a damp leather wiping one of the thick glass scuttles.

Villar tapped his teeth with his pencil. There was probably a story there, he thought, although he doubted that he would ever take the trouble to discover it.

The rating who was cleaning the glass turned and looked at him.

'Anything else, sir?'

Villar regarded him severely. 'That cabinet. Better being in here than out on that cold deck, right?'

Ordinary Seaman Alan Mowbray was young, and looked no more than a boy, although Villar knew he was almost nineteen. Even in his working overalls, he always looked smart, his hair neatly combed and clean. How he had ended up in a battlecruiser was beyond Villar. He had been listed as a former officer candidate who had been rejected, 'dipped', somewhere along the way. Villar had often wondered why. Mowbray had qualities equal to many of those officers Villar met every day in the wardroom, a pleasant manner, and he was quietly well-spoken. Perhaps he had simply lacked the ambition of his classmates.

He watched him polishing the cabinet. He had delicate, almost feminine hands, but he seemed to have fitted into the crowded, roughly ruled world of the messdecks. Otherwise, Villar would have heard about it.

He said suddenly, 'What did you do before you joined up, Mowbray, if anything?'

The youth looked at him. 'I was a student, sir.' He hesitated. 'An art student.'

'I see. And were you very disappointed when you lost your chance of a commission?'

He considered it. 'It was something that happened, sir. I'm not sure what I really wanted.' He continued his polishing.

'Were you any good? As an artist, I mean?'

The duster stopped again. 'I think so, sir.' He looked up, frowning, vulnerable. 'I still do some work when I can get the time.'

Villar was losing interest in the conversation. 'You'll have to show me one of your masterpieces some day.'

He looked round as someone rapped on the door.

'Yes?'

It was a total stranger, a sub-lieutenant so new that the single wavy stripe on his sleeve looked like pure gold.

'I was looking for the Commander, sir. I've just come aboard to join. Sub-Lieutenant Peter Forbes . . .'

'Wrong place. I'm the admiral's secretary.' The phone rang by his elbow, shattering the sudden silence.

Villar snatched it up. It was Howe, the flag lieutenant.

'The Boss wants you down aft, chop-chop!'

But Villar barely heard him. He was looking at the newly appointed subbie and the rating, who was on his knees by the cabinet.

Forbes was saying, 'Alan, it's you! I didn't know you were in *Reliant*! You should have told me . . . written or something!'

The boy stood up, twisting the duster in his hands.

'I'm sorry, Peter . . . I mean, sir. I couldn't . . .'

Villar said softly into the telephone, 'I'm on my way, Flags!' But he was still observing them covertly, saw them reach out and touch hands; sensed the pain and the dismay at this encounter. And something more.

He put down the telephone loudly. 'I'm going that way, Sub. I'll show you,' and to the young seaman, 'You carry on here. This won't take long. Might need you.'

He saw their quick exchange of glances and was satisfied. There was, indeed, a story.

And while Petty Officer Long packed the captain's case for his trip south, and considered the change he had seen in him, and as Lieutenant Dick Rayner of Toronto dubiously agreed to the proposal of a run ashore with Eddy Buck, *Reliant* carried them all. Twelve hundred officers and men, from Rear-Admiral Stagg to the lowliest rating, they were as strong only as the ship which ruled their lives.

The taxi must have been built long before the war. Every time the driver changed gear, it sounded as though it might be the last. The night was pitch dark, and the shades on the headlights, conforming with the air raid precautions, made it impossible to see where they were going. Rayner wiped the window with his sleeve and peered at a darkened house as it loomed above the road.

'Where the hell is this place, Eddy?'

Buck said hopefully, 'I think we're nearly there, Dick.'

Rayner grimaced in the darkness. 'Yeah? Well, I think we're lost!'

It had all sounded straightforward, but then most things suggested by Buck usually did. It was the Malcolm Hotel, 'just a few miles up the Queensferry Road'. There would be music and dancing. Mostly men from the local army camp, and of course girls, from as far away as Dunfermline, which Buck had made sound like Las Vegas.

The driver, withdrawn to the point of surliness, had made it clear from the start: pay in advance, and double fare for the return trip to Rosyth. Buck had dismissed it, saying, 'You can always get a lift back with somebody, army or R.A.F., easy.' It was only later that he admitted he had only been to this hotel once before, and that had been in broad daylight.

Rayner said, 'We should have stayed aboard, or gone across to that cruiser for a drink. It would have been more fun than this.'

At least it wasn't raining, for a change. A sort of wet mist clung to the windscreen; not that it mattered, Rayner thought, there was nothing to see, anyway.

He had been intending to write home when Buck had badgered him into going ashore for a run. He had wanted to tell his parents about his experience, even though he knew there wasn't a cat in hell's chance of it getting past the censor. He only knew that he wanted to confide in them, to share the fact that he had killed two Germans, two airmen like himself. Not to make excuses, or justify his action. War wasn't like that . . .

Buck said, 'Ahah. I recognize *that*, Dick. Not long now!'

Rayner grinned. 'You and your goddamned short cuts!'

It was funny when you thought about it. Two young men from the opposite ends of the earth groping around in Scotland for some momentary release from machines and routine, boredom, and sudden danger.

He would write to them about that.

He heard the driver muttering something, and then Buck saying, 'Some fool parked on the corner. Bloody dangerous, with no lights.'

Rayner said, 'Well, it's not exactly busy around here, is it?'

They groped past the car, which was pointing the other way. Somebody who could still get gas, he thought, in spite of the severe rationing.

127

He reached out and jabbed the driver's arm. 'Stop the taxi!'

The driver applied the brakes. 'What d'you see, man?'

It was the same feeling, ice cold and alert, an instinct.

Buck said, 'Oh, for God's sake. Can't you wait till we get there?'

But Rayner was out of the taxi, his shoes slipping on loose stones as he crossed the road toward the darkened car.

It all happened in a second, even though his mind recorded every small fragment, like touching down to land, twisting to avoid an unexpected burst of flak. He wrenched open the door and saw the man staring at him, his eyes wild in the safety light; he was lashing out with his fist but Rayner scarcely felt the blow. Instead, he saw the girl, bent back in the passenger's seat, her skirt dragged up over her legs, one shoulder bare where her dress had been ripped.

She seemed to be trying to scream, or speak, her mute terror matched only by her disbelief.

Rayner tasted blood on his mouth, and was suddenly, blindly angry. 'You bastard! You son of a bitch!' He felt the pain lance up his arm with the force of the blow, and was vaguely aware that Buck was trying to reach round him to lend a hand.

Rayner did not need a hand from anybody.

The man was falling from the car, hitting out wildly, his fury giving way to fear as Rayner hit him again, and again. Buck called, 'Easy, you mad bugger! He's out for the count!'

Rayner was on the other side, wrenching the door open. She made no attempt to resist as he put his arms round her, nor did she utter a sound as he attempted to cover her legs with her skirt. Only her eyes moved, their expression hidden, shadowed, although Rayner sensed her realization,

128

the shock, when she allowed herself to believe that she was safe.

She stood beside him on the road. Rayner dragged off his blue raincoat and guided each of her arms in turn into the sleeves, covering her with the coat, then buttoning it slowly, his fingers hesitant as they touched the skin where her dress had been torn.

He said, 'That's better,' and to Buck, 'Get the taxi, Eddy.'

Buck said, 'He's done a bunk. A big help, he was!'

She looked at the inert shape on the ground. 'The hotel is just round the corner.' She spoke very carefully, as if afraid of what it might arouse. 'It was a birthday party. There are quite a few of our people there, but I had to get back. He offered me a lift.' She pointed suddenly, and the cuff of Rayner's raincoat slipped over her hand. 'My purse is in there. Could you get it, please?'

She swayed slightly, and Rayner held her gently upright while Buck recovered the purse.

Buck reached into the car again and removed the ignition key. 'I'll ring the cops, Dick.'

They walked around the bend, and there was the hotel. It was not much of a place, and there was certainly no music or dancing, not this particular evening, in any case.

They pushed through the smoky black-out curtains and into the harsh light. There were several people there, most of them in uniform, some of them nurses. One of the latter was standing by a birthday cake, and Rayner thought irrelevantly that it must have taken all of their rations to produce it. He had learned a lot since coming to Britain.

She turned, and he saw her face for the first time. She was pretty, with hair as fair as his own.

Then she took the handkerchief from his reefer pocket and dabbed his mouth, very gently but firmly. 'You'll have a bad bruise there tomorrow.'

Buck grinned. 'So will that bastard outside!'

She glanced down and saw the wings on Rayner's sleeve. It seemed to surprise, even discomfit her. 'You're a flier. I – I thought – when I saw the uniform . . .'

Everybody was crowding round, asking questions, wanting to help; someone handed her a glass of something. In the next bar, Rayner could hear another voice speaking on the telephone, asking for the police.

He said gently, 'Hey, what's the big deal? Don't you like fliers?' It was something to say, to hold on to the moment. She was trying to swallow the drink, and he felt the senseless anger again when he saw the scratches on her throat and cheek.

She choked, and eventually said, 'No . . . it's not that. I work at the new hospital . . . it's not far from here. It's for recuperation . . . burns. We get a lot of fliers sent to us.'

He said, 'Yeah. Off the beaten track,' and could not disguise his bitterness. He had known pilots who had been badly burned, disfigured, who were sent to remote places like this, where they wouldn't embarrass people.

He said, 'That man. Did you know him?'

'I don't think so. He knew I was a nurse . . . must have been listening.' She closed her eyes as if to erase the memory. 'You must never tell them you're a nurse. They think you're anybody's.'

Someone called, 'I'll drive you back right now, Andy!'

It was getting out of hand. Rayner heard doors banging, the authoritative voices which differed very little from cops in Toronto.

She was holding his arm, searching for the words, like people being parted at a railway station, when those words would never come.

She said, 'I'll send you your coat. I don't even know . . .'

'Dick Rayner. I'm in *Reliant*.' He could almost read the

warning posters. *Careless talk costs lives! Be like Dad, Keep Mum!* But he did not care.

'I'll call you. Tomorrow.' He saw her uncertainty, the fear and shock coming back. 'I don't want to lose you. Not now.'

She said, very softly, 'I'm Andrea Collins.' Again, she attempted to smile. 'My friends call me Andy.'

She gripped his arm so tightly then that he could feel her pain, her revulsion.

'He tried to rape me . . .' Then she fainted, and would have fallen but for Rayner's arms around her.

'It's all right, Lieutenant. We'll take care of her.' The speaker was an older nurse; she must have been very pretty when she was young, he thought. She was the one who was having a birthday celebration.

'Take this card,' she said. 'It's the staff quarters. That was a fine thing you did.'

Then suddenly the place was empty, except for Buck and two large policemen.

One of the constables said, 'Did I hear ye say H.M.S. *Reliant*, sir? Now there's a thing, eh, Jamie? A real hero!' He fixed the landlord with a stare. 'A bottle of your best, Alex.' He beamed at the two naval officers. 'An' then I'll be troubling you gentlemen for a wee statement.' He shook Rayner's hand warmly. 'But first, the malt. And dinna fret aboot the ship. We'll take ye back.'

Rayner looked at his sleeve, remembering how she had gripped it. Then he grinned at his friend. Even Eddy would never be able to top this for a run ashore.

My friends call me Andy.

He said, 'Well, I'll be *damned*.'

And they all laughed.

The Cathedral Church of St Thomas à Becket was small,

131

even intimate, when compared with its contemporaries in other cities, but in the years of war it had risen to become a powerful symbol to all who knew it. During the relentless and continuous bombing of the first bitter months, when the city had seen its famous Guildhall reduced to a smoking shell, and streets and whole neighbourhoods were flattened, it held out hope, and gave strength to Portsmouth, to survive, to eventually fight back. Like H.M.S. *Victory* in her dry dock, with most of the buildings around her either blasted to rubble or burned to the ground, the cathedral was like a beacon.

On this bright, cold morning, it was almost full, the congregation consisting of senior officers, two Members of Parliament, government officials, and a small group of men and women, some very old, who still managed to join in the well-known hymns, their medals, from another war, making a brave display in this place which had known and honoured so many heroes.

Toward the rear of the cathedral sat most of the younger naval officers, many from ships in the dockyard. Sherbrooke was standing beside a massive major of marines, and glanced round briefly at the others. Probably detailed off to attend, to make up the numbers at this service, which must have been arranged with an almost unseemly haste.

The Commander-in-Chief, Portsmouth, read the lesson, and the senior chaplain gave a short but moving address. Sherbrooke recalled the old man he had last seen at Rosyth, and found it hard to reconcile the memory with the hero whose life was now being celebrated.

They would never have dared to hold an assembly like this in those early days of the war. So many important people under one roof would have been tempting more than fate.

He had been at sea when that last raid had been launched

against the city and its dockyard. Over three hundred bombers had kept up an almost continuous onslaught for most of the night, and many people had been killed and injured, and over three thousand made homeless. One stick of bombs had fallen across the Point, where his father had a small house overlooking the Solent. He had kept an old telescope on the verandah, so that he could watch the comings and goings of warships, most of which he knew by sight.

They must have died together, instantly. It was little consolation.

Portsmouth had erected a memorial for those who had died, and he wondered if he should walk down and see it. He glanced around at the busts and the memorial plaques, illustrious names, victories to match, the very history of a city and a navy.

Reliant was a Pompey ship, but like most major war vessels, she seldom came here. Even with growing air support and strong anti-aircraft batteries and barrage balloons, there was always the risk of a hit-and-run raid, when a battlecruiser in dock would be too rich a target to miss.

He looked down at the card in his hand. The last hymn would be *For Those in Peril On The Sea*. He smiled privately. It was just about the only hymn sailors spared their own crude translation.

He wondered how Frazier was coping. He had looked very much on edge at their last meeting. It was something personal; it had to be. Something outside the world of the ship, something beyond his own influence or comprehension. If you had a wife or family, and were separated by war . . . He stopped the thoughts right there. He had neither.

And after this, another convoy. The opportunity to

exercise the ship in southern waters, without the constant threat of U-Boat attacks. To get to know her better, to put names to all those faces who passed him, or who chose to avoid his eyes.

He recalled his flight south from Scotland, in an R.A.F. Lysander, with a crew so casual and cheerful they could have been on a holiday jaunt. To them, he had been just so much cargo, a passing responsibility. Stagg certainly had a lot of pull, although it had only extended one way. He would have to return to Rosyth by train.

The cathedral seemed to quiver as the combined voices of servicemen and women rose with those of the veterans who had attended this memorial service because they had been a part of it, and their lives had been touched by the man whose life and death were commemorated.

For those in peril on the sea.

He was surprised that it could still move him.

He heard someone sob as the organ died away, and glanced across the aisle. Almost hidden by a pillar, he recognized her, and saw that she was looking at him. And yet, he had not seen her before this. Perhaps she had wanted it that way.

She raised her hymn card, and smiled. Almost shyly, nervously.

He picked up his cap and waited for the great and the powerful to lead the way down to the doors, back to their various messes for a drink, and the chosen few to something more substantial. The veterans walked together, one in a wheelchair, craning his head to peer up at the trappings and the past glories.

He heard a young lieutenant say, 'They should have had the Last Post. *I* would!'

His friend said sardonically, 'I'd have thought Joe Loss was more in your line!'

Sherbrooke smiled. It was good to know that the spirit was still there, as it had been in Portsmouth after the bombing.

Then she was beside him, almost touching as they walked in the slow-moving press of people.

'I heard you were coming, Captain Sherbrooke. We had a message. It was good of you.'

'You must miss him, Mrs Meheux.'

She glanced up at him. 'Yes, I think I shall. He could be difficult, but that was just his way. I think he overdid things.'

'What will you do now? In your work, I mean?' He looked at her, saw the hair hidden by her thick coat and a long strand which had blown across her brow.

'Oh, I'll get used to my new boss, I expect. Although from what I've heard . . .' She touched his arm. 'Never mind that. When are you going back?'

'Tomorrow. There's a lot going on.'

They walked out into the crisp air, the crowd lingering or dispersing in groups as the mood took them. The doors closed and the organ stopped. It was over.

She said, 'It's been a long trip for you. Where are you staying?'

'My case is at the naval club. I was just going to get it.'

She watched, aware of his uncertainty.

'What is it? Is something wrong?'

Why should he explain?

'I was going to walk to the Point. There's a memorial.'

She said, 'Your father?'

He said, after a moment, 'I just thought . . . Well, you never know.' He was conscious of her hand on his sleeve, the wedding ring shining, like a warning.

'Don't talk like that. You're alive. It *matters*.'

'Thank you for that. I didn't mean to be such a drag.'

She watched him very steadily. 'You're not.' She hesitated, then said abruptly, 'Take me with you, will you? I won't intrude.'

He was about to speak when someone said, 'Why, Captain Sherbrooke! It *is* you, isn't it?'

He swung round and saw a woman in a long fur coat and black hat coming towards him. She was not old, but she had a quality of hardened confidence which might soon make her so. Light brown hair, a treble row of pearls displayed at the neck of her coat, a crisp, persuasive manner. He had no idea who she was.

She said, 'It was some time ago.' She held out her hand. 'At Cowes, I believe. You were a three-ringer then.' She laughed. 'Just.'

It was like turning back the pages of an old photograph album.

Olive, he thought, her name was Olive.

He said quietly, 'Mrs Stagg – of course. I came today because . . .'

She stared with a keen interest at the girl. 'I know why you came. He rang me. And this is?'

She answered for herself. 'Emma Meheux. I was Sir Graham's assistant at the Admiralty.'

'A Wren officer?'

'No.' She seemed very calm. 'I'm a civil servant, Mrs Stagg.'

'There now.' Stagg's wife turned to Sherbrooke, as if to shut her out. 'I have a car. Johnnie will drive us. We could lunch somewhere before you head north again.'

Sherbrooke saw a heavily-built army officer, probably a lieutenant-general, loitering, watching the progress of the conversation. *Johnnie*.

The girl said, 'I have to accompany Captain Sherbrooke to an appointment, Mrs Stagg.'

'I see.' Her eyes flashed between them. 'Quite so. To be questioned about my husband's victory again, no doubt.' She thrust out her hand. 'Never mind. Some other time.'

Sherbrooke saluted, and watched with relief as Stagg's wife was escorted to a waiting staff car.

'Thanks. I can see why you got the job with Edwardes!'

She smiled. 'Forgive me, Captain Sherbrooke. I was feeling rather protective – selfish, if you like.'

He took her arm, and together they walked toward the street, of which nothing remained but the kerb stones to mark where people had once lived, loved, and hoped.

She said softly, 'If I had known, I would have brought some flowers. But there's nothing much in the shops at this time of year.' She fell silent as the captain beside her removed his cap and knelt by the recently erected stone.

Passing sailors looked over; some saluted; others respected his complete isolation.

She watched him, her hands clasped, more deeply moved than she could have imagined. She saw him trace the name listed with all the others. *Commander Thomas Sherbrooke, Royal Navy, Retired.* She waited, holding her breath, as his hand moved over and down. A fine, strong hand; a hand, she thought with strange, sudden pain, which had nearly died.

He said, 'They should have put their names together. But they didn't know, you see. She was visiting. There were so many that night.'

She saw him touch some dead flowers at the base of the stone, as if he were lost in some memory. She noticed that his hair was touching his collar, longer than she might have expected of a naval captain. The hair was brown, but the sideburns were grey.

She could not stop herself. 'Who was she?'

He stood up, and replaced the cap with the bright gold oak leaves on its peak.

'A girl I knew a long time ago. I was thinking of her just now. When I think of her sometimes I can only see her in her school uniform, green blazer and a floppy panama hat. Ridiculous, isn't it?'

She waited, wanting to take him away from this place, knowing that if she did, some fragile contact might be broken.

'I don't think so. My husband was a Territorial before the war. He was called up immediately. We got married on his first and only leave, and on the third day he was recalled to his unit. So you see, I do understand. Very well.'

They walked on, past the remains of the famous old inn, The George, which had also been a victim of the bombing. It had been Nelson's last stop before he had joined *Victory.*

He said, 'You'll probably laugh at me.'

'I won't.'

'I want to see you again. I have absolutely no right, and with the war moving as it is, it might be just another heartache for you. But I do want to see you, to know you. It matters to me.'

When she remained silent, he looked down at her, and was shocked to see tears on her cheek.

'I'm sorry.'

'Don't be. But we both know it would be wrong to hope. To do something . . . might harm something special. It would be cruel . . . unfair to us.'

'Suppose . . .'

She wiped her cheek with her fingers, a young girl again. 'Suppose?'

'If I was able to get some leave. We could meet. Have

138

meals together, talk and understand each other, like other people.'

'As friends, you mean?' She stopped and waited for him to face her. 'And how long would that last?'

'As long as you'll put up with me, Emma.'

She shook her head. 'I'm not ready. I thought I could handle things. God knows it's easy enough to go off the rails – the two girls I share rooms with never stop talking about it. How do you think I would feel? Being with you, but not *with* you?' She held out her hand. 'No. I'm strong – I've had to be.' Then she lifted her head, her eyes dark, and yet luminous, burning him. 'I was watching you just now, you know. Sharing it, because some of it was like my own experience. I wanted to put my arms round you. I didn't care about all your gaping sailors and your rear-admiral's wife. And then I knew I couldn't. *We* couldn't.'

She gripped the ring on her finger, and twisted it.

'In my heart, I know he's still alive, no matter what those bastards say about being missing. If half of what I've heard and read is true, he'll come back eventually – to me. And he'll need me, something that might not have been true before. Three days . . . that was all we had.' She added sharply, as though punishing herself, 'Two nights. That's all I really knew of him. Before that, like your girl, he was just someone I grew up with!'

She stared down at her watch, like that first time.

'I have to go. My new boss will expect it. I came here in case it was you instead of Stagg . . . I told myself not to be such a witless idiot, but you did come. Maybe it would have been better . . .'

He felt her stiffen as he put his arm around her shoulders.

'Please,' she said, 'don't.'

He said, 'No bargains, and no promises.' He raised her

139

chin with a gentle hand. 'But I won't pretend, either.'

She nodded slowly, her eyes never leaving his.

'Friends.'

He watched her walk away, and waited in case she looked back.

This time she did, or perhaps he imagined it. When he looked again, she was gone.

Then he returned to the memorial stone, reasoning that it was on the way to the naval club.

But he paused there for some time, thinking many things, reliving it moment by moment.

Then he touched his cap, and said aloud, 'Thanks.'

His father would have understood.

8

Fast Convoy

Sherbrooke walked out on to the port wing of the bridge and levelled his binoculars on the nearest destroyer. He could feel the sun's heat on his shoulders and his cheek, and a sense of release, something he could scarcely remember. He watched the destroyer lifting and dipping over the glittering water, deep, deep blue, with a sky so empty that it looked almost colourless.

Tomorrow, according to Rhodes, they would sight land, and Table Mountain the following day.

It was three weeks since they had left Scotland's damp and cold, and it was almost impossible to accept such a difference, let alone what a change of circumstances could do for *Reliant*'s ship's company. There were even a few cases of sunburn.

Six thousand miles. Each day they had exercised with their six destroyers, five destroyers now, as one, the *Mediator*, had been forced to leave the group and head for Gibraltar after reporting a shaft defect.

Sherbrooke had been in the chart room with Stagg when he had been informed of it.

Stagg had said scornfully, 'God, they don't make ships that can stand up to everything, not any more!' Then, grinning, 'Nor the men to go with them. Not like *us*, eh, Guy?'

Perhaps it had been the cue he had been looking for.

'I heard that you met up with old Edwardes' assistant when you were down in Portsmouth. Quite young, I gather?'

Sherbrooke had not found it easy to keep a straight face. Mrs Stagg was as sharply observant as her husband, in some things, anyway.

Stagg had pressed him. 'Pretty, is she?'

'*I* think so.' It had surprised him how easily it had come out.

Even if he had been able to see her again before *Reliant* had left for the Cape, it was just an illusion, a conceit. But a moment he would never forget.

Stagg had shaken his head. 'You're a dark one, and no mistake. But then, you always were. Stay with the ship. It's safer in the long run!'

Sherbrooke let the glasses fall to his chest and allowed the destroyer to dwindle into the distance.

Around him, he could hear the signalmen talking amongst themselves, and Yorke, the yeoman, comparing his log with that of his leading hand.

Despite the intake of new recruits and recently qualified ratings, this passage had done much to draw them together. They had observed the Crossing the Line ceremony when *Reliant* had steamed across the Equator. Most of the hands had never been so far south before: *Reliant*'s war had been fought in the North Atlantic, in the Norwegian campaign in support at the second battle of Narvik, in clashes with German cruisers preying on Russian convoys, and only once down to Africa, an unhappy mission, when *Reliant*, with other heavy units, had bombarded the French fleet at Dakar, in case they might later attempt to join up with the Germans and their Italian allies. When France had surrendered, leaving Britain quite alone, the loss of the

French fleet to Germany had posed a major threat. Its destruction was necessary, they had said, but there would be many a Frenchman who would recall that incident with hatred.

He heard the tannoy echo up from the maindeck.

'Up spirits! Senior hands of messes muster for rum!'

That brought a few grins from the watchkeepers.

He considered the convoys. So many troops: it had to mean something. The German Afrika Korps was still falling back in North Africa. Allied victory in the desert was not a fluke, no longer merely wishful thinking. The convoy they would be escorting would consist of ex-liners and modern cargo vessels, fast, more than a match for any would-be raider, and *Reliant* could defend it against any such attempt.

He looked up, shading his eyes against the glare, and saw Stagg's flag streaming out in the strong breeze. If there was to be an invasion, Stagg would expect to be in the thick of it.

He heard Frazier's voice from the bridge, occupied as usual with his lists and inspections. Today had begun for him with Requestmen and Defaulters. He was both mayor and magistrate again.

There were not many defaulters. The men were on their best behaviour, rather than lose the chance of a run ashore at Cape Town. It would seem like another world to most of them.

He leaned out, watching the mechanics working on the Walrus flying boat. They were supposed to be getting another plane when it was available. *Reliant* had sufficient hangar space for three aircraft. He thought of Rayner's surprise and astonishment when he had sent for him and told him that he had been put forward for a Mention-in-Despatches, both for his action against the *Minden*'s float

143

plane, and in response to a glowing report from his previous captain in the old cruiser.

Rayner had touched the livid bruise by his mouth. 'Gee, thanks, sir.' Then he had grinned. 'It was worth it.'

All in all, a good ship's company. As good as . . . He cut the thought from his mind, and walked into the bridge.

Frazier was standing with a solidly-built, stiff-backed chief petty officer. But this was no ordinary C.P.O. It was Keith Glander, the Master-at-Arms, nicknamed the Jaunty. As head of the regulating branch, he was policeman, father confessor, jailer, and if he could have his way with certain names, he would certainly be happy to act as executioner as well. Feared, hated, respected; he could match each challenge with practised authority. He had always wanted to be a policeman, even as a boy. When his chance had come, and he had discovered he was an inch short of the required height, he had joined the Royal Navy instead, out of pique or sheer disappointment he could not now remember. But in his neat uniform, with the crown and encircling laurels on either lapel, he had, by a roundabout route, achieved his original ambition.

It was wise even for young officers to abide by his word. Ignore it over a request or complaint, or believe that the lower deck should know its place, and that officer was as good as sunk.

Seeing him with Frazier now, it was hard to imagine him a few days ago with bright gold crown and a red beard, as King Neptune coming over the side to hold court in the time-honoured fashion.

Frazier said, 'Nothing very exciting, sir. One seaman requesting permission to marry. But he's under age. Just a kid.'

The master-at-arms gave a broad grin, something not often seen on his face.

144

''Sides, sir, she's a tom, like her mother was when I was in the old *Revenge*. I'll give him a quiet talking-to.' The grin vanished. He waited for Frazier to sign his folder, then he saluted and marched from the bridge.

Sherbrooke said, 'He's priceless.'

Frazier glanced round restlessly as the tannoy intoned, 'Cooks to the galley!'

Sherbrooke drew him aside.

'Everything all right, John?'

'Why?' He recovered immediately. 'My wife and I had words, sir. Not exactly front-page, is it?'

'If you feel like a chat, you know where I am.'

Frazier said, without smiling, 'Thanks. I appreciate it, sir.' He saw a petty officer trying to catch his attention. 'Must be off. I'm going to exercise the foc'sle party. Don't want any foul-ups when we drop the hook in Cape Town.' He was gone, to his world again.

The bearded navigating officer was waiting.

'I've got the convoy listings, sir. Seven large ships in all. Should manage eighteen knots, by the look of it.'

Sherbrooke glanced through the ships' names. This was not like those early days in the North Atlantic, where the speed of the convoy had always been that of the slowest ship in it. Some could only manage about eight knots, and most of them had paid for it.

Rhodes was saying, 'We'll be joined by the light cruiser *Diligent*. She was built around *Reliant*'s time ... useful, but not very beautiful. Six single six-inch guns on the centre line. No protection for her crews.'

It was a bleak but accurate summing-up. Another ship of an almost similar design, *Curaçao*, had been acting as a fast escort for a troopship in the Atlantic some four months ago, when Sherbrooke had been recovering from his own experience with *Pyrrhus*. But this had not been

145

just any troopship; she had been Cunard's pride, *Queen Mary*, packed to the deck beams with soldiers. It was still pretty much a secret, and there was some doubt whether *Curaçao* had 'zigged' instead of 'zagged' across the path of her giant charge, but the light cruiser had been cut in half by the collision. It was rumoured that some of the troops in the liner had not even felt the impact.

It was not something any captain in a fast convoy could afford to forget.

He looked up as Frazier reappeared, a pad in his hand. They walked toward the chart room without speaking, and Sherbrooke beckoned to Rhodes.

'You too, Pilot.'

He read the chief telegraphist's neat, schoolboy writing.

Then he said quietly, 'A neutral ship, Spanish, sailing alone, was fired on yesterday by what is alleged to have been a German raider.' He saw Rhodes leaning over the chart table. 'Some two hundred miles south-west of Freetown, Sierra Leone. No further action was reported.'

Frazier said, 'We must have passed him, the cheeky sod!'

Rhodes grunted. 'No chance of being anywhere near, sir. That Spaniard was lucky.'

Sherbrooke was thinking aloud. 'Scaring him off, I shouldn't wonder.' He looked out of a scuttle. The sea was as blue as before, at peace.

Frazier said, 'Could have been intending to steer west, to have a go at the Caribbean, or South America maybe. Might even be a supply or mother-ship.'

Rhodes tapped the chart with his dividers. 'No reports of any, sir.'

Beyond the door, the telephone squawked. Stagg had received his copy of the signal.

Sherbrooke heard a tap on the door. 'We'll have more information soon, with any luck.'

Just one ship, probably a converted merchantman. The raiders usually were. One of *Reliant*'s fifteen-inch shells would finish it.

But suppose . . . He recalled what he had said to Emma at Portsmouth.

He ignored the watching faces as he strode across the bridge and took the handset from the duty midshipman, the boy who had been so afraid.

His voice gave nothing away to Stagg. 'Captain, sir.' Nor must it.

It was afternoon, and *Reliant*'s big wardroom was strangely deserted. Lunch was over, and the long curtain drawn across the dining area separated it from the place where a few officers not required for duty were lounging in the deep chairs, dozing, or raking over the much-thumbed magazines, some of which were months old. *Lilliput*, *Men Only* and *London Opinion* remained the firm favourites.

Lieutenant Dick Rayner wandered over to the notice board and empty letter rack. He could feel the ship beneath and around him, moving fast, her bows pointing north once more, Cape Town a bright memory, too brief to be more than a dream. And lights everywhere. To men who had become used to blackouts and the shabbiness of their own country at war, Cape Town had been breathtaking. Hospitality, food and drink, where a sailor had only to open his money belt and someone would offer to buy him a round, or show him a good time.

And *Reliant*, perhaps enjoying a return to the life she had once known, had basked in the middle of it. Awnings spread, the Royal Marines marching up and down to some lively tune, hemmed in by boats full of sightseers, she had been in her element.

That had been three days ago. Now, with the convoy of seven large troopers steaming in two uneven lines, they were going back to the war.

Rayner glanced round, and after a brief hesitation crossed to a chair beside the one in which Lieutenant Gerald Drake was reading a battered book with obvious interest.

Rayner had not had much contact with the ex-barrister, or possibly, he had been avoiding it. Drake was round-faced and had a gentle, almost diffident manner, with deceptively innocent eyes. They were about the same age, and yet, in his company, Rayner always felt vaguely clumsy and unworldly.

Drake peered up at him. 'Take a pew, old chap. That was terrible coffee!'

Rayner slumped down. 'I didn't notice.'

Drake said, 'I heard about your forthcoming award. Congratulations.'

Rayner shifted in his chair. 'Nothing's settled yet.' Then he smiled. 'My folks would be pleased, though.'

The deck shivered slightly, and Rayner imagined the great stem ploughing through the deep water. The battle-cruiser would be quite a sight, especially from the air.

He asked, 'Why did you join the navy?'

Drake regarded him mildly. 'I liked the uniform better than the other services. And now I'm in, I want to do what I was trained to do. I'd only been commissioned for five minutes and someone was assuring me that there would soon be a vacancy in the Judge Advocate's department!' He sounded indignant. 'That wasn't what I joined up for.'

Rayner looked round, but nobody was listening; some were fast asleep, catching up between watches, or still recovering from the parties at Cape Town.

'You were a lawyer. I hope you don't mind my asking . . .'

Drake examined his immaculate fingernails. 'Are you interested in the law?'

'Not exactly. In Scotland, before we left Rosyth, I was involved in some trouble ashore. There was a girl, a nurse, as it happened. A guy was trying to . . .' He dropped his eyes, and did not see the sharp flicker of interest. 'I stepped in. The rest you probably heard about.'

Drake nodded gravely. 'I did notice the bruise.'

Rayner hesitated, but Drake was not making light of it. 'Eddy Buck and I gave statements to the police. It would be attempted rape, wouldn't it?'

'A serious charge. Very serious in wartime, with so many servicemen on the loose.' He sensed the concern, desperation, in the Canadian's tone. 'Go on.'

'He was a civilian. A businessman of sorts. Expensive watch.'

Drake glanced at Rayner's own watch. Obviously, he knew one when he saw one.

'Then undoubtedly he would hire a defence. Otherwise, it might ruin him.'

'But he *would* have raped her if I hadn't been there! She was terrified.'

'Scottish law has a lot of back alleys, so to speak.' He paused. 'The man in question would be wise to get the best advocate he could.'

'It doesn't seem fair.'

Drake smiled. 'Well, it probably isn't.' He added abruptly, 'You didn't know this girl.' He saw the quick shake of the head. 'And she accepted a lift in his car?'

'Yes, but only to the hospital. Everyone knew . . .'

'In this case, the destination is irrelevant, Dick. May I

call you that? Maybe she gave him the come-hither, encouraged him.'

Rayner looked away. It was like hearing her voice, her contempt.

Never tell them you're a nurse. They think you're anybody's!

Drake reached out and touched his knee kindly. 'I'm only saying what his lawyer would suggest.'

'It wasn't like that. She's a nice girl. Works at the burns recuperation hospital there.' He stared at him angrily. 'Is that what *you* would suggest?'

Drake leaned back in his chair. 'They will cross-examine her, in detail. The prosecution should be able to deal with it. A lot depends on the witness.'

'The victim.'

'Exactly. But your statements are all they'll have to go on. That, and her side of the story, and whatever physical evidence there might have been.'

Rayner looked down at the well-worn carpet. Where these same officers rested between their watches, concealed their worries with varying success from one another, and waited for the day when war reached out to claim them again.

'I wish I could attend that court, or whatever it is. *I'd* have told them!'

Drake glanced at the clock. 'Then tell *her*, Dick. Write to her. It might mean a lot to her.'

The wardroom speaker came to life. 'Lieutenant Rayner report to the bridge immediately.'

Drake watched him. 'You must take me up for a flight some time.' He added gently, 'Sorry I wasn't more help.'

Rayner turned and smiled. 'You were, believe me. I'll do just that.'

Drake saw him stride toward the door, snatching up his

cap on the way. A very nice chap. He looked at the coffee cup distastefully.

All the same, if it were my brief, I'd rather defend than prosecute.

Rayner reached the upper bridge, surprised that, for the first time, he was out of breath. No exercise, too much stodgy food. He would have to watch it.

He thought of his conversation with Drake. He had felt an enormous guilt at sharing it with him. Why had he asked, if not for reassurance? And there had not been much of that. He tried to recall her face, feature by feature. Her hair was short and fair, jutting forward over her cheeks like wings. He paused on the ladder, composing himself. Where he had seen the scratches, and the beginning of a bruise. He leaned back on the ladder and stared at the battlecruiser's ruler-straight wake, the two lines of heavy merchantmen following astern. The small cruiser *Diligent*, which had joined them from Simonstown, was Tail-End Charlie, and the destroyers, spread out on the bow and the quarter, were almost lost in the hard, reflected glare.

Rain, he thought, who needs it?

He saw the captain with Commander Frazier, while the bearded navigating officer was writing something in his pad.

Sherbrooke said, 'Sorry to drag you up here. Quite a climb, isn't it?'

Rayner grinned. 'I guess I've been living too well, sir.'

'I'm glad somebody is!'

Rayner realized that Rear-Admiral Stagg was also present, sitting in the captain's tall chair, moving restlessly, his foot beating a silent tattoo.

Sherbrooke, ignoring him, said, 'We're making good speed. Tomorrow, around first light, we shall be about six hundred miles due west of Loango.'

151

The navigator put in cheerfully, 'French Congo, sonny. I'll show you on the chart, if you like.'

Sherbrooke said, 'After that, we shall alter course to the nor' west, before another alteration south of Freetown, and then out into the Atlantic. There will be two other convoys on the move.'

Stagg muttered, 'Storm in a bloody teacup, to all accounts!'

Sherbrooke looked across at him. 'We can't afford to take risks, sir.'

Rayner thought of the heavily-laden troopships. He had been watching them through a pair of binoculars as they had steamed past at speed to take over the lead position.

Soldiers, thousands and thousands of them, and aboard one ship there had been women too, waving like mad as *Reliant* had steamed past. He had been told about the alleged German raider, and the ship it had fired on. It did not seem much of a threat when you looked up at *Reliant*'s formidable main armament. But certainly no risks, with all those men relying on them, and nurses as well. Like Andy.

Sherbrooke said, 'I want you to be ready to fly off around first light. Weather should be good. I'll give you the details then.'

He looked over at him, and added, 'We may be getting another aircraft to keep you company, take a bit of the weight.'

Rayner saw the others watching him, and thought suddenly of his brother, shot down defending a Malta convoy. And of the girl who cared for airmen like himself, but who had no faces. And he was moved by it, proud.

He said, 'We can manage, sir.'

Stagg grunted. 'Depending on it!'

Sherbrooke said, 'We depend on each other.'

Rayner clattered down the ladders again.

He would write to her. That was it. He would write to her about the captain. What he was like. And about *us*.

Sherbrooke walked out on to the port wing of the bridge and looked at the sky. First light was always a favourite time; he never tired of watching the dawn. To port, the ocean was still dark, like unbroken velvet; it was only when you leaned over the side that you saw the surge of white rolling back from the stem, and regained the sense of power and speed. Through the bridge on the opposite side, the horizon was a fine gold line, not even bright yet, like molten metal. Another hot day, but not for long: another week, and they would be into the Atlantic, and that bitter world they all understood. The real war, as the Jacks called it. U-Boats, and long-range Focke-Wulf Condors to home them on to their targets, and the overstretched escort groups of frigates, destroyers and corvettes, fighting back all the way.

He turned as the Walrus's Pegasus engine coughed, and then roared into a healthy growl. He pictured Rayner with his three-man crew, recalling his words on the bridge yesterday afternoon. *We can manage, sir*. He would, too.

Sherbrooke had heard about the incident while *Reliant* had been at Rosyth, but had not mentioned it to Rayner. He had read the report from the provost people, and seen Rayner's bruise for himself. Officer-like qualities, OLQs, did not come into it. It was a natural reaction.

'Ready, sir!'

'Carry on!'

The bridge shuddered very slightly, as with a jarring bang the Shagbat lurched from its catapult and immediately began a shallow climb. They would have a good scout round: Rayner might even sight the other convoy, but it seemed unlikely. When he looked again, the aircraft had vanished into the remaining shadows to port.

Rhodes was at the bridge door. 'Time to alter course, sir.'

'Very well, Pilot. Inform the convoy commodore.'

The commodore's ship was the old liner *Canberra Star*, well known to cruising enthusiasts before the war, those who could afford her. He wondered what her old master would think of her now. Dazzle-paint and rust, and more than a few dents gathered along the way. But she could still offer over twenty knots when need be.

He half-listened to the orders and acknowledgments.

'Course to steer is three-one-five, sir.'

'Port ten. Midships. Steady. Steer three-one-five.'

Apart from a leaping spectre of spray over the flared bows, he would hardly know that they had altered course.

The others would follow in their obedient columns, with the light cruiser *Diligent* turning to keep the nearest destroyer on her proper bearing.

He thought of Stagg, still aft in his quarters, probably enjoying a good breakfast. How much did 'Olive' know – about Jane Cavendish, for instance? Perhaps his suspicion was unjustified. Nothing was that certain. Stagg had his eyes on a much higher target. Surely he would not risk any scandal.

But he remembered Stagg's keen interest at the mention of Emma Meheux. *Pretty, is she?*

He walked into the bridge and saw faces, where there had been only unrecognizable shadows earlier.

The navigator's yeoman was sharpening pencils; a boatswain's mate was helping one of the signalmen to splice a frayed halliard. Another day, with the memory of Cape Town becoming more and more blurred with every turn of the screws.

Lieutenant Frost was watching the gyro repeater as it ticked soundlessly back and forth, while far below his feet the quartermaster held the great ship on her course, not an easy task in the stuffy confines of the armoured wheelhouse.

Somebody gave a yelp of alarm as a tremor echoed dully against *Reliant*'s flank.

For an instant, Sherbrooke imagined that a ship had been torpedoed in the convoy. No U-Boats had been reported in the area, but there was always a chance. He hurried to the wing again and trained his glasses astern. The other ships were growing in size and personality; he could even see the hundreds of khaki shirts that festooned the stays and upperworks of the trooper leading the port column.

Frazier had come to the bridge, and was staring round with the others.

Sherbrooke said, 'An explosion. But I don't see anything.'

They both turned as the leading signalman called, 'Signal from Commodore, sir. Outbreak of fire on board *Orlando*. Believed serious.'

Sherbrooke said, 'Acknowledge. Signal the commodore to maintain course and speed. *Will assist.*'

He heard another gasp from someone as a spark of fire exploded as if from the sea itself.

Rhodes said, '*Orlando* carries vehicles as well as troops, sir.'

Petrol, too, he thought. He said, 'Reduce to seven-zero revolutions, Pilot. Make to *Diligent*, take station ahead of convoy.'

Lights were already clattering, and brief replies blinked back. It would take too long to turn *Reliant* and take station on the *Orlando*, which was the sternmost ship in the starboard column. He could imagine the excitement aboard *Diligent* when his signal was received. Elation, perhaps, at taking *Reliant*'s place in the lead, away from the boredom of 'following Father'.

It was an uncanny sensation. The big merchant ships which had been half a mile astern were already passing *Reliant* on either beam, as if they had managed to put on an impossible head of steam.

Sherbrooke crossed the bridge again. 'I'll get as close as possible, Pilot.'

Rhodes was watching the new outbreaks of fire, and this time they did not diminish. Thank God they were servicemen on board. Had they been ordinary passengers, they might panic, and start a stampede to the boats that nobody would be able to control.

Frazier commented, 'It could be too dangerous to go alongside, sir.'

'I know. But none of the escorts is big enough for the job. We might have to lift off every man jack. No destroyer, not even *Diligent*, could manage with a ship that size.'

'I see, sir.' He had made his point, which he saw as his duty, both to *Reliant* and her company.

'I want every fire-party you can muster, starboard side. And a full boarding party.' He saw Frazier's concern, his doubt. 'Volunteers, but men who know what they're doing.'

He saw the commodore's ship over Frazier's shoulder, like a pale cliff, her decks already crammed with people even though they might not understand what was happening. On the other side, another lithe shape was moving up fast, smoke dipping from her raked, unmatched funnels: *Diligent* at full speed.

There was mercifully no wind, but the breeze was strong enough to carry the stench of burning. Fire was hated and feared by sailors more than any other peril on the sea.

'And have the boats turned out, port side, Carley floats too, just in case some of them jump for it.' He touched

Frazier's arm, and felt him start. 'She's all yours, John. Clear lower deck – full damage control procedure.'

Out on to the wing again, his eyes seeking order from what landsmen might imagine was chaos. Men running to their stations, fire hoses, extinguishers, first-aid teams and stretchers. On the other side, the lowering parties were already turning out the pulling boats on their davits.

In the strengthening sunlight he could distinguish small islands of authority among the mass: Farleigh, the surgeon commander, being helped into his white coat by one of his sickberth attendants. The chief boatswain's mate, the Buffer, waving his arms and calling to seamen with ropes and wires, fenders and strops: the true sailor.

And here was *Orlando* at last. Sherbrooke switched on the loud-hailer, seeing the crowds of soldiers being assembled by the forward derricks. *Orlando* had been a cargo liner in her day, owned by a New Zealand company, and had been trooping since the outbreak of war. She had been a lucky ship, until today. What had happened? Somebody smoking where the petrol for the vehicles was stored? Carelessness, stupidity? It made no difference now.

He pressed the switch. '*Orlando*, ahoy!' He saw faces peering across at him and felt something brush against his elbow. It was his cap, which he must have left on the chart table. The young signalman who had offered it gave a sheepish grin and withdrew.

Sherbrooke tugged the cap onto his hair. He should have remembered it himself. The sign of authority. Perhaps, of salvation.

'This is the Captain!' His voice, hard and metallic, bounced back across the water. 'I am coming alongside, starboard side to. Are your pumps still working?'

The other captain's voice answered, 'Aye, sir. For the moment. 'Tis Number Four hold.'

Sherbrooke watched as *Reliant* fell further astern, until the bridge was directly opposite the leaping flames. It was too far to feel a sensation of heat: he knew that. But he felt it, with, perhaps, more than his skin.

He called, 'Tell the Commander to begin!'

The long hoses bucked and then spouted water, curving columns which felt their way toward the other ship.

He could hear Rhodes speaking to the wheelhouse. Macallan, the coxswain, would be depending on each direct order, unable as he was to see the nearness of danger.

Closer, closer, until Sherbrooke could see the extent of the damage, a huge hole in the main deck caused by the explosion. Anyone down there would have been killed.

He switched on the other microphone and saw men peering up at him.

'Boarding parties, up forrard!' He saw them begin to move, as if to some remote control. The sheer of *Reliant*'s starboard bow was so close to the other ship that the water between the two hulls was churning in trapped torment.

The hoses were finding their mark, scattering flames, dousing equipment and upperworks, swinging back again as more blazes broke out elsewhere.

Stagg was suddenly beside him, hands in his reefer pockets, his fine cap tilted over in the Beatty style.

'I didn't call you, Guy. I could see you were busy.' His eyes glowed in a fresh outbreak of fire, untroubled, and without pity. 'Our Canadian should get a good view.' He grinned fiercely. 'Go easy, Guy, or the poor chap won't have any ship to come back to!'

The men around them heard him, and laughed, despite the other ship, the suffering, the danger to themselves. *The Old Man isn't bothered, and the admiral obviously doesn't give a monkey's, so why should we?*

'First party's across, sir!' Rhodes was peering through

the screens, bunching his fist as if to urge them on.

Sherbrooke saw the seamen running and skidding on *Orlando*'s unfamiliar decks as other hoses doused them to protect them from the heat. Some of the troops were moving as well, N.C.O.s in bush hats yelling above the din as they dragged smouldering planking and hatch covers to the opposite side.

Stagg snatched some binoculars from a flag locker and peered toward the smoke.

'My God, Frazier's over there with them!' He sounded astonished, angry. 'I'll not have my senior officers behaving like first-year subbies!'

Sherbrooke watched Frazier's cap among a squad of seamen who were squirting foam through an open hatch, demonstrating by his mere presence that he was with them, *of* them, and all the sweat and training had been worthwhile. He wondered if Frazier's wife had ever pictured him like this. He doubted it.

There was another muffled explosion, and more figures blundered down into the hold, which must now be awash with water from the hoses. Minutes later, the first casualties were carried up, some held firmly while dressings were applied, burns covered, others hitting out, unable to comprehend what was happening. There were several who lay where they had been dropped, discarded. He had never become accustomed to it, not even when the hard men joked about the casual brutality of war.

Lieutenant Frost shouted, 'They're winning, sir!' He waved his cap in the air and yelled, 'Come on, Reliants! Let's be having you!'

The yeoman gave a grim smile, and one of his signalmen made a circling gesture with his finger to his forehead.

There were more hoses on *Reliant*'s forecastle now. Some of her side would be scorched and blistered, not so far from the splinter holes and dockyard repairs. Stagg would not be pleased if it meant another delay in what he perceived to be his mission.

The *Orlando*'s loud-hailer echoed against the bridge. 'Fire under control! Fifteen casualties.' The speaker broke off, and shaded his eyes as if staring across the smoky water. 'Thank you, *Reliant*! God bless you!'

Sherbrooke could hear cheers from the soldiers: even the Aussies were impressed.

Stagg sniffed at the smoke. 'I'd like to speak to Frazier when he comes aboard, Guy.'

Sherbrooke said quietly, 'My job, I think, sir. But I believe he was right.'

Stagg gave him a piercing stare. 'Very well, *you* deal.' The fierce grin reappeared. 'After all, we'd be in real bother if we lost a troopship, eh?' The grin disappeared, like a dropped mask. 'We can always get another commander!'

Sherbrooke watched him stride away, pausing to speak with a messenger, a youth who gaped at his admiral with awe. He never stopped performing, he thought. Maybe he could not.

He said, 'Tell the T/S to report progress, Pilot. We'll stand by for another hour and then recover our boarding parties. They did well.'

The navigating officer nodded. 'I thought so, sir.' As Sherbrooke crossed to the opposite side, he added under his breath, 'So did you, my son!'

He thought of the corpses he had seen laid out on the other ship's deck. At least Beveridge, the God-bosun, would have something to keep him busy.

He sighed. You shouldn't have joined if you can't take a joke, they always said.

9

Your Decision

Dick Rayner banked the Walrus slightly and stared down at the sea. In the harsh glare there was little sign of motion, just power and depth, reaching away from horizon to horizon.

He said, 'Time to turn back soon, Eddy. The ship won't want to hang around too long.'

Buck said dryly, 'That has a familiar ring to it!'

Rayner glanced at his instruments, his ear automatically tuning in to the engine. They were flying north-west, at some four thousand five hundred feet. You got your best out of the Shagbat like that. She could manage one hundred and thirty knots under these conditions, with a following wind anyway.

It had been a temptation to loiter in the area with the convoy when the fire had broken out aboard one of the troopers, but Rayner had learned the danger and the folly of being distracted by something, no matter how impressive, if there was nothing he could do to assist.

'Any juice left?'

Buck shook his head. 'The other two gannets have scoffed it!'

Rayner licked his lips. His mouth was like dust. He rarely drank anything but juice, despite what the Chief had said about the mess prices, except that night when the two Scottish cops had persuaded the barman to part with some genuine malt.

That was something else he had discovered in Britain. Scotch whisky had vanished from all the pubs. Gone, for the duration of the war. For export, he wondered? He had noticed that senior officers seemed to have no difficulty in obtaining it.

But if you asked for it in an ordinary pub, they would probably think you were a German spy who'd just dropped by parachute, or that you'd been in prison since the outbreak of war. He thought of the girl, Andrea, nearly choking on it when she'd been given a full glass. What was she doing right now? Who was she with?

He sensed that Buck was pointedly studying the pad strapped to his leg.

He said, 'O.K., I'm turning back. Don't you ever think of anything but your belly?'

Buck was staring out now, his eyes narrowed against the glare.

'*Ship!* Port bow!'

Rayner frowned. 'Use the glasses. Come on, get the lead out!'

Buck raised them carefully and peered through the smeared perspex. 'Freighter. Hold on, she's got a flag painted on the side.'

Morgan had climbed up behind them with another pair of binoculars.

'Red and yellow. She's a Spaniard, a bloody neutral.'

Buck grinned. 'Is that what Wales should be?'

Rayner glanced at his gauges again. 'Better take a look.' Even neutrals took a risk every time they ventured into the combat areas.

He guided the Walrus into a slow, controlled descent,

until they could see their own shadow flashing across the undulating water like a twin.

It was an untidy vessel, and there were men working on deck, some of whom looked up and waved as they turned across her bows and flew down the opposite side.

The ship's name was painted on a large canvas awning, *Cabo Fradera*. Probably for the benefit of nosy bastards like us, Rayner thought.

Then something clicked. 'That's the one that reported being fired on by a raider! Never learn, do they?'

It was rare for the Germans to interfere with Spanish vessels; they had too much in common. Churchill had called it 'one-sided neutrality' in one of his fiery broadcasts.

Hardie, the other member of their little crew, said, 'They were ditchin' their gash, sloppy buggers!'

Rayner eased the stick over. The small figures working on the freighter's deck had been covering something with another piece of canvas, he imagined to protect it from the sun. For only a second, it had registered. 'Look at her stern!'

Buck sounded startled. 'I can't see anything, Skip! What is it?'

The 'gash' being dropped over the stern; the canvas which had almost covered something. Metal tracks, like narrow railway lines.

He exclaimed, 'She's laying mines, for Christ's sake! Rob, call up the ship! We're getting out, fast!'

He felt the engine responding loudly and saw the sea's glistening face slide away like the side of a steep hill.

His mind was almost too full to cope. Laying mines, and the launching rails had been empty. The Spaniard had dropped the lot. They were not for mooring. The ocean was too deep in this area; he had checked it on Rhodes's chart before they had taken off. Three thousand fathoms. They would stay on the surface, drifters, uncontrolled and mindless, and lethal to the unwary. He tried to swallow, to get the words out to Morgan.

'Mines, Rob! Tell the ship!'

There might be dozens of them, hundreds, for all he knew. Or he might be making a bloody fool of himself. But if he was right . . . He heard the splutter of static and wondered if they would be able to make contact. The Spaniard might have been laying the mines for hours, or ever since their reported encounter with the raider.

Reliant had to know.

He did not feel the explosion. It was more like being lifted violently, and then dropped again. There was foul-tasting smoke in the aircraft, and for another instant Rayner imagined they were on fire. But the smoke was thinning even as he struggled with the controls, and stared with shocked disbelief at the jagged holes, feeling the inrush of cold air. They had been hit. And with the realization came the pain, like a hot iron in his side, probing and burning, and making him throw off his goggles as if he were choking. Buck was holding him, staring into his face while he dragged at the leather flying jacket.

Rayner gasped, 'You know the course, Eddy? Hold her on it!'

'I can manage, O.K.?' He withdrew his hand and saw the blood.

Rob Morgan, one-time milkman in Cardiff, was back again. He looked pale, transfigured, in some way. 'The radio's smashed.'

Buck said, 'How's Jim?' He put his arm round Rayner's shoulders and held him upright. Morgan's brief shake of the head said it all. 'Up to us then, Rob. Here, give me a hand. Get a dressing.' He darted a glance at the compass and altimeter. The old Shagbat was flying herself. He wanted to laugh, or cry. But he knew he would not be able to stop.

Rayner blinked, hard. 'How long, Eddy?'

'Half an hour. Don't worry. I've got her.'

Rayner let his head drop back. That long? How could it be? It had only just happened. Flak. He should have known. Guessed.

He had felt his trousers filling with the blood running into his groin, thick blood. He bit back the pain. Obscene. But there was a dressing on the wound now. How had they managed to do that?

Morgan said, 'Convoy in sight, Skipper.' There was neither relief nor emotion. He was beyond both.

Rayner tried to move. 'What about Jim?' The Walrus was turning, losing height. As it did so, the sunlight lanced through the splinter holes and passed slowly across the other seaman's open eyes, but they did not close to it, or blink.

Rayner said, 'Aldis. Call them up . . .' His voice was little more than a whisper.

I have to get them down. I must. It was only when he felt Buck's grip tighten that he realized he had spoken aloud.

'Hold me up. Watch the flaps . . . nice and steady.' If the depth charges exploded, it wouldn't matter anyway.

Vaguely, he heard the clack-clack of the Aldis lamp, and Morgan's voice.

'They've seen it!'

It was not even possible to know if they were badly damaged. They would have to ditch, and wait to be picked up. Or left, like the Germans in their Arado. Tit for tat . . .

He said quietly, 'See that girl for me, will you, Eddy? Tell her I would have written.'

Then they hit the water, and Buck felt spray spitting through some of the holes.

Rayner might be dying, but Buck watched his gloved, bloody hand retaining control as if it alone was alive. He stared at the sea as it corkscrewed up and down, tossing the little flying boat like a leaf on a millrace, and held the bloodied hand in his own as the engine coughed and shuddered into silence.

'We're down! You did it, you crazy bugger!'

Morgan said, '*Reliant* has to send somebody.' It was getting to him now.

Rayner murmured, 'She'll come. You'll see.' And then he passed out.

Buck tried to wipe his friend's face with his one clean handkerchief, but his fingers were shaking so badly that he gave up the attempt.

'You tell her yourself,' he said, and afterwards he convinced himself that he saw Rayner's lips curve in a faint smile.

Lieutenant-Commander Clive Rhodes lowered his glasses, and watched more smouldering debris being manhandled and levered over the *Orlando*'s side, *Reliant*'s seamen working easily with the Australian soldiers, as if they had been doing it for years.

He heard the captain speaking to the transmitting station on one of the bridge telephones, obtaining a clear picture of any damage sustained when the two big hulls had touched one another. It made Rhodes sweat just to think of it. *Reliant* was of thirty-two thousand tons displacement, and the old cargo liner had not been built with that sort of ship-handling in mind. And yet Sherbrooke had conned his ship so close that her great flared bow had hidden the men who had been waiting to assist the boarding parties.

One error of judgment, one freak gust of wind at the moment of impact, and it could have been a disaster. He had handled her like a destroyer, or, perhaps, like the ship he had once commanded.

Sherbrooke joined him, and said, 'We will recover our people now. *Orlando*'s master seems to have everything in hand.'

Rhodes remarked, 'I wouldn't have believed it if I hadn't been here.'

Sherbrooke looked at him, or through him, his eyes distant, as if he were reliving it.

Then he smiled. 'I did have a few doubts myself, Pilot.'

'Aircraft! Green four-five! Angle of sight three-zero! Approach angle zero!'

Across the gunnery speaker they heard Evershed's voice, clipped and tense, as if he had been waiting for it.

'Follow Director!'

But it was Bob Yorke, the yeoman of signals, who grasped the situation. Snatching up the long, outdated telescope which he preferred to any pair of binoculars, he hurried on to the bridge wing, his lips moving silently as he found and held the slow-moving flying boat in the lens. Sherbrooke thrust his hand into his pocket and clenched his fingers around his pipe as the Walrus's kite-like outline dipped towards the searing water, as if it could no longer stay airborne.

Yorke did not even blink in the glare. 'From Walrus, sir.' He frowned, unused to the slow, hesitant flashes. '*Have sighted minelayer to the north-west. Mines on convoy route.*'

Somebody said in a whisper, 'Poor bastard's been hit.'

Rhodes was watching the flying boat also, much closer now to the sea. It must have been tricked into getting too near the minelayer, whatever she was.

Sherbrooke said, 'Signal, Yeoman. Make to commodore. *Convoy will alter course in succession. Steer two-five-zero.* Then find a flare to shake up the lookouts.'

Rhodes waited by the wheelhouse voicepipe, missing nothing.

Sherbrooke added curtly, 'And call up Captain (D) and tell him what's happening.'

Stagg's telephone came to life and a signalman reached for it.

Sherbrooke said, *'Wait.'*

'All acknowledged, sir!'

A quick glance at the clock. How many minutes? *'Execute!'*

Sherbrooke strode out on to the wing and seized the loud-hailer.

'Orlando, ahoy! Boarding parties will remain on board!'

He watched the troopships wheeling round after their commodore, with a kind of ponderous dignity.

Somebody gave a nervous laugh. 'That'll get the Bloke on the hop! He'll think we're leaving him behind!'

There was a muffled bang, which touched *Reliant's* hull like a nudge.

Sherbrooke watched the tall waterspout rise directly alongside the light cruiser's bows. It seemed to take an age to cascade down, and then there was smoke. No flash, but as *Diligent* thrust out of the falling spray he could see that she was already slowing down, her curving wake dropping rapidly until finally she was stopped altogether.

Sherbrooke observed her coldly. 'Half speed ahead both engines. Steady on course . . .' He hesitated, and looked over at Rhodes. 'Where's the Walrus, Pilot?'

'Down, sir. In a bad way.'

'Signal Captain (D) to stand by and assist *Diligent.* Report extent of damage.'

He shut out the clatter of signal lamps, and levelled his glasses on the sea. The Walrus was rocking about, her power gone. It was a marvel they had made it at all.

He seemed to hear Rayner's voice. *We can manage.* Then he made up his mind. 'Alter course for the Walrus, Pilot. Reduce to seven-zero revs in five minutes. That should do it.' He turned away and saw a boatswain's mate staring at him. 'You – Oldfield, isn't it? Pipe the seaboat's crew and lowerers to clear away the port whaler.'

He moved quickly to the radar repeater, thinking only of the pleasure in the man's eyes, because he had called him by name. His father had once told him, *remember their names. It's just about all they own!*

Stagg walked across the bridge. 'How is *Diligent* making out?'

Rhodes called, 'Down by the bows, sir. *Montagu* is standing by.'

'Seaboat's crew ready, sir!'

'Very well.' He looked over at Rhodes. 'Slow ahead. Dead slow, if you think fit. Tell the Chief what's happening.'

Stagg said sharply, '*I'd* quite like to know, too.'

'We can't recover the Walrus, sir. It's probably too badly damaged. I'm picking up its crew.'

Stagg stared at him, then stalked out on to the open bridge wing.

The orders were very faint when heard from up here. 'Turns for lowering! Lower away! Avast lowering!'

Sherbrooke had seen it done a thousand times, the boat dangling at the full extent of the falls, swinging gently above the sluggish bow wave. The five oarsmen in their bulky life-jackets, their coxswain ready to shout his commands.

'Out pins!'

Stagg raised one hand as if to prevent it, as if he could still not believe what was happening.

'Slip!'

Then the boat dropped freely onto the receding bow wave, veering away on the long line which would carry her clear of *Reliant*'s side and towering superstructure. A lonely moment for any boat's crew.

Rhodes said, 'They're almost up to the plane, sir.' He sounded completely absorbed. 'Boat's cox'n is signalling.' He snatched up his glasses again as the tiny figure in the whaler's sternsheets semaphored with his hands, while the whaler lifted and rolled against the drifting Walrus.

'One dead, sir. *One wounded. Am returning.'*

Stagg snapped, 'Get that boat hoisted and alter course after the others immediately!'

He walked to the door and paused. 'And then, I should like to see you in my quarters as soon as is convenient, and provided it does not interfere with the safety of this ship!'

Rhodes and his assistant, Frost, had heard every word, and Sherbrooke knew that Stagg had intended it that way.

'Whaler's coming inboard now, sir!' That was Yorke, his eyes unusually grave, as though moved by what he had just witnessed.

'Carry on, Pilot. Bring her round and increase to one-one-zero revolutions.' He felt the instant response, like a shiver pulsing up through the bridge from the very keel.

He heard Rhodes say, 'Port ten . . . midships . . . Steady.' Relaxed once more, now that the ship was moving again and gathering speed.

Frazier must have witnessed it all, from his isolation aboard *Orlando*.

What would he have done in my place?

He trained his glasses on the listing *Diligent*. It would

be her captain's decision, to abandon and transfer his men to the destroyer *Montagu*, or to try and make it into harbour unaided. Halfway between the light cruiser and *Reliant*, the battered Walrus flying boat might remain afloat for weeks until another storm found it, yet another victim of the Atlantic.

He heard Rhodes speaking on a telephone, and waited.

Rhodes said, 'The man who was killed was named Hardie, newly joined this ship. Lieutenant Rayner was wounded.'

It had probably been no more than a fluke; none of the mines dropped by the unknown enemy might ever have found a contact in this convoy. Only one would have been enough to turn a triumph into disaster. He looked at his hands, but they were quite steady, which surprised him. He felt the ship slicing through the water, overhauling the passive merchantmen like a greyhound, resuming her rightful place at the head of the convoy. Where *Diligent* had been when she had struck the mine.

One of the young signalmen said, 'I was thinking just now, Yeo . . .'

The yeoman of signals patted his blue collar. 'Leave thinking to horses, my son. They've got bigger heads than you have!' He smiled, knowing what was puzzling him. 'Go an' wet some tea for the watchkeepers.'

Sherbrooke said, 'Take over the weight, Pilot. I'm going to see the admiral.' He paused. 'But first, I'm going to the sickbay.'

It was not until eight bells of the first dog watch that he finally made his way aft toward the admiral's quarters. Every muscle and bone ached, and he felt as if he had been on his feet for days without respite.

The flag lieutenant and Stagg's swarthy secretary, Lieutenant Villar, were already there, but they left immediately without speaking. As if this scenario had already been rehearsed.

Stagg said, 'Everything on top line again?' But his eyes seemed to ask, *what took you so long?*

'Yes, sir. I made sure that your signals were sent off, and I received a few more details of the minelayer. It seems as though it was either the Spanish *Cabo Fradera*, which reported being shelled but was in fact being used by the enemy, or a German raider camouflaged to look like her, so they could slip between two convoys without being questioned.' He saw Stagg nod sharply to his chief steward, Taffy Price, who withdrew at once. So it was going to be that sort of confrontation.

The Walrus's observer, the New Zealander, had looked even younger when Sherbrooke had spoken with him in the sickbay. Buck was having a gash dressed on his wrist, about which he could recall nothing.

He had been able to give a good description of the minelayer, even down to the launching rails, and the makeshift identity painted on a large bolt of canvas. He had not seen the gun which had fired at them, but that was hardly surprising. The German gunners could not have missed.

The Admiralty would have to decide what further action to take. One of the new escort carriers like *Seeker*, still being repaired in Iceland, would be ideal. But they themselves could take no further risks where this convoy was concerned.

He said, '*Diligent* is making for Freetown. Tugs will be available for her.'

Stagg said, 'That's not what I wanted to see you about.' He raised an eyebrow. 'Well?'

'I thought you would like to know that Lieutenant Rayner survived, and should make a full recovery.'

Stagg gave him a hard stare. 'I was coming to that, of course!' He reached out restlessly and moved a paperweight to align it with the gold edging on his desk.

'You took a great risk when you went alongside the *Orlando*. It was your decision, and it was, in many ways, a courageous one. Had the fire got out of control *Orlando* might have had to abandon. An ugly situation. But I backed your decision and I shall say as much.'

Sherbrooke felt the tiredness washing over him. *Or you'll say it was your decision.*

Stagg continued, 'But to stop *Reliant* in that fashion, when an escort had already struck a mine, to drop a boat and expose the whole ship to immediate danger was inexcusable.'

'It was a risk. Justified, in my opinion, sir.'

Stagg did not seem to hear. 'My God, we wouldn't even stop for a ship torpedoed in convoy, you know that! Don't stop, and never look back – you of all people should know that!'

'I do, sir. I saw men die because nobody came until it was too late.'

'That was an entirely different situation!'

'Perhaps. But if it hadn't been for Rayner, we would never have known, until it was too late. Perhaps there were only a few mines laid, or maybe there were hundreds, none of which might have crossed the convoy's route. But one did!'

'There is no need to raise your voice!'

'I'm sorry, sir. When I was given *Reliant*, I was not merely surprised, I was grateful. It makes you like that. I wanted this command more than I can put into words. It seemed like an old friend, something reaching out for me.'

He was suddenly angry with Stagg, but more with himself for trying to explain what it had meant to him, what it had cost him. It was private, and should have been shared with no one.

'I stopped for Rayner and his crew because we owed him that much.'

He thought of the drifting Walrus, as he had last seen it from the bridge, with its one dead crewman for company. Like the airman Rayner had described, frozen in his little dinghy. So many faces of war.

Stagg pushed the paperweight aside, bored with it. 'I always knew you were the sentimental type, Guy.'

Sherbrooke closed his fingers slowly and tightly into a fist. First names again . . .

'I think we could open the bar an inch or so, eh?'

Sherbrooke said, 'I'd better not, sir.'

Stagg pressed the small bell button and Price appeared like a genie.

'Suit yourself.' He smiled broadly. 'But remember what I said, eh? Just between us.'

The door closed behind Sherbrooke. He had made an enemy, or perhaps the enemy had always been there, waiting. Like the mine.

It was midnight when Sherbrooke returned to the sickbay. Everything seemed startlingly white and sterile here, almost peaceful, with a sickberth attendant dozing in a chair, head nodding in time with *Reliant*'s easy motion.

He had been right round the ship. *I must be getting like John Frazier.* Unable to stop, to let go.

He halted by the one cot with a light on beside it. How different from the bruised and bloodied figure he had visited before going aft to Stagg.

Surgeon Commander Farleigh had described the wound in his usual meticulous, sparing fashion. Clean enough; caught just in time. But it had missed an artery by an inch or less, and Rayner had lost a great deal of blood. There were savage bruises on his body too, from the impact when the Walrus had made its last efforts to ditch, although, like Buck, he would probably not remember how they had happened.

He realized that Rayner's eyes were open, gazing at him, trying to penetrate the fog of drugs, the only barrier against the pain.

He said hoarsely, 'You came earlier. They told me.'

Sherbrooke touched his bare shoulder. The skin was hot, as though he had fever.

'I'm glad they told you. They told *me* you'll be fine.'

He saw the sudden concern, anxiety, returning, perhaps with memory.

'I heard about Jim. I feel terrible about that. I should have known.'

'Don't blame yourself. You may have saved a lot of lives.' He glanced around. In his mind, he saw the German survivors sitting on their beds in this cool, antiseptic place.

'You might even have saved *Reliant* from damage, or worse. It's worth remembering. You were in charge, so you always tend to blame yourself. I know. I've been there.'

'I won't get sent to another ship, will I, sir?'

'No, of course not. We should get some new aircraft now – a little more quickly, thanks to you!' He stood up. Rayner was drifting again, and his own fatigue was intense. 'One more thing, and then I'll leave you to sleep.' He saw Rayner struggling to remain alert, to listen, and understand him. 'That Mention-in-Despatches. I don't think you'll be getting it.' He leaned a little further over the cot, so that Rayner could see his fingers on the blue and white ribbon on his own jacket. 'I think one of these would be more suitable.'

Rayner stared at him, unable to grasp it.

Sherbrooke stepped back into the shadows, remembering Stagg's final words to him. *Just between us*.

A messenger murmured, 'Captain? You're wanted on the bridge.'

Sherbrooke looked down at Rayner's face, now relaxed in sleep.

It had been worth it.

10

Survivors

The uniformed doorman examined the girl's official identity card and letter of introduction, and said, 'If you'll wait in the office, miss . . . er, Mrs Meheux, Captain Thorne will not keep you waiting too long.'

As she walked through the other door he glanced at her approvingly.

Very nice. Some people have all the luck.

She sat down on a chair and looked around the office, like so many places commandeered for wartime use.

On the door a small sign stated, *Director of Naval Information – Restricted*. It was afternoon, and she had walked here from her old office in Grand Buildings, Trafalgar Square, where she had been concluding Sir Graham Edwardes' affairs before handing over to another woman who had seemed totally disinterested in the work, or what it might offer.

She stuck out one leg and regarded it critically. This was her last good pair of stockings, and yet the girls she had shared rooms with had never seemed short of a supply. The Americans could be very generous, she gathered.

She smiled to herself. That had all changed. This new position was described as promotion, but what was more important to her was the small flat that went with the job. It was in Chelsea, off the King's Road, where lodgings were even harder to obtain than good stockings. She could not see the river because of surrounding houses, but it was pleasant simply to know that it was there.

She loosened her blouse. The change in the weather was amazing, and she had walked here without a coat. The sky was overcast, with low cloud, so that the barrage balloons were invisible, but it was April. Another spring of war. Where had the time gone?

She had written to her father, about the new job, about London, and concerning the most recent letter she had received from the War Office. She allowed her mind to explore its subject. Philip . . . There was still no news of him, and it seemed that the only sources of information were the Swiss Red Cross and other neutral agencies. Lieutenant Philip Meheux, Royal Engineers, had last been seen with his unit, or what had been left of it, on the day Singapore had fallen. He had not been reported killed or captured, and there had not even been a rumour of it. He was simply missing. The War Office had told her that there was still hope, but she wondered if anyone in her situation really believed that.

In her previous work with the hero of the Great War, she had searched through all the records released on Singapore: many, she knew, would remain classified. She had learned about the navy's part in that hopeless attempt at defence, and the tragedy of those two great ships, *Repulse* and *Prince of Wales*. With their destruction, the balance of naval power had shifted. Singapore had been as good as lost from that moment.

She had been thinking of Singapore when she had visited Rosyth. *Reliant* was *Repulse*'s sister ship, but she could not remember if she had merely read that, or if Guy Sherbrooke had told her. She could not forget her visit to the Portsmouth cathedral, and afterwards, when she and

Sherbrooke had walked together to see the memorial stone marking only one of so many terrible air raids.

She knew very well that her father would write back from Bath with the usual words of consolation, giving her news about the place she had grown up in, where she and Philip had been to school, and where they had become friends. What might have happened, but for the war? Even the wedding had been a rush, another urgent part of the call to arms. Philip in uniform, the ceremony and the brief stay in that hotel, the confetti falling from her suitcase where some well-wisher had planted it so that everybody should know they were newlyweds.

Three days, two nights, and he had gone. She thought of Sherbrooke again, how he had described the girl who had died with his father. It was something they had in common. She sensed that, like herself, he had not truly known her, perhaps had not even truly loved her with the love of maturity.

She did not know where *Reliant* was now, or even if he still remembered that day when they had met Stagg's wife. She had been shocked at her own cheek, the way she had dragged him away from the other woman on some pretext or other. But she knew he had been glad of it, relieved; and in his face in those moments afterwards she had seen something very youthful, a shadow of the boy he had been.

A man came through the other door, and said, 'He'll see you now.'

Pompous, she thought. Why was it that, behind the scenes, the armed forces seemed to be run by civilians? She stood up, straightening her skirt. Civil servants. *Like me.*

It was a spacious office, and she guessed that had the curtains been fully opened she would be able to see the Thames from the windows.

Captain Roger Thorne stood up to greet her, his eyes never leaving hers as she walked toward him from the door. He was a tall man, his hair almost grey, his face keen, intelligent, most people's idea of the perfect naval officer. His voice was deep and resonant, and she thought he must have been very good-looking in his youth. Thorne was obviously another retired officer brought back to serve, when he had probably long ago given up hope of ever wearing a uniform again.

'Do be seated, Mrs Meheux. You were early – I like that. Punctuality is like duty, a must, for me, anyway.'

She relaxed somewhat. There was a framed print of Nelson on one wall, a map of the world on another. There was also a fine model of a four-funnelled warship, which she guessed had once been part of his life.

'This department is growing, finding its place in affairs. When the Allies launch their invasion into Europe our contribution will be even more important. I've read all the reports about your work as Graham Edwardes's assistant. You did a great job. From what I knew of the old devil, he could be a difficult chap to serve.'

There was a pause, and she answered, 'He wanted more than anything to present the navy and its achievements in wartime in a manner that ordinary people could understand, and identify with.'

He walked to the window. 'I sometimes think we tell people too much.'

'They have a lot to contend with, too, sir.'

He looked at her, his expression hidden by the light coming in over his shoulders.

'I have to tell you, Mrs Meheux, that I originally asked for a Wren officer to be allotted to this section. No disrespect to you, of course, but their lordships decided otherwise.'

She smiled at him directly. 'Yes, they told me.'

He looked away. 'I see. In that case . . .' He tried again. 'I think we shall get along very well. But I can't get used to calling you "Mrs Meheux" all the time, not unless it's something formal.'

She nodded. *I never got used to being called it, either. There was no time.*

She said, 'My Christian name is Emma.'

He smiled, and glanced at the portrait of Nelson.

'Very appropriate.'

She thought of the woman who had first told her about this appointment. 'Captain Thorne is O.K., dear. But when he gets a few gins inside him, he can be a bit of a groper, d'you know what I mean?'

She did know.

Thorne said, 'I can always have you driven to your quarters in Chelsea, y'know. We sometimes have to work late, meetings, preparing releases, that sort of thing. Not too lonely out there, is it?'

'I think I shall like it.' She tried to describe it as she would to her father. 'Chelsea is more like a village. Except for the bombs – but there's a good shelter in the building.'

She watched him, and knew his thoughts.

He knows all about me. My age; that my father and brother are doctors; that Philip is in the bag. And now he knows what I look like.

He folded his arms, but did not notice the expression that crossed her face, the sudden little shock of recognition. There were four gold rings on his sleeves, exactly like Sherbrooke's, and yet so completely different.

'Well . . . er . . . Emma.' He smiled again at her. 'Let's see how it works out, shall we?'

'Of course, sir. They told me that I could always go back to Armaments Supply in Bath, if I choose.' It was a lie, but it worked.

'We'll have some tea. Nothing stronger, I'm afraid.'

She uncrossed her legs and saw his reaction. Groper, she thought. Just let him try.

He pressed a button, and said, 'One of your last jobs with Graham Edwardes was to fix that interview and broadcast on board *Reliant* – couple of months back, if my brain serves me right?'

She looked at her hand on her lap, the left hand, with its ring.

'Yes, sir.' She was quite grateful when a messenger came in with a tray of tea and some biscuits on a plate. It was like someone knowing a secret, but there was no secret to know.

Thorne was saying, 'I understood Rear-Admiral Stagg was supposed to be there. I believe he was tied up at the Admiralty.' He paused, and then said with something like admiration, 'He's a real goer, that one! We'll see him in high office before this lot's over, you mark my words.'

She leaned forward to take a cup, and winced as her long hair caught on one of the buttons at her collar. Thorne moved as though to assist her, but she freed it, and said coolly, 'My fault. I should cut it short.'

He said, 'That would be a terrible thing to do. It looks delightful. Suits you, too.'

She heard herself change the subject. 'Is *Reliant* back in harbour, sir?'

'Well, yes, she is, as a matter of fact. She's been working up with her group. Done pretty well, to all accounts.'

She held the cup carefully to her lips. *What's the matter with me? Why do I have to think that every man is after me?* Or was it that the guilt and loneliness were tearing her apart?

Thorne said, 'I'll let you see my reports, but you understand that they must never leave this room. It's all very hush-hush, but then, you have top security rating, so that's no bother.'

'Has she been in action?'

He stirred his tea, his face full of curiosity.

'Well, you read about the German cruiser, the *Minden*? Made quite a splash, if you'll excuse the pun. Then she did some fine work with a very important convoy. You won't be able to read about *that*, I'm afraid. Top secret!' He grinned hugely as if to say, *although I know all about it.* 'Now, where was I?' He felt for some cigarettes. 'Care for one of these?'

'No, thank you, sir. I don't.'

He clicked his lighter, and smiled at her through the smoke. 'Not one of your vices, eh?'

She smiled back. Yes, she could handle this. 'Not yet, sir.'

Either the smile or the answer seemed to disconcert him. 'Well, anyway, as I was about to say, Rear-Admiral Stagg is coming to London.' He gave a knowing smile. 'Again.'

He glanced at his watch. 'I must go – I have to see the Second Sea Lord. Might not be back. You can hold the fort, right? Mr Cousins can help with any problems. In at the deep end, eh?'

She walked to the window, and saw the river. The Savoy Hotel was along the Embankment to her left. She and Philip used to joke about going there before they had been married. She had been rather shocked by the suggestion, the implication; it had not been like him. But the thought had been oddly exciting, too. So where had they lost their way?

She listened to the persistent murmur of traffic. Peace or war, fog or air raids, London never slept.

Thorne picked up a briefcase. 'Sign out when you go ashore. Ted will fix transport for you.'

When sailors like those to whom she had spoken aboard *Reliant* referred to going ashore, and even those who lived in barracks, the term had seemed quite natural. From Thorne, captain or not, it sounded too pat. False.

The phone rang loudly, and Thorne put a finger to his lips.

'I've gone. Take a message, or tell Mr Cousins!' He opened the door. 'I'm off!'

She picked up the telephone and a voice said, 'A call for Captain Thorne.'

She replied, 'I'm afraid he's not here.' She reached for a pencil. 'Put it through, please, and I'll take a message.'

A different voice said, 'I was told that Mrs Meheux had been appointed to your section.'

She stared at the pencil in her fingers.

'Speaking.'

There was a long pause.

'Emma?'

She said faintly, 'It's you, Captain Sherbrooke.'

He said, 'Are you all right? If this is an awkward time, I'll . . .'

She shook her head, as though he could see her. 'No . . . no, it's not. Please, tell me how you are.'

'Fine.' He sounded unsure. 'A bit tired, but otherwise, just fine.'

Somewhere in the background a whistle shrilled, and she heard the hiss of steam. So he was at a railway station.

He said, 'I'm coming to London. I'd like to see you again. Very much.'

He waited, and then asked, 'Are you still there?'

'Yes.' She glanced at Nelson's portrait. 'I'd like that. I've thought about you, wondered how you were.'

Don't be such a stupid fool. You'll both be hurt. Think what it might do to him.

She heard herself saying, 'Call me when you get here.' Somebody was speaking urgently in the background: perhaps it was Stagg.

He said, 'Did you get my letter, Emma?'

'No.'

'When you do . . .' But there was too much noise, and he said quickly, 'Goodbye!'

She put the phone down as if it were something brittle.

He was here. And she was frightened.

She looked toward the portrait of Nelson again. *And he called me Emma.*

The army ambulance with the bright red crosses painted on its canvas sides swung around a wide bend and lurched across a section of newly repaired road.

Lieutenant Dick Rayner clenched his teeth and felt the pain throbbing in his side. God help any wounded man in this crate, he thought.

He glanced around. How different it all looked from his one and only visit to Eddy Buck's 'lively hotel'. He felt strangely lost, light-headed, as if he no longer belonged anywhere.

When *Reliant* had handed over the convoy to the local escort group he had been put ashore, and had eventually ended up in the Royal Naval Hospital at Haslar. A surgeon had praised *Reliant*'s medical team, saying how fortunate he had been. *An inch or so this way or that, and that would have been it.* Rayner wondered how many times those words had been used, and to how many men.

After a week at Haslar he had been told that he was to be moved north, to the R.N. Sick Quarters at Rosyth. He had been feeling so depressed that the news could not have come at a better time. He kept thinking of *Reliant*, and the friends he had made aboard her. He knew how it was: they would soon forget him, and he might never be sent back to her, despite what the captain had said. *Just another pilot. So who cares?*

He had fretted for two whole days after arriving in Rosyth, enduring all the usual tests and inspections, the formalities of being alive, then he had cadged a lift from this army ambulance. The driver had watched him with obvious amusement when he had broken the journey in order to buy some flowers from a small shop. It was April. Spring. He looked at the flowers again, tulips. She might think he was being stupid. Perhaps he should have tried to get hold of something less ordinary.

The driver asked politely, 'Goin' to a weddin', are we, sir?'

It had given him a strange feeling of loss when he had seen the anchorage where *Reliant* had been. There was a carrier there, and a battleship, but nothing to compare with *Reliant*'s grace and power. He had written to his parents about those recent events, but had omitted any mention of his injury, and the captain's visits and their conversations in the sickbay. And the medal.

The soldier said, 'Not far now.'

Rayner smiled nervously. That was exactly what Eddy Buck had said that night. She might not even be free to see him, or want to, for that matter. A girl like her, always working with servicemen, would have plenty of offers.

He asked, 'Do you come here very often?'

The driver shrugged. 'I've been a few times. Most of our lot go to the military hospital. I've taken a couple of cases, though.' He had seen the wings on Rayner's sleeve when he had asked for a lift. 'Breaks yer 'eart, sir. What it can do to a bloke.'

A Londoner. The accent, too, held memories, of Jim Hardie from 'the Smoke'.

'I know,' he said.

The man glanced at him, and said, 'I think I'll go to Canada after this little lot's over an' done with. Room to breathe. Raise a family, maybe.' He grinned. 'Bloody pipe dreamin', that's me, sir.'

And suddenly, they had arrived. The building had probably been built between the wars, and was solid, unattractive, functional.

The driver leaned on his wheel. 'Used to be a mental 'ospital. Says it all, dunnit?'

Rayner gave him a pack of cigarettes and thanked him, then walked through the open gates, where a uniformed porter was regarding him and his bunch of flowers with interest. Behind him, he heard the ambulance drive on.

The porter looked out from his cubbyhole. 'Can I help, sir?' His eyes assessed Rayner in a second. No suitcase, no attendant; no obvious reason for being here.

Rayner glanced past him at the main building, larger than he had expected, and obviously added to over the years. It was extremely unwelcoming.

'I've come to see Nurse Collins . . . Andrea Collins, if it's convenient.'

The porter frowned. 'Sister Collins, you mean. Is she expecting you, sir?'

Why did they always call them 'sister', as if they were a bunch of nuns?

'Well, not exactly. I've been in hospital myself.' He broke off. 'Sorry. I'm not making very much sense.'

The porter smiled, for the first time. 'I'll see what I can do.' He picked up a telephone and turned away, so that Rayner could not hear what was said.

He shivered. It seemed very cold here, or maybe it was just him. She would make some excuse and tell him to get lost. What else had he expected?

187

The porter regarded him gravely and then spoke into the mouthpiece again.

'Yes, it certainly appears to be him.' He put the telephone down. 'Up the drive, sir. Second entrance on your right.' Then, severely, 'Sister Collins is on duty, but she sent word that you were to wait for her.'

A white-coated orderly met him at the door, and Rayner guessed that the porter had been speaking to him.

'Have a seat, sir. Newspapers aren't in yet, not that they make light reading these days.'

Rayner tried to smile. *Tell me about it.* 'Oh, it'll probably get better,' he said.

The orderly sighed. 'I sometimes wonder how we all got into this mess.'

He picked up a uniform jacket on its hanger and resumed brushing it. It was an R.A.F. officer's jacket, and Rayner studied it with professional interest, although he knew it was more to control his sudden attack of nerves. A flight lieutenant. He recognized the bright medal ribbons as a D.F.C. and the A.F.C. They didn't hand those out with the chocolate ration, he thought. The guy was obviously a hero.

He said, 'Someone's done a good job on that. It looks like new.'

The man regarded him without expression. 'He can't wear it, of course. He just likes to have it with him.'

Rayner watched the orderly walk away with the jacket, something for a survivor to cling to.

He looked away, and saw her standing in the entrance, her hands at her sides, almost unrecognizable in the starched uniform and the funny little cap English nurses wore. And yet, so familiar . . .

He got to his feet, saying hurriedly, 'See, I'm back. Just like the bad penny. Sorry it had to be this way . . . I should have given you more notice. But that's the navy for you!' He heard the words tumbling out, as if he could not contain them, and knew he was being stupid. He held out the flowers. 'These are for you. There wasn't much choice, I'm afraid.'

She took them and held them to her face, although they had no perfume that he had noticed. 'They're lovely. Thank you so much.' She seemed to be studying him. 'You've lost weight.' They walked along the room, side by side, like the strangers they were.

Rayner said, 'I got into a bit of trouble.'

He saw one wing of fair hair escape the pins and fall across her cheek, as it had done before.

She said, 'I know. Your friend Eddy called me. He told me you'd been hurt. He was afraid to say too much in case he was cut off – they do that kind of thing, if they think they're intercepting careless talk.' She stopped and faced him. 'Are you really all right?'

He said, 'Sure. I feel great. I was lucky.' Then, 'I thought about you all the time.' He saw the scepticism in her eyes. 'No, really. It's not just a line. I thought about that night – I wondered how you made out afterwards. Did you go to court?'

She smiled, but he sensed that it was only for his sake. 'He turned out to be "a very respectable citizen", and he'd been working *so* hard. He'd had a glass or two too many.' She paused, and said bitterly, 'He *apologized*. The charge was dropped, and he was found guilty of being drunk and disorderly instead.'

Rayner said, 'I don't believe it. I was *there*. I saw what that bastard did to you, and was trying to do!'

She said, 'Thank you for that. But I had no choice. I had to accept it. My job is here, and my mother might have heard about it if the police had pressed the issue.'

Rayner said, 'I'd have killed him. If I ever see him again . . .'

She gripped his arm, as she had that night at the hotel.

'Try to forget about it. You were there. You saved me. I should have been more careful, but it was Mary's birthday. I should have known better.'

She opened a door, and he guessed it was some kind of staff lounge. He waited while she brought tea, he assumed from a canteen nearby.

He watched her intently, afraid it was all part of some hallucination, like the hours in *Reliant*'s sickbay after his wound had been stitched and he had been drifting in a haze of drugs. Faces had come and gone through the mist, Eddy, almost in tears and trying to make jokes at the same time, Rob Morgan, with his lilting Welsh accent, his hand resting on his bare shoulder as if to share his own great physical strength. And the captain, who had visited him several times, although Rayner thought some were probably in his imagination.

And always, in each lull between the intervals of pain, he had seen her. This girl.

'I'm in the R.N. Sick Quarters now,' he said.

She put her hand on the back of his. 'I know. I found out.'

She turned as one of the canteen staff came in, carrying a vase for the flowers.

He watched her, her lashes, the fine curve of her skin, enjoying the cool pressure of her hand on his. It was real. It was happening.

She asked, without looking at him, 'How long?'

'I'm not sure. The ship's been at sea again. I'm supposed to be rejoining when I'm cleared by the M.O.'

She said softly, 'You miss your ship, don't you? I can understand that.'

'I missed *you* . . .' He hesitated. 'Andy. How we met doesn't count any more. I just know that I want to see you again.' He dropped his gaze, unable to look at her. 'And again. Please don't laugh at me. I mean it. I've never been in love with anyone before.'

Her grip tightened on his hand. 'You're so nice. Like fresh air. Like . . . *living*.'

He said, 'Have you been up here long?'

'No. I was at the big hospital at East Drayton.'

'Where's that?'

'Down south. They asked me to come up here when they opened this place.' She shrugged lightly. 'So here I am.'

'Can we meet somewhere? Have a meal, or something?'

She withdrew her hand, smiling at him. 'A meal? I can see you don't know this area very well!'

She watched his emotions, so easy to read, and yet so obviously sincere that it made her want to cry. But she was past tears: she had to be.

She relented, and said, 'Yes. I'd like that.' She tried to lighten it. 'But you'll see, once you're back aboard your precious ship you'll soon forget all about me.'

She saw his sudden hurt, like something physical. 'I'm sorry. That was a bitchy thing to say.' She looked up as a shadow fell between them.

'Number Seven, Sister. Getting a bit fraught. He's upset at leaving.'

She was on her feet. 'I'll come at once.'

The orderly said, 'Give me a few minutes, Sister. We're a bit short-handed on the block until the relief comes on duty.'

Rayner stood up. 'I'll give you a hand.'

The orderly said, 'No, sir. I don't think you'd understand.'

She said sharply, 'Of course he'd understand. He's one of them. We're not.'

They walked together into an adjoining wing of the building, with the same polished floors and lines of numbered doors. The orderly Rayner had met was sitting outside one of them.

'It was the jacket,' he said. 'I knew this would happen.'

She said to Rayner, 'Flight Lieutenant Bowles is being transferred to another recuperation hospital today.' She consulted the small watch pinned to the bosom of her uniform. 'In an hour's time.'

The orderly said, 'I'll get the duty M.O., Sister.'

She shook her head. 'He hates doctors, don't you understand?'

Rayner watched her, so small and pretty, but with a strength and compassion he was seeing for the first time.

'Why are they getting rid of him?'

She said, without emotion, 'Because there's nothing more they can do for him. This is the only place he knows. To him, it's like the end of the line.'

Something fell and shattered in the room. Rayner said, 'Let me.'

She opened the door, and he followed her inside. It was clean but spartan, like the rest of the place. The suitcase and the neatly pressed uniform jacket said it all.

The officer was sitting on the edge of the bed, staring at a sunlit crack in the black-out curtains, so that he appeared to be crossed by a single yellow line.

He said, 'Good. I told them you'd put a stop to it, Andy!' He turned his head and shoulders, and asked sharply, 'Who's this?'

She said, 'Lieutenant Rayner. A Canadian pilot.'

He nodded, dealing with it. 'We had a few of your bods at Biggin Hill. Not a bad bunch, considering.'

Rayner said, 'We try.'

The flight lieutenant named Bowles appeared to laugh, but no sound came.

'What sort of kite do you fly?'

Rayner thought of the listing Walrus drifting away.

'Walrus amphibian.'

'Christ, rather you than me. Bit long in the tooth for our sort of war, I'd have thought. Give me a Spit and I'll back it against any damned thing that flies!'

'Yes, my brother was a Spitfire pilot. Well, the naval version of it.'

There was a silence, then the other man said, 'Was? He bought it, did he?'

'Yes. Over the Med.'

The girl stood motionless, hardly daring to breathe. Two pilots talking, as if it were the most natural thing in the world.

Rayner heard the breeze against the window, and saw the sunlight probe the heavy curtains and enter the room for the first time. He had seen it before: most of them had, and the lucky ones counted their blessings. But you never got used to it.

The eyes were blue, like his captain's; how they had survived the fire and the surgery unblinded was a miracle. Of the face, only a grotesque mask remained. No wonder there were no mirrors in these places.

Rayner said, 'They tell me you're leaving today. That's too bad. We could have had a drink somewhere. I could tell you about a real plane, my Shagbat!' He could feel the others tense. 'Another time, maybe.'

Unexpectedly, the flight lieutenant held out his hand. That, too, was horribly scarred. 'Another time, that's the ticket.' He peered around the room. 'Mustn't forget anything . . .'

Then he said in a different, harder tone, 'You just watch

193

your back, my lad. Give the buggers half a chance and you're done for. *Watch your back.*'

There were sounds in the corridor, voices; the relief had arrived.

The flight lieutenant said, 'So, Andy, I'm losing you again. Bad show, damn bad show, but there you are.' He glanced at Rayner. 'This the chap?'

He did not wait for an answer, picking up his uniform jacket. All that was left.

He said lightly, 'Don't forget me, Andy. You can't trust sailors, you know!'

She put her arms around his neck and held him closely for several seconds.

'We'll miss you, Jamie. Don't lose faith. They all care, you know.' Then she kissed him.

Rayner looked away, unspeakably moved, and saw an orderly picking up the case, and what looked like a folded photograph frame.

Outside in the corridor, there were suddenly others like the man who had just walked out, some in uniform or parts of uniform, in dressing gowns or careless mixtures of civilian clothing.

As the flight lieutenant walked down towards the entrance some of them came forward and patted him on the back; a few of them raised a cheer, their terrible injuries momentarily forgotten. They were themselves again, young men, some very young, who had given so much. Too much.

The door closed, and when he looked around Rayner saw that the corridor was empty, as though they had been spectres from some battlefield somewhere, saying their last farewell.

She said, very softly, 'You were wonderful just now. I was so proud of you. You made him feel wanted again.'

'So did you. No wonder they all love you.'

She was watching a small light flashing at the other end of the corridor. 'I must go, if nobody answers that.'

Like Stagg's malevolent little red light, Rayner thought.

But he said, 'And I love you too, Andy. You realize that, don't you?'

'You hardly know me.' But she did not pull away when he took her hand.

'I can change that, given the chance.'

She studied him, her eyes calm.

'Yes. I want to give you that chance.'

A voice called, 'Sister! Number nineteen, quickly, please!'

She reached up, and touched his mouth with those cool fingers. 'Call me. Tomorrow, if you can.'

He watched her hurry away, then he turned back and walked into the flight lieutenant's empty room.

He said aloud, 'I won't forget. I'll watch my back, for both of us.'

He found a taxi outside, from which an elderly couple, perhaps relatives, had just emerged; the driver was glad of a return fare.

As they rattled back along the road to Rosyth, he recalled every moment separately.

Like a first, perfect touchdown; nothing would ever be the same again.

He thought of her with the flight lieutenant, the man with no face, and was filled with gratitude.

11

Hit-and-Run

The first day at the Admiralty in London seemed endless to Sherbrooke. Most of the time he remained with Rear-Admiral Stagg, although on two occasions he was required to examine some reports in another office. He suspected it was so that Stagg could speak more freely in his absence.

Reliant and their new escort carrier *Seeker* were lying at Greenock, not all that far from Clydebank where the battlecruiser's keel had first tasted water nearly thirty years before.

It had been a long and uncomfortable journey from Scotland to London, and although Stagg said nothing on the subject, Sherbrooke had sensed that he was privately fuming about the failure to lay on a plane for him.

They had spent all morning with Vice-Admiral James Hudson, who was the Chief-of-Staff as well as personal naval adviser to Winston Churchill. A tall, reedy man with the appearance of a much put-upon schoolmaster, he soon proved that he was the right person for the job.

Maps were brought, minions coming and going silently, while traffic occasionally rattled the windows and suggested the other world outside. North Africa, then, no longer just a rumour or an empty hope. It was all true: the much vaunted Afrika Korps, Rommel's unbeatable army, was in full retreat. Secret information had reached the reedy vice-admiral through intelligence sources that Rommel himself was to be replaced by Hitler's order. That was, perhaps, the most significant piece of news. Rommel *was* the Afrika Korps. It was as simple as that. Throughout all the initial German triumphs along the North African coastline, Rommel had always been there, with his men and his armour, so that they all knew he was sharing the same dangers. British generals had often been criticized by certain outspoken M.P.s and journalists for spending too much time in Cairo and very little at the front, which was a very fluid description in any case. There were no trenches or static positions in this war. Armour, supplies, and infantry equipped to keep up with both were the key, and something which the British lacked, until Monty had arrived on the scene. General Montgomery might not have had the dash and style of his German counterpart, but he had something equally important: compassion. He had fought through the mud and horror of Flanders as a young man, and was determined that the lives of his soldiers should not be thrown away on a whim, or merely to make headlines.

At El Alamein, at the very gates of Alexandria, with the Germans and their Italian allies already contemplating a victory march through Cairo, Montgomery made his stand. The position, with the sea on one side and the tank-devouring Qatar Depression on the other, was his choice. El Alamein was not much of a place, but now its name was written in history. The Afrika Korps had been forced into retreat, by-passing all those familiar, disputed places, Sollum, Tobruk, Benghazi, Tripoli. For the Allies, it was the long way back.

Now, at last, unless some unforeseen disaster could turn the tables, the Germans were slowly being forced towards the jutting peninsula of Cape Bon in Tunis, the only point from which they had any hope of evacuation to Sicily, one hundred miles across the Strait. British convoys had been decimated trying to force that same route to relieve Malta, and wrecks were strewn across the seabed for every mile of the way as a testament to their courage, when courage had not been enough.

Vice-Admiral Hudson had stared at his big map. 'When the day comes that every enemy soldier is dead or captured, Africa will be ours.' He spoke without emotion, but Sherbrooke thought his quiet simplicity made it all the more moving.

After a brief lunch in that same room, Hudson had outlined Stagg's part in the final stages of the master plan.

Ever since their disagreement aboard *Reliant*, Sherbrooke's contact with Stagg had been limited to the necessities of duty, and when exercising at sea with *Seeker*. The news which had awaited them in London had changed all that, and Stagg had become his old self again to the point of geniality. He was finally getting what he wanted, not a role to merely fill in the gaps, or to act as a long-range heavy escort for 'a bunch of squaddies', as he had sarcastically called the convoys. He was about to take his rightful place in things, where they could hit hard at the enemy, and the revelation had made him a different man.

Now there was to be a small reception at a flat in town, some of Stagg's friends and other senior officers. Sherbrooke watched Stagg's strong fingers rifling through yet another file. Emma Meheux would be there with her new boss. He examined his feelings, pleased, and yet very aware of the danger. *Friends* . . .

Hudson was saying, 'I'll need you with me for a few days, Vincent. The P.M. will want to see you. He always does, with these pet projects.' He almost smiled. 'Won't do you any harm, will it?'

Stagg grinned. 'Point taken, sir.' He looked at Sherbrooke. 'You'll have to get back to Greenock, I'm afraid, Guy. General recall, and the reprovisioning plan we discussed on the way down.'

Sherbrooke smiled faintly. A few grunts and nods had been about the full extent of that particular conversation.

Stagg relented, his good humour apparently fully restored. 'Take a couple of days, eh? Staying at the club?' He did not wait for or expect an answer, his mind already busy with the next question for the vice-admiral. 'And we're to have a top war correspondent with us, sir?'

Hudson nodded, and pressed his fingertips together. 'Pat Drury. He's good, I believe.'

Stagg rubbed his chin. 'I wonder if our young barrister knows him as well.'

Hudson opened an envelope. He had left it until the end.

'By the way, your minelayer was sighted and torpedoed by a U.S. submarine last week. It must still have had some of the cargo on board – it was blown to pieces. No survivors, I'm afraid, so we'll not find out much else about it. The Germans have said nothing, but then they wouldn't, would they? It's against every clause of the Geneva Convention to lay unmoored mines where any neutral vessel might fall victim to them.'

Stagg snorted, 'Those rules went out the window long ago!'

Hudson regarded him curiously. 'Not in my book, Vincent. Otherwise, all this is a sham.'

Again, no emotion, no anger. But it was there. He looked over at Sherbrooke and said, 'I read the reports. The behaviour of your Walrus crew was commendable. They're not exactly old salts, are they?'

Stagg said, 'I've put the pilot up for a D.S.C.' He glanced

at Sherbrooke. 'Seemed only right, at the time.'

Sherbrooke said nothing. This was the Stagg he under-stood best.

Stagg said, 'I hope you'll be coming to our little reception, sir.'

Hudson shook his head. 'Meetings, I'm afraid. But give my kind regards to your wife.'

And then, they were out of the office and hurrying down the stairs toward the entrance, with its barriers of painted sandbags.

Stagg said bluntly, 'Thank Christ for that! He'd put the blight on any party!'

He shot Sherbrooke another sly glance. 'But *you're* coming. Thought you might.' He did not elaborate. There was no need.

An Admiralty car was waiting at the kerbside for them, and as they climbed into it a platoon of soldiers marched past. Sherbrooke saw that they were from the Free Polish Army. London was like that, full of uniforms, every colour, every nationality, every service. What must it be like for them, fighting for a homeland which was already occupied, and dominated by the enemy?

Stagg was lighting a cigar, while the Admiralty driver watched him covertly in the mirror.

'Poles, eh?' He puffed contentedly. 'A right lot of bastards where women are concerned!'

They drove off, and Sherbrooke noticed that no words were exchanged between Stagg and the driver. *Maybe I'm being naive.* Stagg had quite a reputation with women himself, or had, when they had been lieutenants together.

Stagg remarked, 'I kept the flat on. Useful if I'm in town. Can't stand the hotels these days, full of shagged-out officers and moaning Americans.' He laughed shortly. 'It was my wife's idea. One of her better ones.'

Familiar scenes were rolling past the smooth-running Humber, like old, pre-war postcards. Trafalgar Square, with pigeons everywhere; uniforms and more uniforms, soldiers with their girls, sailors watching a busker outside a theatre; Hyde Park Corner and the first evidence of bombing, a house completely gutted, a mere shell, with an A.F.S. water tank outside where nannies had once pushed their prams.

Stagg said, 'Thank God, this part of London doesn't change much!'

They approached and passed the Dorchester, aloof behind its own barricade of sandbags. A capital at war.

The car swooped into a side street and Stagg said, 'Some have arrived early, I see.' He chuckled. 'That'll give 'em a chance to talk about me behind my back!' It seemed to amuse him.

They walked into a spacious entrance hall, with a uniformed porter who almost saluted when he saw them.

The flat was on the first floor, and Sherbrooke could feel his muscles tensing even before the door was opened. Voices, people he would not know. When would he get over it? When he had come out of hospital it had been like this, not wanting to see or speak to anybody, but knowing all the time it was his last chance, not to forget what had happened to him, but simply to survive it.

At first glance, the flat looked as huge as *Reliant*'s wardroom, and it seemed to be full of men and women, some in uniform, some not. There was obviously plenty to drink, and there would be food, too. Stagg had a lot of pull somewhere.

He recognized a couple of faces, and saw one bending to speak to an attractive Wren officer. *That's Sherbrooke, Reliant's captain.* Or perhaps, *the poor chap who lost his ship. Only eight picked up, you know.*

He should accept it. It would never leave him.

Stagg had charged into the fray like his namesake, his arms waving, his grin like a beacon.

And then Sherbrooke saw her. She was standing with a tall naval officer, a captain: that must be Roger Thorne, her boss.

Thorne strode over and thrust out his hand. 'You look well! Don't suppose you remember me. I was your horrible first lieutenant in the old *Montrose*!' He turned and grinned at the girl beside him. 'Just a stroppy young subbie he was then! Look at him now, eh?'

Sherbrooke said carefully, 'Yes, I remember *Montrose*. Just before I joined *Reliant* in the Med.'

Thorne made an extravagant gesture. 'This is my assistant, Mrs Emma Meheux, of D.O.I.' He frowned. 'But you've met, haven't you? I forgot!'

She held out her hand, and smiled. Her eyes said, *no, you didn't forget.*

'It's very good to see you again, Captain. We've been hearing some very nice things about you.'

'Probably lies,' he said. He watched her mouth, and the small pulse beating in her throat. She was ill at ease, perhaps unhappy at this arranged meeting.

Thorne said, 'Damned long ship, this one. I'll get some service over here,' and left them alone.

Sherbrooke said, 'I've thought about you a lot, Emma. Wondered about you.'

She reached out impulsively and gripped his hand. 'How was it . . . really?'

'It could have been worse. Much worse.'

She smiled, but it did not change the expression in her eyes. 'You'd say that anyway.'

'And you?'

She shook her head with a little shrug, and he saw the long hair down her back. 'No news.' She was looking past him. 'How long will you be in London?'

'Two days.' He saw what he thought was disappointment in her face, or maybe he imagined it. Perhaps she was remembering the last time she had seen her husband.

Then she said, almost urgently, 'I know it's all secret, but you're off again very soon, aren't you?' She saw him nod. 'I think about you and your ship. I feel I know both of you.' Her eyes flashed a warning. '*He's* coming back.'

'What's he like?'

'Easy-going, most of the time.'

Sherbrooke said, 'I didn't know him all that well. *Horrible first lieutenant* or not, I can't really remember him.'

She laughed, and the tension drained visibly from her face. 'He's as jealous as hell of you!'

Thorne was carrying a tray of glasses; there seemed to be about six of them.

'Gin all round. Still, there's nothing better here by the look of it.'

A woman's voice said loudly, 'Why, Mrs Meheux, here you are!' and Stagg's wife joined the group, staring keenly from face to face. 'Well, this is quite a meeting place! I'm so glad you came.' She looked up at Sherbrooke with a little, arch smile. 'You're making quite an impression on my husband, Guy. Don't let him have it all his own way!' She gave the girl another lingering glance. 'Take good care of her, Captain Thorne, won't you?'

Thorne gave a fierce grin. 'I certainly will!'

Sherbrooke watched Stagg's wife moving through the crowd to join her husband.

A lieutenant found Thorne and murmured something.

Thorne downed another gin and exclaimed, 'Bloody hell, they never leave you alone! I'll be back in a second.'

She said softly, 'You're hating this, aren't you?'

203

'I wanted to talk, be with you.' Sherbrooke looked around, and she saw it in his eyes again. *Trapped*.

The black-out shutters were up, and they had not even noticed. The room was becoming very stuffy and hot, and the food had still not made an appearance.

She looked at Sherbrooke with something like defiance, and said, 'There's not much at my place, but I can make you a sandwich. I have some Scotch, too – Sir Graham gave it to me for Christmas. I haven't touched it.'

He took her wrist, but shielded her and the gesture from the others.

'I would love that.'

'But remember what we said. I don't want to spoil it.'

He closed his fingers gently on her wrist. 'I've only just found you. I don't want to spoil a single moment of it.'

Stagg's voice interrupted, 'I don't blame you.' He grinned hugely at the girl. 'See you tomorrow.' He almost winked. 'Remember the old ship's motto, Guy!'

Heads turned to watch as they made for the door. His cap was lying with others on a table. Beside it was a telephone, and Sherbrooke glanced at the Mayfair number. Very posh, Petty Officer Long had said. It was the same one. This was the place where Jane Cavendish had answered his call.

She was saying, 'What's the motto? Tell me.'

' "We will never give in." ' He felt her slip her hand through his arm. 'Don't worry about it. He's that kind of man.'

She thought of Olive Stagg's assessing eyes, and Thorne. *With a few gins inside him*, she would never hear the last of it. People could be so cruel, and already had been, to her.

They found a taxi near the Dorchester.

The driver, who was towing an auxiliary fire pump behind

his taxi, regarded them without curiosity. 'Chelsea, Squire? May 'ave to charge double fare if they needs me pump!'

They sat in the deepening shadows and held hands, like any sailor and his girl, Sherbrooke thought.

She whispered, 'Please kiss me, Guy.'

Uncertain, nervous, afraid it might begin something that knew no rules, and which, like the mysterious minelayer, could destroy them both.

She withdrew, and he could taste the sweetness of her mouth on his.

She said, 'I was thinking . . .'

The inside of the taxi lit up and Sherbrooke saw small pinpoints of shellfire, far away, probably in south London somewhere.

The cabbie swore to himself. 'I'll drop you in the King's Road. Best I can do.'

They stood on the darkening pavement, and Sherbrooke heard the insistent drone of air raid sirens.

He gripped her arm. 'I don't like this, Emma.' But when he looked down at her, she was laughing.

'It's always like *this*, Guy. It's not as bad as it used to be, but they still sometimes have a go.'

She looked up and he saw the moon, very faintly above the river.

She said, 'Bomber's moon, that's what they call it.'

'I see.' But he felt like some innocent recruit.

She guided him into a narrow street, and said, 'It looks much nicer around here by daylight.'

A bell jangled, and a shop door opened and closed furtively.

She said, 'Let's try the off-licence. They might have some wine.' He was aware of her sudden, delicious excitement, rather like a child's. Perhaps they both were, for the moment . . .

There was a man in an apron standing behind the counter, chatting to a tall, heavily made-up girl, whom Glander, the master-at-arms, would probably describe as a tom. She looked round and glanced at the girl and the officer, and then ignored them.

The manager spread his hands. 'Wine, lady? I'll see what I can do, but you know how it is!'

She murmured to Sherbrooke, 'Now he'll strike a bargain.' Then she stared at him, her eyes suddenly wide, frightened. 'What is it?'

Sherbrooke wrapped his arms around her and pushed her into a corner.

'Get down!'

That was all he had time for. Then the world exploded.

It was impossible to know how long it took for his senses to recover from the immediate blast. He was conscious of the pressure, his lungs unable to draw breath, and a total loss of balance. And yet he knew exactly where he was, and that he was holding her tightly in his arms although they were on their knees against some sort of wall, with dust, fragments of wood, and plaster falling all around them. The whole scene was made unreal and stark by the one remaining light bulb that had survived, even though its shade had been blown to pieces.

Then, as his hearing returned, Sherbrooke heard the sound of shattering glass, someone screaming and screaming like a tortured animal.

He held her face in his hands and used his sleeve to wipe some grit from her mouth, repeating her name over and over, although he did not realize he had spoken a word.

She opened her eyes and stared at him, the first shock giving way to terrible fear.

He said, 'It's all right, Emma. I've got you. I think it's over.'

He looked past her and saw the cascade of broken glass, the shelves emptied by the bomb, if that was what it had been. There was no smell of drink, and he guessed that most of the bottles had been empty and for display only, due to the shortages the manager had mentioned. He saw the man lying face down on the floor, groping amongst the glass and scattered debris as though he were blind.

She whispered, 'You're filthy, Guy. There's dirt all over you!'

He knew they were both near to breaking down. He said, 'Can you move? Give me your hands. I'll help you.'

They stood up together, their shoes slipping on splintered glass. There were voices now, the sound of a car engine, and the distant clamour of bells like those fitted to ambulances and police vehicles.

She clutched his shoulder and exclaimed, 'Oh, my God, that poor woman!'

The girl they had seen earlier . . . Sherbrooke tried to clear his mind. *Earlier* was just minutes ago. The one the Jaunty would have labelled a tom lay with her legs apart, her skirt up to her waist, her eyes staring at the solitary light bulb as if fascinated by it.

She said, 'Help her, Guy. I think . . .'

Sherbrooke bent over her and felt for a pulse, for a heartbeat. He could smell the perfume; it was very strong, like Stagg's aftershave.

He dragged her skirt down over her bare thighs and stood.

'She's dead, Emma.' He held her again, knowing she was feeling the full effect of shock.

She said in a small voice, 'But she's not marked. She was just standing there. Talking.'

The manager staggered to his feet, shaking himself like a dog, then he looked at the damage and exclaimed, 'Bloody hell! That was nasty!' He picked a long needle of broken glass from his hand, and saw the dead woman for the first time. He looked at her for a long moment, and then said softly, 'Poor old Mavis. Never did no 'arm to nobody.'

Torches flashed, and helmets appeared in the sagging doorway.

The first one was a policeman, who looked at Sherbrooke and the girl clinging to his arm and said, 'You two O.K.?' and then bent over the corpse. 'Direct hit round the corner. The rest of the street is unmarked.' He straightened his back and took out his notebook. 'Hit-and-run. Probably going for the power station or the railway – they just follow the river on bright nights like these. But this time they drew a blank.' He glanced down at the staring eyes, watching him from the floor. 'Except for a few poor souls, that is.'

A car squealed to a halt outside: reinforcements. The policeman said, 'Got somewhere to go?' and then, as though noticing Sherbrooke's four gold stripes, 'Sir?'

She replied, for both of them, 'Number seventeen.'

He grinned. 'Oh, well, that's all right then. No damage there.'

Figures passed them, ambulancemen carrying a stretcher with a red blanket, a fireman with an extinguisher. To them, it was all routine.

'Let's get out of here.' Sherbrooke put his arm around her shoulders and guided her toward the doorway, shielding her from the sight of the dead woman being rolled onto the stretcher. A fireman put one of her shoes and a handbag under the blanket and covered her face. As they crunched out into the street, he heard one of the stretcher-bearers whistling softly to himself. His own gesture of defence.

A hand reached out, and someone said, 'Your cap, sir.'

'Thanks.' He had not even noticed it had gone.

He jammed it over his unruly hair and felt the grit around the rim.

'Can you make it, Emma? If not, I'll carry you.'

She looked at him, her face very clear as the moon showed itself again beyond the river.

'Just hold me, Guy. Don't leave me. Not yet.'

There were people everywhere, when earlier the street had been like a grave, calling to one another, some laughing with relief when a familiar face showed itself.

Sherbrooke walked through the crowd, knowing he would never forget this, his only experience of the civilians' war. It was something which had always remained at a distance, reaching him only across a table when some rating lost his parents or wife in one of these raids, which were so frequent that they rarely got a mention in the press. Hit-and-run. Like that day in Portsmouth . . .

Some wag called from the darkness, 'Up the navy!' Another gave a cheer.

Sherbrooke called back something, although he could never recall what he had said, and no words, however jocular, could relieve what he felt.

They stopped in front of an undistinguished house, and she said, 'It's all right, thank God. Just as he said!'

He waited while she searched for her key in the darkness. Blast was a strange thing. The bomb had fallen around the corner, but in a narrow intersection the blast could have gone in any direction. These houses were untouched. He was reminded of an incident aboard *Pyrrhus*, when German bombers had attacked a convoy of empty ships returning from Murmansk. Strange that the memory had become lost, swallowed up by everything else that had happened, and that it should choose this night to return to him.

Minutes before the air attack, he had been talking with a young signalman on the cruiser's bridge. Another bitter, bitter day, when any contact between bare skin and instruments or fittings could end in frostbite. The signalman had been holding up an old magazine to shield Sherbrooke while he tried to light his pipe.

Then the attack had begun, the air torn apart by chattering pom-poms and Oerlikon guns, so that the solitary bomb had exploded almost unnoticed between the bridge and B Turret. Sherbrooke had scarcely felt the blast, but the young signalman had been killed outright. His body was completely unmarked, like the woman in the wine shop.

'Got it!' She pushed open the door. 'Come in and close it, will you?'

She sounded breathless, as if it had only just happened. She called, 'It's only me, Ellen!' There was no reply and she said, 'She must be out. She has the other flat, you see. I feed her cat when she has to be away.' Again, she was speaking fast, as if afraid she might break down.

They climbed the stairs in the darkness, and he tried to imagine her living here or in some other temporary place, getting up and going to work, wondering each day if the flat would still be here when she returned. And Captain Thorne, sharing her official life while she thought only of her missing husband, a man she said she could hardly remember.

Another door, and she switched on a light, her eyes moving quickly to a window to make sure that the curtains were drawn.

She turned towards him, and said, 'Your hand! What have you done?'

He looked at his right hand, covered with blood, some already dry, but with a deep cut just below the cuff of his shirt.

'Sit here.' She led him to a chair. 'I'll clean it. It must have happened when you were looking after that poor woman.'

Sherbrooke tried to ease the pain in his back; he seemed to ache all over. Then he raised his arm, afraid that some of his blood might stain the furniture. It all seemed so ridiculous that he wanted to laugh.

She knelt by the chair and held out a small, dainty towel. 'It's only damp, I'm afraid. The water's cut off. It often happens during a raid.' Then she said, 'What is it?' and looked up at him, her eyes suddenly very calm, her voice steady. 'Tell me.'

He shook his head. 'Nothing.' He tried to control it, but his hand was trembling so badly that he could not stop it. 'I – I can't . . .'

She wrapped the towel around his bloody wrist and held it with both hands, and with great gentleness. He could feel himself giving in, breaking. *Please, not now. Not in front of her. Please . . .*

She said, 'Don't talk, Guy. Don't try to explain. Not to me. You don't have to. It makes you more of a man, not less.' She continued to grip his hand. 'Do you have any cigarettes? I could light one for you.' She saw him shake his head. 'I don't smoke, myself.' It triggered off another small memory. 'Not one of my vices.'

He said, 'I'm a pipe-smoker . . . used to be, anyway.' He saw her reaching into his jacket pocket. 'Splashed out and bought myself a really good one after I came out of hospital.'

She looked directly into his eyes. 'I know. I understand.' She took away the rough bandage and said, 'It's stopped, I

211

think. But don't move. I'll get something for it in a minute.'

He watched her as she placed the pipe and pouch of tobacco on the floor beside her knees. Her hair was still hanging down her back, dishevelled by the blast. He wanted to touch it. To hold her very tightly, as he had in the shop.

She was saying, 'My dad smokes a pipe. I've done this for him a few times.' She smiled, perhaps at another memory. 'I like to see a man with a pipe.' She held it out, pleased with her efforts. 'There. Try that.'

They shared it in silence, Sherbrooke holding her hand while she watched the smoke drifting up to the ceiling.

He said, 'I feel better already.' He squeezed the hand he held. 'Really.'

'I don't know whether to believe you or not. I promised you a drink.'

She stood up, undecided.

'I must go, Emma. If you think you'll be all right.'

As if to mock their anxiety, they heard the distant wail of sirens sounding the All Clear, and from nearby there was a spurt and gurgle of water as the supply was switched on.

'That settles it,' he said. 'I'll need to find a taxi.'

She frowned, and came to a decision. 'You can't go looking like this. Give me time to clean up your uniform. I'll wash your shirt – it will be ready before you leave. No arguments now. I mean it.'

'I promised you this wasn't going to happen.'

'It *won't*. Now go to the bathroom and take off your jacket and shirt. I'll find the Scotch.' She smiled at him. 'Truce?'

He washed his hands and then his face in the basin, and saw her personal things arranged on a shelf below the mirror, the carefully hoarded cologne, her cosmetics, a few yellow daffodils in a jug. He heard her call, 'I've got an old robe you can put on. My brother gave it to me for wearing in the shelter – it's miles too big for me!'

Then he saw her reflected in the mirror, looking in at him.

'What are those marks, Guy?'

He swung round and took the thick robe from her, embarrassed, not wanting her to see.

She asked again, 'What are they? You never told me.'

He glanced at his injured hand, but it was quite steady now. He answered, 'When I was in the water.' He let the blood and dirt flow out of the basin, not looking at her. 'The ice.'

She said, 'Never be afraid to tell me . . . to show me.'

He allowed her to take him back to the other room.

'Let me hold you, Emma.'

She did not resist as he put his arms round her, in a close embrace, like the moment when she had first realized what had happened in the shop. The screams and the falling glass, the staring eyes, the stretcher-bearer who had whistled in defiance of death.

And here, in this room she still hardly knew, there was peace. The sense of what was happening, the danger it would bring, was replaced by yearning.

She felt his hand on her spine, and imagined how it would be to make love with him. Strong, sensitive hands, holding, caressing, demanding of her . . .

She said, 'I really will get that drink now.' She leaned back in his arms and looked into his face. 'We both knew this would happen. I told myself I should end it before it began, but I thought we might still . . .'

He said, 'Be friends?'

She did not respond. 'Of course I find you attractive –

what woman wouldn't? Some of the people I meet . . . What I'm trying to say . . .'

He touched her mouth with his fingers. 'Don't say it. I *know*. I feel so alive when I'm with you that I want to ignore all the risks, all the pain that might come to you because of me.'

She slipped away from his arms, and he walked to the window and peered through a slit in the black-out curtain. Moonlight, no beams sweeping the clear sky, no bright sparks of flak above another part of this great city.

He heard her voice somewhere, and thought for a moment that somebody had called to see her. He stared down at her brother's dressing gown. *Oh, this is Captain Sherbrooke, who's just dropped in for a drink.* How would that look?

She came in, smiling at the confusion on his face. 'I phoned the night staff. They'll send a car for us in the morning, and drop you off at the Admiralty first.'

'You are a very smart girl.'

She brought two glasses and filled them carefully. She seemed happy, at ease, until she asked, 'The day after tomorrow, then?'

So easily said, and yet it meant so much.

'Yes, back to Greenock. Get the machine in motion.'

She took a sip, and said, 'This will knock me out, and I promised you some sandwiches.' She tried again. 'You know, I think I'm beginning to see your ship as a rival.'

He smiled, feeling her leaning against him on the small sofa.

'Don't. She's my protector, in a way. I can't explain it.'

She saw that his glass was empty. 'I'll bet you didn't even taste that!'

She watched him refill it, watched his hand, his serious profile. *Stop it now.*

214

He said, 'I'll remember this when I'm away.'

'Until the next time.'

He looked at her over the rim of the glass. 'Yes. The next time.'

'Promise?'

He said, 'I think you should turn in.'

She nodded gravely. 'Aye, aye, sir.'

'I'll bunk down here. That will make it quite safe.' But the humour eluded him.

'I agree. Call me if you need anything.' The door closed, and he was alone.

Nobody would believe it. *Least of all me.*

He did not hear her come in later and switch off the light, nor feel her remove his shoes.

She crouched by the sofa, looking at him as he slept in the darkness, remembering him with his men and with the dead prostitute in the off-licence, and whispering to him.

'We both knew this might happen. I love you, but I can never say it. Our future could have ended tonight, if that bomb had come our way. It would be all over without ever beginning.' She wanted to touch his hair, but dared not. 'So why do we have to pretend? If you wanted me now, I wouldn't be able to resist, because I want you, too. And you, dear man, ashamed as you are of your honourable scars, might hate me for it.'

The following morning they were both awake early, he unable, at first, to remember where he was. They barely spoke, and then only like two people who had just met.

The car arrived on time, and dropped Sherbrooke at the Admiralty as arranged.

He walked past two saluting sailors, scarcely noticing them, and made his way to the operations office where he was to meet Stagg.

Much to his surprise, Stagg was already there, tapping his watch with one finger.

'Where the hell have you been, Guy? I've had half of London out looking for you! The club said you hadn't even been there!' It was like a cruel game, and he knew Stagg was enjoying it.

He continued, 'Never mind, I can guess. Can't say I blame you.' He changed the subject. 'You'll have to go north today. The intelligence is ready. I want you to brief the captains, all of them, and explain what we're taking on. It's top secret, of course, so make sure it sinks in!' He gave his famous fierce grin. 'Operation *Sackcloth* – rather apt, I thought!'

He looked pointedly at his watch again. 'I must see Hudson. If you want to hang about, I'll drive you to the club for your gear.' He winked. 'Can't have you vanishing again, can we?'

Sherbrooke walked around the outer office until he found what he thought was a friendly face at one of the telephones.

'Could you get me a line to the D.O.I.? It's rather urgent.'

She studied him. 'It's Captain Sherbrooke, isn't it? I saw your picture in the paper, about the German cruiser.' She smiled. 'I'll see what I can do.' She picked up the telephone. 'My brother was in a battlecruiser.' Then, into the mouthpiece, 'Can you get a number for me, Ann?'

Sherbrooke wondered what he should say. If she would even be there.

'Which one was that?'

She looked up, and did not blink. '*Hood*, sir.' She held out the telephone. 'Don't be too long, sir.'

You never got used to the ambush of memory.

Her voice said, 'I knew it would be you.'

216

It was a good line: she sounded very close, like last evening, her head on his shoulder.

'Can I talk, Emma?'

'Yes. I'm alone at the moment.' Another pause. 'You're going away, aren't you?'

'Yes. I only just found out. I'm so sorry.'

'We should have understood. Accepted it, and not fought against it.' He started to say something, but she said, 'No, listen, Guy. I've only got a minute. We will meet again. We must.'

'Yes. It's all I care about.'

It was as if he had remained silent. 'I just wanted you to *know*. I want to be with you. *With* you, d'you understand?'

He said, 'I love you, Emma.' But the line went dead.

He replaced the telephone. 'Thank you very much.'

The operator watched him walk away. Lucky girl, whoever she is, she thought.

That evening, Captain Guy Sherbrooke was on a crowded train heading north. He was no longer alone.

12

Operation Sackcloth

Sherbrooke moved restlessly around his large day cabin, patting his pockets, trying to remember if he had all the notes he might need, and some clean handkerchiefs. The shape of the new pipe, smoked for the first time in her flat, brought her sharply to his mind. He could see her filling it for him while he had sat with his hand wrapped in the towel, afraid that the shameful trembling would return. All around and below him, he could sense, almost more than feel, the ship stirring, preparing for sea once again, the shouted orders, muffled by watertight doors, the occasional trill of a boatswain's call, the squeal of a winch.

In a moment, he would leave this private place and join the rest of *Reliant*'s company, as they raised the anchor and made their way from Greenock into the Firth of Clyde, to skirt the Isle of Arran before changing course to the west, and into the Atlantic.

How good was security this time? *Reliant* always drew attention, and with the new carrier *Seeker* in company and the six powerful destroyers ready to take up their stations in open water, somebody might put two and two together. Stagg would be sailing aboard *Seeker*, and would then make the transfer at sea, a suitably dramatic beginning to Operation *Sackcloth*, and so typical of the man.

Another glance around the cabin. Little more than three

months since he had taken command, and yet it felt as if he had always had her.

He thought of the pile of Cavendish's personal gear, the broken picture frame.

And Emma's voice on the telephone, very controlled, and yet he had sensed the emotion. *I want to be with you.* All the risks held at bay, so that she could make him understand.

Petty Officer Long hovered in the doorway of his small pantry.

''Nother cup before you go up, sir?'

He grinned at Long's mournful face. 'Better not. Might disgrace myself!'

Long nodded, satisfied. It was not a passing mood. Something had happened to the Captain, as if he had shed something – or found it, more likely.

He had been discussing the change in Sherbrooke with Dave Price, the rear-admiral's chief steward.

'Well, it has to be a woman, Dodger.' He had given a wintry smile. 'Not like my guvnor, like bloody quicksilver, he is.'

Long understood what he meant. Price had served the rear-admiral before, and had told him a thing or two. *Like a rat up a pump*, as he had often described his master's insatiable appetite for women.

Sherbrooke looked at the clock. Frazier would be down soon, ready to proceed, all loose ends tied up. Even the destroyer *Mediator*, which had been forced into Gibraltar with shaft problems, was waiting to slip with the others. Stagg had made it absolutely clear that there would be 'no more bloody excuses'.

There were voices outside, and Long said, 'They're too early, sir.' He sounded quite outraged at the intrusion.

It was not Frazier but a bluff, squarely-built man with

thin, sandy hair and a weathered face, deep crows' feet etched around the eyes.

'Sorry to make a pierhead jump, Captain Sherbrooke.' He held out his hand. 'Pat Drury, B.B.C. I'm supposed to be sailing with you.'

The handshake was hard and rough, more like a farm worker's than that of a top war correspondent. He could have been any age from the mid-thirties to fifty.

Sherbrooke said, 'This is Petty Officer Long. He'll look after you while you're aboard, Mr Drury.'

He could sense Long's disapproval, and added, 'We shall be weighing anchor shortly. I've passed the word: you can visit the bridge any time. Just let us know where you are if the balloon should go up. *Reliant*'s a big ship. You might get lost.'

Drury smiled. 'I'll find my way.' He glanced around the spacious cabin and gave a silent whistle. 'This is the way to live! You should see some of the dumps I've ended up in during this war!'

Sherbrooke could not look at Long's pixie face. He said, 'It's yours, until this jaunt is over.'

He noticed that Drury's eyes were grey, like slate, and seemed to miss nothing. Hard, like his handshake: a man who probably liked to be thought tough, and unable to be impressed by anything, or anyone.

The deck gave another shudder, the Chief testing something, taking no chances.

Drury dropped a suitcase on the carpet. 'My guess is that you feel a bit isolated from your crew sometimes, Captain. Maybe you couldn't afford to lower the barrier, even if you wanted to?'

Sherbrooke picked up his favourite binoculars. They had been ashore for an overhaul when *Pyrrhus* had gone down, which made them doubly valuable to him now.

'My ship's company can make up their own minds about that. A barrier, as you describe it, is an obstacle. That's no use to any captain.'

There was another tap at the door. Long bustled away, muttering, 'Like bloody Piccadilly Circus!'

It was the Canadian lieutenant, Rayner.

'I just heard you wanted to see me, sir. I was in the sickbay – the doc was checking me out.' He glanced without interest at the civilian. 'He says it's all great.' He grinned, his relief and his pleasure at catching the ship at such short notice very obvious.

Sherbrooke said, 'I'm glad. As you saw, we've got you a new Shagbat, and there's another one on board to keep you company.'

Drury interjected, 'When I was aboard the *Seeker* yesterday, I saw a lot of fighters, Lieutenant. I would have thought they'd be more to your taste.'

Sherbrooke sensed Rayner's caution, if not actual resentment, and said gently, 'It's all right. Mr Drury *is* on our side. He's with the B.B.C.'

Rayner, unimpressed, said, 'That's good to know, sir,' and then, to the correspondent, 'No, Mr Drury, the Walrus'll do me just fine.' He faced the captain again. 'I've met my new gunner, sir. I think we'll hit it off all right.'

Sherbrooke knew what he was thinking, of his old Walrus drifting at the mercy of the sea, with the dead gunner still inside.

He said, 'I wanted you to know right away, Lieutenant Rayner. You'll be getting a gong. The D.S.C.'

Rayner swallowed, momentarily lost for words. Finally he said, 'Thank you, sir. We all shared in it.'

'I know. But it goes with the job, remember that. Now carry on.'

The door closed, and Drury commented, 'He liked

221

that, coming from you, personally, I mean.'

Sherbrooke said, 'So did I.' Drury was experienced, and some said uncompassionate in his reporting of the war as he saw it. But for once, at least, he had been unable to conceal his surprise. Not a barrier in sight.

The door opened and Frazier stepped into the cabin, his cap beneath his arm.

'Ready to proceed, sir. Tugs standing by.' Just the hint of a smile, something private. 'A formality, of course.'

Sherbrooke picked up his cap.

'Hands fall in for leaving harbour, John.'

They climbed to the broad quarterdeck together. Seamen and marines were already forming up, without fuss or any outward show of excitement. They walked along the familiar deck, beneath the angled muzzles of the four-inch secondary armament and the squat multi-barrelled pom-poms, nicknamed 'Chicago Pianos', with the great tripod masts and layered bridges waiting to receive them. A glance here and there, a nudge from one seaman to his oppo, a formal salute from a petty officer or some divisional lieutenant. It was routine, part of their lives, but even to those who understood it, this leavetaking was no less inspiring. A great ship was preparing for sea. Operation *Sackcloth* was about to begin.

Down in the cabin, Pat Drury dropped into a deep chair and scratched his leg. It was still hard to understand why the captain of *Reliant* should have to exchange all this for a tiny cabin on the bridge, where he would never be allowed to rest.

He smiled broadly. But a gift horse was just that.

He said, 'I'll have a drink – er, Long. Something strong.'

Long almost smiled with pleasure. 'Sorry, sir. The bar's closed.'

Right on time, with signals flashing back and forth to

and from the shore, *Reliant*'s massive anchor clanked, dripping, from the water to be brought home into its hawse pipe. She was free of the land.

Rear-Admiral Vincent Stagg stood by one of the polished scuttles in his day cabin and stared into the distance.

Sherbrooke watched him, very aware of Stagg's mood, and in some measure sharing the frustration he was unable to conceal.

He knew what Stagg was looking at, the familiar, unchanging profile of the Rock of Gibraltar, a refuge to generations of sailors, and the guardian at the gates of the Mediterranean. Stagg would not be regarding it in that light. After their fast passage from Greenock, out into the Atlantic before altering course again and anchoring here, it was an anti-climax. To a man with Stagg's lack of patience, it would seem like something far worse.

Stagg's swarthy-faced secretary and his flag lieutenant were also present, sitting on opposite sides of the cabin as if they disliked any sort of contact. And the new boy in Stagg's force, Captain Thomas Essex of the *Seeker*, had also come across from his ship for this meeting.

Sherbrooke liked what he had seen of Essex, a lean, serious-faced officer who had spent most of his war in the Atlantic, and nevertheless retained a dry sense of humour.

Sherbrooke knew he was not the only one to share Stagg's frustration. After all the dash and the promise of action, Gibraltar seemed to represent the very opposite. The weather did not help. It was hot, even sultry after the cold to which they had become accustomed, and with scuttles and watertight doors opened wide, a kind of torpor seemed to permeate every part of the ship.

Stagg said, 'In spite of everything, the Germans are still holding out. They're being attacked by the R.A.F. and

American bombers, and any attempt to run supplies to them from Sicily is chased and harried by our M.T.B.s and destroyers around the clock.' He stared out of the scuttle again. 'Look at them ... more troopships than you can shake a stick at. All waiting to go to Alexandria, and even Malta, to prepare for the next move.' He faced them, his forehead damp with perspiration. 'The enemy is pinned in on the peninsula. They can't break out, or hope to win, and the longer they leave it the more resources fall to us. The harbours they left full of wrecks and the facilities they demolished are being occupied and put back into use by our light coastal forces – even destroyers are involved, although not without risk, and some expected losses.'

What remained of the Afrika Korps was clinging to its last toe-hold in North Africa. Even the old French naval base at Bizerte was still operating despite the bombing raids, and a chronic shortage of supplies and ammunition. If the Desert Fox had indeed been replaced by General von Arnim, as intelligence had claimed, then his spirit lingered on.

Stagg said, 'The Commander-in-Chief is well aware of the danger in delaying some strong course of action. If the Admiralty could see its way ...' He glanced sharply at Captain Essex. 'You were about to say?'

Essex smiled gently. 'You know what Jack says about the Admiralty, sir. That it's like the cinema – the best seats are high up and right at the back!'

Paymaster Lieutenant Villar laughed, but choked it short as Stagg shot him an icy look.

He said, 'I have intervened personally with the C-in-C, Admiral Cunningham. He, at least, will see the sense of my argument. Enemy installations around Bizerte are well-defended, and can still give a hot reception to any of our smaller craft if they move inshore to find a target.'

He looked directly at Sherbrooke. '*We* could knock them out. Right up *Reliant*'s street, wouldn't you say, Guy?'

The casual use of his name was no accident. Essex would feel outnumbered; the others did not count.

He answered, 'It would be very hazardous without air cover. We don't know for certain how many aircraft the enemy have at their immediate disposal, but with *Seeker* in close company I think it could be done. Without air cover . . .'

Stagg said irritably, 'I know, I know, Guy. I haven't forgotten *Repulse*. Who could?'

Essex said, 'Fast in, fast out, at first light, sir. I can put up some fighter-bombers.' He was apparently unrepentent at Stagg's cold reception of his comment on the Admiralty. 'A rapid-fire bombardment would be far more effective than high-level bombing. Might even block the harbour. That would really finish them.'

Stagg looked across at Sherbrooke again.

'Any other observations, Guy?'

'E-Boats, sir. They've been reported in the area of Cape Bon. Our M.T.B.s have clashed with them a few times.' He was surprised at his own calmness, as if it had already been decided. 'But we can handle them with our secondary armament. The destroyers will take care of the rest.'

Stagg said, 'One destroyer, Guy. The others will look after *Seeker*. We'll do this one alone. It's what she was built for, eh?'

It reminded him sharply of the girl whose name was carved on the stone at Portsmouth Point, the girl he had once believed he might marry, but now could remember without emotion. He recalled what he had said to her when they had walked and talked together, about the future, and how their lives might change. Of the navy, he had said, 'It is what I do. What I am.' Nobody had ever spoken of risk in those distant, sunlit days.

Stagg was wearing the predatory grin, now that action seemed imminent. 'Not a word to anybody until I hear from the C-in-C. Not even to Mr Drury.' His grin grew wider. '*Especially* Mr Drury!'

They all stood up, and Sherbrooke said to the carrier's captain, 'I'll see you over the side.'

Stagg shook Essex's hand, playing the admiral again. 'We shall make a bit of history together yet, you'll see!'

Sherbrooke walked out with Essex, and saw a messenger dash away to warn the quarterdeck so that *Seeker*'s boat would be ready and waiting. With Frazier as the commander, it was pleasant to know that he himself never had to remember such matters.

They stood together in the hot sunlight, looking at the lines of troopships, some of which *Reliant* had probably escorted at some time during the war. Beyond, and dwarfing every ship, was the Rock itself. Sherbrooke had been in *Reliant* at Gibraltar several times in the years of peace, when life had consisted of regattas and races, contests with other warships, and mess bills to make a lieutenant weep.

He realized that Essex was watching him. He was only a few years older than himself, with an experienced, energetic face. His hair was going grey. That wasn't just the war. That was the Atlantic.

'How do you get on with him? Stagg, I mean?'

You should never ask a flag captain that, and Sherbrooke liked him for it.

'He gets a bit carried away sometimes.'

Essex turned as his boat cut across the blue water, the bowman stiffly upright with his boathook.

He said quietly, 'I'm glad to know you.' Then he looked

at him with steady, penetrating eyes. 'And I'm damned glad Rear-Admiral Stagg's got you in command. I think you know why.'

They faced each other and saluted, then Essex was going down the long accommodation ladder, his eyes already looking across at his own ship.

Frazier joined Sherbrooke in the shadow of Y Turret. 'Go well, sir?'

'I think so. Bombardment, by the sound of it. Nothing's decided.'

A petty officer hurried up and saluted Frazier. 'Beg pardon, sir, but the admiral will want his barge in half an hour. Going ashore, sir.'

'Pipe for the lowering party to muster.' He turned as the P.O. strode away. 'I'll tell the O.O.D. Don't want to be caught out!'

It is what I do. What I am.

Rhodes was waiting for him, to sound him out about what charts might be needed, he thought. And the admiral's secretary, Villars, was hovering nearby. Sherbrooke spoke to him first.

'Problem, Sec?'

Villar shrugged. 'Rear-Admiral Stagg suggested I should take on another officer to assist me.' He hesitated. 'In view of what was discussed, sir.'

'You'd better speak with the Bloke.' He saw Villar's unwillingness. 'Do you have anyone in mind?'

Villar smiled. 'Well, yes, sir. A young subbie named Forbes, just out of *King Alfred*, I understand. Good experience for him.'

Sherbrooke summoned the face to his mind. 'Well, tell Commander Frazier anyway. I don't see that he'd object.'

Rhodes waited until the secretary had gone, and then asked, 'About charts, sir?'

Sherbrooke smiled at him, and said, 'I thought it might be.'

The porter on duty looked up from his desk as he heard the girl's shoes clicking across the bare floor.

'Good evening, Mrs Meheux. Working late, then? Another flap on, I'll bet.'

She smiled absently, thinking of the river path where she had been walking, the river dark, ever-restless, the black, shapeless barges moored with other craft, and only one small boat moving, the river police or the Home Guard. For once, she had been scarcely interested.

She had only been back at the flat in Chelsea for an hour before receiving a message that Captain Thorne needed her to return to the department offices, 'unless it's impossible, of course.'

It had been cold by the river, and she could not stop shivering, even though she was wearing the blue denim trousers and jacket she kept for fire-watching, or those rare occasions when she joined other residents in the shelter. She had told herself that it was stupid not to take cover when a raid was in progress, but she hated the thought of being trapped, unable to see or hear what was happening. Some people actually seemed to enjoy it, and went regularly to the shelters, well supplied with blankets, food and drink, making a night of it. Maybe they were lonely. At least the war had broken down a few social barriers.

The lift was not working; they always turned off the power when the building was empty, just in case. She gripped the handrail and began to climb. She should have telephoned her father in Bath, but she could not. She was barely able to think about it, or what it might mean to her now.

The letter had been waiting for her, with its official stamps. She was carrying it in her shoulder bag at this very moment, and could still see the carefully worded information printed in her mind, as if someone were dictating it to her.

It was too early for optimism, and all information took such a long time to filter through to London that much of it was out of date, useless. She had tried to test her feelings, to prepare herself one way or the other. But nothing came.

Some facts had been passed through a Swedish agency; the remainder was speculation, something to which the authorities had become hardened since the Japanese victories in Singapore, Burma, Malaya, Hong Kong, and every other colony and territory which had fallen to the Rising Sun. Lieutenant Philip Meheux of the Royal Engineers was thought to be alive and working as a prisoner, not where he was captured, but in Japan. Separated from his own unit, he had been transported from Singapore in a naval supply vessel, which had been torpedoed by an American or Dutch submarine. Philip had survived, and had been identified by his dog-tag before being put ashore in Japan, for treatment, or for forced labour, no one knew.

Perhaps he was ill, or had been badly injured when the ship had been torpedoed. It was possible that he had since died.

To have some hope was often worse than having no hope at all. She had thought of the moment in the off-licence when the bomb had fallen. He had held her, protecting her from something he had known was about to happen. Instinct, experience, who could tell? But she had realized that if she had been going to die on that particular evening, she would have wanted it to happen with him, and with no other man. It made her feel ashamed, disloyal, but convinced.

She had reached the office without being aware of it, and was strangely glad that she had been recalled. Tonight she needed it, like an escape.

Captain Roger Thorne was sitting at his desk, and looked up as she entered.

'Oh, it's you, Emma. Sorry to drag you back. Your fault really, for making yourself indispensable!' He laughed, studying her trousers as she walked into the pool of light by his desk. 'All prepared, eh?'

He waited for her to sit down, his eyes still on the trousers as if he were disappointed in some way. 'I had a chat with the Chief-of-Staff. James is a bit cagey, but he knows he can rely on this department.'

She tried to relax. Vice-Admiral Hudson seemed a very upright and dignified man, always courteous on the rare occasions when she had met him. He was not the sort of officer Thorne would ever call by his first name.

'How are we involved, sir?'

He sounded vague. 'Usual thing, full details to be reported to our selected list of department heads. Restricted, of course.' He gave what might have been a wink. 'Very.'

She said, 'Well, I still have some work to do, so I'll be in the next room if you need me.' She knew at once that it was the wrong thing to have said.

'Who wouldn't need you, my girl?' He changed tack, and said, 'You know Captain Guy Sherbrooke quite well, I expect?'

She sat completely still, but could feel her heart pounding against her ribs like a fist.

'I've met him a few times, yes. Mostly in connection with the ship, and the *Minden*. Has something happened?'

He watched her curiously. 'The Chief-of-Staff confirmed that Rear-Admiral Stagg's force is involved in an operation. If I know Vincent Stagg he'll make a mark for himself. He's a real goer, that one, and he has quite an eye for the ladies, I'm told, so don't say I didn't warn you!'

He's playing with me. Enjoying it.

She said, 'Is it dangerous, then?'

He stood up, and walked across the office to adjust a picture above the empty fireplace.

'I knew Sherbrooke in the *Montrose*, you know. That takes me back a bit.'

'Yes, you told me.'

He did not seem to hear. 'Good officer, a bit of a quiet one, but I quite liked him.'

He walked behind her chair and she felt his hand brush against her hair. It was not an accident. Surprisingly, it made her feel sad, rather than angry.

She said, 'Have you told your wife you're working late, sir?'

He laughed sharply. 'She understands. A navy wife has to accept these things!'

Faintly, they heard the dismal, undulating dirge of sirens.

Thorne grunted, 'The nightly hate begins!' but her remark seemed to have had an effect. He slumped into his chair and watched her across the desk. 'It must be hard on you, Emma, your husband being a prisoner of war. Damned difficult, not knowing what the hell is going on.'

She felt her bag beneath her elbow. The letter: polite, concerned, cold.

'They think he's alive.'

He stared at her. 'Do they, by God. Now there's something to celebrate!'

She saw him dragging open a drawer. Not for the first time this evening, it seemed.

'These glasses are clean. Have a drink with me, Emma. It's only gin, I'm afraid, but what d'you say?'

Like hearing somebody else, she thought. 'Just a small one. Thank you.'

He splashed some water into her glass, or it could have all been gin. He was saying something and beaming over his own glass. But all she saw was Sherbrooke, kneeling by the stone in Portsmouth.

And when she felt the gin, raw across her tongue, she was tasting in memory the whisky which had been Sir Graham Edwardes's present to her, and sitting beside that same man in her flat in Chelsea.

Had it really happened?

Thorne was pouring himself another generous measure.

'I expect you get a lot of bright lads trying to make a pass at you. Can hardly blame them. You're a very pretty girl, you know.'

He glared at his telephone as a small light blinked just once, and exclaimed, 'God damnit! Who the hell can that be?' He almost snatched her glass, and put it with his own into the drawer.

The door opened without a knock, and Vice-Admiral James Hudson strode into the room.

He saw the girl and held out his hand. 'No, please don't get up, Mrs Meheux.' He nodded to Thorne, his eyes taking in the half-empty water jug, and the wet marks where the glasses had been. He would smell the gin, too, she thought.

He said, 'Glad you got your people together, Roger. Red alert has just been sounded, too, so don't hang about if the planes come this way.'

He laid a thin file on the desk. 'Operation *Sackcloth*. The details, such as they are.' He waited, watching Thorne's discomfort. 'Raids or no raids, I want this dealt with.'

She asked quietly, 'When is it, sir?'

He studied her gravely before answering. 'It was

232

brought forward by one day. The operation was carried out this morning.'

Thorne had used the exchange to recover himself. 'Satisfactory, I trust, sir?'

'Signals are still coming in – security. You know the score, Roger.'

They both looked at her as she said, 'Was it *Reliant*, sir?' and then, 'Is she all right?'

Hudson seemed to make up his mind. There was something in this young woman's face, in her eyes, that made him realize this was no casual question.

'She is reported safe. There was some damage, and we have reports of casualties. Next of kin will be informed as soon as possible.'

She stood up, thinking of the cascade of broken glass, the prostitute who had given her such a searching glance when they had entered the shop. Next of kin . . .

'Captain Sherbrooke, sir?'

I need you with me.

She should have told him earlier. Now, it might be too late for both of them.

Hudson smiled. 'Safe.' So that was it. He was surprised that such simple truths could still move him. 'In fact, for a captain who's just fought the enemy and managed to save his own ship, I'd say he was feeling pretty good!'

He saw the fingers of her right hand close over the plain wedding ring on her left, but sensed that she neither saw nor felt it. Then she closed her eyes briefly, and opened them.

You see, I love him so much. And he loves me.

But all she said was, 'Thank you. I'm so happy that he's safe.'

She remembered him telling her the ship's motto after Stagg's pointed little comment. *We will never give in.*

She excused herself and left the room.
Nor will we.

13

Blood and Congratulations

H.M.S. *Reliant*'s bearded navigating officer straightened up from his voicepipes and said, 'Steady on new course, sir, one-three-zero, one-one-zero revolutions.' He sounded unusually formal, very aware of the rear-admiral's pale figure cross-legged in the captain's chair.

Sherbrooke glanced at him. 'Very good, Pilot. Still damned dark, by the look of it.'

Rhodes grunted. 'Guns won't thank us. He'll have the sun right in his eyes when it does appear!'

The ship seemed very quiet, even though she was thrusting through the water at half-speed. The sea was remarkably calm, and only the occasional tremble of power through the bridge deck gave a hint of her movement.

Officers and men had changed into white clothing, which only seemed to deepen the tension aboard *Reliant*: Stagg had made his wishes known in this respect when they had eventually been ordered to leave Gibraltar. Sherbrooke envied the ratings in their simple rig; his own heavy white drill was already clinging to his body. It would be worse when the sun came up. Most of the junior officers were wearing only shirts and shorts, unwilling to purchase extra uniforms which they might never wear again, once this operation was over.

He wondered why Stagg was here instead of enjoying

the privacy of his own small bridge. Maybe the delays and the postponement of his plan had finally got to him. When they had at last been ordered to bring the bombardment forward by twenty-four hours, he had expected Stagg to explode. Instead, he had vented most of his anger on Howe, his flag lieutenant, and in confidence had snapped, 'I'll be rid of that jellyfish at the first chance I get, just you watch me! I don't owe his father a bloody thing!'

Another little insight. Howe's father was an admiral.

Sherbrooke glanced at the radar repeater, the revolving beam reaching out like a blind man's stick. He saw their accompanying destroyer, *Montagu*, appear momentarily and vanish, leading the way, on a regular zig-zag some four miles ahead of the flagship. It still felt as though they were all alone: the carrier *Seeker* and the other destroyers were deployed well astern to the north-west. Beyond *Montagu*, there was only the land. The enemy.

A quick bombardment, in and out, before Jerry realized what was happening. It never seemed so simple once it was staring you in the face.

Up in his control position, Evershed, the gunnery officer, was waiting. All six guns were loaded with high-explosive shells, far more effective than armour-piercing projectiles when used against land targets.

The enemy had been under constant attack, from the air, and from the tightening jaws of tanks and infantry pushing up from the south. German aircraft had been reduced to using the beaches for landing and take-off; landing craft had to risk being wrecked by sunken or grounded vessels whenever they tried to run supplies or evacuate survivors from broken and demoralized units.

Evershed would be in his element, Sherbrooke thought, packed into his armoured control position with his assistants, who would sift the information as it came in.

Range, rate, deflection, like a single machine, with Evershed's hand on the trigger.

Sherbrooke looked at Rhodes by the voicepipes, his features and uniform tinged green by the shaded lights of repeaters and dials. Men he had come to know, in so short a time; men he trusted, like Onslow, the Chief, down below the waterline in his confined world of racing machinery and roaring fans. And Farleigh, the surgeon commander, who had proved his worth many times over with survivors, no matter what uniform they wore. He would be down there now, arms folded, his S.B.A.s and first aid parties placed throughout the ship like extensions of himself, listening to the constant rattle of instruments, the tools of his trade; waiting in that glaring, white place.

He walked to the opposite side of the bridge. There it was, the first real hint of dawn. It was misty as well; Rhodes had prophesied as much during the afternoon watch. He licked his lips. *Yesterday*. His mouth was dry, which was always a bad sign. He had to be above it all. He almost smiled. *Inhuman*. Most of them probably thought he was, anyway.

All hands had been called early and the watchkeepers relieved, to have a quick meal and swallow gallons of sweet tea before going to action stations. Many of the old hands would be glad that the waiting was over, until the next time. Others would be dreading it, but more afraid of showing fear in front of their messmates and friends than of fear itself.

Rhodes said, 'Half an hour, sir.' He, at least, sounded calm, unworried.

Stagg remained silent. He could have been asleep, one leg swaying in time with the slow tilt of the bridge.

Sherbrooke watched the light exploring the forecastle, giving colour to the anchor cables and stanchions, the point where the master-at-arms had come aboard as Neptune with his villainous-looking 'court'. It seemed like a year ago.

Rhodes's assistant, Frost, jammed a handset under his cap and called, 'W/T office reports signal from *Montagu*, sir!' In the strange, filtered light his wispy beard looked even more absurd. '*Enemy vessels ahead! Small craft, moving right!*'

Sherbrooke said, 'Tell *Montagu* to disregard! *Do not engage!*'

Stagg snapped, 'Landing craft?'

Sherbrooke listened to the rasp of static from one of the speakers, then Evershed's voice, clipped and unemotional. 'Six or seven small craft, bearing one-three-zero, range one-double-oh.'

Sherbrooke repeated, 'Signal *Montagu*! Now!' He could see it clearly enough. The hope of every destroyer's commander: ships pinned down by radar, probably having run the blockade from Sicily. *Montagu* must be right on top of them. Their distance from *Reliant* was ten thousand yards: five miles.

Stagg waved one hand in the air. 'What's that fool doing now?'

Frost said, 'No acknowledgment from *Montagu*, sir.'

Sherbrooke raised his binoculars as bright stars of red and green tracer exploded through the mist like fireworks at a regatta.

Montagu's R/T had either been deflected by the nearness of land, or her captain had no intention of throwing away such easy targets.

Rhodes slid back part of the screen, and above the muted din of machinery and the surge of water alongside, it was possible to hear the double crack of the destroyer's paired mountings, and an unbroken exchange of automatic fire.

Sherbrooke held his breath as the image strengthened in the lenses: *Montagu*, increasing speed, her funnel smoke dragging astern like a cloak, turning slightly to port as she charged for the rearmost vessels in the convoy. Low, chunky shapes, still too dark to identify, but probably Siebel ferries, landing craft which were heavily armed against air attack. To engage a powerful destroyer like *Montagu* would be like a mouse squaring up to a charging bull.

They heard Evershed cough, or perhaps it was one of his officers in Control. Somebody had left a key down, all eyes intent on the miniature battle.

A boatswain's mate said, 'Land! I can see land, sir, dead ahead!'

Another brushstroke, undulating and yellow in the growing light.

The speaker said, 'A, B, and Y Turrets stand by. Follow Director!'

There was a vivid flash, and seconds later the explosion boomed against the hull. One of the enemy vessels had blown up, perhaps carrying ammunition or fuel. The convoy must have slipped across the Strait of Sicily and around Cape Bon during the night, their crews risking everything, only to meet disaster at the end.

Another explosion, and a towering sheet of flame and sparks, which illuminated *Montagu* even as she fired and fired again.

The rest was like a sequence in a bad dream, distorted and unreal, because of the initial silence in which it took place. Three tall waterspouts burst from the sea as if propelled from the depths, and bracketed the wheeling destroyer like white pillars. They seemed to fall very slowly, and only then did the crash and shock wave of those big shells quiver against *Reliant*'s flank.

Stagg muttered, 'They've done for *Montagu*.'

Sherbrooke called, *'Open fire!'*

He tensed as the foremost turret moved slightly, one gun rising a little higher than its companion.

It was not possible to see the hidden battery, but Evershed's spotting team had marked the flashes, and marked them well.

'Shoot!'

Evershed again, icy calm. 'Deflection seven left! Up two hundred!' A bell jangled in the distance. *'Shoot!'*

The bridge shook violently as the marines in Y Turret trained around as far as they could, the shells ripping past the ship to join the other vivid orange flashes on the shore.

Sherbrooke said, 'Stand by, Pilot. We'll alter course after the next salvo. Tell Control to engage on the opposite side!'

Stagg was right beside him, his eyes glittering in the reflected explosions from the stricken destroyer.

'Not so fast! We might lose the chance if we turn too soon!' He stared at Sherbrooke angrily. 'Hit them again! It's what we came for!'

Rhodes watched them, and then turned away.

Sherbrooke said, 'I am increasing speed, sir.'

Stagg did not reply. He was training his glasses on the *Montagu*. The destroyer had fallen onto her side, steam and flames spurting out of her bilges, where there was a hole big enough for a London bus. Tiny figures were running along the tilting deck or clambering onto the rails; some threw up their hands and dropped out of sight, and Sherbrooke guessed that the buckled plating was furnace-hot. As *Pyrrhus* had been.

'Full ahead together, Pilot. Tell Control.' Through the smeared glass he saw two signalmen cover their heads and duck down; simultaneously, he heard the rising whine of aircraft as two of *Seeker*'s Seafires roared from astern and headed into the smoke.

Stagg said, 'That'll show the bastards.'

'Time to turn on to new course, sir.' Rhodes made a point of ignoring the rear-admiral. 'We don't know how many wrecks are littered about here.'

A burning landing craft drifted quickly abeam. In fact, it was motionless, but swayed over as *Reliant*'s mounting bow wave surged across it, dousing flames and sweeping away dead and wounded alike.

'Half speed ahead! Starboard twenty! *Steady!*'

Sherbrooke watched the ticking gyro repeater but saw only the destroyer, all grace gone, a wreck, a sinking coffin for her company. They might never know if *Montagu*'s captain had ignored the signal to break off the action in order to seize the chance for himself, or if his R/T procedure had failed at the critical moment. Either way, it had cost him his ship and most of his men.

It was like having ice-cold hands against his skin, although his body was sweating.

'Steady on three-zero-zero!'

This great ship had come about with an agility even *Montagu* could not have matched. The three turrets were even now training round, another shell and its charge already in the hoist from magazine to breech.

They had come to destroy the remaining port facilities in a harbour already full of wrecks, and to bombard the surrounding defences, where soldiers had lived like rats for weeks. The enemy could always have been expected to do something, but a powerful shore battery had never been suggested. But for *Montagu*'s folly, they would never have found out, until it was too late.

'Shoot!'

The bridge fittings bucked violently again, and flakes of paint fell from the deckhead like snow. Sherbrooke raised his glasses and saw the flashes from the explosions.

There was so much smoke and dust in the air that it was like firing into a fog.

Some one yelled, '*Montagu*'s gone! Poor bastards!'

Sherbrooke gripped a handrail, and saw Stagg turn to stare at him.

Like the bomb, there was no warning, no sensation; he simply knew. He saw the water falling across B Turret in an endless cascade, and yet he had seen no fall of shot, heard no explosion. Two more hideous shockwaves jarred through his shoes, and he saw a glass screen shiver to fragments, men falling, mouths wide in silent screams, faces cut to bloody ribbons. The guns fired again from forward and aft, but below the bridge, B Turret, the barrels steaming now in the flung spray, was unmoving.

'Training mechanism out of control, sir!'

The other guns recoiled again. Evershed was still firing, doing what he loved, and lived for.

Sherbrooke said harshly, 'Report damage!'

His hearing was almost normal again: someone was screaming, the sound suddenly cut off as if a door had been slammed against it. Damage control and first aid parties were picking their way over broken glass.

A messenger said, 'The admiral's bridge has been hit, sir.' He faltered. 'Three casualties.'

Sherbrooke heard the chattering voicepipes, and imagined his men throughout the ship, then he turned and saw the war correspondent, Pat Drury, hands in his jacket pockets, the blood of a seaman who had fallen beside him splashed over his shoe.

'Get some people down there, Pilot, and tell T/S what's happened.'

He saw a sub-lieutenant and a few spare hands running for the ladder, faces frozen in the same emotionless masks as they prepared themselves for what they would find.

More muffled detonations, and moments later the two Seafires roared past, low over the water, heading back to their carrier. There were no more shells from the land, only a serried bank of flame and the sound of exploding ammunition, and the occasional fireball of an ignited fuel storage shelter.

Sherbrooke called, *'Cease firing!'* The stillness and the sudden intrusion of pain was almost worse.

One shell, fired at a very high trajectory, had hit *Reliant* on the superstructure, exploding as it burst through the searchlight platform and shattering the admiral's bridge, leaving only smashed communications gear and trailing wire, with the sunlight breaking at last through mist and smoke to reveal the full extent of the damage. A few feet in either direction, and the shell might have continued, barely hindered by *Reliant*'s thin plating, to explode finally in the magazine below B Turret.

One of the first in the party to be sent from the bridge was the seaman Alan Mowbray, for a brief period of his young life a promising art student. Like most recruits selected as potential candidates for wartime commissions, Mowbray had spent very little time at sea before being pitchforked into the training establishment, *King Alfred*. His ship had spent most of Mowbray's sea time in dock, undergoing repairs after months on escort duty.

He had never been in action before. He had heard the old Jacks in his mess talking about it, embroidering it for his benefit. They had pulled his leg about his posh manner of speaking, and a gentleness which they had wrongly regarded as innocence; but in the navy the lower deck had its own rules, and a justice as rigid as any in the K.R.s and A.I.s. Leg-pulling was accepted: bullying was not.

He clung to the side of the steel door. There were holes punched through it, like the fingerprints of a potter in clay, and blood on the broken furniture and splashed like paint across the deckhead. One man lay crushed beneath an upended wireless receiver, the back of his head smashed open, the bone protruding like the shell of an egg. The admiral's secretary sat in one corner, his face in his hands, groaning but otherwise unmarked, even though the sunlight piercing some of the splinter holes was only inches away.

'Out of the way, laddie!' A sickberth petty officer and two stretcher bearers pushed him aside. The P.O. said curtly, 'Leave that one. Get the admiral's sec out of it. You, Toby, lend this chap a hand.'

Mowbray would have fallen but for his grip on the steel door. It was his friend, Peter, now Sub-Lieutenant Forbes, who had been told to assist Lieutenant Villar with his extra duties. He sat with one leg doubled under him and his face pressed against the steel side, his eyes closed, while he gasped for breath as if he were drowning. There was a small hole halfway down the side of the compartment, and a smear of blood where he had slithered to the deck.

Fear and shock forgotten, Mowbray flung himself down and cradled his friend in his arms. He did not know what he was saying; the words seemed to flood out of him. And all the time he was holding him, willing him to speak, to open his eyes.

The petty officer knelt down and tore open the young officer's shirt, and with surprising gentleness prised his interlocked fingers open and away from the wound. Another man was standing nearby, ready with a large shell dressing. For Mowbray, it was a moment locked and motionless in time.

Two things happened. Forbes opened his eyes and stared at his friend, and in that small instant there was complete recognition. Then the frantic breathing stopped, and the eyes were closed again.

The P.O. said, 'Save the dressing, Toby. He's bought it.'

Mowbray stared at him, and then into his friend's face. *'Don't leave him!* He'll be all right!' He tried to drag the torn shirt across the wound. 'Must get him to a doctor!'

The P.O. stood up and exchanged a glance with his assistant.

'We're needed down there.' But something held him back. He said, 'It's no use, my son. He's dead. Nothing anyone can do.' He looked round as a messenger hurried past. 'Better tell the bridge. He was an officer, after all.'

Mowbray tried to fight them as they dragged him to his feet, but his strength was gone.

He felt the sea air in his face, the ship beneath him still surging ahead.

There was a lieutenant and another working party clambering along a broken ladder, and when the petty officer described what had happened, he looked at Mowbray and said, 'You knew Forbes, eh? Hard luck! Could have been worse.' He stared at the sea far below the bridge. 'For all of us, remember that!' Then he was gone, running with his men.

Mowbray cried out, *'He was my friend!'* Then he collapsed.

His words seemed to linger outside the door with the holes punched through it, like an epitaph.

Lieutenant Dick Rayner gripped a stanchion and stared up at his Walrus flying boat, perched on the catapult like some tethered bird of prey. The plane was untouched; not even the smallest splinter had damaged it, although one enemy shell had exploded directly alongside the ship.

He felt the mounting pressure under his hand and knew *Reliant* was turning again, and still working up to her full revolutions. It was a strange reaction, now that it was over, he thought, but he had felt a sense of helplessness. Here, but not a part of it. While the guns had roared and thundered, shaking the battlecruiser from masthead to keel, and the reports of the first hits on the enemy had been shouted down to them, he had been conscious of a peculiar remoteness, rather like the Walrus, painted in her new markings, a mere spectator.

Splinters had penetrated one compartment, which had been used as a paint store, and for a moment Rayner and his fellow airmen had imagined the whole area would be engulfed in flames. He had sent some of his own deck crew with extinguishers and had watched as a grubby leading hand had emerged, giving a thumbs-up.

He wondered what had happened to the survivors from *Montagu*, if there had been any. She had made a terrible sight going over, explosions and shattered machinery tearing her apart as she took the last plunge.

Like the dead airman he had seen in his dinghy, or Jim Hardie in the broken Shagbat. Somebody would miss them, perhaps keep hoping . . .

Rayner turned away from the sea, and saw the new pilot banging his cap against his thigh to remove some of the paint chippings that covered it.

Lieutenant Leslie Niven had the additional Walrus, which had remained in the hangar during the bombardment. R.N.V.R., with what Eddy Buck had described as 'a typical uppercrust drawl', he would be considered dashing by many women. But 'uppercrust'? Rayner thought of some of the other officers he had met, and had learned to judge for himself. Affected might be a better description. It was unfair, and he knew he was wrong to make such snap decisions about someone he hardly knew, except for an occasional meeting here by the catapult, or across the table in the mess.

Niven said, 'My God, *Seeker*'s Seafires made a picture!' He jammed the cap onto his head at a rakish angle.

If he was an R.A.F. type he would probably grow one of those ridiculous moustaches too, Rayner thought.

'They made a lot of noise,' he said. 'I thought they went in too fast to be really sure of a target.'

Niven gave an amused smile. 'Loyal to the old banger to the end, aren't you?'

Rayner leaned over a rail and saw two more stretchers being carried aft. There was no urgency this time, and the faces were covered.

'How many do you think?'

Niven shrugged. 'Twenty, I'd say. One of the stokers just told me the flag lieutenant was killed, with another officer.' He gestured toward the bridge, around which they could see the motionless barrels of B Turret, a hose playing water on something below the forward funnel. 'Blown to bits, apparently.'

Why is he trying to shock me? Why pretend that he doesn't care, that he's above it?

Rayner said, 'That's one job I couldn't do. Trotting around after some admiral, wiping his ass for him if you're told to. Not for me. I'd tell them to stick it!'

Niven's smile broadened into a grin. 'I think you would, at that!'

They looked up as a speaker squeaked into life. 'D'you hear there? Stand by for the Captain!'

It goes with the job. Rayner glanced down at the spray-dappled planking. There were several deep scars on the quarterdeck: the Bloke would have something to say about those. He looked up again toward the scattered parties of seamen and marines, some filthy and bedraggled after dealing with splinter holes along the waterline, and restoring communications where voicepipes and telephone lines had been broken. And the line of bodies, wrapped in blankets or pieces of canvas. Anonymous, except to the men who had found and carried them there, and then they, too, would forget them, out of necessity. The ship came first.

'This is the Captain. We are rejoining the group without delay. I want you all to know that the attack was a success, there can be no doubt about that. Some of you are quite new to this ship – something your captain can share and understand.'

Rayner saw some of the men grinning, and he heard an ironic cheer from one of the gun mountings. He hoped Sherbrooke would hear it, too.

'I have to tell you that it was not without cost. *Reliant* had twenty-eight casualties, half of which were fatal. *Montagu*'s losses must have been considerable. It is something we have to accept, but to which we can never become accustomed.'

He heard Niven say, 'Told you. I was about right!'

Rayner did not reply. He wanted to hit him, like the man in the car, who had been trying to rape the girl. *My girl.*

'There will be an issue of rum shortly.' Rayner thought he heard or imagined a catch in Sherbrooke's voice, distorted as it was over the tannoy. 'I am very proud of you.'

Buck had joined them, in an unusually serious mood. 'That's what I like about him. No bullshit.' He did not look at the other pilot. 'Not like some!'

He would tell Andy about it when they next met. *Why am I so sure we will?* Don't write about it, *tell her.* She would understand, better than most, what it cost men who had to fight, and give, and keep on giving. Like the pilot called Jamie.

He leaned out to see all that he could. There was no cheering, nothing heroic or dramatic. They had lost some men they had known, but they had survived. Until the next action. And now there would be an extra rum ration. The silence made it all the more memorable, he thought. As he was about to turn away he saw two seamen coming around the after turret, who almost collided.

Obviously, they were seeing one another for the first time since the cease-fire gongs had sounded. One was carrying a broom, the other a canvas bucket. But they stopped, oblivious to everyone else and to the silent, shrouded shapes laid by the rail to await burial, and then they shook hands, as if they were meeting on a street or in some country lane. Rayner thought he would tell her that, too. It said it all.

Surgeon Commander Farleigh stood by the chart room door, and observed the activities of some seamen clearing up broken glass. He was still wearing his white coat, and there were spots of blood on it.

He said, 'Two amputations, sir. I did not count the cuts and bruises brigade. They'll mend quickly enough.' He held out a list. 'Here are the others.'

Sherbrooke reached out for it, but Stagg, who was sitting on the chart locker, said, 'Here, let me see it.'

Sherbrooke watched the flecked eyes moving over the list.

Stagg asked, 'And my flag lieutenant died instantly?'

Farleigh regarded him without expression. 'He was directly beneath the point of impact, sir.' He sounded almost surprised at the question. 'An explosion like that would leave nothing of the body. Total disintegration. Oblivion.'

Stagg nodded gravely, and returned the list to Sherbrooke.

'I see. I shall write to his father, the admiral. A sad loss. I shall tell him what a promising officer Stephen Howe turned out to be.'

Sherbrooke glanced through the list, able to put faces to most of the names, and recalling Stagg's vicious comments on Lieutenant Howe. A violent, terrible death had given the 'jellyfish' unexpected status.

Stagg stood up. 'I shall be down aft if you need me,' and to the surgeon, 'Good work.'

Sherbrooke heard someone laugh, probably in the W/T office; the shock was dissipating.

He saw the correspondent writing rapidly in his notebook. He seemed to feel Sherbrooke's gaze, and looked up, his eyes like slate in the reflected glare.

'Not too many casualties, Captain? In those circumstances you might have suffered far worse, I'd have thought.'

He recalled *Montagu*'s failure to acknowledge the order to avoid action, and later, Stagg's insistence that *Reliant* should remain on the same course. But for the gunnery department's quick observations and reactions, *Reliant* could have been crippled before a target had been selected. *Could have been. Might have been . . .*

He was tired and feeling the strain, a bruising of mind and body, like that evening in London after the bomb had fallen.

He said, 'I accept that. Did you get what you wanted?'

Drury looked away.

'More than enough. I recorded some of it, but the first message will tell my people what to expect . . . what to do.'

Sherbrooke said, 'You make it sound easy.' His hands were very steady, something he observed without emotion.

'We can't afford to clutter up valuable space on naval

250

wireless, Captain. We use codes, a bit like your chaps.'

A messenger called, 'Chaplain requests permission to come to the bridge, sir.'

Sherbrooke saw Yorke, the yeoman of signals, pause in polishing his telescope and give a grimace. They all knew what that was for.

Sherbrooke said, 'Ask him to wait, please. I have things to do at the moment.'

Drury raised his book as though he had found something else to write, and then decided against it. He looked instead at the broken glass, the smoke still rising above the place where he had felt and heard the shell explode. He had thought for a moment that the whole bridge would go. He must have dropped to his knees, a reaction born of experience, just by being with, and watching, men at war. Men with faces slashed by flying glass, somebody screaming, and screaming, until he could feel his mind cringe from the sound as if in physical pain.

When he had opened his eyes again, Sherbrooke had been by the voicepipes with the navigating officer; order had been returning; the effects of the explosion and another alongside were being assessed and dealt with. He almost smiled. *I have things to do at the moment.*

And he had seen the signals petty officer they called a yeoman make a disparaging face at one of his team. They shared the humour and the reason for the joke; they knew, also, that Sherbrooke would be down there with them when the bodies went over the side. It would make a moving story, broadcast, and in print.

He said casually, 'I understand you know somebody in the D.O.I., Captain?'

He felt Sherbrooke's eyes settle on him. 'Yes.'

Stagg must have been talking. Surprisingly, he felt no resentment. It could not hurt her.

Drury understood. He was not getting any more. Yet.

'Signal in W/T, sir. Immediate.'

Drury watched the grave profile for some revelation of strain or anxiety.

Sherbrooke said, 'Tell them to send it up right away.'

Frazier appeared on the bridge, his white uniform as filthy as any stoker's. He had come to report the damage which he had investigated for himself.

The C.P.O. Telegraphist, Cliff Elphick, who had been born and raised in Rutland, which was about as far as you could get from the sea in England, brought the signal in person.

Sherbrooke took it, remembering all the others.

Frazier said, 'Shall I inform the admiral, sir?'

Sherbrooke looked at him, and then smiled. 'Not yet, John.' He opened it, and said, 'It's addressed to *Reliant*. The ship.'

He listened to the beat of engines, the muffled clatter of hammers, the sound of temporary repairs.

Soon he would go and bury their dead.

He said, 'It's from the Commander-in-Chief, on board H.M.S. *Warspite*.'

Yorke's leading signalman would like that; he had served in the old *Warspite*. He glanced around at their faces, seeing only the ship, another veteran.

'It reads, *Congratulations Reliant. You turned the tide. They're on the run.*' He folded the signal. '*Ends.*'

Only Admiral Cunningham, the C-in-C, would find the time to make a signal like that. He had never forgotten what it was like; what it cost.

'Take over, Pilot.' He looked at Frazier. 'Come with me. We'll tell the admiral together.'

Drury watched them leave. He had enough for the moment; anything else would be an intrusion. He grinned, and dragged a shred of cloth from his torn sleeve. *Even for me.*

14

No Turning Back

Andrea Collins paused by a window that overlooked the hospital driveway and adjusted some flowers in a vase, left, she thought, by a visitor. In this place, a touch of colour was always welcome.

She could see her reflection faintly in the window, and made certain that her hair was properly confined. Not too flippant, as one old matron had called it.

She was aware of warmth on her skin through the glass, the sun brilliant on these drab buildings, the shrubs, and the clothing of a few visitors who were getting into the bus that would take them to the station. They were parents, for the most part: few of the men who were brought here seemed to be married. And they all had the same anxious, drained faces. She often wondered if they were more concerned for themselves than those whom they were visiting.

She turned and looked back along the passageway at the line of doors, where the smell of fresh paint marked the retreat of the carpenters and workmen who had finally completed a whole new wing. She had noticed that most of the patients avoided contact of any kind with the workmen. As if they were ashamed of what they had become, afraid of kindness, or the eyes of people they did not know or see every day.

The construction of an additional wing meant more

casualties were expected. Here they could offer better facilities, and a saline bath unit equal to the one where she had trained, at East Grinstead. It seemed a million years ago now.

She thought of the letter she had received from the Canadian airman, although she had no idea where it had begun its travels. He had been careful to say nothing about the climate or anything else that might arouse the attention of a censor.

She had read it several times and was still surprised that it had moved her so much. It was a sincere, simple letter, but it had been like hearing him talk. A strong, outwardly confident naval officer; she had seen that strength that night at the hotel when the 'respectable citizen' had attacked her. He never mentioned the incident any more, as if he wanted to shield her from the memory, and had never seemed to expect any gratitude for what he had done. But there was also a sort of gentleness, which came through in his letter, a quality she had found rare in the young men who came and went here, who wanted only to be again as they had been once, and could not come to terms with what they were.

Dick Rayner had been more concerned about his dead crewman than himself. He had seemed unable to accept it, to leave the blame elsewhere. She had heard some of them making jokes about death. *What did you expect? D'you want to live forever?* Or, *you shouldn't have joined if you can't take a joke!* Maybe it helped them in some way, callous though it seemed.

She paused at another window; the bus had gone. As if to a signal, two figures in blue dressing gowns emerged from the opposite building and walked amongst the flowers, as if they hadn't a care in the world. She knew them both, and had been proud of the courage with which

255

they had ticked off the dates as their transfer to a final recuperation hospital drew near.

One of them, a veteran of twenty-one, had told her, 'You have to see the world through your own eyes. It hasn't changed. Try not to think what *they* see when they look at you!'

Did he really believe that?

Two nights ago, sitting in her small room with her feet bare after standing all day, she had been half-listening to her wireless, and the well-modulated tones of the announcer recounting the latest news of the war in North Africa. He had mentioned some of the ships which had been taking part, and she had heard *Reliant*'s name mentioned, and that she had been involved. No details, not when, where or why; but she had sat upright in her chair, shocked, and deeply apprehensive.

The following day, the news had broken in every headline around the country. The German forces and their Italian allies in North Africa had surrendered: the legendary Afrika Korps was defeated. As Churchill proclaimed, 'Africa is ours!'

What would it mean now? The new wards and operating theatres told their own story. There would be an allied invasion somewhere. Wherever it was, there would be more casualties . . . many more.

She heard somebody whistling softly and, without looking, knew it was Nobby, one of the senior orderlies. He must have another name, but to everybody from surgeon to trainee nurse and to the patients themselves, he was simply Nobby.

'Hello, Sister! I was just thinkin' about you!' He regarded her cheerfully. 'I often does, of course!'

A Londoner. How he had arrived up here in Scotland was another mystery.

'Trouble, Nobby?'

He shrugged. 'The usual. Some ambulances are coming in. We just had the buzz about them, but everything's lined up an' ready.' Then he grinned. 'That young feller who come 'ere to see you, Sister. The Canadian chap?'

'What about him?' She tried to remain calm. It was like hearing the news on the wireless.

Nobby beamed at her. '*Reliant*, the battlecruiser, right?'

'Yes.'

'She's *in*, Sister! 'Ere, back in Rosyth!'

'But how can that be? I heard just a few days ago that the ship was involved in the North African campaign. I *heard* it.'

'Well, she's 'ere now, large as life. I 'eard *that*. One of the drivers told me. Bit knocked about, she is – probably 'ere for repairs.'

She stared at him. *How badly knocked about?* She thought of the announcer's voice and the glaring headlines. *Africa is ours*. It was suddenly meaningless.

One of the senior surgeons appeared in the passageway, and glanced at her over his glasses.

'Ah, Sister Collins. Glad you're still about. I know you should have been off duty an hour ago. But these ambulances. Got waylaid somewhere. Can't rely on anything.' He always spoke in short, staccato sentences, even in the operating theatre.

'That's all right. I – I was just saying . . .'

He peered at her. 'Been overdoing it? I've had my eye on you. No good to anybody if you crack up.' He broke off and stared out of the window. 'Here they are. I wonder what the excuse will be this time.' He strode away, calling over his shoulder, 'Get things started, Nobby!'

The orderly said, 'Course, sir,' then he looked at her again. 'I reckon 'e's right, though, for once. You 'ave been on the go, ever since that disgusting court case. We'd 'ave known what to do with the likes of '*im* down in Paddington Green!'

It was a well-practised drill. The ambulances wheeling into line, orderlies and nurses with lists, and one doctor on the steps, hands in pockets to show how calm he was.

It did not take long; there were only seven of them, two in wheelchairs, the others being guided toward the steps, the nurses chatting inconsequentially. It was something to which they had had to become accustomed, no matter what they saw or felt.

Then the orderlies with the few bags and items of personal clothing. Something these men always clung to, to give them reality and purpose and identity, when their world had exploded.

Doors opening, the murmur of voices. Thank God all the visitors had departed. It was bad enough without witnesses. The way the burned and wounded looked around, as if seeking something familiar, nodding to acknowledge what was said, one staring at the floor, not wanting to see or to be seen.

She said, 'Well, Nobby, it looks as though we're going to need the extra space.'

Nobby grimaced. 'Least it's not bloody well rainin', makes a change for this place.' Then he said sharply, ''Ere, what is it? 'Old on, I'll get someone!'

She barely heard him; she was looking at the clothing draped over one of the other orderlies' arms. Not pale blue like most of them, but dark, like *his*, with two wavy gold stripes on the sleeve. Like his.

The man halted and looked anxiously at Nobby. *'What?'*

She stepped forward and lifted the sleeve of the uniform jacket. It was not a dream. She saw the gold pilot's wings above the curl.

A phone was ringing somewhere, and Nobby was saying, 'For Christ's sake, get somebody!'

Another nurse was here, with one arm around her waist, as he had done that night beside the car. 'Andy, love, what's the matter?'

She tried again. *I must go to him. He must know I'm here*. But no words would come.

She felt Nobby touching her arm, heard him saying, 'There's a call for you, Sister. If you want me to get rid of 'im, say the word!' He was peering around. 'Like a bloody copper, you can never find a doctor when you needs one!'

She shook her head and gripped the phone. She must hold on. Not let him see her like this. *He needs me now*.

'Yes?'

Rayner's voice was right in her ear, as if they were standing close together.

'It's me, Andy! The bad penny!' He hesitated. 'Is this a bad time? I'm sorry, Andy . . . I just wanted you to know . . .'

She was crying and laughing in the same breath. 'It's not! It's a perfect time! Don't go away!'

When he spoke again, his voice was very even, gentle. As if he were here, and had seen it for himself, and understood.

'I'll never go away. I've thought about you so much . . .' The slightest pause. 'I love you, girl.'

As though from another planet, she heard someone calling her name. She straightened her back, and tried to smile at Nobby and the nurses.

'Come for me tomorrow. I'm free.'

'Sister Collins, please!'

She said softly, 'Thank you so much for calling.' She replaced the telephone and walked quickly to the open door. A swift glance at the little card, and she stepped into the room.

'Well, what's it to be? Do I call you Lieutenant Carter, or just Paul?'

She did not look at the uniform jacket on the chair: she dared not. One bandaged hand reached out and covered hers.

For him, it was a beginning. For her, it had been a very close thing.

The dockyard manager was a short, almost squat man, hardened to the demands and the suspicions of naval officers, particularly the captains of the various ships that passed through his hands for repair and overhaul. The list was endless, the work equally so. Ships bombed or torpedoed, others almost cut in halves, having been rammed in convoy on pitch-black Atlantic nights, and always the work was urgent, vital, and any delay was looked upon as a betrayal of the war effort.

Apart from that, there were the dockyard workers: men dragging their feet to obtain overtime pay, union representatives plaguing him with complaints, even threats of strike action. No wonder sailors hated them. *They* took all the risks, with precious little to show for it on their pay days.

But that was not his concern. Repair the ships, turn them round as soon as possible, and make room for the next casualties.

He sat in one of the chairs in the captain's quarters, watching as *Reliant*'s commanding officer turned over each page of his report. Men like Captain Sherbrooke had no idea what dockyard managers and engineers had to contend with, he thought. A captain could say 'jump' and a man would jump, to another, 'do this,' and he would do it without question. Another world.

He said abruptly, 'Most of the damage is in the forrard superstructure. It's all there in my report.' He glanced around the cabin. It was comfortable, restful, after the noise and dirt of the yard. Hard to believe that men had died in this ship. But then, it always surprised him how the navy always managed to tidy up after a bombing or a battle.

Sherbrooke looked at him. 'Some of the plating is too thin. It's an old story, but nobody ever seems to hear it.'

The manager concealed his surprise. It was not usual for a four-ringed skipper to criticize the system.

He said, 'I worked on *Reliant* as a lad, you know. Even then, I used to hear the old gaffers saying the battlecruisers were too thinly armoured. Jutland proved them right.' He peered around again, seeing with the eyes of the past. 'I can remember when they brought *Reliant* here for a refit and reconstruction. She was in and out several times, and the story was always the same. More armour plating, but never enough. We were proved right, though. *Reliant* and *Renown* are the only two left now.'

Sherbrooke closed the file. 'How long will it take?'

'Month, maybe more, maybe less. It all depends on the resources and the priorities.' He eyed him resentfully. 'Can't perform miracles, you know.'

Petty Officer Long appeared by the pantry and glanced meaningly at the clock.

Sherbrooke looked at his visitor. 'A drink, perhaps?'

He smiled for the first time. 'I wouldn't say no, Captain.'

Sherbrooke listened to the dockyard noises outside the hull, rivet guns and saws, drills and rattling cranes. Some of the other ships here looked as if they might never move again.

He thought of the bombardment, the crash of a direct hit on Stagg's bridge, the splinter holes, which he had seen for himself, like knives through butter. The guns and the waterline were protected up to a point, but high-velocity shells, dropping like those which had destroyed *Montagu*, were something very different. He had said as much to the rear-admiral. Stagg had been reading the newspapers with obvious pleasure. One headline said of *Reliant*'s swift action, *The fighting admiral does it again! Stagg shows his horns!*

Stagg had said, 'Operation *Sackcloth* was a success, everybody knows that now. The C-in-C followed it up. Sink, burn and destroy! Let nothing pass! That was Operation *Retribution*, and it worked! You can't fight a war with promises – we fight it *with what we've got!* You of all people must know that!'

It was hopeless. *Reliant* could not be spared for a long refit: Stagg was right about that, at least. Sicily would be the next obvious point at which to attack, and invade, the enemy. A month? Two at the most, before the weather changed sides again.

The dockyard manager was enjoying his Scotch. 'Good stuff, Captain. You do well for yourselves, and no mistake!'

Sherbrooke smiled. 'No drydocking, then?'

Their eyes met. 'I'll see what I can do.'

Sherbrooke saw him to the door and they shook hands.

If they kept out of dock, *Reliant* could still run a daily routine, and remain as a unit. An empty ship at the mercy of the dockyard was without life.

Frazier could arrange local leave, and longer periods for those overdue for visiting their homes in other parts of the country. But *Reliant* would remain a living ship. That was what really mattered.

Long was busy clearing up his drinks cabinet, glad that Pat Drury had left the ship. Hopefully for good, in his view.

He asked guardedly, 'Will you be taking some leave, sir?'

Sherbrooke said, 'I should think that's unlikely. I don't want anybody making excuses that a job can't be done properly because the skipper's away enjoying himself!'

Stagg would be going to London. *The fighting admiral* would be in great demand.

Frazier tapped on the open door and entered. He looked tired, strained, as if contact with the land was a burden rather than a blessing.

'Postman's been aboard, sir.' He put a letter and an official-looking envelope on the desk.

Sherbrooke picked up the letter. He knew Frazier was watching him, waiting without being obvious about it until he opened the other envelope.

Sherbrooke read the document slowly and exclaimed, 'Bloody good show, John. Rayner's gong has come through. He's to go to London.' He looked up, pleased more than he could say. 'He'll get it from HM the K in person!'

Frazier said, 'I'm glad.' Then he hesitated. 'Because you put him up for it, sir.' Again, the smallest pause. 'I think you should have got something.'

Sherbrooke said, 'Forget it, John. We get our share.'

Frazier looked at the clock. 'I have to see some request-men. All the usual, I expect. My wife is coming up for a few days. But I'll be available at any time, sir . . . you know that.'

He said gently, 'Yes. I know.'

Long said, 'Admiral's secretary to see you, sir.'

Frazier left, and Lieutenant Villar strode briskly into the cabin.

'I just wanted to know if there's anything you might need, sir. I shall be going to London with Rear-Admiral Stagg.' He did not conceal his surprise. Stagg rarely took anybody with him.

'I'm glad you're quite recovered. It was very bad down there.'

Villar gazed past him, apparently at the ship's crest. 'Yes, sir. Still can't remember much about it.' He indicated a large folder held under his arm. 'I've gathered some of Sub-Lieutenant Forbes's gear together. I'll have it sent to his parents. He was only standing a few feet from me when it happened. Makes you think, doesn't it?'

And if Stagg had been there, as he should have been, he too might be dead.

Villar was saying, 'I'll be glad to get away for a few days, sir. I spend more time in an office here than I would in barracks ashore!'

Long followed the lieutenant out and closed the door ostentatiously behind them, leaving Sherbrooke alone.

He slit open the envelope and unfolded the letter. Her handwriting was very unfamiliar.

Dear Guy, I am taking some time off. They tell me I'm due for it.

He could hear her voice in her writing, and sensed that she had been nervous when she had written this. She was probably regretting it now.

I can come and see you if you think that might be easier. Things have happened. I had some news about my husband. She never spoke of him by name. *I have been reading a lot about you lately. What you did.* He could almost feel the hesitation. *I'm so proud of you, I really am. I would love to see you again. Soon.*

There was a sharp tap at the door. 'Captain of the dockyard, sir!'

Sherbrooke folded the letter with care and put it inside his jacket. She was coming. He tried to examine his feelings. Her husband was alive, otherwise she would have said that he was dead. It would make all the difference. It must.

Long opened the outer door, and the tannoy intruded noisily, 'Leave for the starboard watch from 1600 to 2230, Chief and Petty Officers until midnight. Duty part of the Port Watch will muster for fire drill at 1430.'

Sherbrooke stood up to meet his visitor, and felt his hand brush the steel bulkhead. *A living ship*. And Emma had written to him. If either of them had wanted to, there was now no turning back.

Lieutenant James Villar lit a cigarette and thought of his forthcoming trip to London. Until a new flag lieutenant was appointed, he would be doubly important to the admiral. There were endless possibilities in this.

He looked at the folder and then touched it, preparing himself, searching for the risks, considering what could go wrong.

He did not mix much with the other wardroom officers, and he knew they regarded him as a spy in their midst. He accepted that, and actually enjoyed it. Where Stagg was concerned, Villar kept his ears and eyes wide open, and his mouth shut. That had been poor Howe's problem. Too high an opinion of himself, always making suggestions and offering advice. An admiral's son, maybe, and from an illustrious naval family, but he hadn't a clue about men like Stagg. He smiled. Howe had not even realized that one of the reasons Stagg disliked him was because he was several inches taller than himself. Absurd? Not with men like Stagg.

There was a tap at the office door.

'Enter!' He leaned back, letting the cigarette smoke filter straight up into the vent.

It was the young seaman, Mowbray, looking strangely different in his best uniform, and not the usual working gear.

'You sent for me, sir?'

Villar nodded. 'Shut the door. Sit down if you like.'

Mowbray did not sit down, but stood gazing around the office as if it were completely new to him, although he had worked here for Villar, and had been united here with his friend.

'Going on leave, I understand. Guildford – that's in Surrey, isn't it?'

The young face seemed to return with difficulty to reality.

'Yes, sir. Seven days.'

'Good. I was concerned about you after we broke off the action.'

It sounded good, he decided. Authentic: the old campaigner.

Mowbray smiled faintly. 'It was kind of you to visit me in sickbay, sir. I – I was surprised. You see, I never . . .'

Villar watched the smoke. 'It was quite understandable. You'd never been in combat before. Then losing your friend like that . . .' He watched each word going home. What that robot Evershed would call the *fall of shot*. 'Matter of fact, I've just been collecting some of his personal belongings. I was recovering some of the files I had given him to study. For his new duties. However . . .'

He saw Mowbray's eyes on the folder, well used and stained in crayon. It had been in the bottom of the subbie's suitcase.

He pulled one of the tapes loose, feeling the eyes watching each move. Fascinated. Afraid.

'You once told me you were an artist. But, of course, some people say things just to impress.' He opened the file. 'These drawings are good. Some would judge them excellent.' He looked at him calmly. 'If a trifle explicit for some tastes.'

266

'He was a good artist, sir.' His shoulders seemed to sag. 'Very good.'

'I can see that. This one of you, for instance – rather daring, wouldn't you say?'

'We often modelled for each other, sir. It was the only way to . . .'

Villar leaned forward in his chair. 'I'm not judging or probing, but you must see, Mowbray, that others *might*, if these fell into the wrong hands. Forbes was young, but he was an officer. This sort of . . . involvement . . . is not accepted or tolerated in the service. Even you must realize that.'

'Yes, sir.'

Villar felt his muscles relax slightly. 'And you *were* involved, weren't you?'

'We were friends.' There was no defiance, no sort of challenge.

'And there is a photograph of you, Mowbray, one he used to finish the drawing, right?'

'Yes, sir.' He looked up suddenly, his eyes brilliant, pleading. 'If his family found out, even thought there was any kind of . . .' He could not continue.

Villar smiled. 'I don't know why I'm doing this, Mowbray. But I shall see that these pictures are placed somewhere secure.' He placed the photograph on one side. 'This one I will keep.'

Mowbray left the office. What could he do? Who could he turn to? Nobody would believe him. His eyes filled with tears of anger and despair. And Peter would be disgraced, even in death.

He heard voices, someone laughing, and saw Glander, the master-at-arms, talking to a group of seamen and a petty officer, all of whom were wearing white belts and webbing gaiters. Then he remembered hearing about it on the messdeck. A man who had deserted the ship when they had been in Greenock had been found and arrested, and was being held to await an escort.

He could see it, in his shocked and troubled mind. Being dragged back on board in handcuffs, being humiliated and hated by everyone.

Glander said, 'What's up, my son? You look like a bloke who's lost a quid and found a tanner!'

The others grinned. They didn't give a damn. They had been in action and some men had been killed; two had lost their legs. He had watched them being carried ashore at Gibraltar on the way back. And it was as if nothing had happened, as if death could never touch them. It was their way. Mowbray walked past them and straightened his uniform, ready for the inspection of libertymen.

So why not me? None of it was my fault. I did it for Peter, and now he's dead.

He knew what Villar expected, what he was really like. He had known when they had first met. There was always a Villar around, officer or not.

Glander saw him walk away. 'We'll have to watch that one, Ted.'

The Regulating Petty Officer, always known as the Crusher, grinned broadly.

'What, you, Master? I thought your weakness was women!'

They both roared with laughter. They had seen it all.

They lay side by side on the bed, their small, private world confined to a circle of light from a solitary lamp. The girl was propped on one elbow, her hand on his shoulder, her fair hair almost silver in the lamplight.

There was a great sense of peace between them, and a new awareness, which their nudity only enhanced. Only beyond the circle of light was the other part of the story, the embrace, the lingering disbelief that it was happening to them. A pillow knocked onto the floor, his uniform jacket tossed carelessly onto a chair, her stockings across his shirt.

The flat was above a dentist's surgery and waiting room, comfortably furnished, and yet vaguely old-fashioned in some way. There was a photograph of an R.A.F. officer in the next room.

As she had closed and locked the door behind them, he had asked, 'A flier?' Something to say, more than any curiosity or suspicion.

She had replied, 'No. He's a wingless wonder at some bomber station down in Kent. His wife owns this place. She adores him. Even though he can't keep his hands off all the little Waafs!'

Then she had said, 'Just hold me, will you. I can't believe it, can you?'

The food and the wine he had bribed out of the wardroom pantry were still in the other room, untouched. The rest was still pounding through him like a receding madness. He had held her on the bed, torturing himself while he had explored her, before lifting her against his body.

Neither could withstand the ferocity of desire. She had wrapped her arms round his neck and had kissed him hard, and harder still.

'I can't wait!' She had been gasping. 'Can't wait!'

He knew he must have hurt her, and she had cried out when he had entered her, their bodies one, until, completely spent, they had lain together, unmoving, each unwilling to part from the other. He saw her looking down at him, her left breast slightly reddened where he had kissed and sucked it.

She said, 'I wanted it to last forever . . . but I couldn't

wait. I wanted you to go on and on, to take me any way you wanted.' She smiled, as though remembering something. 'You're quite a man, you know.'

She leaned over him, and he knew she was looking at the scar in his groin where the splinter had pierced him. She caressed it, and said, 'I'd kill anyone who did this to you.'

He smiled. The curve of her back, the shadow between her breasts, the secret hair where he had found and taken her. 'I couldn't wait, either.'

Then he said, 'My jacket. I have to get it.'

'No.' She slid from the bed and walked into the shadows. He did not see her hesitate as she folded the jacket over her bare arm, and touched the pilot's wings.

She must have come to this place several times, with somebody . . . or maybe visiting the dentist who was married to the wingless wonder. She would have picked up that expression from some of her patients.

She gave him the jacket and knelt on the bed beside him. 'Secrets?'

'No.' He pulled out the small, flat case and gave it to her. 'You might not even like it, Andy.'

She looked over it at him, touched by the simplicity, the honesty of this man who was so refreshing after some of the line-shooters she had met.

She took it out of the box: it was a silver necklace, designed like overlapping leaves. He watched her holding it to the light, finding and opening the clasp.

He said, 'I got it in Gibraltar. The guy said it was Spanish silver. But if it's not your kind of thing . . .'

She held it out, her eyes shining. 'I love it, silly! Put it on for me.'

He fastened it at the nape of her neck and kissed her on one shoulder.

He said, 'I bet they won't let you wear that on duty!'

She faced him again, the necklace fitting closely below her throat.

She said, 'That was a lovely thing to do. You certainly know how to make a girl happy.'

He rested his head against her. 'I just wanted you to have something. So you could look at it sometimes, and remember me.'

She gripped his shoulder, afraid he would see the tears.

'It's beautiful.' She looked away. 'You spoke of London. Is it important?'

He thought of the way he had planned it. What he would say, how she would respond. Did it never happen according to plan?

'It's kind of hard to explain.' Then, 'I mean, it was no big deal.'

She stroked his arm. 'Tell me. I won't bite.'

He grinned, and afterwards she thought he looked embarrassed. 'They're giving me a medal.'

'*What?* Why didn't you tell me sooner?' She tried to look into his face. 'Who's giving you this medal?'

He touched her cheek and pushed some hair from her forehead.

'Well, I guess it's the King. That's what it says.'

Her voice was very low, muffled. 'And you want me to go to London for it. Is that what you're saying?'

He said, 'Well, there's more to it than that.'

'You want to seduce me?'

'That goes without saying.' He faced her, with sudden determination. 'I want to get a ring for you.'

'Do you really know if that's what you want?'

'I've always known it. You're my girl. I want to take this all the way. I want to marry you, Andy.'

'You mean it,' she said. 'Those eyes couldn't lie to save your life!'

271

She put her arms around him and hugged him, very tightly. 'What a perfect way to propose to a girl!'

'Tomorrow I have to report back to the ship. I'll call you when I get all the info.' He lay back as she pushed him down flat on the crumpled sheet.

'That's tomorrow.' She climbed over and sat astride his body, her eyes never leaving his as she settled against him. 'I can see you're getting the message— in fact, I can feel it!' She moved against him, while he reached up to hold her. 'And this time I *will* make it last.'

The rest was lost as they came together.

The Bond

The first two weeks at Rosyth were anything but restful for *Reliant*'s ship's company, other than the lucky ones who were on leave. Every day the dockyard workers swarmed aboard as if solely intent on destroying rather than repairing the ship, while at other times disgruntled seamen and marines stood firm against the invasion, with paint and polish to cover up the worst of it.

For Sherbrooke, there had been no respite either. He had unexpectedly been requested to sit on a board of inquiry after a suspicious officer at the base had discovered that his stores of rum were seriously depleted. The inquiry had led almost inevitably to the formation of a court-martial. One officer and two petty officers were found to be involved. It was often said that more people were 'busted' over rum than anything else.

Emma's hoped-for visit had been postponed, but they had managed to speak on that notoriously busy line for a few minutes at a time. And then, quite suddenly, she had called him again. She was coming, but in a semi-official capacity, as Captain Thorne's assistant.

If he were being reasonable, he would have known that it was the right thing. Perhaps she had even arranged it herself. The facts were always there. She was a married woman, and her husband was a prisoner of war, probably existing under the worst conditions imaginable, if half the rumours were true.

Any attachment would be seen by others as just another sordid wartime affair. The wife who couldn't or wouldn't wait for her man to come home. Cruel, unfair, but it would stick.

And what of the naval officer who would take advantage of her, knowing as he did that it was dishonourable, and selfish beyond description? This way, at least, he would be able to see her without damaging her reputation. He was *Reliant*'s captain; there would be plenty of eyes watching for what might be regarded as a moral lapse, or something even less charitable. Under no circumstances would he allow her to be wounded by empty and stupid gossip.

As one officer had said at the court of inquiry, to do wrong is one thing; to continue to do it is another, and, for a trusted officer, is unforgivable.

Easy to say, when you were on that side of the table.

Perhaps they could find a few moments to be alone together.

And now there was the party, this very evening. Lieutenant Dick Rayner had returned from London with his Distinguished Service Cross, and a strange air of disbelief, as if it had all happened to somebody else.

Frazier had arranged the party to celebrate Rayner's decoration, but it was as if the whole ship was sharing it. Some Wrens from the base had been invited, as well as nurses from two hospitals, and a couple of wives. There would be some very costly mess bills afterwards.

Sherbrooke had said, 'Don't you think you could have waited a few more days, John? Rear-Admiral Stagg will be back by then.'

Frazier had given a tight little smile. 'You know, sir, I forgot all about that!'

And the war seemed very far away. After the surrender of German and Italian forces in North Africa, it had been a question of clearing up. Vehicles, equipment, guns and ammunition, and thousands of prisoners. The victory was complete.

When Stagg returned from London, there might be real news. The next move, and where.

They would be into June soon. It was easy to criticize, but Sherbrooke knew from first-hand experience that vacillation in war did not encourage success. To plan and begin such a large-scale operation as an invasion would be an awesome task, but every week that passed gave the enemy time to recover from defeat on one front, and to build up massive resistance and power on another. It seemed madness to delay until the weather worsened.

No matter where an invasion was launched, it would be left mainly to British, Canadian and American forces to execute. No such large-scale invasion had ever been undertaken before.

Sherbrooke was restless, even nervous, as the hour for the party approached. Frazier would let him know when it was timely for his captain to visit the wardroom, when the first skylarking was over, and when to leave, before the real bedlam began.

There would be several senior officers in attendance, and it was well known that the admiral commanding Rosyth and the coast of Scotland was extremely keen on parties.

He reflected on what they had all achieved together in *Reliant*. She was a happy ship, most would agree. There were the usual bad apples, persistent defaulters, the hard men, found in any ship. There were some who had been afraid when *Reliant*'s main armament had thundered out at the enemy, and others who had been able to contain it, conceal it, until the next time.

He thought about the wardroom, the junior officers like Drake the ex-barrister and Frost, the assistant navigator, and Steele, the lieutenant of marines, who entertained his gun crews with a tin whistle. Howe, the flag lieutenant who had been blasted into nothing, and the young subbie who had died close by, killed by a single splinter. It was as good a crowd of men and youngsters as you could hope to find in any big ship. He still shut it from his mind. He must not make comparisons. That was in the past. Gone.

His steward peered in at him. 'Sorry to disturb you, sir. Shore telephone call.' He scowled. 'In the lobby, I'm afraid. Some dockyard matey has severed a line!'

'Who is it, do you know?'

Long's face was expressionless. 'A lady, sir. I didn't get the name, wot with all the din!'

Sherbrooke walked quickly to the lobby where two workmen were finally clearing up their rubbish for the day.

One of them was whistling loudly until Long said bluntly, 'Unlucky to whistle on board a warship.'

The man grinned. 'To sailors, maybe!'

Long saw Sherbrooke pick up the telephone and hissed, 'Well, shut your gob while the Captain is speaking an' clear off!'

They went.

She said, 'It's me. I'm in the admiral's house. I hope it's all right, about my boss, I mean.'

He smiled. 'Just get here as soon as you can. It seems so long.'

'I know.'

Somewhere in the far distance he heard a bugle, and realized that the dockyard was silent, the workers making their way home. The manager who had been in charge of *Reliant*'s repairs, and who had once worked on her as a boy, was no doubt telling his wife all about it, what it was like to work alongside stuck-up naval officers who never lifted a finger themselves. If the relationship between sailors and dockyards ever changed, it would ruin everything.

He said, 'Any more news, Emma?'

'No.'

She was probably sick to death of being asked that question.

'I must go, Guy.' She was speaking very closely into the telephone. 'They're leaving now.' She was about to hang up when something made her add, 'I must be alone with you. To talk. To be together. That's not so wrong, is it?'

He did not get a chance to answer.

Long was waiting for him. 'All ready, sir? I'm glad for Mr Rayner, nice chap . . .' He realized what he had said and almost blushed. 'I'm sorry, sir, what I meant was . . .'

Sherbrooke touched his white sleeve. 'You were right. He *is* a nice chap!'

Long watched him leave. *Not too dusty yourself*, he thought.

Then he picked up his tray and made his way to the wardroom to give a hand. It was going to be a long evening.

'Excuse me, sir, but I think the admiral is about to leave.'

Lieutenant-Commander Rhodes, who was the O.O.D., grinned broadly. 'Again.'

Sherbrooke nodded. 'I'll be ready, Pilot. Have you managed to get a drink?'

Rhodes looked around at the shining faces, the stewards pushing manfully through the crowd with their trays. 'Just about, sir. Good party, I thought.'

Sherbrooke turned as he saw her coming through the

door, her eyes seeking his, sharing it, feeling it. She glanced quickly at her boss, Thorne, and then hurried to join him.

'I hate it, being here and not able to be with you.' She studied him, feature by feature. 'But I'm so glad I came. To see you as the captain.' And then, very quietly, 'My captain.' She shook her head, so that the long plait of hair shone in the bright overhead lights like a silk rope. 'No, don't say anything. I'm just being stupid. I blame myself . . . have done, ever since that day you went to the Admiralty. You were in Chelsea with me all night and I acted like a prude . . . a fool. And I'm paying for it now.' She looked at him again in her direct way. 'We both are.'

Frazier appeared from the other side of the wardroom, and said, 'Went well, sir.'

Sherbrooke looked at the young woman who had come with him, and was standing with her arm through his. Alison, Frazier's wife. She was almost doll-like, and very pretty, well dressed, and apparently very much at home in this noisy, mostly male gathering. She was not quite what Sherbrooke had been expecting, although he was not sure why. Perhaps because he only saw Frazier as the thorough, efficient second-in-command, a slightly withdrawn, self-contained man who needed time to make up his mind about everyone he met.

She said, 'A few thick heads tomorrow, I shouldn't wonder!' She looked at Emma, and said, 'You must see a lot of this kind of thing. I used to more than I do now, of course. With a young family to think of, and in wartime, you can never afford to relax too much.'

Frazier said quietly, 'One daughter, actually. It's hardly a brood.'

Sherbrooke saw the sharp exchange of glances. She said, 'Well, that's not my fault, is it?' She looked at Emma again. 'Do you have any family?'

Emma replied, 'No.'

Frazier's wife put one hand to her mouth. 'I'm so sorry, I forgot. Stupid of me. Your husband is a prisoner of war.'

Frazier took her arm. 'I want you to meet the Chief, Alison. He knows more about the ship than anybody!'

When they were again alone, Emma said, 'It seems everybody knows.' Then the shadow left her face. 'Your Commander Frazier certainly has his hands full there!'

The admiral and his guests were taking their leave. It would soon be over, and she would be going away with her chaperone. He could see Captain Thorne towering over two small Wren officers, his face creased with smiles as he launched into yet another dubious story.

Sherbrooke asked, 'What's he like? With you, I mean.'

'No trouble, really.' She touched his sleeve, and did not remove her hand. 'He means well, I suppose. There's nothing quite so damning, is there?'

She gazed past him, her eyes suddenly saddened. 'They look right together, don't they?'

Lieutenant Dick Rayner was standing with the nurse he had brought as his guest, as though completely alone with her. Sherbrooke had realized that what was between them was far deeper and stronger than mere friendship, seeing the way they looked at each other, the unspoken messages passing between them.

At one point in the evening, the admiral had made a short speech, something almost unknown for him.

He had spoken only briefly of Rayner's Distinguished Service Cross, which he had, indeed, received from the King himself in London.

Sherbrooke had seen Emma turn to look at him, and at the blue and white ribbon on his left breast. It had been impossible to guess what she was thinking for those few seconds. But, for Rayner, he had felt only envy.

The admiral had been saying, 'This was not some spectacular mission of the sort to which we have become accustomed recently. Perhaps for that very reason, it was all the more inspiring to the rest of us.'

Sherbrooke had watched the nurse with the short, fair hair grip Rayner's arm; had noticed the new ring on her finger, felt her emotion as the admiral had summed it up in his old-fashioned manner. 'For gallantry, skill and devotion to duty against a determined enemy, and although wounded himself, his concern for his crew remained paramount.' He had given a smile. 'Well done, sir!'

Sherbrooke looked now at the hand resting on his gold stripes. People would see, gossip, form conclusions.

He said, 'I have to deal with the admiral. I'll be as fast as I can.'

Frazier came back, without his wife. 'All right, Mrs Meheux?'

'Fine. It was good of you to arrange it.' The admiral had gone, and there was an outbreak of raucous cheering and laughter. She could see Thorne peering round, his audience of Wrens departed.

Frazier said, 'The Captain asked me to take you aft to his quarters.' He smiled awkwardly. 'My wife is there. Freshening up.'

'I'd like that.'

Frazier watched her looking around the wardroom as if to remember every aspect of it, every moment. Evershed, gesturing and stabbing the air with his hands, explaining the intricacies of muzzle-velocity in feet per second to a civilian who appeared to be past understanding anything. The Chief, glaring at strangers using the Club, and *his* chair. Drake, the pink-faced ex-barrister, and another lieutenant he had not immediately recognized. It was Frost, beardless and looking strangely furtive, enduring all the comments and the insults.

Frazier said, 'I was sorry just now . . . about my wife's comment on your husband. It was not intended.'

She looked at him, and thought what a nice man he was. Someone you could talk to, eventually.

Of course it was intended. 'Will you lead the way?'

She glanced around her. How still the ship was, a few figures moving in the shadows, the incessant clatter of glasses and plates from the officers' galley.

A sentry, leaning on a tiny desk, a revolver hanging from his belt, brought his heels together and said, 'All quiet, sir.' But his eyes were on her.

Frazier smiled. 'Thank you, Mason. There's a tot for you in the lobby.'

She sensed their familiarity, stronger than rank or status.

Frazier called back, 'And hide that trashy magazine before the Captain sees it!'

The deserted, white-painted passageways; the ship's crest; a photograph, certainly not a new one, of a football team, an unknown captain sitting in their midst.

'You've been aboard for some time, Commander?'

'Longer than most. I was with Captain Cavendish. You need to know, *really* know a ship this size.'

'What does your wife think about it?'

He glanced at her curiously. 'Alison? Well, she wants me to take promotion.' He laughed, but there was no life in it. 'A good shore job, with stewards running about after me like slaves!'

'Not for you?'

He paused and she saw the polished plate. *Captain.* 'I'd loathe it.'

They found Frazier's wife in the cabin, sitting, legs crossed, examining her make-up in a mirror. She did not look at them, but said over her shoulder, 'I hope you haven't forgotten, John. The admiral asked us to join his party. Are you ready?'

Frazier said, 'I'm waiting for the Captain.'

She gave a small shrug. 'I'm sure I don't know *what* they'd do without you!'

Emma saw Frazier's discomfort, and said, 'Are you staying long up here, Mrs Frazier?'

She smiled and made a little mouth into the mirror. 'A few more days, then back to the south.' She closed the compact with a snap. 'Civilization.'

The door opened and Sherbrooke stepped over the coaming and tossed his cap onto a chair. It fell on the deck but he did not seem to notice.

Alison Frazier said, 'We're all going to the admiral's house, Guy. Are you coming?' Her glance shifted to Emma, only for a moment, but it said everything.

Sherbrooke seemed to drag himself back from somewhere.

'No. I can't.' He looked at Frazier. 'Make excuses. I've something to deal with.'

Emma stood up and walked to another chair to give herself time. Even the use of his name was offensive. But she would not show her resentment. She picked up the cap and held it, remembering the dust and smoke, the great cascade of broken glass in the off-licence, the dead eyes staring from the floor.

Frazier seemed at a loss. 'I'm not all that keen, sir. I've sunk enough gin to float the *Queen Mary* as it is!' He tried to grin. 'All in the name of duty, of course!'

Sherbrooke said, 'I'll catch you up. Tell the O.O.D. for me.'

The door closed behind them, and he took her hands in his. 'Your faithful escort will be here before you know it, but I just wanted to see you alone. It's been bloody difficult, hasn't it?'

She waited, thinking of the closed door. The woman's amused, backward glance, and Frazier's discomfort. They could think what they liked. They would, anyway.

'What is it?'

'I want to hide, to be away from it with you. I think we've earned it.' He tightened his grip, as if afraid they would be interrupted. 'All evening I've been watching you, Emma. Imagined us together, as it might have been. Just now, when you turned your back, I thought of your hair, loose and across your shoulders, and with only me to see it.' He hesitated. 'More like a bumbling midshipman than the iron captain, eh?'

She leaned her head against his chest; he could feel her breathing, the pressure of her breast, the warmth of her.

'If it was honour that held us apart, it is love which defies even that!'

She laid her fingers on his lips as though to stop him, but he added, 'I'm not proud of the fact, but if I could take you from your husband, or anyone else, I would.'

There were voices outside, muffled by the door, the sound of someone singing.

She said, 'I'll have to leave when they do. Can't you come? Just to see you, to know you're there?'

Sherbrooke released her very gently. 'No. I really do have something to deal with.'

The door opened and Thorne made a great show of peering around it.

'Just being discreet, old boy!' He glanced between them, but his eyes did not focus very well. 'Don't want to be a spoil-sport!'

Then he stared around, his jovial confidence deflated. 'Point me towards the heads, will you? Won't be a tick!'

Alone again, they faced one another beneath the ship's crest.

She said, 'Come to me again, Guy. Like we promised?'

'And you take care of yourself.'

She lifted her face.

'Kiss me. As you would. As you wanted to.'

It was impossible to know how long it lasted, but it seemed as if they had been lovers over and beyond time itself.

Then she stood back and wiped her lipstick from his mouth with gentle fingers. 'That *would* make people talk!'

Sherbrooke heard Long's voice from the other cabin. So he knew about it. *About us*.

Long was saying, 'Here we go, sir, nice an' easy like!' Then they heard Thorne's slurred reply, and Long said, 'The old ship's rolling a bit tonight, sir, an' no mistake!'

She looked up at Sherbrooke again, torn between laughter and tears.

Sherbrooke watched Long guiding the other captain through the door.

'He's quite incorrigible, that one.'

She was looking through the other door, at the neatly made bunk, the reading light, and his enemy, the telephone. His world, which she could never share.

He saw her eyes, and took her arm. 'I know, Emma. I know.'

After he had seen them down the brow to the waiting cars, he returned to his cabin and removed his jacket, as if he hated it. Long came and went without any comment, but left a decanter by the blotter on the desk.

The party slowly faded to an end, and the last visitors left or were half-carried ashore. Thorne was not the only one who was upset by the ship's 'rolling'.

He thought about her, even as his eyes skimmed through

his notes, thinking of her here, right here, in the cabin. And in Chelsea: how it might have been.

He sighed and massaged his eyes, and then began reading once again. Perhaps he had missed something. No captain could afford carelessness.

He poured another drink and knew he had had too much.

He stood up and paced around the cabin and heard Long give a discreet cough in his pantry. He slid open the hatch and said, 'Go and turn in. You must be dog-tired. God, it must be a mess in the wardroom!'

Long, framed in his little pantry hatch, regarded him gravely. 'The last for a bit, probably, eh, sir?'

Sherbrooke glanced at the desk, the pile of papers. No, he had not missed anything.

Long disappeared, and the ship was in silence when Frazier came aft to the cabin.

Sherbrooke did not remember any knock, or how long Frazier had been sitting there.

Stupidly he said, 'You're back then?'

Frazier glanced at the decanter and the empty glass. 'Thought I should, sir. If you don't need me, I'd better go to the hotel.'

Sherbrooke nodded, then touched his mouth, where her lipstick had been. 'What the hell is the time, anyway?'

Frazier smiled. 'About three, sir.'

'Christ!'

Frazier said quietly, 'Is something wrong, sir?'

'Wrong? Why should there be?' He attempted to stand but it was too much for him. He was tired, strained to the limit, and quite drunk.

He said, 'We shall be leaving the yard.' He pushed the signal across the desk. 'Here, read it for yourself. It came when the admiral was going ashore.'

Frazier made himself look at the signal. 'I'll not be sorry

to leave, sir. Get back to sea.' Then he exclaimed, 'It's three weeks earlier than expected. I never thought those idle sods would get the new plating fitted in time!'

Sherbrooke stared at him, and remembered what she had said about Frazier's pretty wife. *Got his hands full there*. He replied, 'Because *they're not going to do it!* Take too long. Can't spare the time. You know the bloody excuses – you should do, by now!'

Frazier persisted, 'I don't understand, sir. They agreed to the report. It was all arranged.'

'It was overruled apparently, John. At Rear-Admiral Stagg's insistence.'

Frazier ran his fingers through his hair. It made him look about twenty.

'I suppose he must know what he's doing?'

Sherbrooke stood up very carefully. 'Well, I don't, and neither, I suspect, do you!'

Petty Officer Long appeared as if by magic, wide awake, and still in a spotless white jacket.

'Time for a doss-down, sir?'

Frazier took one arm and Long the other. If Long had not still been around, he would have had to manage somehow.

They must have looked like three tipsy libertymen returning from a very wet run ashore.

Frazier said, 'I must make a shore call, Long. I'll be staying aboard tonight.' He grinned. 'What's left of it!'

He paused at the door and saw Long swing Sherbrooke's legs up on to the bunk. He did not switch off the light. He had heard about that custom from somebody.

He had never seen the captain the worse for drink before, and was surprised that he was moved by it in some way.

Long let out a deep breath. 'You'll have a head on you

in the morning, Captain!' He smiled. He was human, anyway. The nice little party who'd been with him would see him all right.

He glanced around the cabin and said quietly, 'Off again, old girl. No peace for the wicked, is there?'

There was a little brandy left in the decanter and he carried it with him to the pantry.

It went with the job.

Rear-Admiral Vincent Stagg sipped some coffee and grimaced. 'Muck! Don't they teach people anything these days?'

Sherbrooke glanced around the big cabin. It looked as if it had been hit by a whirlwind: uniforms on hangers waiting to be stowed away, golf clubs and a case of wine, and almost every chair was covered with files and signal folders. He had seen the admiral's secretary hurrying back to his office, his arms filled with other material relating to the ship's readiness, or lack of it.

Stagg looked at him curiously. 'You've done well while I've been away, Guy. Knew you would.' He wrinkled his broken nose. 'Whole ship stinks of paint, most of it still wet, by the look of it. You'll have to have a quiet word with Frazier. Too much harbour time, that's their problem. Practically gone native!'

'It's been a rush, sir. I'm still not happy about . . .' He stopped as Stagg's chief steward appeared in response to the bell on the desk.

'Sir?' Price sounded wary.

Stagg said, 'More coffee. I'd have something stronger, but the sun's hardly over the yardarm yet!' He laughed shortly. 'Not even for me!' He glanced down at some papers. 'I hear the party went off all right. For that Canadian chap, what's-his-name?'

'Rayner, sir.'

Sherbrooke watched him: he was on edge about something. The rest was bluff.

'I'm told the admiral was pleased. Good show. And what about replacements for the men killed in the Med? Your job, I know all about that, but I'd like to *know*.'

'Still two to come, sir.' He waited while Stagg searched for his cigar case. 'Did you find another flag lieutenant when you were in London?'

Stagg shrugged. 'More or less. He'll be joining us later. Good record, and the right background. We'll have to see.'

Price came and went; the coffee remained untouched.

'You'll hear soon enough, Guy, but it's right at the top of the secret list. It's to be Sicily, no surprise to us, of course, but the brains of Whitehall intend to provide a few diversions to keep the enemy guessing. It will be hard, no matter how it goes. But *it must work*. Everything will depend on this first step and the navy's role will be paramount. Nothing new in that, but I want every man jack to know it!'

'We will begin to reammunition tomorrow, sir.'

Stagg was not listening. 'I was reading the dockyard report.' He gave him a searching glance. 'And your comments about it. I must be frank, I thought they were well out of line. Not what I would have expected, from you, anyway.'

So that was it. Sherbrooke said, 'I thought . . . I still believe that the refit and repairs were skimped. Our last engagement showed what kind of damage we might expect. Frankly, sir, I think it puts the ship at risk.'

'Do you?' He smiled. 'This from the man who goes hell-for-leather against a German cruiser, and then practically stops the ship to pick up three men. Now that I *would* call a risk!'

'Justified, sir.'

Stagg stood up, and ignored the papers which fell from his lap.

'*Reliant* is a good appointment for you, Guy. What you needed, maybe more than you realized. I've seen what the other business did to you. I understood, but you know as well as I do that where I am concerned, the rap stops here. You command my flagship, and I know I'm not all that easy to serve under. That can't concern us. The next months, weeks even, are vital, and I don't just mean to the progress of the war. Later on, perhaps, *Reliant* can go into dock for a proper overhaul, *but not now!*'

'Is there something else, sir?'

Stagg sat down and stared at the papers around his feet.

'Between us, Guy, I'm not even sure myself!' He grinned suddenly, as he did when he was speaking with some dumbfounded sailor on his unofficial rounds. 'I may not be staying in *Reliant* for much longer. It depends . . .' He shrugged. 'Well, it *depends* – let's leave it at that.'

Sherbrooke said, 'Another flag officer is taking over?'

Stagg looked away. 'I doubt it. *Reliant* will probably get her well-deserved refit, and the extra armour plate we're always being promised. After that, who can say?'

Sherbrooke waited, surprised that he could remain so calm. The big push, and then *Reliant* was to be written off, left to perform less important duties.

Stagg continued, 'There will be a post in Washington, an important one, in view of the situation with the Americans in the Far East. I was astonished, of course, when I was suggested for it. Proud too, I must say.'

Sherbrooke thought of all the faces at Rayner's party: the Chief, not only the oldest member of *Reliant*'s company, but one who probably knew her better than anyone. Frazier, who had turned down a command of his own, perhaps out

289

of the same loyalty, and Evershed, the gunnery officer, who had not rested or taken a day's leave while the ship had been here at Rosyth until B Turret was fully operational again, and every circuit had been double-checked. Rhodes, the navigating officer, like a rock, and highly skilled; one who could handle this great ship like a schooner. So many faces he had come to know: men who all had one thing in common. The ship.

And what of dead men's shoes? Cavendish, who had killed himself, no matter what the recorded verdict claimed. He had given so much to *Reliant* in the most dangerous days of the war, and had been betrayed by the woman he had loved.

Stagg said, 'You have your own future to think about, Guy. You can't keep running only to stay in the same place, eh?'

'Then there will be no change in sailing orders, sir?'

'None. This is our big chance. I'll not see it screwed up.' He gave his famous grin. 'By anybody!'

Sherbrooke picked up his cap. When he looked at Stagg again, there was no trace of uneasiness. *The fighting admiral.*

Stagg said, 'We are going to Scapa, where we shall join *Seeker* and our destroyers.' He frowned. 'I've been promised a replacement for *Montagu*. It all takes too long!' And then, dismissing it, as if he had just thought of something more pressing, 'The cruiser *Assurance* is to be part of the group. Her skipper, Jock Pirie, is an old chum of mine. Things are looking up.'

As he left the cabin, Villar passed him with barely a glance.

Stagg said to him, 'Did you arrange that shore telephone for me? Good show!'

Sherbrooke closed the door. A call to whom, he

wondered. Stagg's watchful wife or the elegant Jane, or someone else entirely?

It did not matter. It must not. There was too much at stake.

He turned away from his own quarters and went out on deck, where the afternoon sunshine was very bright, but without warmth.

The beardless Lieutenant Frost, who was the O.O.D., straightened up as he saw the captain walking across the quarterdeck below the guns of Y Turret. For a moment he thought he had missed something, that the captain had spoken to him.

Overhead, the tannoy speaker reminded him of his duties.

'Out pipes! Hands carry on with your work!'

Sherbrooke grasped the guardrail and looked down at the oily, littered water between the ship's side and the pier.

In fact, he had spoken aloud, although he had not realized it.

'I'll not leave you, my lady. Depend on it.'

The thick wire back-spring tightened suddenly and grated around the quarterdeck bollards.

Sherbrooke looked toward the White Ensign, hanging limp and still from its staff. Stagg's flag, too, was motionless. There was not a breath of wind, and yet *Reliant* had moved.

The bond was here. As strong as ever.

16

Storm Warning

Despite the number of officers present, *Reliant*'s wardroom seemed unnaturally quiet. There were no stewards in attendance, and the pantry hatch and all doors were closed, with a Royal Marine guard in the outer lobby to ensure that this gathering remained undisturbed.

Frazier said, 'All present, sir.' He sounded clipped, formal. By 'all', he meant the battlecruiser's senior officers and heads of departments, those who fed, armed and drove this great ship, or cared for the injuries of her company if the worst should happen.

Sherbrooke remained standing by a small table and looked at them, waiting for them to settle down. Even the ship seemed quiet, only the fans purring softly to give any sense of her movement.

The action with the German cruiser *Minden*, the near-miss with the disguised minelayer, and even the nerve-jarring bombardment of the old French naval dockyard at Ferryville outside Bizerte, the culmination of Operation *Sackcloth*, had been mentally shelved, if not forgotten. After a too-brief work-up with the rest of the group, they had headed south once more, and but for the curtains drawn across the polished scuttles to hold back the glaring sunlight, the impressive natural fortress of Gibraltar would be the backdrop, the setting for the next stage of naval operations.

Sherbrooke had never seen such an armada of ships, nor so many types and classes: escorts and storeships, tank landing craft, and the larger vessels which carried their own flotillas of box-like boats for ferrying infantry to beaches held by the enemy. In the Eastern Mediterranean the deployment would be the same, from Alexandria to Malta and the captured bases along the North African coastline, the forces of invasion were poised to attack, and as ready as they could ever hope to be.

Secrecy was a matter of conjecture; success was the only goal. There was no alternative.

And in every ship at this moment, the other commanding officers would be doing the same, telling their people what was required of them.

Stagg was ashore with the admiral, and Sherbrooke was surprised that he should feel so relieved at his absence. Stagg, after all, was a past master at this kind of thing, and would have added the right flavour, in a style which they had all come to know.

He said, 'Gentlemen, knowing the navy, I feel quite certain that you are all aware of my reason for calling you together. In fact, you probably knew before I did myself.'

He gazed at them, the men who ran and controlled the affairs of his ship. Onslow, the Chief, massive in his chair, Farleigh, the tight-lipped surgeon commander, and Rhodes. Evershed, gunnery officer, Palliser, the major of marines, looking more like a soldier than ever in his lightweight khaki uniform. Bearcroft, the supply officer, who would know to the ounce how much corned beef would be needed to supply every gun position with sandwiches; and of course, the Bloke, John Frazier. All of them wore white drill, and looked like strangers after the scuffed sea boots and duffle coats of the North Atlantic.

'I have a signal here from Admiral Cunningham, the Commander-in-Chief, which he has made to all ships and naval units taking part in this great operation.' He saw Rhodes lean forward slightly, his strong fingers interlaced, intent on his words, no doubt remembering Cunningham's signal of congratulations, not to any name or single person, but to the ship. 'We are to embark on the most momentous enterprise of the war – striking for the first time at the enemy on his own territory.' He smiled, and felt the tightness in his jaw. 'For us, gentlemen, this will be Operation *Husky*. The invasion of Sicily.'

Perhaps when Nelson's ships had paused here before the savage battle of the Nile, there had been cheering, or some other outward demonstration of loyalty and trust. Today, there were only a few quick glances, and the Chief uttered a heavy sigh, either of relief or because of the demands *Reliant*'s participation would make on his departments in boiler and engine rooms.

'You will be fully briefed when the operational signal is received. Our main task will be to support the landings of troops on the south and south-east beaches, the Eighth Army, with our Canadian friends on their left flank. The U.S. Seventh Army will attack and land further to the west. There will be full airborne and glider support, and as much fighter cover as is required. Tell your subordinates as much as you think fit, no more. There will be a lot of men out there. Let us try not to lose them for the want of a little care.' He paused. 'Any questions?'

It was the Chief, as he had known it would be.

'About how long, sir?'

He replied without hesitation, 'Three weeks at the very most. I think it will be less.'

There was a gasp or two this time. It was not a rumour, or something vaguely planned for next year or in a few months' time. As far as this ship and her consorts were concerned, it was now.

There were no more questions. Sherbrooke said quietly, 'I would like to add that if *Reliant* is called to action again, there is no better company I would choose.'

Rhodes was on his feet. 'That goes for us too, sir!'

They were all standing, and Evershed looked as if he was about to applaud in support.

Sherbrooke walked to the door. 'Thanks, John. It's never easy to ask people to die for you. It never was.'

He gave a quick smile. *Perhaps not even for Nelson.*

The Royal Marine sentry's eyes followed him beneath the peak of his cap.

I was there when the Old Man came out. Looks me straight in the eye and says, Sicily – tell the lads. We'll murder the bastards!

On the catapult deck, Rayner watched the mechanics checking over the two Walrus amphibians. Stripped to the waist and wearing shorts, they looked quite at home in the sun.

Eddy Buck wiped his hands with a rag and said, 'Over there across the Bay – d'you reckon the Spaniards are making a note of all this? Calling up their pals in jackboots? God, what a killing they could make amongst this lot!'

Rayner saw his new Telegraphist Air Gunner clambering out of the aircraft. He was a regular, a leading hand, very stiff and unused to the informality of their small crew. His name was Percy Moon, and like his predecessor Jim Hardie, he was a Londoner. When he had first heard him speak, Rayner had almost expected to see the dead gunner back again.

They both looked over at one of the destroyers as a burst of cheering broke out across the crowded anchorage.

Rayner said quietly, 'It's on, then. I wondered what our

skipper mustered the senior officers for.'

Buck looked at him, unusually grim-faced for one who was rarely without some witty rejoinder.

'Won't end it, though, will it?'

Rayner grinned and slapped his bare shoulder. 'Hardly! It'll go on for years and years. You and I will be too old to climb into a bloody Shagbat by then!'

Buck's mood did not lighten.

'If anything goes wrong . . . I mean, if I got the chop . . .'

Rayner looked at him. 'Yeah, yeah, I know. I can have your egg for breakfast.'

Then he gripped his shoulder. 'Listen, Eddy. We'll be together. No matter what.'

They both looked up at the Rock, the peak of which was drifting in a freak heat haze.

Rayner said, 'Remember. I'm banking on you to be best man.'

They both laughed, and the other crewmen looked up and grinned, although they had not heard what was said.

'Launch coming out to us!'

Rayner shaded his eyes against the reflected glare. It was the familiar green barge with the rear-admiral's flag on either bow, the one he had shared with Sherbrooke when they had joined *Reliant* together on that cold day in Scotland.

'His lordship's coming aboard.' He watched the side-party forming up just clear of the tightly-spread awnings, so that the marines' bayonets would not poke holes through the canvas.

Buck glanced at him. 'You don't much like Rear-Admiral Stagg, do you, Dick?'

'Not much. He's dangerous.' He groped for the description he wanted. 'My dad used to talk about the generals in his war. All bullshit and no brains.' He turned away, angered and distressed without understanding why. 'Never thought of the poor bastards they sent over the top. Well, he's like that. If bullshit was music, he'd be the whole bloody brass band.'

Buck smiled. 'Run ashore in Gib, that's what we need, old son!' He saw the mood passing. 'Remember that other time? You ended up getting engaged! Full of surprises, that's me!'

The silver calls trilled and the Royal Marines presented arms in a small cloud of blanco.

Stagg saluted and glanced along the deck, where various working parties had been called to face aft and stand to attention.

Then he looked keenly at Sherbrooke. 'So you told them, did you?'

'Yes, sir.' He knew Stagg was not listening to him.

'Those lunatics over aboard *Marathon* were all cheering their heads off! Send for her C.O. and give him a bloody good bottle. *Security!*' He sniffed. 'It's a wonder they don't put the invasion date on the front page of *Reveille*!'

They walked into the cool shadows, and Stagg said, 'We'll use your quarters. I've got my secretary and Flags waiting for me in mine.'

Sherbrooke stood aside and watched him stride into the day cabin.

Long appeared by the pantry and asked, 'Can I get anything, sir?'

Stagg said rudely, 'You can get out!'

Then he turned and glared at Sherbrooke. 'I've been with the admiral. He had a long screed for me from their lordships at the Admiralty, all about the Rosyth refit, and your comments on the standards of work! Really enjoyed himself, I could bloody well see that!'

'As *Reliant*'s captain, I had no choice, sir.'

'As far as I am concerned, the only choice was mine! How do you imagine it made me look? I'll say this, Guy, and I'll say it just once. I got you *Reliant*, so remember that, the next time you want to play God!' A lock of hair had fallen across his eye but he seemed too enraged to notice it. 'And remember, I can just as easily take her away from you and get a captain who knows the score!'

Sherbrooke said quietly, 'Who does what he's told, right or wrong – is that closer to it, sir?'

Stagg swept the hair from his face and jammed on his fine cap with the twin rows of oak leaves. 'Exactly. Yes, I say *exactly!*'

Sherbrooke stood by an open scuttle for several minutes after Stagg had slammed out. Perhaps somebody in high places at the Admiralty did not much care for Stagg, or maybe another name had been suggested for the plum job in Washington.

He gazed out at the lines of troopships and landing craft, the countless khaki figures lying or walking on their crowded decks. An army on the move, an armada such as the world had not seen before.

He touched the letter folded inside his pocket, which had been brought aboard today, and which he had not yet had time to open, then he sat down and looked at her writing, no longer unfamiliar to him. In the far distance, he thought he heard Stagg laugh. Acting on cue again.

He had always known it would be like this. Maybe he had been too afraid of losing the ship.

He forced himself to relax, muscle by muscle. It should have been obvious; Stagg was the one who was afraid.

It is a lovely day here in London, and everyone feels better for the sunshine. I am writing this in the office as I wanted to reach out to you as soon as possible. Today I had some news . . .

Later, Long peered in at him, anxious and worried.

'I'm sorry about earlier on, sir.'

Sherbrooke looked at him. 'Not your fault. I should have seen the storm clouds for myself.' He turned the letter over again. 'Brandy, Long.' As the petty officer hurried away he added, 'Two glasses. You can share in the celebration.'

Long's eyes were like saucers. 'Celebration?' he repeated.

Sherbrooke said quietly, 'I'm going to get married.' Then he smiled. 'Eventually.'

Long almost ran into the pantry, and Sherbrooke looked for several seconds at the framed photograph of the ship at full speed, taken between the wars.

But first, my lady, Operation Husky.

It was a perfect morning, fine, sunny and warm . . . perhaps a little too perfect. Emma Meheux had joined her neighbour in the other flat for breakfast; nobody else could make powdered egg look and taste like the real thing. Small, precious moments, like watching Ellen's cat enjoying the pieces of fish she had queued for; talking about clothes and the grim reality of coupons; the black market; the reshowing of *Gone With The Wind* at the local cinema.

When she had entered the requisitioned building by the Thames, she had felt it immediately. Like a cold wind.

The porter on duty said, 'A visitor for you, Mrs Meheux. I put her in your office.'

When she walked through the waiting room she saw Captain Thorne's door closed, but somehow she knew he was inside. That in itself was unusual. He always seemed to be lying in wait when she arrived, no matter how early, or how late when she left.

She pushed open the door and saw a woman in uniform sitting with a magazine unopened on her lap. A Wren officer, like those she had seen on board *Reliant*.

She stood up and held out her hand. 'Sorry about this, Mrs Meheux. There was no time to call you.' She smiled. 'I'm Second Officer Slade, Julie, if you like. I'm from Welfare.'

She removed her smart tricorne hat and shook her hair out; she was only in her thirties, but the hair was iron-grey. She had a strong, intelligent face, beautiful in a striking sort of way.

Emma said, 'Welfare? Is there some news?'

The Wren sat down again. 'This is not strictly a naval business, but Welfare covers all three services, and Major Wallis thought it right that I should see you. Do you know him?'

Emma shook her head. Another name, a different uniform. 'Perhaps he wrote to me. So many people have tried . . .'

'I understand. Anyway, the C-in-C, Vice-Admiral Hudson, agreed. You are a top classified and highly regarded person here, so it's only right and proper.'

'It's my husband, isn't it?'

'Yes. There will be an official letter, of course. In fact, due to some idiotic foul-up somewhere, one was sent to your home in Bath by mistake.'

She said, 'I think I knew. I'm . . . not sure.'

The Wren said, 'There are many cases like this, I'm afraid. When the Japanese invaded Singapore they completely overran all lines of communication. Your husband's unit was separated from the main force, and during the fighting he was wounded.'

'But how do you know? Why did it take so long?'

'Many of our troops tried to escape from Singapore, in naval vessels, native craft, even junks. Most of them failed. The nearest land not controlled by the Japanese was Java.'

She nodded, remembering the cuttings and the files she had studied, when she had tried to understand it and why it had happened.

'But a few managed it, and were looked after mostly by Javanese fishermen, not always for patriotic reasons.' The Wren looked at her steadily. 'We now know that during a secret operation on one of the islands, three British soldiers were found alive, and in reasonable health, to all accounts. They have described what happened when Singapore fell. Lieutenant Meheux was wounded, but he insisted on staying behind to blow up their supplies and equipment. The diversion allowed others to escape.'

Emma was on her feet, but did not recall having risen. She touched the anti-blast tape on the window and stared at the street below, the red buses, the uniforms, the carefree movement of people in the sun, the scars of war hidden away for the moment.

She heard herself say, 'There was an identity disc. They told me. On a ship that was torpedoed.'

'Yes.' The Wren had come to stand beside her, and had placed one hand on her shoulder, not a gesture of pity or sympathy, but of understanding. Strength. 'They believe he gave it to somebody. To let people know.' She watched her, and the hand on her shoulder told her what remained unspoken.

Emma said, 'And it's taken all this time. Over a year, and nobody knew. Or cared.'

She realized that the Wren officer was looking at her, her hand quite still.

'Sorry, Julie. This has been rotten for you too, hasn't it?'

The Wren gave a slight smile. 'It gets to you at times like this.'

'Do his family know yet?' She was shocked that she could barely remember Philip's mother.

The other woman glanced at the clock. 'About now, I should think.'

Emma walked to her desk and stared at the letters and files, the paper war.

'They killed him, didn't they? Because of what he tried to do.'

'Yes.' She picked up her hat. 'The survivors witnessed most of it.'

She wanted to put her arms around her, to offer some kind of comfort, but Emma Meheux had strength in her own way, and was now freed of something which had been hanging over her, like so many others the Wren had visited. It would be difficult to face the next part, but not impossible. It would do no good to tell her that her husband had been beheaded by the victorious enemy.

She asked suddenly, 'Is there anyone? Somebody you can contact? If not I'll hang around. We could have a drink, or something.'

'I shall be all right, Julie, but thank you. Yes, there is someone.'

'I'm glad.' She held out her hand. 'Call me if you need anything.' Then she was gone.

How long she sat at the desk Emma had no idea. The telephone remained silent, and Captain Thorne did not trouble her.

She touched her eyes with her fingertips, remembering her lipstick on his mouth. *Yes, there is someone*. It was so easy to say.

Then she pulled out her writing paper and unfastened the cap of her pen.

Dear Guy . . . She wiped her eyes with the back of her wrist as a tear fell on to the paper. She screwed it up and began again. He must not be distracted now, of all times.

My dearest Guy, It is a lovely day here in London.

She looked up as the door opened very slowly and Captain Thorne stood just outside it, his face anxious, and suddenly very old.

'If there's anything I can do, Emma? If you like, I could arrange a long leave, perhaps a transfer to Bath, near your family?'

He was trying, but it saddened her to see him like this. The Groper she could cope with.

'I'm all right, sir.' She looked at the letter. 'I want to stay here. To know what's happening. So that he'll always remember that I'm with him . . .'

But the office was empty. It was not over. It was only just beginning.

If only . . . She shook her head again, and wrote, *Today I had some news.*

She glanced down at the ring on her finger, then very deliberately removed it.

Commander John Frazier strode aft, and paused by the quartermaster's lobby to look at the Rock, the glittering lights in the town and reflected across the darkening water, where ships' boats were cutting long phosphorescent wakes like comets' tails. Did they know how lucky they were here, he wondered. They only saw the war at a distance, in the burned or listing ships creeping into the harbour for refuge, or in the eager faces of young servicemen searching for souvenirs, or merely a good time. Did they ever ask themselves what had happened to all those soldiers, sailors and airmen?

He paused by the table and the open log book.

The quartermaster watched him warily. Frazier was all right, a lot better than most, but you could never afford to be slack where he was concerned.

He said, 'All libertymen ashore, sir. Duty boats' crews have just fallen in.'

Frazier acknowledged it. He kept thinking of the captain, how he had asked him to his cabin for a gin, and then had told him about the girl he had met when Alison had been so bloody rude.

He glanced aft. 'Are they at dinner yet, d'you know?'

The quartermaster shook his head. 'No, sir. I saw Chiefy Price take another bottle from the pantry.'

A quartermaster, the ship's gatekeeper, knew everything. He had to.

Frazier sighed, and went down to the cabin flat. Where he had taken the girl who was married to a P.O.W. He had never dreamed . . .

Price opened the door for him, and called over his shoulder, 'Commander, sir!'

There were four of them, Stagg, looking unusually flushed, Captain Essex of the carrier *Seeker*, Sherbrooke, and the newcomer to the group, Captain Jock Pirie of the eight-inch gun cruiser *Assurance*. The latter was known, affectionately or otherwise, by his ship's company as Punch, because of the huge nose that dominated his face and made all his other features seem incidental.

Frazier tried to adjust to it. The beautifully laid table, fit for a royal review, the officers in their ice-cream suits, the wine and the polished silver. Petty Officer Long was here, too. *Lending a hand*, as he would call it.

And they had all heard the news this morning. They had been expecting it, cursing each dragging delay, which to the average Jack seemed like sheer bloody-mindedness.

Husky was on, about to become a fact. They even knew the date: the tenth of July. Just like that.

Stagg looked at him cheerfully. 'Come for a tot, Commander?'

Frazier answered, 'Signal, sir. Thought you should see it.' As Stagg seized it, he looked at Sherbrooke, and

304

said, 'Weather report. It's not too good.'

Stagg slapped the signal down on the table. 'Lot of old women! I heard from the C-in-C myself. There's too much involved. We can turn the invasion fleet round, even delay it, but once the balloon goes up, *we go*, weather or not!'

Frazier had heard a rumour about friction between Stagg and Sherbrooke. He could guess most of it: Rosyth, the armour plate, the rear-admiral's determination to be in the vanguard of *Husky*. You didn't need a crystal ball to fathom it out.

He said, 'I've spoken with Pilot, sir. He's keeping book on the weather conditions.'

Sherbrooke smiled. 'I guessed as much.'

Captain Pirie trained his nose towards them. 'I hear your war correspondent, Pat Drury, is coming with you again?'

Stagg interrupted, 'If he gets a move on. I think he must have invented the pierhead jump!'

Captain Essex said thoughtfully, 'So the ships at Gib will be leaving tomorrow. Hard to believe the waiting's over.'

Frazier said, 'All leave's cancelled. The redcaps will be out now rounding up the late drinkers.'

Stagg said sharply, 'And then we can weigh. Twelve hundred miles, and we make some more history!'

Sherbrooke said quietly, 'Thanks, John. I'll see you later on.'

His eyes said, *as soon as I can get away.*

It was a few minutes to nine o'clock when Sherbrooke eventually made his way aft to join Frazier by Y Turret, as if the meeting had been arranged.

It had been an angry sunset, and the sky was streaked in long bars of copper. Most of the harbour was in shadow, with few boats running back and forth at this time. It was normal, harbour routine: what they had both been trained to accept, from Dartmouth to this moment.

A few figures stood on the quarterdeck, the duty signalman, the O.O.D., quartermaster and sentry. Standing apart from the others, the Royal Marine bugler stood on the little rope mat which had been thoughtfully provided to protect the planking from his heavy boots.

Sherbrooke recalled Stagg's threat, for that was what it had been. To undertake a long overhaul and restructuring at some later date would mean that *Reliant* would be paid off, her company scattered to different depots and barracks to await drafts to other ships and new companies. In Rosyth they could have managed some of it; the squat dockyard manager had as much as promised that he could complete such a refit in time, even before they had discovered that *Husky* had been delayed.

The O.O.D. had at last realized that the captain and second-in-command were present, and coughed nervously.

'Sunset, sir!'

The O.O.D. called, *'Make it so!'*

The marine, his eyes on the White Ensign, began to sound the Last Post, as was the custom in big warships in harbour. Routine, part of their lives.

But it was more than that, much more. Sherbrooke and Frazier saluted together as the flag was lowered, and scooped up by the signalman before it could touch the deck.

'Carry *on*!'

They walked along the deck together, and Frazier said, 'I wouldn't want to leave *Reliant*, sir. Not now that we've come this far.'

Somebody said, 'The other captains are coming on deck, sir!'

Sherbrooke was glad of the interruption. 'I'll deal with it. Man the side!' Frazier's words were still in his mind. He could have spoken them himself.

On the morning of *Reliant*'s departure from the Bay, the
weather had changed considerably. The wind had risen,
and blew from the north-west, which was unusual to say
the least; even Rhodes was disturbed by it. A short, choppy
sea, broken by the wind, would make the going hard for
the landing vessels, especially the smaller ones, and some
might find it impossible to make the final rendezvous in
two days' time.

Reliant had led the way from Gibraltar, followed directly
astern by the carrier *Seeker*, with the cruiser *Assurance*
bringing up the rear. The flotilla of destroyers, still depleted
by the loss of *Montagu*, were deployed on either beam, an
impressive sight, even to the buffs amongst the many
onlookers lining the shore. It was as close to the peacetime
navy as Gibraltar had seen for years, with all hands fallen
in fore-and-aft in their white uniforms, and keeping perfect
station on the battlecruiser. All it had needed was a band.

Once clear of the bay, the serious business of preparing
for anything that might challenge them got under way.

Sherbrooke walked out on to the flag deck and looked
along his command. The awnings had gone, and a slightly
frayed ensign replaced the one flown in harbour; the anti-
aircraft and short-range weapons were manned, and the
whole ship at Defence Stations.

He saw one of the Walrus flying boats on the catapult,
mechanics crawling over it like predators. There was an
officer with them, and when he removed his cap to scratch
his fair hair, Sherbrooke knew it was Rayner. Something
made him squint up at the lofty bridge.

Sherbrooke raised his hand, and turned away to join the
bridge team. He knew their strength now, too. Yorke, the
capable yeoman of signals who had emerged as quite a wit
with a dry sense of humour. His signalmen, seasoned hands

and mere boys as well; the boatswain's mate by the bridge tannoy speaker; a messenger with the inevitable tray of tea. Lieutenant Friar, the second gunnery officer, had the watch, and Drake, whose pink face defied sun and wind alike, was assisting him. The chain of command: up to the invisible radar, down through the W/T office and the wheelhouse.

He heard Yorke murmur, 'Here comes our front-line reporter, Jack. Now we can get on with the war!'

Pat Drury, as untidy as ever, clambered into the bridge and grinned.

'Sorry I was a bit late off shore last night, Captain. Got involved with another chap I used to work with in Fleet Street.'

Sherbrooke raised his binoculars and watched the nearest destroyer as the diamond-bright signal lamp began to stammer.

'Thought you'd missed the boat?' He turned. 'What's *Marathon* got to say, Yeo?' To Drury, he added, 'I think the weather's going to get worse. Just what we don't need.'

Yorke lowered his telescope. 'From *Marathon*, sir. *Permission to exercise guns.*'

'Granted.' He half listened to the rapid clatter of the lamp. You had to be good to keep up with Yorke's team.

Drury said, 'Will it make that much difference?'

'To the landing craft, yes, it might.' Most of the soldiers would be keyed up to the limit anyway, without having to stagger ashore seasick and then be expected to fight, but there was no point in saying as much to Drury. He probably knew already. And most of the landing craft were commanded by young, temporary officers, like Drake and all the other Wavy Navy officers who had been 'forced up under glass', as Rhodes had put it. They were all inexperienced, simply because an invasion of this magnitude had never been attempted before.

'Could you spare a few minutes, Captain?' Drury glanced at the chart room. 'In there, maybe?'

Sherbrooke nodded to the O.O.W., a stiff-backed and very formal lieutenant, a true product of the Whale Island gunnery school.

It seemed peaceful and remote after the bridge with its busy watchkeepers.

'Close the door.' He smiled as the destroyer shattered the silence with the staccato rattle of anti-aircraft weapons. 'It'll be quieter.'

Drury closed it, regarding him with interest. He had always made a point of remaining cynical, and was rarely impressed or manipulated into forming the wrong conclusions. Soldiers and sailors of all ranks, none was above a bit of bullshit. But Sherbrooke intrigued him. He had seen him wave to one of his officers, the pilot who had received the D.S.C.; had watched him shift his attention in the space of an instant to the destroyer which was now pooping off the taxpayers' money. And he was still able to detach himself from it. *Like now*.

A pair of parallel rulers rolled suddenly across the chart table and clattered to the deck. Drury saw Sherbrooke's eyes move to it, aware of the motion, hearing the metallic creak of the entire bridge structure, seeing all those landing craft in his mind. Whatever anybody else had told him, Drury knew that they could not reverse this undertaking.

He realized that the blue eyes were watching him.

He said, 'I was in London, Captain. I was briefed there before they flew me out.'

'They must trust you a great deal.'

Drury wondered why he felt so awkward. It was unusual for him.

He said, 'Some more than others, apparently.' He opened

his jacket and took out an envelope. 'For you.'

There was utter silence.

He said, 'Before you open it, I must say something. She asked me to give it *to you*, and not to tell anybody.'

She. Sherbrooke opened the thick, official envelope with the Admiralty fouled anchor on it.

It was a photograph. It must have been taken in the office, her office, where no cameras were ever allowed.

'Thank you . . . very much. Did you take it?'

'Of course. Then I got the press lab to make a print for you. This job does have some perks!'

He watched him turn over the photograph to read what she had written on the reverse. It was just an ordinary press glossy. But Sherbrooke was holding it as if it was beyond value. So this was the private man. Not the one they had written about. *I wrote about*. The man Drury had seen for himself in action, and during the aftermath with his men.

Sherbrooke said, 'You take a good picture,' and placed it carefully back in the envelope.

Drury was about to remark that she was a good subject, and that he hoped they might find happiness, when so many had lost it. But that kind of sentiment was not for this moment, nor was it for this man.

'Can you tell me what we're heading into, Captain?'

Sherbrooke seemed detached, absent in spirit. 'A bombardment. Covering fire for the troops once they get ashore. That sort of thing.'

He heard the wind sigh against the superstructure, and saw the signalmen pulling down their chinstays to stop their caps from flying over the side. In for a blow. Bad timing.

But when he spoke again, he revealed nothing of his thoughts. 'The first few hours will tell.'

Someone was hovering outside the door.

Sherbrooke said, 'Anything else?'

Drury wondered how he would describe this private moment, but no facile words came to his mind. Instead he said, 'I'm glad I'm coming with you,' and found that he meant it.

And so, H.M.S. *Reliant* went back to war.

17

Of One Company

Paymaster Lieutenant James Villar leaned back in his office chair and opened his white tunic. With most watertight doors shut and deadlights and ventilators sealed off, the ship was like an oven. He wiped his throat and chest with a damp handkerchief and felt his stomach contract painfully as *Reliant* dipped steeply in a swell. It was unusual for him to feel like this, but then, the weather was not helping.

If he let his mind dwell on it, he knew he would throw up. Look outboard, keep your eyes on the horizon, the old hands always said, and you would never be seasick. Down here in his office, there was no horizon, and it would be as black as pitch on deck in any case.

He glanced at the clock and swallowed hard. It was an hour before midnight, but he did not feel like turning in, nor did he want to go to the wardroom where a few of the off-duty watchkeepers would be dozing, fully dressed, and waiting to be roused for their next tour of duty.

Reliant had been closed up at Defence Stations since leaving Gibraltar, four hours on, four hours off, with only a brief respite during the two-hour dog watches. Despite the hardship of watchkeeping with so little time for anything else, the men seemed to prefer it. Villar had never been able to understand this. He kept to fairly regular hours, in harbour or at sea, and was left alone to plan most of his routine. And this office was his retreat, unlike his cabin, which was so full of extra filing cabinets that he often felt he was in one of them.

He pulled out his key ring, and after some hesitation opened a drawer in his desk. A *retreat*, something which most of the young officers who shared the wardroom would never appreciate. They were juvenile and immature, no matter how they might see themselves.

He lifted out his leather writing case. It still had a fine, rich smell, and was pleasant to touch. He smiled. It had been expensive as well, but Villar had always liked nice things.

He considered the invisible ships, heading toward their chosen area of battle. Tomorrow they would catch up with the landing vessels he had seen at Gibraltar. After that, it was anybody's guess.

He had been surprised, rather than pleased, that he had not collapsed into complete terror when the enemy shell had exploded against the admiral's bridge. In his memory, the experience was recorded only as a kind of numbness, a shock, with only distorted pictures to illustrate it. The young subbie gasping for air, the telegraphist who had fallen and been crushed when the side had caved in on them. The flag lieutenant had simply vanished.

He smiled again. The new flag lieutenant was not much better, but Stagg seemed to approve of him so far. He was, after all, a few inches shorter than the admiral.

He had seen very little of Stagg during the visit to London. He had been to a few shops listed in Stagg's diary, and had collected some clothing from Gieves, and several cases of wine from Berry Brothers & Rudd in St. James's Street.

And then . . . He shook his head as if someone had

questioned it. It had not been an impulse; he had planned it. He had telephoned Mowbray's home in Guildford. Mowbray himself had not been there, or so his mother had said. She had had a strong, cultured voice, not quite what Villar had expected, and had been vaguely suspicious until he had explained that he was one of her son's officers, who had shared his experience, when others had died.

Since Rosyth and Gibraltar, he had seen very little of ordinary Seaman Alan Mowbray. Perversely, that told him that the telephone call had been a success.

He opened the writing case and touched the matched fountain pens, and the neat rank of envelopes. Everything tasteful, tidy. Then he withdrew the photograph and studied it, his nausea momentarily forgotten.

Mowbray had been surprised when he had visited him in the sick quarters, nervous too. But not outwardly hostile.

The deck tilted again and he heard things in his cupboards falling in confusion. One of his writers could clear up the mess tomorrow.

Villar wiped his face and throat again. They must have been very close, very intimate, to share such pictures. And now his friend was dead.

He sat up with a jerk as somebody tapped on the door. 'Yes!'

He tried to contain his surprise. It was Mowbray, carrying his cap, his eyes moving quickly around the office.

'I'm sorry, sir. I thought you might be working late. I know you do. It's just that . . .'

'Come in.' He closed the writing case. 'Shut the door. I was just finishing, anyway.' He watched the youth, making up his mind, not sure how to proceed.

Mowbray said, 'I'm on the Middle Watch, sir.' He looked at the clock. 'I heard about your phone call, sir.'

Villar smiled gently. 'You didn't mind, did you? It was

something we both went through. I was in London. I thought we might meet.'

'People would think . . .'

Villar said impatiently, 'I don't care what people think. Neither should you. What's your station on the Middle Watch?'

Mowbray seemed taken aback by the question. 'Damage control, sir. There's a lot of gear to move before we're properly ready.'

'I can imagine.' He made his decision. 'You shouldn't be using your hands for that kind of work. You have a real talent. It's like a pianist digging for coal.'

The youth glanced at his hands. 'I'll be careful.'

'Come over here.' Villar watched the sudden apprehension. 'You're not afraid of me, are you?'

Mowbray stood by the desk. 'I don't want anyone to think it was like that, you see, sir. It was different.'

Villar reached out and took his hand. 'How different? You and young Forbes . . . Peter, wasn't it?' He saw him nod wretchedly. 'You were often together. More than just friends, I'd say?'

Mowbray murmured, 'There was an old boat on the river. It belonged to his uncle. We used to go there. Take some food, and our sketching things.'

His eyes were distant, and his hand in Villar's quite relaxed, unafraid.

'And then what did you get up to?'

Mowbray looked at him steadily; resigned, submissive, it could be either.

'You *know* what we did, sir.'

'Well, that wasn't too bad, was it?' He smiled. 'Get it all out of the way.' He saw the youth stagger and heard more objects falling somewhere. '*Christ*, what was that?'

Mowbray stooped and recovered his cap while Villar

stared around, unable to assemble his thoughts.

Mowbray said simply, 'The engines have stopped, sir. Something must have happened.'

To make it worse the telephone buzzed, seemingly twice as loud as ever before.

Villar snatched it up, his fingers so slippery with sweat that he almost dropped the receiver. It was the new flag lieutenant.

Villar said, 'Of *course* I'm still here!' He nodded, still dazed. 'Right away!'

He was just in time to see the door closing.

Lieutenant-Commander Clive Rhodes made another neat calculation on the chart and swore quietly to himself as a drop of sweat splashed down by his dividers. Even with the bridge screens lowered or wide open, the air was stifling, and the motion, even for him, uncomfortable. The north-westerly wind was as strong as before, and they had twice reduced speed so that the group could retain its formation.

He leaned on the table and glanced at his tools, freshly sharpened pencils, pads, estimates of speed, time and distance, all kept in perfect order by his yeoman, a very serious young seaman from Southampton.

In his mind's eye, Rhodes could picture the vast armada of ships moving from both ends of the Mediterranean. The organization was enough to make your head swim. Thousands of troops, armoured vehicles, guns and supplies, all of which had to be dumped on the beaches. *Reliant* would lie off and offer support like the other big ships. For the poor bloody infantry, it was a grim prospect.

And after that? He thought of what the captain had said about putting him up for a command. He had often considered it himself, but something always seemed to get in the way. Rumour had it that *Reliant* would be sent for a long refit soon, and Rhodes knew it was on the captain's mind; he had a thing about this ship. He grinned through his beard. *Listen to me*. But if that happened, it would not be the same afterwards, everyone scattered, faces you had come to respect, to like, or to hate. All a part of something, the whole.

A command of his own, then. He glanced around the familiar chart room. No, it would not be the same.

The midshipman of the watch said, 'Captain's coming up, sir.'

'Thanks, Tim. I'm about ready.' He looked at the clock. Another alteration of course. He examined his feelings. The attack would begin on the morning after next. No recall, no turning back; it was on.

Rhodes was not married, although he had been close to it a few times. It had not fitted in with his service life, or so he had believed. Now, after seeing the Canadian two-ringer with his nurse, and the captain and the striking girl who had come to the party, he was not so certain.

He picked up his pad and walked into the bridge. His eyes moved unhurriedly across the pattern he knew so well: men at voicepipes and telephones, his assistant, Frost, peering through the screen, signalmen, messengers. They were all puny when he considered the ship that ruled their lives.

He saw Sherbrooke, and said, 'About ready to alter course, sir.'

Sherbrooke climbed onto his chair, and felt the metal arms pressing against his ribs as the ship rolled heavily. Aboard the destroyers it must be impossible to keep dry.

He saw the correspondent Pat Drury talking quietly to one of the signalmen. Drury knew how to avoid disrupting the routine, and had a casual, almost offhand manner of approach when talking to the ship's company; it made a big change from some journalists he had known. He wondered if Drury's eventual broadcast would be any better for the experience, or have any real significance in the end.

Drury said, 'I hope I'm not intruding, Captain.'

Sherbrooke smiled. 'I thought you'd be down aft enjoying a good sleep. I know I would!'

Drury glanced across the bridge. 'Your steward keeps a sharp eye on me, right enough. He'll make a good butler one day!'

Rhodes heard him and grinned privately. If Long was like many other senior stewards he had known, he would probably end up wealthy enough to employ a butler of his own.

A messenger spoke into the big voicepipe, and then turned to Frost.

'Wheelhouse, sir. Permission to relieve the quartermaster.'

Frost grunted. 'Very good.'

'Wheelhouse – bridge.'

Frost touched his face as if still expecting to feel the stubble of his beard. 'Bridge?'

'Leading Seaman Justice on the wheel, sir. Course zero-four-five.'

Frost glanced at the ticking gyro repeater. 'Steady as you go.'

Sherbrooke asked, 'What is your next assignment?'

Drury thought about it. 'A victory parade, I hope. I've seen all the other aspects of it – Dunkirk, Norway, Crete. And it was almost touch and go in North Africa at one time. I want to see it, smell it, and be able to write about it, so that people will never forget.'

He stepped aside as Rhodes said, 'Time, sir.'

Sherbrooke nodded. 'Carry on.'

Rhodes leaned over the gyro. 'Starboard twenty!'

'Starboard twenty, sir. Twenty of starboard wheel on.'

Rhodes watched the moving gyro tape. 'Ease to five. Midships!'

Frost exclaimed, 'She's not answering, sir!'

Sherbrooke slid off the chair and rested one hand on the wheelhouse voicepipe.

'What's the matter, Justice? Opposite helm, *port fifteen!*'

The gyro repeater was still moving, *tick, tick, tick.*

'Not answering, sir!'

Reliant was still turning to starboard, her rudder locked over.

Sherbrooke said, 'Stop engines!'

Even that seemed to take an eternity, the engine room staff dulled into the same revolutions and speed, watch after watch with barely a change. The bridge gave a shiver, and the sounds of the sea and the ship intruded like strangers.

Sherbrooke pressed the red handset to his ear. 'This is the Captain.'

'Sinclair, sir!'

Sherbrooke saw the face in his mind, Onslow's second in command. A very experienced engineer.

'What is it?'

Sinclair sounded miles away. 'Steering won't answer, sir. I've sent my lads to the tiller flat. Until then, I'm not . . .'

Sherbrooke swung round as a voice yelled, 'Ship at Green four-five, sir!'

Rhodes muttered, 'Christ, it must be *Mastiff.*'

Sherbrooke said, '*Emergency.* Full speed astern!' He heard the distant clang of bells and strode to the bridge wing, his glasses already raised. Then he saw the other ship. The destroyer appeared to be turning inwards, her

319

bow wave like a great white moustache against the darkness. In fact, she was still on course. *Reliant* was the one which was swinging round, as if intent on ramming her.

'Shall I clear lower deck, sir?'

Sherbrooke re-entered the bridge and stood by the voicepipes, his eyes on the compass.

'No time, Pilot. *No time.*' He gripped the voicepipes and listened to the mounting clatter and scrape of the bridge structure, as from her keel to this point *Reliant* shook like a mad thing, all four screws thrashing astern.

Sherbrooke saw the destroyer's dark outline appear to change direction. Another minute or so, and *Reliant* would have sliced her in half.

Sherbrooke said, 'Stop engines. Make a signal to *Seeker*, repeated to the whole group. *Keep clear of me – I am manoeuvring with difficulty.*'

'I'll do that, sir!' It was Yorke, naked to the waist and barefooted; he must have run all the way from his mess. What had brought him? A sound, a movement, or was it his signalman's instinct?

'Admiral's on here, sir!'

Sherbrooke glanced at the dark water. 'Good lookout for other ships. With luck, radar will earn its keep tonight!'

Somebody gave a short, frightened laugh.

'Captain, sir?'

'What's wrong?'

'Not under command, sir. No steering. Engine room thinks the rudder is jammed.'

There was such a long pause that he thought Stagg had forgotten him.

'How long?'

'The engine room has people aft right now, sir. I can't ask them to enter the tiller flat without stopping the engines.'

'*Ask?* Bloody well tell them!' Stagg seemed to control himself with a great effort. 'I'll come up. Inform *Seeker.*'

'I have, sir.'

Stagg was thinking aloud. '*It must be fixed!* There's no room for delays, or for the people who cause them, either.'

It sounded like a threat, but Sherbrooke knew what was really troubling Stagg. He had commanded three ships himself; he knew as well as any captain what the risks were. All he could see was his overall control of the landing forces slipping away.

Stagg said sharply, 'Well, carry on. Fast as you can.'

Sherbrooke realized that Drury was still loitering by his chair.

'Rough, was it?'

Sherbrooke felt his mouth crease into a smile. 'He's not pleased.'

Drury listened to muffled orders being shouted beneath the bridge, the slap of running feet. Men dazed by the realization that *Reliant* was stopped, and rolling slowly like any abandoned hulk, her power and strength suddenly gone.

Stagg slammed into the bridge, his eyes red-rimmed with anger.

'What the *hell* is going on?'

Sherbrooke saw his new flag lieutenant hovering in the background, his appearance marred by the collar of his pyjama jacket, which protruded over his uniform.

'The Chief's down aft, sir. We should know soon.'

Stagg strode about, brushing against wary watchkeepers without apparently noticing them. 'Soon? Soon? What the hell does that mean?' He grasped Sherbrooke's arm and said, 'What was it? The bloody dockyard, or some oversight *on board this ship?*'

'From *Seeker*, sir. *Request instructions.*'

Sherbrooke said, 'Nothing they can do for us, sir. I would suggest they continue as before. The landing ships will be depending on it.' He watched the emotions and the arguments. 'We cannot break radio silence at this stage.'

'I *know that*, dammit!' Stagg ran a finger around his collar as if it was choking him. 'Very well. Tell *Seeker* to assume command.'

Sherbrooke pictured the carrier's captain. Had he expected something like this?

They all turned as the Chief appeared in the bridge. His cap was awry, and his uniform streaked in grease, and there was a bandage on his wrist.

'Sorry it took so long, sir.' He sighed as the ship dipped heavily, not from the wind this time, but from the surging wash of a destroyer as she gathered speed to take station on *Seeker*.

Stagg snapped, 'Well, get on with it!'

Onslow regarded him more with sadness than anger.

'The rams that control the tiller and rudder head are locked solid.' He held his greasy fingers together to demonstrate. 'I've got my best tiffies working on it, but for the life of me I can't think what caused it. It wasn't damaged by the shellfire . . .'

Stagg held up his hand. 'Did you check it yourself?'

Onslow studied him calmly. 'Yes, sir.' It sounded like *of course*. He looked at Sherbrooke. 'The dockyard would have found it, say what you like about them!'

Stagg snapped at the navigating officer, 'Show me on the chart where the group will be tomorrow morning.'

Rhodes showed neither surprise nor hesitation. 'According to the orders, sir, they will make contact with the landing vessels tomorrow at eighteen hundred.'

Stagg repeated, '*Tomorrow morning*. As soon after first light as possible.'

Sherbrooke followed them into the chart room, and watched Rhodes pointing out bearings and landmarks which they had studied endlessly since *Husky* had become a part of their destiny, north of Bizerte where *Reliant*'s six big guns had destroyed the last of the German defences, and south of the Tyrrhenian Sea, to the narrow approaches of Sicily itself.

Stagg straightened up, his hands on his hips like crabs.

'If the steering gear can be repaired by first light,' every word seemed measured, 'and I am not at all certain that the Chief is too hopeful . . . God, he makes Job sound like a bloody optimist!' He seemed quite composed again. 'Could *Reliant* still make the rendezvous on time?'

Sherbrooke said, 'With our speed, yes, sir. Otherwise . . .'

'Very well.' Stagg turned as if to leave. 'Chase them up!'

'May I ask what you intend, sir?'

'Of course. I intend to lead my section of the invasion forces up to the allotted beaches, no matter what. If *Reliant* cannot do it, then I will shift my flag to a ship that can. Understood?'

'You intend to fly in one of our aircraft, sir?'

'The Americans do it all the time.' He smiled. 'So why not?'

When he returned to the bridge, Sherbrooke found Frazier waiting for him.

He listened in silence, and then said, 'We shall be without escorts, sir. And no chance of calling for assistance until the invasion has started.' He winced as a booming crash echoed through the hull, as if something was bumping along the keel. 'I know the area is supposed to be clear of enemy submarines, or so they tell us, but any U-Boat commander would have to be stone-deaf not to pick that up!'

Sherbrooke walked out on to the flag deck. He heard Rhodes saying angrily, 'That bloody man! Shift his flag? I'd bloody shift *him* if I had my way!'

And Frazier's calm response. 'I didn't hear a word of that, Pilot.' Then they laughed, and Frazier added, 'Ask me again later!'

The watches changed, and those relieved crouched or lay where they could, fully dressed, and with their lifebelts loose and ready.

A great ship, drifting and helpless in the darkness. Impossible to believe. And when daylight returned, they would still be drifting, stark and vulnerable.

Sherbrooke spent most of the night on the open bridge wing, the sea air and the flung spray keeping all thought of sleep at bay. He had his unfilled pipe clenched in his teeth, remembering the brief moments he had shared with the girl named Emma.

People came and went with messages, requests and questions. He acknowledged them, and barely heard them.

Another one who dared not rest was the war correspondent, Pat Drury.

He sat in the chart room, his stomach adjusting to the uncomfortable motion.

He wrote a lot in his much-used pad.

I watch this man, this quiet hero, a man who lives only for his ship, and would just as willingly die for her.

He closed the pad. *He even gets to me.*

John Frazier gripped a guardrail and watched the Chief and some of his men emerge from the hatch. He could not ever recall seeing Onslow so troubled and weary. His overalls were filthy, and there were streaks of oil on his forehead.

'You look as if you've had a hard night, Chief.'

Onslow did not rise to it; he could not. 'I've got everybody working on it, stokers, torpedomen, tiffies, as many as can get down there safely.' He stared at the sea, as if he had not noticed it before. Dark blue, with the first hint of dawn on the horizon. The wind was still blowing, the ship heavy and lifeless under their feet.

He said, 'My Chief Stoker has narrowed it down, he thinks, to the pump gear telemotor. He's a good man, but I'm not sure of anything any more.' He gazed at the water beyond the stern, usually so alive with *Reliant*'s wake. 'She did this before, you know, at Jutland.'

Frazier said, 'She was under fire then, Chief.'

Onslow stifled a yawn. 'I'm going down again. See what we can sort out.' He saw the question on Frazier's face. 'It might take another two hours just to strip it. They didn't build this sort of gear for amateurs!'

Frazier walked towards the sheltered side-deck. There were off-watch men hanging about, waiting, trying to gauge what was happening. Usually they would stay in their messes until the last minute before they were piped to work or to watchkeeping duties.

Frazier thought of his wife and wondered what she would think if she could see this side of things. He smiled tightly. What she usually said. *Oh, John, you and your old ship!*

A seaman came sharply to a halt and said, 'Captain's compliments, sir, and would you join him on the bridge?'

He felt the wind whipping around him as he climbed the first ladder. This time tomorrow, the landing craft would be going in. The smaller ones steered like shoe-boxes, one skipper had told him, and that was in perfect conditions.

He saw the gun crews watching him as he climbed past their mountings. They had put up with most things, but this was something very different.

Sherbrooke was waiting for him as he entered the bridge, which seemed very hot and humid after the spray-dappled quarterdeck.

Frazier said, 'Nothing, sir. Two more hours, and the Chief thinks they might reduce the possibilities. That's about all he can offer. He's taking it badly.'

Sherbrooke said, 'He would.' Then, 'Well, we'll have to put up with it. I'll speak with the ship's company later on.' He glanced at the listless figures by the voicepipes, the revolving beam of light on the empty radar repeater. 'In an emergency we can move the ship. But using engines alone in a vessel this size would be a disaster.'

The chart room door opened, and Frazier turned with surprise as Rear-Admiral Stagg walked to the centre of the bridge.

He looked cool and relaxed, when compared with his first appearance, freshly shaved, and wearing a pristine new uniform. Frazier thought it was like seeing a different person.

Stagg said, 'No joy, then?'

Sherbrooke replied, 'The Chief is working on it, sir.'

There was a thump, and Frazier saw the new flag lieutenant with two suitcases. He felt suddenly angry, sickened by what he was witnessing. It was all true. Stagg was leaving.

Stagg said, 'Have my gear put aboard the Walrus, Flags. The rest can wait here.' He looked directly at Sherbrooke, excluding everyone else. 'You may require tugs. Eventually. There is nothing more I can do here.'

Several of the men on watch started with alarm as the Walrus engine coughed and then roared into life. They might not understand, or be able to reason why the officer whose flag flew over their lives was suddenly leaving them. *The fighting admiral.*

Pat Drury had also appeared from somewhere, tired and unshaven, but oddly cheerful.

Stagg regarded him impassively. 'There's room for another passenger, Mr Drury. You will miss the main event, otherwise.'

Drury shrugged. 'My assignment is *Reliant*, sir. I'll stay here, if the Captain can stand it.'

Stagg looked away. 'You can go to hell!'

Drury said, 'I very probably will, sir. So we might meet again, in that case.'

Stagg retorted coldly, 'I shall have a word with your superiors about you!'

Drury turned his back to conceal his sudden rage. *I'll do the same for you, you bloody bastard!*

Sherbrooke said, 'Take over, John.' Then he followed Stagg and his aide to the ladder.

Frazier had looked for some sign which might reveal Sherbrooke's feelings at this moment. Stagg was entitled to take all available measures to retain his control of the group and the crowded landing craft which would be in his care. Suppose it had been Sherbrooke's choice? He didn't even have to ask.

Sherbrooke waited inside the hangar space forward of the catapult, while some seamen hoisted the admiral's luggage into the Walrus. The other flying boat was standing under cover, and in the faint light he could see the red maple leaf painted below the cockpit. He knew Rayner was here too, with his friend the New Zealander. *Of one company.* So Rayner had chosen to remain in *Reliant*. The fact that it pleased him revealed more than anything how badly he had been hurt.

Stagg hesitated, seeking the right words. Something to be remembered.

'You'll be safe enough. I'll see that assistance is

available as soon as possible. No submarines anyway – that's something, eh?' But the mood eluded him. He touched the peak of his cap in a casual salute. 'Come and see us when this is over!'

Sherbrooke saluted. *Us?* Who did he mean?

Stagg would never request him as his flag captain again. He walked away from the hangar, and glanced up at the masthead. Stagg's flag had vanished.

Neither would anybody else, after this.

With a crash, the catapult hurled the Walrus outboard and into the air, where it flew in a wide arc before turning into the first true sunlight.

It seemed to take an age before the flying boat was out of sight. Without it, the sea seemed totally empty. Hostile.

Hot coffee and toast had arrived on the bridge, and he saw two of Yorke's young signalmen tucking in without hesitation. Admirals could come and go, but food came first.

Even from the upper bridge, he could hear the din from the tiller flat. He sipped the coffee and thought about Stagg. He had got what he wanted, or soon would. After that, the plum job in Washington, or a vice-admiral's flag in the Pacific.

He saw Lieutenant-Commander (E) Roger Sinclair enter the bridge and peer round like an intruder. He had been on watch when the steering had jammed, and had been working down aft ever since.

'Sorry, sir. I was looking for the Chief.'

Frazier said, 'Don't look so glum. You weren't to blame.'

The man grinned at him. 'You don't look too chirpy yourself!'

Eventually Sherbrooke left them and went to his small sea cabin, where he found his shaving gear and a fresh drill uniform waiting for him. Long was trying to care for him in the only way he knew.

When he had changed, he took out the photograph again and held it to the light.

On the reverse she had written, *For my Captain, with so much love.*

'Could you come, sir?'

Sherbrooke replaced the photograph and strode out to the bridge. The watch had changed. Different faces, different voices. Everything else was the same, or was it?

He saw the Chief sitting on a locker, his big hands on his knees, staring with a wildness Sherbrooke had never seen.

'What is it, Chief?'

Rhodes had returned to the bridge, too. 'Tell the Captain, Chief! *How it was!*' Even he sounded excited.

Onslow said, 'I was in the wheelhouse. Checking right through the telemotor lines, the telegraphs, every bloody thing all over again.' He shook his head. 'Just for the hell of it, I turned the wheel to port. The others down there were all looking at me as if I'd gone round the bend!' He wiped his face with his sleeve. 'Maybe I had. I'm not sure of anything after today!'

Sherbrooke felt something like a chill on his spine. 'Warn the engine room and wheelhouse. Pilot, course to steer?'

'Wheelhouse, sir. Cox'n on the wheel!'

Onslow had managed to reach the red handset. 'This is the Chief. Stand by.' He looked at the deck as if he could see right down to his world of machinery and power. 'Clear the tiller flat. *Now.*' He nodded, sharing the other engineer's incredulity. 'I know, *I know.*' He replaced the handset and sat down again.

Sherbrooke walked to the voicepipes. 'Slow ahead both engines.'

He felt the sudden shiver through his shoes, the

329

companionable rattle of signals gear and loose fittings. She was moving again. *Moving*.

'Slow ahead, sir. Seven-oh revolutions.'

Rhodes said hoarsely, 'Course to steer zero-eight-zero,' and then, as though to himself, 'Jesus, I don't believe this.'

Sherbrooke looked at the compass. 'Starboard fifteen.' He watched the empty jackstaff in the bows of the ship; it too was moving, edging across the hardening horizon like a conductor's baton.

He said, 'Ease to five. Midships. *Steady*.'

'Steady, sir! Course zero-eight-zero!'

Pat Drury exclaimed, 'Well, I'll go to the top of our stairs! She's answering again!'

Sherbrooke looked over at Onslow. 'You knew, didn't you, Chief?'

Onslow licked his lips. 'I'd stake my purple stripes on it, sir. There was not a bloody thing wrong with the steering gear!'

Rhodes said, 'We'll not make the rendezvous, sir, not even at full speed.' Then he grinned. 'But at least we're moving again!'

He turned, angry at the interruption as a messenger said, 'W/T office, sir.'

Drury yawned. 'Rear-Admiral Stagg won't be too happy about this, Captain.' He smiled. 'Too bad, eh?'

It was a wildness, infectious, running through the ship like a shouted message. Somebody gave a cheer; even some of the older hands were peering down at the creaming bow wave as if they had never seen it in their lives.

Rhodes said, 'Captain, sir. Important signal, restricted.'

'Tell him to bring it up.'

Nothing could halt the proposed landings now, unless the troops were unable to pinpoint their beaches. Even then . . .

He turned as Elphick, the chief telegraphist, hurried on to the bridge. He was wearing his gold badges, as if to suit the importance of his signal.

Sherbrooke read it quickly in silence. Testing it, word by word, and then himself.

He said, 'From the Admiralty. It is reported that the Italian battleship *Tiberio* is known to have left Naples yesterday in company with one, perhaps two, *Oriani* Class destroyers.' He looked at each of them. 'They were heading south-west.'

Frost asked, '*Tiberio*?'

Frazier took the recognition manual from Yorke's shelf.

He said quietly, '*Littorio* Class, nine fifteen-inch guns, speed thirty knots.' He closed the book with a snap. 'Big.'

Sherbrooke walked to the chart room. 'Show me, Pilot.'

Tiberio was not merely big, she was a battleship, built just before the war for Mussolini's expanding navy.

Rhodes said, 'She was last reported as being in Taranto. The R.A.F. and the U.S. Air Force were supposed to have her bottled up.'

Sherbrooke watched the strong hands adjusting his rulers and dividers, his pencil moving like *Reliant*'s jackstaff when she had come back to life.

'There, sir. I'd say she was out to intercept our group's landing ships. She could do it, too. It would be murder.' He raised his eyes from the chart. 'There's nothing that can stop that brute!'

Sherbrooke said, 'There's us, Pilot.' Then, 'Lay a course to intercept.' He glanced at his watch, but he had left it in the sea cabin, and he saw the pale Atlantic skin where the strap had been. 'I'll speak to the ship's company before we exercise action stations.'

Rhodes felt dulled by the speed and the change of events.

'Tell them what they're up against, sir?'

The blue eyes settled on his. 'Fight they must, Pilot, but they should be told why.'

Rhodes looked away. It was hopeless, of course, and the Captain of all people would know it. His gaze fell on the remains of a cigar stubbed out by Rear-Admiral Stagg, perhaps as a parting gesture of contempt.

Well, damn him to hell!

And suddenly, like the correspondent, Pat Drury, and the young Canadian flier, he was glad he was here.

18

'The Violence of the Enemy'

The Walrus's solitary 'pusher' engine had settled into its usual throaty drone. At a mere two thousand feet, they could even see the reflection in the sea below whenever they crossed a smooth stretch of water, but, for the most part, since leaving *Reliant*, the sea had been choppy, with endless ranks of short, serried waves.

The pilot, Lieutenant Leslie Niven, checked his instruments and tried to ignore Rear-Admiral Stagg, who was sitting in the observer's seat, studying a folder of typed information. Either Stagg knew it all by heart or he had no wish to converse with a subordinate, it was hard to tell. Niven smiled. But the admiral's eyes hardly moved.

Niven could feel the others shifting about behind and below him, but he did not really concern himself with them. He had hardly got to know his crew before being sent to *Reliant*, and that suited him well enough. The battlecruiser had been a dead-end for him, and this unexpected mission flying Stagg to rejoin the group and the landing ships would change everything, if he was careful and kept his wits about him. For one thing, it was unlikely there would be any time and even less inclination to delay the ships while he manoeuvred the Walrus alongside to be hoisted inboard, even if there was room. And he would not be expected to fly back to *Reliant*, even if he could find her, drifting out of command as she was. And there was the problem of fuel. It would be cutting it too fine.

They would find something for him to do. He might even get an appointment in *Seeker*, but only as a stepping-stone; he would not get forced into a corner again.

He thought of his fellow pilot, Rayner. He was happy where he was. He had his medal, and would end his war flying a Shagbat, if it didn't fall to pieces under him.

Stagg said sharply, 'Much longer?'

Niven peered at the pad strapped to his knee. 'According to the calculations, sir, another hour. Touch down in good light. Then tomorrow, sir, the big attack!' He bit his lip. Stagg was back with his folder again.

He beckoned to his observer and said loudly, 'Don't forget the lamp, Mike! The recognition signal is vital with those trigger-happy bastards!' He nodded toward the engrossed admiral. 'We wouldn't want any mishaps, would we?'

He moved the controls slightly, his eyes on the compass. The old girl was heavy today. Hardly surprising with the extra passengers, the suitcases, not forgetting the bloody depth charges!

Niven switched on his intercom. 'I'm going up to five thousand. Might be a bit steadier, and we'll get a better chance to see the ships!'

He switched off. The others were probably fed up with having Stagg aboard, and with the unexpected mission, leaving all their kit and friends behind them.

Niven sighed. *But not me.* They all spoke about 'sea time' as if it was God's greatest gift. They could have it. After this, a nice air station in England perhaps, or on one of those flash advanced courses in the U.S.A. Either would suit him very well. *Sea time . . .*

Rear-Admiral Vincent Stagg stared unseeingly at his

papers. He knew the lieutenant wanted to talk, perhaps to ask him for a favour. They usually did. But there was no point: after this, it was unlikely that they would ever meet again. He thought of Pat Drury's hostility, his comment about hell. Well, they could all go there. After *Husky*, there would be a whole new venture. He could do it, just as their lordships knew he could.

He shifted his thoughts to the letter he had received from his lawyer in London. Olive was going to sue for divorce. He grinned. She could bloody well whistle for it. When she saw how his career was expanding, and all that went with it, she would soon climb down, as she had done before. And there was Jane. No wonder poor Cavendish hadn't been able to cope. She was too intelligent, too beautiful for him to understand.

He licked his lips, recalling the hours in bed with her at the flat in Mayfair. Tender one minute, demanding the next. He must not lose contact with her completely.

The other officer, the observer, was hanging over the pilot's shoulder again, gesturing, grinning hugely and showing him his watch.

Necessary, Stagg thought. But only good for wartime.

Niven switched on again. 'There are your ships, sir. Red four-five!' He smiled as his observer wriggled forward with his signal lamp.

Stagg grunted. 'Must be the second group, Vice-Admiral Lacey's command.'

They had been at Dartmouth together, although in different terms.

He said, 'Disregard! Remain on course.' He added patiently, 'But make your signal, if it seems safer!'

Niven consulted the compass and altimeter. *Ahead of time*. Full marks for Leslie!

The observer was scrambling back again, his mouth like

a black hole as he tried to yell above the engine's roar.

He reached Niven and banged on his shoulder.

Niven could just make out the words, *Enemy!* and *Eye-Ties!* when suddenly his small world blew apart.

Stagg reeled about in his seat; he was unused to wearing a harness. His mind seemed frozen, unable to deal with the next thought or instinct.

He stared around, beyond belief as they flew through small clouds of smoke. *Flak*, his mind recorded, but nothing else. He felt the explosions, the sharp thumps against the side and bottom of the aircraft. He tore off the flying helmet, and even above the din and sudden vibration he heard someone screaming, so shrill and agonized that it could have been a woman.

He reached out and seized the pilot's arm. Niven lolled over in his harness and looked at him. But there was blood on his mouth, and only a blank stare.

Another vivid flash and more swirling smoke, but this time it was inside the aircraft, filling it, choking it and throttling the terrible screams.

Stagg could not understand. First there was the sea and then the sky, and there was blood everywhere, on the perspex and across the scattered papers, and when he stared down he saw it pouring over his seat.

He tried to call out, but his mouth was blocked, scalding, final. Then the Walrus hit the water and exploded like a bomb.

With the north-westerly wind still blowing, there was not even smoke to mark the grave.

Rhodes reported, 'Steady on new course, sir. Zero-two-zero.' He saw the captain scanning the sea with his binoculars. How many times did they do it in every watch, he wondered. 'We could try another sweep, sir. Maybe the

336

Tiberio's captain changed his mind, or the intelligence reports were misleading.'

'I don't think so, Pilot.' Sherbrooke lowered his glasses and rubbed his eyes. Rhodes was only voicing what the rest of the ship's company must think, or hope. That the enemy battleship had returned to harbour, if it had ever been at sea.

The light was angry, like copper again, the short wave crests almost gold in the sun. Plenty of daylight left, but when darkness fell it would be sudden and complete, and their chance of encountering the enemy almost nonexistent.

He walked to the front of the bridge and looked at the forecastle, bare and empty, with the ship at full action stations. The jackstaff and guardrails were laid flat on the deck, and although they were out of his vision he knew the leaky hoses would be playing across *Reliant*'s beautifully laid decks to help withstand the shock of heavy gunfire.

Apart from that, the ship seemed deserted, all those thousands of officers and ratings, marines and boy seamen, sealed up until they were told otherwise.

It had been different when he had spoken to them over the tannoy system earlier. He had seen faces upturned from the guns, men pausing in their tasks to listen, men around him on the bridge, all watching for a sign, a hint of what they might expect.

Now that they had had plenty of time to think about it, how might they feel? He had told them bluntly that *Reliant* was the only ship of any size that could challenge the Italian battleship. Once amongst the landing ships, the enemy could destroy every one of them, even if, in the end, *Tiberio* was caught and overwhelmed before she could reach a safe harbour. The invasion forces would be in enough difficulty with the prevailing weather conditions.

To have one complete group wiped out might throw the entire operation into chaos.

The Canadian, Rayner, had pleaded with Frazier to be allowed to fly off and add to their span of search. Sherbrooke thought perhaps he was fretting simply because the other pilot had taken Stagg to the group, and he had been left to kick his heels.

He had said, 'Tell him, John. It's not on. If *Tiberio* really is coming this way, it's worth remembering that she carries four aircraft of her own, any one of which could put his Walrus in the drink.'

He recalled what he had said to Frazier. *If Tiberio really is coming* . . . Did that mean that he was doubtful himself?

How would Stagg respond to it, if he were still aboard? Make light of it, no doubt. Put it down to too much caution. But Stagg would not be sparing a thought for any of them now: he would have hoisted his flag over *Assurance*, sharing the joke with his old chum, 'Punch' Pirie.

Suppose we fight? Every captain must have asked that question of himself at moments like these. *Reliant* would give of her best, as she and her consorts had done at Jutland, and as *Hood* and *Repulse* had tried to do in this war. *And for what?* Ask that, and there was no hope. For him, or for the men who had no choice but to obey.

Pat Drury was in the chart room; he had seen his shadow on the steel plating, crouched and brooding, probably cursing his decision to remain in *Reliant*.

In his mind, he could see his men throughout the ship, at shell hoists and sitting at their gunsights and rangefinders. The damage control parties, the 'odds and sods'. Surplus stokers, supply assistants, and stewards, cooks and anyone who was not required to serve the guns. The transmitting station, the T/S, deep down and behind armour plate, would dictate the workings of damage control, just as it would take over the radar and the plotting if the bridge was wiped out.

And Emma ... Where would she be? In her Chelsea flat near the bombed off-licence, or in her office, helping Thorne? It was strange to realize that she would be one of the first to know, when the news reached the Admiralty.

High above the bridge in his armoured director control tower, the gunnery officer, Lieutenant-Commander Christopher Evershed, was plagued with no such doubts or misgivings.

It was a crowded place, but the metal seats were fitted with great care so that nobody was overlooked or restricted. The phone man, a seaman gunner, the spotting officer, the rate officer and the director layer as well as the trainer and his minion, and above all of them, with his own powerful sights, was Evershed. The touch of a button could swing the three big turrets on to the required bearing in seconds; the director layer could raise or lower all six guns to the exact elevation required.

Evershed knew all about the Italian battleship, *Tiberio*, and her sister ships, although he had never laid eyes on any of them. Heavily protected, like most battleships, *Tiberio* was faster than most. She had nine fifteen-inch guns compared with *Reliant*'s six, but they shared the same restriction. Each ship had three turrets, so that, although stronger gun for gun, *Tiberio* was confined to the same arcs of fire as *Reliant*. That was the way Evershed's mind worked, in a series of equations. Like the bearing, range and deflection which could drop shells onto an enemy after only one straddle.

He wondered what would become of *Reliant* after this. Rumours about the rift between Stagg and the captain were rife in messdeck and wardroom alike. Evershed settled himself firmly in his seat; he never allowed himself to slouch, unlike his assistant, the spotting officer.

The lieutenant in question jerked upright, his hand to his ear.

'Radar. Ship at zero-three-zero, range two-one-five!'

Evershed nodded. About eleven miles. How did the brute get so close?

'Rate closing!'

Evershed was very calm. 'All guns, with semi-armour-piercing, *load, load, load!*'

He felt the seat quiver and knew Sherbrooke was increasing speed. He looked at his hands, quite still, and then adjusted his sights.

'Begin tracking.' He glanced down. 'What's the wind force? Could be tricky.'

'Wind force Four from red nine-oh.'

'All guns loaded, sir.'

He heard the captain's voice, clear and unhurried on the control speaker.

'Open fire!'

Evershed smiled grimly. That was the way it should be. No bloody dramatics.

He pressed his forehead against the rubber pad and watched the image begin to sharpen, and become real and dangerous.

Blink – blink – blink.

All three turrets. The enemy had opened fire.

Evershed concentrated his mind on this moment.

'Shoot!'

No sooner had the guns hurled themselves back on their springs than they were ready to be reloaded, men, machines, and gleaming rammers working as one to fill the gaping breeches, and fire again.

Evershed turned quickly to watch as the enemy shells exploded, flinging impressively tall waterspouts hundreds of feet into the air. He did not notice the copper glow on the cascading water and the great churning whirlpools where the shells had fallen: the appearance of the sea did not come into it.

'Short, sir!'

The spotting officer reported, 'Straddle, sir!'

Evershed hid his satisfaction. 'Calm down! Check the deflection!'

Reliant was altering course again, her wake curving astern as she headed towards the enemy.

'Ready!'

'Shoot!'

Two to their one. Evershed was comparing them when the next salvo exploded on either side of *Reliant*'s bows. Even up here, it felt as though they had rammed a submerged wreck.

'Deflection Right Twelve.'

Evershed was satisfied. Nothing else must concern them.

Like leviathans, the two great warships remained on converging courses, as if Rhodes's pencilled lines had been transferred to the glittering, windswept water.

In the early stages of the war most people had regarded the Italian forces as something of a joke, especially after their first defeats in North Africa. There had been so many Italians trying to surrender that there were barely enough British troops available to guard them.

The Italian navy was different; their ships had distinguished themselves in several fierce actions, and even after Cunningham's crushing victory at Matapan, their individual operations had continued. The Italians had been the first to use two-man torpedoes, and explosive motor boats against superior British forces, and there were some in *Reliant* this day who would not now think of the oncoming giant as a joke.

Evershed's gunnery was excellent, largely because of *Reliant*'s greater agility, her ability to alter course at speed allowing all three turrets to engage together. The *Tiberio* had been hit several times, and had turned almost bows-on to offer as small a target as possible.

Of the two reported destroyers, there had been no sign. They had either been sent on another mission or had gone into port to refuel, not that their presence or absence would have made much difference.

When they had failed to appear on the radar, and it was accepted that this was to be a ship-to-ship engagement, someone on the bridge had groaned, 'Is that all? Hoo-bloody-ray!'

Reliant had been straddled by two salvoes, and the damage control parties were working like madmen to shore up buckled metal and drag out any men who had been injured. There seemed to have been hours of tremendous noise from guns and exploding shells. In fact, it was only seventeen minutes after the first shots that *Reliant* received two direct hits.

One smashed into the forecastle deck near A Turret and ripped down into the lower deck before exploding. Seamen's messes, storerooms, fresh water tanks, bulkheads and frames were torn apart in a confusion of flying splinters and smoke.

The second shell hit the ship further aft, penetrating the after superstructure and ploughing through the wardroom where it burst like a huge bomb. Several of the men already wounded had been carried into the wardroom to await treatment. None survived.

On the bridge, Sherbrooke felt the two blows shake the ship with incredible violence, as if *Reliant* had been lifted high out of the water.

'A and B Turrets are out of action, sir!'

The first shell must have jammed the training mechanism. There was no time left.

'Hard a-port!' He saw Rhodes at the voicepipe. 'Bring her round! I must bring Y Turret to bear!' It was all they had; the smaller weapons might never be used again.

A great waterspout shot above the quarterdeck even as the helm went over. From the bridge, it was possible to hear the terrible crack and screech of deadly splinters as they crashed into the hull. Despite the danger, Sherbrooke could see men crouching and running from one emergency to the next. There was smoke now, and the acrid smell of burning.

Evershed's voice again over the speaker. 'Ready, marines! *Shoot!*'

The bridge quivered violently as more shells fell close by. Sherbrooke heard someone yell, 'The bastard's turning!'

It was true; the *Tiberio*'s shape was already lengthening, turning at last to give all her big guns an opportunity to finish it. Not knowing that *Reliant*'s guns were out of action, the Italian captain probably imagined that the enemy was standing away, running for it.

Sherbrooke gripped the rail until his fingers throbbed. It must be that. It had to be. It was all they had.

The two long guns lifted slightly and settled.

'Shoot!'

A shell burst alongside like a fireball, and more fragments jagged against the bridge and punched holes in the funnels.

No wonder the Italian captain thought they were making a run for it. He could see the ship, his ship, as if he were behind the enemy guns, with several fires burning, fanned and urged on by the wind, and with great rents in her plating

343

which, even at a range of eight miles, would be plainly visible in those powerful lenses.

Y Turret fired, and Sherbrooke counted the seconds, his eyes watering as he tried to keep his glasses steady.

'A *hit!*'

He saw the violent explosion on the *Tiberio*'s massive superstructure; it seemed wrong that he could scarcely hear it above all the other noise. Then another, a great gout of dark red fire, swirling up and over the bridge, carried on the same unexpected wind. Another explosion, perhaps a magazine, or more likely some ready-use ammunition near one of the gun mountings. It was enough. The battleship was swinging round, almost hidden in a smoke screen, heading away.

Rhodes said, 'The left gun is jammed in Y Turret, sir.' He held the telephone, unable to tear his eyes away from Sherbrooke's face. 'That last shell, sir.' He did not want to prolong it. 'Director Control was hit, too.'

'Tell them to fire.'

There was a pause and then the turret began to move again, only one gun rising slightly as the range was adjusted: Y Turret, which was manned entirely by marines. Just one gun.

He saw it recoil, the other gun still smoking from the previous shot, as if they had fired together.

There was so much smoke that the spotters could not see the fall of the last shot. But there were no replies from the enemy.

Sherbrooke said, 'Report damage and casualties.'

He made himself walk to the bridge wing, what remained of it. Yorke, the yeoman of signals, was on his knees with one of his young signalmen in his arms. He seemed to sense his presence, and when he looked up, Sherbrooke was moved by the tears in his eyes. Yorke was a true professional and had been in the navy since he was a boy. But he, too, had his limits.

He peered up at Sherbrooke and murmured, 'Why him, sir? He's only a kid!'

Then he lowered the youth to the deck and covered his face with a signal flag.

Lieutenant Frost said, 'Will the *Tiberio* come back?'

Rhodes was watching the captain. 'They might.' He looked around at the jagged splinter holes, the stains, the blood quivering to the engines' unbroken vibrations, as if it had outlived its owner.

The reports were coming in, some by messenger, as even the T/S was all but disabled. They had relied on messengers at Jutland too, he thought.

A fire here; a fire there; damage below the waterline. But the Chief had the pumps going. And they were still afloat. He braced himself and went out into the smoky sunlight.

'Commander Frazier's dead, sir. They're still searching for some of the others.'

Sherbrooke turned, and saw Frost staring from the bridge, his face ashen.

'Take over, Pilot. You've done it before.' He gripped his arm. 'Tell me when you know.'

There had been many casualties. Some died as they had lived, like Frazier, organizing, encouraging, filling the gaps, until a shell splinter had killed him instantly, while he had been helping his men. Others had died in anger and bitterness, cheated without knowing why. Chief Petty Officer Price, the admiral's steward, had been wounded during the first exchange of fire. His friend Dodger Long had helped to carry him to the wardroom for treatment. Price had not believed that Stagg would leave him behind after he had served him so faithfully, and had drawn his

345

last breath cursing Stagg's name, with Long self-consciously holding his hand.

Friends, but entirely different people. The shell was impartial, and had killed both of them.

A few had died quite alone and in terror. Lieutenant James Villar had been assisting one of the working parties, slipping on foam and trapped water as they sought out fires and quenched them before they could reach anything vital. When the shell had exploded in the wardroom he had thought that the ship had taken a mortal blow. As if in a daze, he had seen his office, the door ajar, and had blundered into it. Papers were scattered everywhere; water spurted occasionally from the ventilation shaft and somehow changed into steam as it fell, which was not possible. He had clung to his desk and stared, wild-eyed with disbelief, at the steel bulkhead. The white paintwork was alive, puffing out like something obscene. He had no knowledge of such things. He had not realized that the metal was melting.

There had been a muffled explosion and fire had burst through the hole like a flame-thrower. He had fallen, clutching at his face and eyes, to stop the agony and hold back the new darkness.

When the damage control party had smashed in with their crowbars and axes, Villar had been dead.

The youth, Alan Mowbray, had been one of them. He had ignored the drenching hoses and the extinguishers, the frantic cries of men he had come to know and respect, and had knelt down to cover Villar's terrible injuries.

A leading seaman had looked at him. 'All right, my son?'

And all that Mowbray had been able to remember was what Villar had said about his hands. He had looked at them then.

'I – I think so, Hookey.' He had got to his feet. It was over, and he knew he would never forget.

And there were some who had expected to die, simply because there seemed no alternative as the two great ships had fired point-blank at each other, or so it had felt, at the time.

Lieutenant Dick Rayner had been leading a group of seamen and mechanics who were trying to put out fires which had spread through the deck below from the shattered wardroom, and had suddenly exploded with a vivid flash through the catapult athwartships.

The men had been frightened, or too shocked by what they had already seen and done to respond.

Rayner had shouted, 'Come on, you guys! D'you want to live forever?'

It had almost worked, until fire had exploded amongst some stored aircraft fuel. It was pouring out as the ship tilted over in another wild alteration of course, like a burning stream, and he had felt the heat searing his uniform and hair.

He had snatched up an extinguisher and had jumped toward the flames. He was not sure of what had happened next. He had felt something like a punch, and had been flung down at the feet of the others.

Eddy Buck was not a big man; in fact he was slight, like a boy. He had dragged the extinguisher from him and yelled, 'Not this time, sunshine!' The ship had swayed over again, and the young New Zealander had become a human torch.

Later, when they had wrapped him in a blanket, Buck had opened one eye and had tried to focus it on his friend.

Rayner had put his face to his, hating the stench of burned flesh and of gas. He had held him closely, wanting him to die to be spared this suffering, needing him to live.

He had whispered, 'Don't bale out now, Eddy. I'm going to need you, remember?'

The blistered mouth had twisted into a smile. Just one word. 'Sorry.' And he was gone.

Rayner had been very close to Andy at that moment. She knew it better than anyone.

And up on the bridge, Sherbrooke was a part of them all.

The ship was on her new course, at reduced speed; no one would know the full extent of her damage until she was docked.

When he had told Frost to assume the new course, he had seen the hesitation, the aftermath of fear.

Sherbrooke had said, 'Pilot showed you what to do. *Do it.*'

He had looked up at the director, riddled with holes in spite of its two-inch armour plate. Evershed and his team had been killed before the marines had fired that last defiant shot. Evershed would have approved: he had trained them all.

Back to Gibraltar, then. Relief for some, broken hearts for many more.

He saw Pat Drury helping an injured seaman to hop on one leg as he guided him to safety. Another survivor. Would he ever be able to write again about the war in the same way? Perhaps he no longer believed in anything. Like Beveridge, the chaplain, when Sherbrooke had seen him wandering along the splintered decks with a prayer book, repeating the same line over and over. *'Preserve us from the dangers of the sea, and from the violence of the enemy.'* On and on.

Then he heard a man laugh, and others joined in. They were realizing what they had done. Tomorrow, the whole world would know.

Almost unconsciously, he ran his fingers along the screen. *Reliant* had done what must be done. She had also evened an old score, in some way.

He knew that *Reliant* would never fight again; they both did. But, as is the way with some ships, the legend would never die.

Epilogue

Operation *Husky*, the successful invasion of Sicily, like the landings in Italy which followed two months later, are now firmly placed in the annals of history: great events, which were to lead to and culminate in the D-Day landings, and final victory by the Allied forces.

Reliant's desperate fight against the powerful Italian battleship, like so many single actions throughout the war, was overshadowed, a mere episode in a catalogue of inspiring events, except to those who had been there, and had survived. With the hostilities ended, and with the beginning of what is now remembered as the Cold War, like so many other ships, there was no longer a role for the battlecruiser.

On a bright, crisp day, H.M.S. *Reliant* left her moorings for her last passage, to the breaker's yard. Her sister ship *Renown* had gone to her fate only weeks earlier, so *Reliant* was indeed the last battlecruiser. The end of a dream.

Under tow, she sailed without fuss or ceremony, her past deeds forgotten, except by those who had known her. Stripped of all her guns, engines and machinery, her graceful hull pockmarked with dents and streaks of rust, she was, to the experienced tug masters, just another hulk.

Reliant had covered several oceans, and thousands of men had passed through her in peace and war.

She was the same ship.

At the inquiry which was to follow, the same arguments were repeated which had been reported after Jutland, and in the Mediterranean before *Reliant*'s last fight. It simply could not happen. It was impossible. But it did.

On a calm sea, and without any power of her own, *Reliant*'s rudder went hard over.

The senior tug master described how she had suddenly veered away, the tow had snapped, and another tug had been hard put to avoid a collision. He also said that he had heard something like a rumble, which he was unable to explain. Another witness stated that the old battlecruiser had given a great shudder, like that first day on the slipway at Clydebank, when she had hesitated before sliding into the water.

She had taken on a heavy list, and had started to sink by the stern. There had been nothing anyone could do. In half an hour she was gone; perhaps, like her motto, she had been determined not to give in.

Now, over the years, those who remember her grow fewer. But when ships pass this place, occasionally, you will still hear a voice, bringing it all back.

'The old *Reliant* lies down there. I once served in her. I tell you, she was a *fine* ship!'

A sailor's tribute. None better.